Conversations with My Mother

Center Point
Large Print

Conversations with My Mother

A Novel of Dementia on the Maine Coast

Ronald-Stéphane Gilbert

CENTER POINT LARGE PRINT
THORNDIKE, MAINE

This Center Point Large Print edition
is published in the year 2025 by arrangement with
Rootstock Publishing.

Copyright © 2024 Ronald-Stéphane Gilbert.

All rights reserved.

This is a work of fiction. Names, characters,
places, and incidents either are the product of the
author's imagination or are used fictitiously.
Any resemblance to actual persons, living or dead,
events, or locales is entirely coincidental.

The text of this Large Print edition is unabridged.
In other aspects, this book may vary
from the original edition.
Printed in the United States of America
on permanent paper sourced using
environmentally responsible foresting methods.
Set in 16-point Times New Roman type.

ISBN: 979-8-89164-510-3

The Library of Congress has cataloged this record
under Library of Congress Control Number: 2024951898

For my sister Mary, my wife Leah, my son Nathaniel, my nieces Azia and Jessica, and all the other family members who either supported me in the writing of this book or provided care for my late mother.

". . . one by one, in the infinite meadows of heaven,
Blossomed the lovely stars, the forget-me-nots of the angels."
—Henry Wadsworth Longfellow,
Evangeline: A Tale of Acadie

Author's Note

I began this book in 2016, en route from Boston to Cleveland, after a weeklong stay with my eighty-nine-year-old Francophone mother in the small Maine town where I was raised and where she still lived with my sister in our family home. Over the course of several visits earlier that year, it had become apparent that my mother's frailty was increasing and her clarity of mind decreasing. During my latest stay, she'd experienced multiple instances of confusion, and, just before I left, had been diagnosed with first-stage vascular dementia.

For fear the mother I'd known was fast disappearing, I began visiting and calling her as often as possible. Consequently, from her initial diagnosis through her passing a few years later, I witnessed firsthand and at a greater remove the effects of her illness. Some, such as her growing fatigue, disorientation, and anxiety, I'd expected, but others, like her flights of fancy, startlingly sage pronouncements, and bursts of pitiless candor, caught me by surprise.

These and other changes I observed in her were the impetus for this story: a fictionalized account of one woman's descent into disability and dementia, and the occasionally touching or chilling milestones that marked her journey. Composed of episodic, chronologically ordered chapters and written in the first-person present tense, the book explores how, as its central character's dementia evolves and she herself devolves, her dominant traits recede and resurface, disappear and reappear like reflections on a lake or pane of glass under a variable, fast-moving sky. It details her struggle to cope with her growing limitations, sense of loss, and awareness of her impending demise, but also describes how, even as her identity frays and then fades, her core characteristics—insight, empathy, and kindness—remain intact, preventing her complete loss. This is perhaps the story's central point: that, however deep and tangled dementia's morass, the affected individual doesn't always entirely vanish. He or she might still be present—perhaps only fleetingly and in fragments but present nonetheless. I hope this perspective offers a measure of consolation to the many who've accompanied a loved one down dementia's long and sometimes painfully disturbing path.

PART I

Along a Twisting Trail

CHAPTER 1

Every Road Leads Somewhere

Medium Take

It's a clear fall day, the sky a brilliant blue, the trees along the beach road suffused in bright golds, rich russets, and deep reds. I park the car by the now defunct Wormwoods, my late father's favorite seafood place, the victim of changing tastes, since, even in Maine, old New England favorites like deep-fried fish, clams, and shrimp have largely given way to less-caloric, presumably healthier fare.

My eighty-nine-year-old mother, who's asked me to drive her here, looks seaward through the windshield. "We can't see the water from this spot," she remarks.

"You're right—that new beach house blocks the view," I say, pointing to a tall, gray-shingled building by the breakwater.

Mom's expression is inscrutable behind her big Jackie O sunglasses. "Your father proposed to me here. We'd just had dinner at Wormwoods and were sitting in his car smoking—that was back when everyone smoked." She sighs. "I miss my cigarettes."

"But you stopped smoking forty years ago."

"Bad habits are hard to break." She presses the middle finger and forefinger of her right hand together and gracefully lifts them into the air in eloquent evocation of the vanquished habit and memory of her elegant, now vanished, younger self.

"Anyway, as I'd started to say," she continues impatiently, perhaps irritated at our having drifted off topic. "That evening, after your father proposed, he and I sat here, looking up at the stars shining in the black night sky. We could hear the ocean—the waves breaking against the rocks—but we couldn't really see much. It was too dark." Then she says quietly, almost to herself, "I really miss your dad." Because of her sunglasses, I can't tell if her eyes are misting over with tears, as they sometimes do when she speaks about him.

To distract her, I say, "Why don't we walk over to the breakwater and get a better view of the ocean? After all, that's what we came here for."

She hesitates, then, as if thinking aloud, murmurs, "Pourquoi pas—why not?"

Before she can change her mind, I get out of the car, retrieve her walker from the trunk, and open her door. Putting my arms under hers in an awkward but necessary embrace, I pull her up off the car seat, help her step onto the gravel-strewn berm, and grab hold of the walker.

"Good thing I'm not in heels," she remarks.

"When I was younger, I wore them whenever I went out—even just to the supermarket."

"I remember," I answer, steadying her on the walker as we begin the short walk to the shore.

"Everyone wore high heels back then—when we were all young and stupid," she adds with a laugh.

"You were never stupid."

"Sometimes I feel as if I were never young," she mutters, while we inch forward, skirting small stones and pits in the gravel along the roadside.

The wind off the water is strong today, a force to be reckoned with. As we reach land's end, it flattens Mom's tan trench coat against her frail body, sends the ends of her white scarf streaming upward, and dishevels the few strands of silver hair that jut out from beneath her kerchief, which in all likelihood she wore to prevent just such an occurrence.

"That's a pretty kerchief," I remark.

"It's very old—like me," she replies, breaking into a smile. "No one wears kerchiefs anymore, just like no one goes to Mass."

"You think the two might be related?" I ask.

She pulls her sunglasses down the bridge of her nose and gives me a quizzical look. "Who knows? All the women used to have to cover their heads in church, and then, when we didn't have to anymore, people stopped going. So, yes, maybe." She pauses. "People are strange sometimes—and, of course, the devil is clever."

As we get closer to our destination and the ground underfoot becomes ever more uneven, Mom announces, "This is close enough."

We look out at the breakwater, a half-mile of rough-hewn granite that bisects the bay, separating the river flow from the sea, the water lighter on one side than the other. Toward its end, fishermen—tiny figures in the windswept distance—raise their arms skyward, hoisting rod and reel to cast their lines into air and ocean. Beyond them, the breakwater's endpoint seems almost to disappear into the horizon.

"A road to nowhere," I remark.

"Every road leads somewhere," Mom replies, taking hold of my arm to steady herself against the wind. "Even if it's not where you want to be."

CHAPTER 2

Ask a Stupid Question

Short Take

My mom is lying on the brown leather sofa in her family room. Phlebitis has forced her to rest and raise her legs every afternoon since my childhood—though, in truth, these days, she lies down more to nap than to alleviate leg swelling.

The walls of the family room are hung with photos of deceased relatives, vanished pets, and long-gone local landmarks—a Victorian beach hotel, the old Portland train station, and the town square's white-spired First Congregational Church, lost in a fire years ago.

"I miss them all—the people, the dogs, the places," she remarks, even though she has been staring at the ceiling and hasn't so much seen as sensed me looking at the photos. "A lot has changed, but I like this town. It has everything I need. I don't have to travel anywhere."

After a moment, she turns her head on the sofa pillow, looks at me, and, in a concerned tone, asks, "Do you still travel all of the time?"

Some of my jobs have involved my traveling all over the world, which she hasn't liked. "Not as much as before," I reply.

"Good! It bothered me, your flying all over the place like that. I hate planes!" she says emphatically, then coughs.

"You flew to my wedding in Cleveland," I remind her.

"Well, of course! I would have flown to the moon and back for that!"

"Why?"

She gives me the exasperated look that she typically reserves for errant TV remotes or for faucets that won't stop dripping. "Because you're my son!" Peering at me over her rimless glasses, she adds, "Sometimes, you ask stupid questions!"

"It's my specialty," I answer, smiling.

She considers this. "You must take after me."

We both laugh.

CHAPTER 3

Sic Transit Gloria Mundi

Long Take

Grimacing, Mom shifts her weight in the passenger seat of my old Lotus sports car. "Are you uncomfortable, Mom?" I ask, as the traffic light switches from red to green and I shift the car into drive.

"Yes, a little," she replies. "I can't believe I didn't remember to bring my seat pillow. I'm so forgetful sometimes," she continues, with characteristic self-effacement.

"It's my fault, Mom. Diane handed it to me as we were about to leave but then I got a text message, and I forgot the pillow on the kitchen table."

"We all make mistakes." she says, forever forgiving.

I'm driving Mom to the beauty salon to give my sister Diane, who lives with Mom and is her principal caregiver, a break from chauffeuring her to her many medical and personal-care appointments. I've never taken Mom to the hairdresser's before, so I'm surprised when the GPS guides us into an industrial park instead of to a shopping center. "Are you sure Diane gave us the right address?"

"What address did she give you?"

When I tell her, Mom replies, "Could be. I'm not certain."

"Well, does this look like the way you usually go?"

"Maybe—but who knows?" she answers, resigned to the fact that nowadays she's more likely to recall the details of a long-ago wedding than what she had for breakfast.

With no choice but to follow the GPS's guidance, I pull the car into the gravel parking lot of a corrugated-steel building and scan the list of tenants at its entrance. To my surprise, this includes the "Coiffed Creations" hair salon, "Nine-Inch Nails" manicure studio, "Virtuous Cycle" bike shop, and a vegan-oriented coffeehouse called "Coffee with a Conscience"—all names likely to have engendered laughter among the residents of this small Maine beach town when I was raised here, prior to its invasion by out-of-staters.

"Do you think it's really possible for coffee to have a 'conscience'?" I ask Mom.

She looks at me uncomprehending, and then, reading the building directory, frowns.

"Don't be so literal."

"I can't help it—remember, I started my career as an editor."

"That's just an excuse. You like finding fault—with things and with people!"

"I do when they're actually at fault," I reply, driving the Lotus into a parking space so deeply rutted that it causes us to lurch forward in our seats. "Like the geniuses who decided not to pave this parking lot, for example."

She unbuckles her seatbelt with a sigh. " 'Judge not, lest ye, too, be judged.' "

"But aren't we judged every day, by almost everyone we meet?" I object. "And, anyway, when did you start quoting scripture?"

"I always have," she answers primly.

"Really?" I respond, knowing full well she hasn't. "Then quote me another passage."

" 'Let he who is without sin cast the first stone,' " she replies, without hesitation.

"My, you're on a roll today," I comment, opening the driver's door and walking over to open hers.

"I will be if you don't help me out of this Matchbox Car of yours," she says, trying to maneuver her arthritic legs over the car-door threshold. "Why a tall man like you got a tiny toy car like this is beyond me."

I lift her feet off the floormat and try to ensure that her head doesn't strike the top of the doorframe in the process. "Well, you know me and my obsession with fitness."

"What do you mean?" she asks, grabbing hold of her walker.

"Isn't it obvious?" I tease her. "I bought a

sports car so that I'd stick to my diet—I mean, if I put on any weight, I won't even be able to squeeze behind the steering wheel."

"Said the man in the thrall of a mid-life crisis," Mom counters. "Go ahead, make fun," she continues with a frown. "Those thirty pounds you've lost have left you looking like a skeleton, though—no 'ifs, ands, or buts' about it."

"It's all the exercise," I answer truthfully, since I bike twenty-five miles a day.

She glares at me. "You need therapy—and I don't mean the physical kind!" she exclaims and adds, "You're anorexic!" for emphasis.

"That was Gisele," I say, referring to one of my younger sisters, who was indeed anorexic in her adolescence—a cause of much familial upset at the time and for long afterward. "But that was decades ago," I say in an attempt to calm her. "She's better now and has been for ages."

"Whatever!" Mom mutters, causing me to regret having raised the topic.

I try flattery to distract her. "Why are you having your hair done today, anyway? It looks great!" This is not an exaggeration. Her thick, gray curls put the scraggly coiffures of many women her age—and my own white-haired, balding pate—to shame.

"You must need new contact lenses," she replies, as we negotiate the building's handicap-access ramp. "Maybe it looks OK right now, but, in a few days, it will be a mess of knots and whorls sticking out at odd angles."

"Like that bush?" I point to a bramble whose thorny, unpruned limbs jut out onto the ramp, forming a minor hazard.

She looks at the intrusive branches. "There you go finding fault again—I swear you'll even find something to criticize in heaven."

"Probably," I say as we enter the lobby—a small, fluorescent-lit space with gray linoleum flooring. "If I even get into heaven."

She winces. "Joke all you want—someday you won't think it's so funny!"

"And what day would that be, exactly?" I ask as we head down a corridor.

She glares at me. "I'm serious—it's a character flaw to always look at things so critically."

This strikes me as a critical remark in and of itself but since we've already arrived at the beauty salon, I say nothing.

"Why do you come here, anyway?" I ask, stepping ahead to open the salon door, which is flanked by several Photoshopped coiffeur posters. "Aren't there nicer places closer to us?"

The look she gives me is nothing short of deadly. "There are, but I come here because my stylist, Monique, is a distant cousin, and she could use the money, especially since she got divorced again."

"Again?"

She nods. "It's the third time, I think."

"How is she related to us?" I ask, mostly to avoid saying something that Mom would consider judgmental.

"I don't remember the details, but she is," she replies in an urgent whisper. "Now keep your voice down or, better yet, just shut up, period."

Monique, a tall middle-aged woman with too-dark brown hair, sits in her styling chair, on the far end of the salon, which is filled with women roughly Mom's age having their hair washed, set, or dried. "Hi, Yvette," she calls out, "How're you doing today?"

"Fine, thank you," Mom answers brightly, even though there's only a 50-50 chance that her frail voice will carry over the swoosh of running water, roar of the hair dryers, and the ruckus of general chatter. "This is my eldest son, Rob, who lives in Cleveland," she continues, as Monique draws closer.

Giving me the once over, Monique asks, "How about those Indians?"

"Yeah, aren't they something this season?" I answer, hedging my bets, since I don't follow the local sports teams or any others either.

"Well, that's one way of putting it," Monique replies with a smile, not revealing whether they're winning or losing. She turns to Mom and asks, "What'll it be today, Yvette—the usual?" which makes me wonder if she's ever been a bartender.

"Yes, I think so," Mom replies.

Monique studies Mom's head appraisingly while I guide her towards the styling chair. "You know, your hair looks pretty good this week," she tells Mom. "It barely needs to be set, really."

Mom seems abashed. "Well, a curl can't hurt, though, can it?" she replies, sitting down. "I like to keep up appearances."

"Don't we all?" Monique replies with a bemused smile and then starts to comb through Mom's thick tresses. "We should be done in about forty minutes," she says to me, "if you want to run a few errands and pick her up afterwards."

"I think maybe I'll just wait," I answer, knowing that's what Diane usually does.

"Suit yourself," she replies. "There's coffee and muffins in the waiting area—made them myself."

"You did?" Mom remarks—simply to make conversation, I'm guessing.

"Yeah, I was unusually ambitious this morning," Monique replies, and both she and Mom start laughing.

"Thanks," I tell Monique, and walk to the front of the salon. There I sit down on a tired-looking futon set between two tattered armchairs, one of which is occupied by an elderly woman waiting for a stylist. On a large, flat-panel television across from us, the Red Sox, in the final inning at Fenway Park, are losing by a hair's breadth.

"It's been this way all season," the woman

remarks, pushing an errant strand of gray hair off her wrinkled face with an irritated gesture. "I mean—they tear through most of the game and then fall back and leave you on pins and needles toward the end of it."

I recall that this is how the Sox played through most of my childhood—though, in truth, then, as now, I seldom paid much attention. "Seems like that's their style," I offer, "or maybe their curse."

The woman breaks into a smile, the lines around her eyes and lips becoming momentarily deeper. "Maybe," she replies. "My name's Celia, by the way."

"Mine's Rob," I offer. "Nice to meet you." From the coffee table, I pick up a day-old copy of the *Portland Press Herald*. The lead story is part of an ongoing series on the battle between summer residents and shorefront communities over whether or not seasonal homes should be taxed at market value. Since the positions and arguments of each side are predictable and, by now, tiresomely familiar, I put the paper back down again.

Noticing its headline, Celia comments, "Those out-of-staters will do anything to keep from paying their fair share, won't they?"

"Guess so," I reply with a shrug.

No longer smiling, she looks at me more closely. "You live hereabouts?"

"No," I answer. "I live in the Midwest, but I was

raised here—first, at Hill's Beach in Biddeford and, afterwards, in Saco."

"You get a special dispensation, then," she remarks, her smile returning.

"How so?" I say.

"You're not really from away."

My cellphone vibrates. The call is from my Parisian business associate, Valérin de Courty, so I take it. "Bonjour, Valérin!" I say and then ask how he is "Comment ça va?"

"Trés bien," he responds and immediately inquires whether I have time to talk, "As tu quelques moments á me parler?" Then, without further ado, he asks me a project question far too detailed for me to answer confidently without referring to the client's files, which are on my laptop.

"Écoutez, Valérin! Je devrais consulter le dossier du client pour te répondre avec certitude, mais je ne suis pas chez-moi actuellement. Puis-je te rapeller un peu plus tard?" I interrupt, telling him that I don't have the client file in question with me and asking if we can talk later. He agrees, so I say, "À bientôt!" and click off the cell.

Celia stares. "Are you French?"

"As a matter of fact, yes. French-American," I say.

"Wherever did you learn to speak French like that, then? I majored in Latin and French at

Colby, and it was decades before I could even begin to understand North American French," she says with a pinched expression, as if she'd just caught whiff of an offensive odor.

I consider this lament—not uncommon among some who've learned French in high school or college—both condescending and indicative of limited fluency—but don't say so. "The local accent was beaten out of me," I respond neutrally, since Celia's age warrants a measure of respect—even if, under the circumstances, perhaps only a modicum.

"Beaten?"

"Yeah, at a variety of private universities," I respond, smiling wryly.

Celia laughs. "Well, you speak it beautifully."

Though this isn't true, I humor her. "Thanks—but it's easy, isn't it, with such a beautiful language?" I refrain from adding that, when spoken as a birthright, maybe any language has an innate beauty that becomes self-evident.

On the television, the Red Sox hit a game-deciding home run, and the crowd at Fenway rises in the stands and flings a flurry of baseball caps skyward. One of the hairdressers increases the volume. The game's commentators are speculating on the team's chances of taking the pennant, even though they currently trail behind the league's leader—a situation that, it seems, is often the case for them at this point in the season.

Exclamations of surprise and gratification ripple through the salon.

"You have to hand it to the Red Sox," Celia remarks, "somehow, they always surprise you."

"Apparently," I answer.

Mom, her hair fresher- and fuller-looking, approaches, accompanied by Monique.

"That was fast," I say. "Did you just wash and set it?"

"Not even," she answers. "I didn't really have to. All I did was use a little styling mousse, comb her hair out, then spray it." She turns to Mom, "and it worked out well, n'est ce pas, Yvette?" she asks, with the exaggeratedly upbeat tone that one might use to address a pet or small child.

My mother looks dubious. Maybe she is just uncomfortable because she generally doesn't speak French unless she's certain that all present are conversant, and, having noticed Celia, she isn't sure of this.

Celia's hairdresser walks up. "Hi Celia," she says and then, inevitably, asks, "So, how'd you like your hair done today?"

Celia runs a hand through her thin, loosely tied-back hair. "Make it really beautiful, with a lot of body—like hers," she answers, gesturing toward Mom's full, well-rounded curls.

Perhaps unable to tell whether Celia is serious or joking, the hairdresser answers, "Sure. Why not give it a shot? Who knows what might happen!" Everyone starts laughing.

I turn to Mom. "See? Judgments aren't always bad. Sometimes they're complimentary."

Mom gives me a sharp look. "Yes, sometimes," she concedes, "but things can change quickly."

"How's that?"

"Well, after a couple of nights of being slept on, my hair won't look so great and all of you might have a different opinion."

Everyone laughs again.

"Sic transit gloria mundi?" I inquire.

"Exactly," Mom answers.

"What does that mean?" Celia's hairdresser asks.

Looking bemused, Celia, the long-ago Latin student, translates. "Thus passes the glory of the world."

"Is that in the Bible?" Monique asks.

"No, but it ought to be," Mom answers.

CHAPTER 4

Something to Talk About

Short Take

One afternoon, while sitting at the kitchen table with the newspaper and reading of a celebrity scandal, Mom says, "It's terrible to be famous."
"What do you mean?" I ask.
"Everyone knows all of your mistakes."
"Is that really so bad? Nobody's perfect."
"Right," Diane says. "We all make mistakes."
"That's true," Mom replies, and, then, after thinking a little more about it, adds. "Plus, if someone who's as old as I am knows about them, it most likely doesn't matter."
"Why?" I ask.
"I'll forget about them in a day or so. And, if somebody tells me about them again, I'll say, 'Really, I didn't know that.'"
"That's terrible," remarks my son Ian, who, on break from medical school, has accompanied me on this visit.
"Not entirely," Mom responds, without missing a beat. "It will give us something to talk about."

CHAPTER 5

Common Decency

Medium Take

It's an afternoon in early August, the end of Maine's blueberry season. Beyond the pines, arbor vitae, and shrub roses that border Mom's rolling lawn, women and children in shorts and tees crouch amid long grass and low bushes, bright plastic beach buckets and kitchen containers in hand as they garner the last of the year's harvest. In the shade of a large maple by the barn, Diane, our niece Carrie, Ian, and I sift through a jumble of berries spread atop a picnic table, sorting light from dark, separating sweet from sour, and extracting small leaves and bits of branches, which we flick onto the grass.

"Has it been a good year for wild blueberries?" I ask.

Mom, seated beside us in an Adirondack chair, fingers the stem of the tiger lily that Carrie, who's living here while enrolled at a nearby college, has brought her. "Pretty good," she says, "at least, from the looks of all the people who've come picking." She shields her eyes to peer into the field, where the grass gleams gold in the slanted, mid-afternoon light.

Diane amends this assessment. "The cultivated blueberries have fared better," she says, referring to the high-bush plants that my late father had long-ago planted elsewhere on the property.

"So why aren't people picking those?" Ian asks.

"We don't let them," replies Carrie.

Diane explains further. "Your father and uncles worked so hard to put in the cultivated ones—they transplanted 40 huge plants one summer alone—that Dad wanted to keep them for the immediate family."

"That's right," Mom admits, though then she adds, "but he considered the wild blueberries a gift from God to be shared with everybody."

"Just who is 'everybody' these days?" I ask, gesturing towards the field full of pickers.

"Pretty much the same mix as always," Diane responds. "Relatives, neighbors, and whichever friends they've invited."

"How do they all get here?"

Mom gives me a look typically reserved for slow students. "The way anybody gets anywhere around here—by driving or walking."

"But I didn't see cars in the drive or in front of the house," I protest.

"They usually park on a side street and come into the field through the condo complex," Diane says, referring to the mass—or, as she more typically describes it, the "mess"—of vinyl-sided and faux-stone faced duplexes a developer erected at the field's far end, the objections of neighbors notwithstanding. "Either there or in the parking lot of the Greek Orthodox church across from us."

"How did that church get built there anyway?" Ian asks her. "Aren't the woods across the street part of a nature preserve?"

"They are," Diane confirms. "But the preserve's trustees made an exception for the Greek congregation, so long as what it built wasn't obtrusive," she continues. "That's why the church and parking lot are hidden in the trees and all you can see from the road is a sign." She pauses to remove a ladybug from the blueberries laid out before her, depositing it gently on the grass at her feet. "All things considered, the Greeks aren't bad neighbors."

Carrie smiles. "They're very nice," she says. "Especially during their summer festival, when they send us filo and baklava."

Ian looks surprised. "For free?"

Diane nods in affirmation. "It's in return for our letting their visitors park on our property."

To get us back to our original subject, I turn to Mom and motion toward the field. "Why do you really let all these people pick here, anyway?" I press her.

Mom shrugs. "It doesn't cost anything, and it's what your father wanted," she says. " 'No fences make good neighbors.' "

"I thought the poem went, 'Good fences make good neighbors,'" Carrie pipes up. "That's what we learned in high school."

"You learn a lot of things in high school," Diane says, teasing her. "Not all of them accurate."

"That's true," Carrie admits, gingerly sifting through the blueberries so as not to burst any with her long fingernails, which are already streaked with purple berry juice, in testament to past failure. "Like how the teachers tell you you have to be a leader, when all that really matters is that you follow the rules and be popular."

"Popular?" Mom asks.

"It means something different in English than in French," I explain to her. For Carrie and Ian's benefit, I add, "In French, one meaning of *populaire* is 'vulgar.'"

"Oh," says Carrie. "In English, Mémère, it means people who are liked or admired—you know, like a jock or a cheerleader."

"'Jock'?" Mom asks, perplexed. "Isn't that a kind of men's underwear?"

"Yes," Carrie replies. "Guys wear jocks while playing sports. They're a support for . . ."

"Speaking of vulgar!" Diane interrupts her.

"In this case, 'jock' refers to the athlete himself," I tell Mom. To avoid further explanation, I prompt Carrie. "You were talking about being popular in high school."

She looks up from her blueberry sorting. "I

was only going to say that it seems shallow," she replies, "even hypocritical. The 'popular' kids in my high school only cared about themselves or people who were like them. They didn't seem like leaders."

"That's because being popular and being a leader aren't the same," Mom remarks, still studying the tiger lily Carrie brought her.

"What do you mean?" Carrie asks.

"From what you and Rob have said, being popular is about getting people to like you and putting you up on a pedestal," Mom answers, setting the flower down on an arm of the Adirondack chair. "Real leaders should get people to do what's right," she continues. "That doesn't always make them liked. Often, it leads to the opposite."

Diane picks a leaf from the pile of blueberries spread out before her and flings it groundward. "So, the best way is the hard way?" she asks, with an ironic smile, probably because this pretty much sums up her life philosophy.

"Not always, but often," Mom answers. A cloud moves rapidly across the sky and a wind, redolent of the coming afternoon fog, rustles the maple's leaves overhead and blows through the field grass, rippling it like pond water. Mom looks out across the waving grass, where the blueberry pickers are gathering containers and marshalling children in preparation for departure.

"The best way for whom?" Carrie asks, while she and Diane, having poured the sorted blueberries into Tupperware bowls, start back up the hill to the house.

"For everybody," Mom answers as Ian and I take hold of her walker and follow. "It's like being a parent—you have to pay as much attention to the middle children as you do to the younger and the older. You can't neglect them as if they were outsiders, looking in at the window."

"Why?" asks Diane, herself a middle child.

Before Mom can answer her, I hazard a guess. "Is it because the 'neglected' have the clearest view of what's happening?"

The fog begins to enter the field in earnest, first as mist and then in opaque waves, obscuring the field grass and the pickers as the latter hurriedly exit. Shaking her head no, Mom looks up at the house, already lit against the encroaching darkness. "It's because common decency demands it."

CHAPTER 6

A Question of Fate

Short Take

Mom, who's just finished reading an article about a Beijing gay man who was battered and killed by the Chinese police, lays her newspaper down on the kitchen table in disgust.

"That's horrible," she says. "There was no reason for police to do that—being gay isn't a crime, or, for that matter, a sin, either."

"I agree," I say, "but I'm a little surprised to hear you say the last part."

"Why?" she inquires. "It's not someone's fault if he or she is gay. Gays are born that way."

"Doesn't the Church consider homosexuality a sin?" I ask.

"No!" she retorts. "It's only when they do something about it that it's sinful."

"Do something about what?" I ask.

"About being gay, of course."

"What do you mean, exactly?"

She rolls her eyes and looks at me as if she suspects me of being deliberately obtuse. "You know exactly what I mean!" she exclaims. "When I was young, if a man was effeminate and a woman was masculine, they simply married each other, and that was the end of it. Everybody accepted it, and everything worked out fine."

"But don't you think gay people have a right to live their lives as they want? To marry who they want?" I get bolder here and add, "To have sex with whom they want? After all, perhaps that's their destiny."

My mother peers at me over her glasses. "Having sex is not one's destiny—it's one's fate."

Thinking it best not to disputes this, I ask, "Do you think God loves gay people?"

She glares at me. "Certainly!"

"Do you love them?"

"Of course I do!" she answers indignantly. "Ours is not to judge, but to be judged!"

CHAPTER 7
A Rat by Any Other Name
Short Take

My mother sits in her walnut-paneled den, sunlight pouring in through window mullions that cast a lattice work of shadows across the sand-colored floor, as my son and I sip tea from gray China cups.

"I hear that your sense of smell has come back," I say.

"A little bit," she replies, then adds, "Well, it was never really completely gone."

"It wasn't?"

"No," she answers, looking down at her engagement ring, which sparkles in the light. "For example, I could always smell a rat."

I laugh, but my son, Ian, is shocked.

"But you're terrified of rats, Mémère!"

"Yes," she nods, straight-faced. "That's why being able detect them is so useful."

CHAPTER 8

Speaking the Language
Medium Take

Rain beats relentlessly against the many-mullioned bay window in Mom's family room, coursing downward in rivulets, a visual and audible reminder of this umpteenth day of bad, unseasonably chilly weather.

Exhausted from an afternoon of Mother's Day visitors, Mom lies on the sofa under a woven throw depicting eighteenth-century Portsmouth's harbor replete with sloops, schooners, and frigates, her legs raised to alleviate the persistent phlebitis that resulted from her having long-ago borne seven children. Scenes from the latest chicanery in the nation's capital loom large on the flat-panel television before us, frowning politicians and too-pretty or -handsome newscasters doling out typical helpings of hypocrisy in the first case and trite observation in the second.

"Please change the station," Mom asks Diane, who switches the TV to the Discovery Channel, where Nova's program logo briefly appears then gives way to a computer-generated depiction of Mars adrift in the cosmos.

"I like this show," Mom remarks, turning her

head on a pillow embroidered with fleurs-de-lis and then pushing her glasses up the bridge of her nose to see the television better. On its screen, a graphic of a spaceship wends its way across the solar system as Nova's opening theme fades and a narrator portentously introduces the program's topic: a private company's solicitation of passengers for a one-way colonization mission to Mars. "The company has been flooded with intrepid applicants for this pioneering adventure," the narrator states excitedly and then, in graver tones, says, "Even though the mission's participants will never return to Earth, their home planet," emphasizing, on more than one count, the obvious.

"Ha!" Mom exclaims, "They could never get me to go to Mars!"

"Why?" asks Ian, who's interested in all things scientific.

"Maybe because it's crazy?" Diane offers, guessing at Mom's answer.

Mom stares first at Diane and then at Ian, as if assessing each's sanity. "The reason should be obvious," she replies, deadpan, "I don't speak the language!"

Ian, Diane, and I break out in laughter. "That's exactly what you told Dad years ago when he wanted the two of you to vacation in Washington," I remind her.

Mom draws the throw to her chin. "Case in point," she counters.

CHAPTER 9

Accidents Happen

Short Take

One night, as we sat at the dining room's long mahogany table, lingering over our coffee and vanilla meringue cookies, the after-dinner conversation turns to politics and, eventually, to a prominent politician of questionable competence and suspect ethics.

"When I think of him, I see nothing but a hole," Mom remarks.

"An asshole?" Diane quips.

Above her thick glasses, Mom arches her brows. "I would never say such a thing about anyone! It was funny, though, wasn't it?" she continues with a laugh. Then she muses, "Now, I'll have to go to confession."

"Why?" I ask.

"Because of that remark."

"But you didn't make the remark," I protest, "You just laughed at it—almost by accident, in fact."

"That doesn't let me off the hook," she replies. "Lots of the things we do are accidents."

"Even the good things?"

"Especially the good things."

CHAPTER 10

Law and Disorder

Long Take

I sit in the cramped back seat of my Lotus sports car, my legs folded so tightly that my knees nearly touch my chin, while Mom and my sister Diane sit in front. We are on our way to Portland for a meeting with Nancy Poole, Mom's eldercare attorney, to discuss the structure of my late father's estate.

Diane, who's never driven this car before, is challenged by its standard transmission. "I can't believe you drove this thing all the way here from Cleveland," she says to me, shifting gears for the umpteenth time in the quarter of an hour since we left Mom's house in Saco. "How in hell did you get it through the Catskills and Berkshires?"

"Those mountains are pretty low," I reply defensively, as Diane opens the sunroof and the car fills with a deafening wind.

"Could you please close that until we get off the highway?" Mom asks loudly, drawing the turquoise Pashmina scarf that I bought for her in Paris close around her shoulders to shield herself from the draft.

Once Diane's complied, Mom takes off her

tortoise-shell sunglasses and peers into her compact to check that her hair has not turned into a jumbled mess.

"Those are nice glasses," I remark.

"They're fake," she answers. "Diane bought them for me at the Dollar Store. You don't have to spend a bundle to look presentable," she adds, likely scolding me for the extravagance of both the car and the Pashmina scarf, even though I've told her countless times that I purchased the latter from a street vendor and that it, too, is probably counterfeit.

Diane activates the righthand turn signal and takes the Portland waterfront exit onto the new bridge over the western end of Casco Bay.

"Is this the Million Dollar Bridge?" Mom asks.

"I'm pretty sure it cost more than that," Diane replies, changing lanes.

"The Million Dollar Bridge is east of here," I tell Mom. Then, for Diane's benefit, I explain, "It was built back in the 1930s, when a million dollars was enough money to impress people—well, at least, enough to impress Mainers."

Diane nods. "I remember now. The *Portland Press Herald* ran a story about it a while back," she says as, glancing left, she guides the car onto the bridge. "I think it's supposed to be torn down soon."

I don't often get into Portland or read its paper either, so I'm surprised. "That's a shame," I say.

"Nothing lasts forever," Diane replies, characteristically matter of fact.

"Bien sûr que cela, c'est la vérité," Mom says.

I look out the car windows. On the right, a destroyer and tanker are moored by an oil-storage facility whereas on the left, the Maine Medical Center looms above the Georgian Revival and Victorian mansions of the Western Promenade.

"I hate that hospital," Mom remarks.

"Why?" I ask.

Diane answers. "That was where Dad had his first stroke—the night following his operation," she says, referring to the surgery my father underwent to alleviate a brain bleed resulting from a fall. I'd been in Asia when this happened, and, though Diane had called me, in the rush of all that followed—the eighteen-hour flight back to the States, my father's ultimately pointless stay in rehab, the search for a suitable long-term care facility—I forgot some details.

"How could they not have noticed that he'd had a stroke until the morning after?" Mom continues. "What kind of hospital isn't on top of things like that? If they'd caught it right away, he might have had a chance!"

"Is that right?" I ask, more skeptically than I'd intended.

"Maybe," Diane replies, again answering on Mom's behalf. "Sometimes, if a stroke is detected immediately, the effects can be minimized." She looks into the rearview mirror as we exit the bridge and descend to the Portland waterfront, Commercial Street's cobblestones and disused trolley tracks rumbling close beneath the Lotus's low-slung body. "Mom read an article about it last month in *Newsweek*. Ever since, she's been obsessed with the idea that things could have worked out better for Dad."

"*Newsweek*'s still published?" I ask, astonished.

"Oh, yes," Diane answers. "So are *Time, Ladies Home Journal*—even *Reader's Digest*! We get them all! It's almost like living in the past!"

"We were talking about your father," Mom says, at once taking us to task and bringing us back, "and how much I hate that the hospital wasn't able to help him more."

"Sorry."

Unappeased, Mom says, "You know another thing I hate?"

"What?"

Mom looks out the window at the passing docks, warehouses, and lobster pounds, flocks of gulls circling over all but particularly over the last. "I hate that your father's money came to me before he'd passed. He gave me so much, and I took what was his while he was still alive," she says, referring to the subject of our visit to the attorney: a review of the assets transferred to Mom so that my father could qualify for state-assisted medical coverage and her house be shielded from medical-debt collectors even after his death.

"You gave him a lot, too," I remind her. "Seven children, as it happened."

"God gave him those," Mom replies, still looking through the window glass.

Diane, who has little patience for Mom's self-effacement, chimes in, "I think you helped."

"It was my job," Mom answers flatly.

"Just like it was his to support you," Diane replies. We come to a stop behind a line of cars turning onto the wharf where the *Prince of Fundy*, a New Brunswick-bound cruise ship, is set to depart.

"Dad did a great job," I tell Mom. "None of us ever wanted for anything—all his children went to college, you live in a beautiful house, and you've got retirement savings. Now it's your job—and ours—to make sure Dad's efforts weren't for naught. That's why we're visiting Nancy Poole today—to make certain that, even now that he's gone, the family gets to keep the fruit of his labors."

My mother studies her wedding ring.

"Don't you think that's what Dad wanted?"

She sighs. "After the stroke, when he couldn't speak, it was hard to be sure what he wanted. I just wish he'd have told us!"

"Well, he kind of did, didn't he?" I persist. "Remember how, when we described all this to him, he smiled and nodded? Dad might not have able to talk but he understood!"

"If you say so."

"I say so," I reply. "Because it is so."

Her face is expressionless.

The last of the cars ahead turns toward the *Prince of Fundy* and we head into the tourist-filled Old Port, whose former fishing wharves have been converted into condominiums and dive bars into trendy cafés or shops full of handmade pottery, expensive cookware, and local souvenirs, like lobster pots and bottled sailboats made in China.

In front of a yacht outfitted as a floating restaurant, a white-clad blonde carrying a Harvard tote and an Abacus Art Gallery shopping bag blithely steps into the traffic. Diane hits the Lotus's brake pedal, and the car screeches to a halt.

"Learn to drive!" the young woman calls out with a scowl.

Diane, her face flushed with anger, yells back, "Learn to read! Or don't they teach that at Harvard anymore?"

The blonde raises her middle finger in response, and Diane steps down hard on the gas pedal, driving so close to the young woman that her skirt rises in the car's slipstream as we pass. Surprised, she drops her Abacus bag to the tinkling sound of shattered glass. Diane takes a sharp left at the Old Customs House, and we roar up Pearl Street, pigeons taking flight before us and leaves and litter roiling in our wake. We make the next light, turn onto Middle Street, and come to a stop before a posh brasserie across the way from the renovated 1920s office building where Nancy Poole has her place of business.

"Seigneur!" Mom says to Diane, "You didn't need to startle her like that!"

"Startle her? That smart-mouth bitch?! She's lucky I didn't knock her skinny ass all the way back to Boston!"

"Diane!" Mom protests, as I help her out of the Lotus and attempt to extract her walker from its tiny trunk. "I didn't raise you to talk like that—or to be so unkind either."

Noticing my struggle with the walker, the brasserie's car valet walks over and helps me dislodge it. "Where do you park the cars?" I ask him, as Diane hands over the keys.

"Dockside on Commercial Street, in the direction you came from."

"Any other choices?"

"There's underground parking at Monument Square, but it costs extra."

"Whatever the price, I'll pay it. Here's half your tip in advance," I say, handing him a ten.

"Sure thing!" he replies and drives the car away.

"What was all that about?" Diane asks, helping

Mom steady herself and the walker on the uneven brick sidewalk.

"I'd rather not drive my car back to Cleveland with any unwanted mementoes of my visit—like key scratches left by your newfound 'friend' from Massachusetts."

"You're so paranoid!" Diane answers. "How did you ever travel all over the world?!"

"Very carefully," I say, smirking

Mom looks at us. "If something happens to your car today, you deserve it," she says to me disapprovingly.

"I didn't try to run over that twit back there! I'm innocent!"

"What goes around comes around," Mom responds. "Sometimes, it just hits the wrong target. And, as for being innocent, none of us even comes close," she continues, doubtless referring to the reallocation of my father's assets.

We enter the building's lobby, once a drab passthrough coated in decades of gray paint now transformed into an impressive foyer with marble pilasters, alabaster chandeliers, and panoramic, gilt-framed seascapes. Entering the refurbished elevator, its etched brass walls polished to an almost too-bright sheen, I press the button for the fifth floor as Mom asks, "Do you remember the elevators in the old Porteous, Mitchell, and Braun department store? They were old like this one, but simpler—just beige or white inside, I can't recall which. Anyway, back in the '40s, they were run by young women in bellhop uniforms. It was refined," she concludes wistfully. "Now, all we have to push are these buttons."

"Is this so bad?" I respond. "Think of how boring that job must have been. Now, it's automated," I add, before recalling her aversion to automation and the job losses it often causes.

"And just what do you think those poor women are doing these days?" she asks pointedly.

"I think that they're retired, like you," Diane says to circumvent further lecturing.

"Touché," Mom replies, conceding defeat. "Anyway, this is a lot better than that winding staircase at Nancy's last office."

"The one in the brownstone across from Mercy Hospital?" I ask.

"Yes!" she responds. "Its steps were too high, and I could barely see two feet ahead of me because of the dark wall-paneling. I thought I'd fall and kill myself on those stairs!"

"So, it was the 'Stairway to Heaven?'" Diane teases, eliciting a sharp look.

"I didn't like that place either," I say. "The traffic was crazy and it was hard to find parking because of all of the people trying to get to Mercy."

"Aren't we all trying to get mercy?" Diane asks, in another ill-advised attempt at humor.

Mom frowns. "If we'd had the ambulance take

your father there instead of to Maine Med," she says, ignoring her, "we probably wouldn't be doing this today."

The elevator doors open on the fifth floor, where Diane and I help Mom down the long corridor that leads to Nancy Poole's office. At the hall's end, just before the entrance to Nancy's waiting room, a large, arched window overlooks the nineteenth-century commercial blocks and row houses of India Street. Recently turned into antique shops, apartment houses, and gourmet restaurants, their freshly painted ochre, rose, and chartreuse facades gleam softly in the slanted August light. "Pretty," Mom remarks, looking out. " But I liked it better before."

"You mean when all the buildings were dingy and the alleys full of weeds?" Diane asks.

"At least it was honest-looking then," Mom replies. "Now, it reminds me of an overdressed woman who's trying to impress."

Neither Diane nor I react. Instead, Diane turns Mom away from the window and opens the door to Nancy Poole's waiting room. There, the young receptionist looks up from her computer screen and greets us. "Ah, the Allaires! I'll let Nancy know you're here."

"You've met us?" Mom asks, our half-dozen previous visits having apparently, and suddenly, vanished from her memory.

"Why, yes," the young woman replies, inured

to the foibles of the law firm's elderly clients. "Several times."

My mother studies her. "Well, nice to see you again," she says. After a moment, she adds, "Don't take my forgetfulness personally. Sometimes I wake up not really knowing where I am or how I got there."

"We all have days like that," the receptionist answers kindly.

"I didn't used to," Mom replies, "but life changes, and we change along with it, I guess."

"We do if we're lucky," the receptionist responds, smiling. "Nancy will be with you in a minute. Can I get anyone something to drink—water, tea, or coffee?"

"No thanks," I answer. "We'll just get Mom settled."

Diane and I help Mom sit down in a tall armchair, from which it will be easy to rise, and seat ourselves on a sofa across from her, a coffee table strewn with newspapers between us. Diane picks up a copy of the *Wall Street Journal*, whose headline reads, "Pharma Giant's Stock Plunges After Misleading Earnings Report." She grimaces. "There was a clip about this on last night's news. This is the same company that raised a generic drug's price by 2,000 percent a while back. Now, they're trying to ascribe a billion-dollar product failure to an unforeseeable 'decline in good will.'"

"Who'd they think would buy that story?" I ask. "They didn't ever have that much good will going for them."

Mom looks sanguine. "I guess it depends on one's point of view."

"What do you mean?"

"Just that different people see things differently at different times," she replies.

"How?" I ask.

"For example, when I was twenty-eight and you were just two years old, I remember watching you play on the beach one afternoon and thinking how I was literally fourteen times as old as you. It was almost unbelievable that we could even talk to each other."

"Did you actually talk to each other?" Diane asks, eyebrows arched. "He was only two!"

"Your brother spoke at a very young age—at least, in French," Mom replies. Turning back to me, she goes on, "In fact, you were only a year when you first started talking."

"And, God knows, he hasn't stopped since," remarks Diane.

Mom ignores this to return to her topic. "But now that you're sixty and I'm eighty-six, there's only a 30 percent difference in our ages," she goes on. "What's more, if I live to be a hundred and you live to be seventy-five, the difference will be just 25 percent." She reflects on this. "It's almost as if, even though we started out in different generations, over the years, we'll become near contemporaries. That's what I meant by different perspectives at different times," she concludes with satisfaction.

Perhaps having overheard Mom's off-kilter argument, the receptionist stops typing, whereas I'm speechless.

"What do you call this line of thinking?" Diane asks.

"Variable aging," Mom replies.

Diane stares. "How in the world did you ever think all this up?"

"I used to be a bookkeeper," she answers.

"Well, it's creative accounting, that's for sure," I remark.

Mom glances at the *Wall Street Journal* headline. "Yes—I'd probably be in great demand today if I were still working," she reflects, without a hint of wryness. We all—Diane, myself, and the receptionist—start laughing, but Mom's expression is serious. "Getting back to the point," she continues single mindedly, "even though I don't agree, maybe these pharmaceutical executives only did what they believed was in their company's best interests."

"Not in their own self-interest?" I ask her.

"Is there a difference?" Mom asks. "Think of why we're here today: because we took all of your father's assets and put them in my name so that he could qualify for state assistance.

Peut-être nous méritions cette aide et peut-être pas. Ça dépend de la façon dont on regarde les circonstances."

Diane, who doesn't understand much French, turns to me for translation. "Mom thinks that maybe we didn't deserve the state assistance," I explain reluctantly, dreading her reaction. "She thinks it depends on how one views the situation."

Anger fills Diane's face like a thunderhead rising. "Don't deserve the assistance!?" she exclaims. "Why do you think Dad paid all those taxes?!" she demands. "So that we could take advantage of government programs that would keep his money from falling into the hands of thieves like the guys who run the pharma companies and the rip-off artists who own the nursing homes!"

"Even if others serve their own interests, we don't have to serve ours," Mom pronounces. "We should follow the example of the saints, not the sinners."

Diane's choler deepens. "I'll tell you who the saints are here," she answers, likely alluding to herself and the grandchildren who assist her in caring for Mom, but she stops without saying anything further.

"Where does that reference to 'saints and sinners' come from—the Bible?" I ask Mom, to skirt Diane's ire.

"I have no idea," Mom answers. "I pray every

day but I haven't read the Bible in years. I don't even know where I keep it."

"By the kitchen telephone," Diane says. "Right next to the bills that come in every day—the ones we're here to make sure you'll be able to keep paying!" She pauses to take a deep—and, I hope, steadying—breath. "You know, Mom, we're not talking about money that was stolen from anybody," she finishes, more calmly.

Not so easily dissuaded, Mom asks, "How's that?"

"After Dad's assets were transferred to you," I explain, "he fell below the poverty line, and the State of Maine paid his nursing-home costs at a lower public-patient rate. Once you've died, though, the family will have to pay back the difference. The whole thing is a 'legal fiction' designed to keep you from being bankrupted by Dad's illness."

"Are you sure?"

"As a matter of fact, yes," I reply. "Under the Maine Care Act, you, as Dad's spouse, are protected by the right of dower. This shields your estate—including your real property and investment assets—from healthcare creditors during your lifetime."

Mom looks at me, plainly amazed. "How do you know all this?"

"He went to law school, remember?" Diane answers.

"You're an attorney?!" Mom asks incredulously.

"No. I didn't like law school, so I left before graduating and never practiced."

"I forgot all of that," Mom says sadly.

"That's OK—it's in the past."

She sighs. "Like most of my life."

Nancy Poole's office door opens, and Nancy—a thin 60-year-old in a tailored suit—enters the room, dispelling Mom's wistfulness. "Bonjour Madame Allaire, comment ça va?" she begins, taking the opportunity to practice her French, which she does on each of our visits.

"You remember me?!" Mom asks.

"Of course!" Nancy declares, disarmingly. "I'm your attorney, it's my job to know all about you and represent your best interests!" she adds.

"That's good of you, as busy as you must be," Mom says, "considering the complicated laws you have to deal with in cases like mine."

Nancy smiles. "Eldercare law isn't all that complicated," she replies. "It's really just a matter of rendering onto Caesar what's Caesar's and unto the client's what's . . ."

"The client's," Diane says, finishing the maxim for her.

My mother glances at the headline of the newspaper on the coffee table. "You've never been involved with Wall Street, then?" she asks Nancy.

"Not ever!"

"I guess that's a good thing. For you, me, and maybe just about anybody."

"Anybody?" Nancy asks, raising her eyebrows.

"Anybody who cares about integrity."

"That might be a matter of perspective," Nancy offers neutrally.

"Precisely," Mom answers.

CHAPTER 11

A Pass Time

Short Take

Mom pushes her walker down the hallway that leads to the laundry room. She moves slowly and gingerly over the tan tile floor, having learned from experience that a hard fall can lead to weeks or months in a nursing home. This is why, when she picks up speed, she slows down and murmurs her new mantra, "Haste makes waste"—a caveat that, along with many others, regulates the rhythm of her housebound days.

My sister, Diane, is in the laundry room dropping yet another load of wash—scarcely soiled white face cloths, bath towels, and hand towels—into the washing machine. She frowns at Mom. "It's beyond me how one person can go through so many towels in a single day! We're up to a load of wash every morning and, sometimes, another in the afternoon!"

Mom, who had several siblings and used to help her mother do the laundry with a wringer washer, shrugs, further irritating my sister. "I mean, really, what do you do, Mom?" Diane asks her, "Just toss everything in sight into the hamper?"

As usual when confronted by something unpleasant, Mom smiles. "It's a pastime," she replies, having no better explanation.

Diane's face turns red. "A pastime!" She repeats, incredulous. "Maybe you should try something else to pass the time!" Then, likely not wanting to say anything harsher, she starts the wash and brushes past Mom, who remains in the hallway, leaning on her walker.

"Why did you say that?" I ask.

"Because I'm trying to teach her—us—patience?" she replies, tentatively.

"How's that working?" I ask, my voice loud above the rising noise of the washer.

"It's hit or miss," she answers softly.

CHAPTER 12

Don't Talk to Strangers
Medium Take

It is a mid-July day, the sky cloudless and brilliant, reflected heat rising in transparent, filmy waves from the parking lot blacktop. We pass through the supermarket's glass doors into frigid air-conditioning, making Mom draw her apricot-colored summer cardigan close around her neck.

Mom shopped here for more than five decades but now, because of the number and length of the store's aisles, her children and grandchildren typically shop on her behalf. This afternoon, however, on learning that Diane, Carrie, and I were about to pick up something for dinner, she has asked to come along.

"Are you sure you want to do this?" Diane asks.

"Yes," Mom replies, determinedly. "I want to see the store again. After all, it could be my last time."

"Don't talk like that—you'll come here again," I say in the reassuring tone that I invariably adopt when she teeters toward the morose.

"You never know." She eyes the motorized shopping carts, which she's always eschewed because, in her own words, "I don't like to make a spectacle of myself."

"Would you like to try one of these?" I ask, hoping she might have had a change of heart.

Her expression turns hard. "What do you think?" she asks, in a tone icier than the air-conditioned drafts blowing down from the ceiling.

We walk into the store's produce department, where grapes, peaches, strawberries, and blueberries are heaped high on counter tops in a show of seasonal abundance. "My!" she remarks, grasping her walker more tightly and craning her neck to see into the vegetable section beyond. "This store is much bigger than I remember."

"It's exactly the same size it's always been," Diane remarks flatly.

Mom studies her, trying to determine if this is sarcasm.

"That's strange," I say to break the tension. "When I go somewhere I haven't been in a long time—someplace I haven't seen since I was a kid—it usually seems smaller."

Mom, still holding onto her walker with one hand, squeezes a peach with the other to determine its ripeness. "That's because you're older now."

"So, shouldn't you find this place smaller?" I ask, trying to coax a smile out of her.

The peach having been deemed acceptable, Mom

hands it to Carrie, who places it in a flimsy plastic produce bag that she's pulled from a dispenser.

"It's different," Mom continues curtly. "I'm a *lot* older."

I'm trying to think of a conciliatory comment, when a young woman wearing a halter top and cutoffs short enough to warrant arrest for indecent exposure, barges into the aisle with her cart, nearly bumping into Carrie. Oblivious, she says, "So what are you doing now?" into her cellphone.

My mother, startled, collects herself, and politely answers, "Well, right now, I'm shopping."

The young woman, whom I recognize as the new occupant of a rental house on Mom's street, brushes a strand of frizzy hair off of her face and glares. "I'm not talking to you!" she says, pushing her cart down and then out of the aisle, cellphone still held to her ear.

"Thank God," Mom remarks to no one in particular.

"What makes you say that?" I ask her, since she seldom says anything unkind about anyone, even when confronted with bad behavior.

"Well, it's like I used to tell all of you when you were children, you should never talk to strange people."

I grin. "And you think that she qualifies?"

"Absolument!" she replies, her expression suddenly mischievous.

CHAPTER 13
Alive and Well and Not Living in Paris
Medium Take

My mother and I are in the family room, looking at 1940s snapshots of her and her lifelong friend Jeannine Blanchard posed like bathing beauties—shades of Betty Grable and Jane Russell—at a local beach. We turn a page of the photo album and look at pictures of Mom and my late father with Jeanine and her husband, Ed, at a long-ago New Year's Eve party: noisemakers between their lips, crepe-paper streamers overhead, feathered and glitter-daubed paper hats on their heads—glimpses of the early days of their marriages, captured within the borders of black-and-white photographs. The two young couples seem to me like characters from an early sitcom: Rob and Laura Petrie with their neighbors, Jerry and Millie, setting out on the journey of adulthood, a winding road full of unimagined joy and promise, unsuspected sorrow and disappointment about to unfurl before them.

My mother seems to sense my thoughts. "The world was our oyster," she says wistfully.

"And what did you do with it?" my sister Diane asks.

"We ate it, of course," Mom answers. We all laugh.

Diane asks, "Did it give you indigestion?"

"What do you think?" Mom replies, giving us a look inveighed with the particular irony that perhaps only octogenarians are entitled to summon. "It's been a long time since I've seen Jeannine and Ed."

"Why don't you go visit them now?" Diane suggests.

"Now?"

"Sure. It's a nice, sunny day, and Rob can drive you. Let me give them a call." Every now and then, Diane needs a break from being Mom's caregiver day in and day out.

"Why not?" I join in. "It'll be nice to visit the Blanchards—I haven't seen them in ages."

"All right," Mom says tentatively. "But, I'll need to go to the bathroom first." These days, Mom, afflicted by occasional incontinence and intent on avoiding public embarrassment, spends an increasing amount of time in bathrooms.

I help her rise from her chair, as Diane calls the Blanchards to let them know we will be coming.

Getting Mom in and out of the house is not a simple matter. In winter, such as now, Diane, I, or whoever else is present must help her don the requisite multiple layers of outerwear—

boots, coats and hats, gloves and scarves. Then, because her house and garage are on a hill, with the garage sitting lower on the grade, she must be helped onto the electric lift that she uses to access it. Then, one must get her into the car, an exercise that involves sliding her onto the front seat without bumping her head on the doorframe, and, afterwards, lifting her feet off the garage floor and into the car.

This process completed, I turn the key in the ignition and back the car out of the drive. "It's nice to be out and about," Mom states pleasantly, despite the energy she's had to expend merely to get this far. Taking note of new or renovated houses along the street where she has lived for nearly fifty years, she remarks, "It's interesting to see all the new things." As we drive through town, she continues to comment on the changes that time has wrought over the last few decades: an abandoned church, a repurposed fire station, a new shopping center—though, in truth, she has seen and commented on all of this before.

Arriving at the Blanchards, Mom confronts another physical challenge. Their nineteenth-century Victorian home, a sprawling many gabled structure, replete with several porches and a turret, sits high on a granite-block foundation. Lacking a wheelchair ramp, it is only accessible via stairs. For a moment, she stares at the steps leading up to the back door as if contemplating a climb up Mt. Everest. Steeling herself, she takes hold of the grab bar and begins her ascent. "No wonder Jeannine never goes out," she says on making it up the first step, "She'd never be able to get back in."

With much effort, she raises each of her legs in turn onto the high, brick risers, while I follow at her back, ready to catch her in the event of a fall. Ascending, she calls out every step by number, as if doing so will somehow render her climb less difficult. Finally, she reaches the top step and, winded, exclaims, "Four! Now I know what it's like to rock climb!"

"You think so?" I ask, steadying her against a railing.

"Not really—but as much as I want to know!"

About to knock on the back door, I notice a yellowed, neatly printed note that reads, "Come on in—we're out front." I'm not surprised. I've been forewarned by Diane that the Blanchards—who are Mom's age—are trying to minimize their movements within their large house, which they love but now find too big to manage.

I turn the doorknob. In the far reaches of the first floor, a television blares at a volume set to compensate for elderly deafness. I hope they haven't forgotten we're coming as they've occasionally done in the past. My fears are allayed as I help Mom over the threshold, since someone, perhaps the Blanchards' part-time healthcare aide, has left a "guest walker" for us.

Mom scowls at the walker as she takes hold of it. "I miss my cane."

"You do?"

"Sure," she answers. "It made me look like an old lady, but at least it didn't make me feel like an invalid."

"So, that's why you miss it?" I ask, steadying the walker as we start down the back hall, whose too-pliant carpet runner concerns me the way hidden shoals and currents worry a sailor entering uncharted waters.

"Partly," she replies, sounding tired after the morning's many exertions. "These days, though, I miss a lot of things—the house I grew up in, your father, even a fancy doll I wanted when I was small but that Mom couldn't afford to buy me."

I walk a few feet ahead and bend down to smooth an unruly stretch of carpet. "How can you miss something you never had?"

"People miss all sorts of things—whether or not they're worth missing," she responds, her gaze, like mine, fixed on the runner, the gauntlet we must traverse to get to our destination. "For instance, you miss living in Paris."

"I've never lived in Paris," I answer, standing up to help her with the walker.

"Exactly!" she beams, happy to have driven sense into me yet again.

CHAPTER 14

Something Completely Different
Short Take

This afternoon, sitting in the den with Mom while she watches the Weather Channel, I ask her about a high-school friend of hers. "How is Estelle doing these days?" I inquire.

"Estelle?" Mom replies.

"Yes," I answer. "You know—Estelle, the one who's been widowed a couple of times. I'm sorry but I can't remember her last name."

"I don't know—I haven't seen her in a while," Mom replies, turning her attention from the television, which is airing a show about the dangers of hurricanes, even though there hasn't been a single one this season. "I don't remember her birthdate either," she continues, "because it changed again the last time she got married."

Coming in from the kitchen with a glass of lemonade, Diane harrumphs. "People's birthdays don't change when they get married, Mom," she chides.

"They don't?!" Mom exclaims.

"No," Diane responds. "Only their names. After her last husband died, Estelle went back to using her maiden name."

"What was that name?" I ask.

" 'Côté,' the 'Smith' of the Québécois world," Diane answers with a smirk.

Mom shakes her head. "She would have been better off with the new birthdate."

"How?" I ask.

"It would been something completely different," Mom replies.

CHAPTER 15

At the Home
Long Take

Ian, Diane, Mom, and I ride through the center of Saco in Diane's black Lexus sedan. The town is much changed since my childhood. Many of the colonial-era mansions, which formerly housed lawyers' and doctors' offices, have been turned into B and Bs and decked out with window boxes of marigolds and geraniums. The once uneven sidewalks have been repaved and garnished with plantings of giant canna and hanging baskets of pink petunias and surprisingly long ivy. Though the eighteenth- and nineteenth-century brick and granite commercial buildings remain, they no longer house pharmacies, corner groceries, and hardware stores but giftshops, coffeehouses, and art galleries with names like the Rugged Spruce, the Duck Spoon Café, and the Paintbrush Manifesto—names that in my youth likely would have drawn laughter, not customers.

"Things certainly have been prettied up around here," I remark.

"That's for sure," Diane says. "The Massachusetts and New York retirees who've moved here have driven up real-estate prices, so the locals are trying to make a buck by shaking them down on merchandise and services."

"La plus ça change, la plus c'est la même chose," Mom observes with an air of resignation. "It's always about money."

Diane turns the car into a circular drive and brings it to a stop under the porte-cochère of the retirement facility where my late father's sister, Jeanne, lives. On a porch beneath the building's portico, old men and women sit in white rockers, reading, knitting, and chatting like figures in a Victorian engraving of an old folks' home—except that some are tapping on tablets or talking into cellphones and others have Audis or Mercedes parked in an adjacent lot, just beyond a border of daylilies and hydrangeas.

I open the car door for Mom, who, in concession to the warm early-autumn weather, wears a white cotton shift and sunhat decorated with a pattern of intertwined vines and roses. Taking hold of her walker, she looks at her contemporaries on the porch. "I wonder whether I know anyone. If I do, I should wave."

"Can't you tell whether you know them?" Diane asks.

"Not really," Mom answers. "My cataracts make distant things fuzzy." She sighs. "I don't want to seem rude just because I don't recognize someone."

"Why don't you wave anyway?" Diane suggests. "The ones you know will think you recognize them and the others will assume you're waving at another person."

"Good idea!" Mom replies and waves as Diane's suggested. Several people wave back, either out of recognition or politeness.

Ian holds the building's door open while I help Mom through it and Diane enters the vestibule, where she presses the call button for Jeanne's apartment. After she's pushed it several times, my aunt's voice comes out of the call box. "Allô. C'est qui?"

"Bonjour," I answer. "C'est votre neveu, Rob. Mon fils, ma soeur, et ma mère sont avec moi. Nous sommes venus vous rendre visite," I continue, reviewing who we are and why we're here—just in case she's had a lapse of memory since I called and told her the same this morning. "Je vous a prévenu ce matin. Vous souvenez-vous?" Likely not understanding, Ian and Diane exchange quizzical glances.

"Bien sûr, I remember!" my aunt exclaims. "Entrez!"

With a buzz and a click, the glass front door unlocks and we enter a large palm-filled lobby with a Georgian-paneled reception desk at its center. "We're here to see Jeanne Delormé," I announce to the blank-faced young woman behind the counter. "I'm her nephew, and this is my son, my sister, and Mom," I inform her for security purposes.

Brushing the bangs of her too-long pageboy out of her eyes and off her forehead, she gives us the once over, and then consults her computer. "Third floor, apartment 344," she instructs, eyes still on her computer's screen. "Take the elevator to your left and then a right when you get off of it." She looks up and raises her eyebrows as I struggle to steady Mom on her walker and nearly lose my balance. "If you think you might get lost, sir," she says, in a mix of concern and condescension, "I'll have somebody show you the way."

Her offer doesn't entirely surprise me, because, since my hair's gone gray, some young people seem to assume that I'm elderly and prone to confusion. "That won't be necessary," I say, curtly. Heading off as directed, I reflect on how Mom must feel when we presume she doesn't understand something even if, at that moment, she's utterly lucid.

In the elevator, Diane asks if Jeanne remembered we were coming, confirming my suspicion that she didn't understand the intercom conversation.

Mom gives Diane a sharp look. "You heard Rob talk with her! Don't tell me you've forgotten your French?!"

"I haven't!" Diane protests, appearing affronted,

despite the evidence to the contrary. "It's just Rob's accent that throws me. I understand the Québécois pronunciation, but the Parisian accent he picked up at all his fancy schools is like listening to a brook babbling!" She looks at me to ensure her barb has registered.

"What fancy schools?" Mom asks. "He went to the same elementary school and high school as you!"

"I meant college and grad school," Diane clarifies.

"What's your point?" I ask.

"That you always get what you want—whatever the cost to those around you," Diane replies, implying, not for the first time, that my education drained the family finances, though in fact, beyond scholarships, I covered my expenses.

"Diane!" Mom exclaims, "what Rob spent on his education is his own business."

"What *he* spent is," Diane says, her larger meaning nonetheless apparent.

"I'm glad we're in consensus," I remark archly.

Before she can respond, the elevator reaches Jeanne's floor and opens its doors on a scene straight out of *Town and Country* or the *Maine Antiques Digest*: an eighteenth-century chest of drawers in flame mahogany above which hangs an equally old portrait of a bonneted matron with a dark, patently disapproving stare.

"Impressive," I remark, hoping to move us onto

a new topic. "I didn't realize this place was so high end."

"It isn't, really," Diane replies. "A resident's family probably left the stuff because they didn't want it."

"You think so?" I ask, surprised that anyone would simply abandon what could well be heirlooms.

"Who knows?" Diane replies. "Either that or they left it to settle disputed charges."

"What sorts of disputed charges?"

"For services like extra housekeeping and gourmet meals that the deceased probably never ordered but that were easily added to the bill after he or she kicked the bucket. This place is famous for that and other kinds of crap, which is why we didn't move Dad here after his stroke."

"Is that legal?"

"Of course not," she replies, as she holds the elevator doors open and I help Mom maneuver her walker into the hallway. "But the management doesn't care. It's just focused on profit."

"What are you talking about?" Mom asks.

"How beautiful the furniture in the hall is," I answer, ashamed that I'm patronizing Mom like the receptionist patronized me, not to mention deceiving her.

"I thought you weren't collecting antiques anymore," Diane remarks.

"I'm not," I respond defensively. "But I still

appreciate them—and this bureau is a beautiful example of the Empire style."

"Empire?" Mom asks

"American Empire," I reply. "It's based on the French version."

"Québec had an empire?"

"No, Mom," Diane tells her. "He means 'French' as in 'from France.'" She sighs. "The French had an empire, but, after losing a war with England, they kicked Québec out to keep Guadeloupe."

"Guadeloupe?" Mom repeats, looking at Diane as I straighten the walker on the hall carpet.

"It's in the Caribbean," Diane explains. "The French wanted its sugar and got rid of Québec because the furs it exported were out of fashion."

Though this is an oversimplification, Diane's familiarity with Québec history catches me off guard. Hoping my surprise isn't plain, I remark, "It was a strategic blunder in the long run and an outright abandonment of our ancestors."

"Not surprising—since screwing others over is what the people in power seem to do best."

"Maybe along with robbing everybody else," I offer.

"You've got that right," she agrees.

"This conversation's depressing," Mom remarks. "How far is to Jeanne's?" she asks, sounding tired as we pass one apartment after another without stopping.

"We're almost there, Mémère," Ian says.

"Vraiment?" she asks.

Ian looks at me. "Really?" I translate.

"Absolutely," he reassures her.

At the corridor's end, we come to an apartment whose entrance is marked by a plaster statue of Ste. Jeanne d'Arc, depicted, as is the convention, in armor, a sword in one hand and a banner emblazoned with fleurs-de-lis in the other.

"Think this is the place?" I ask Diane archly.

"Look at the door number," she replies, shaking her head. "It's the apartment opposite—go figure."

We cross the hall and knock on Jeanne's door.

"Just a second," she calls from within. The sound of footsteps follows, then the lock turns and the door opens. "Allô! Quelle belle surprise!" she exclaims, so forcefully that I wonder if she's already forgotten our conversation moments ago not to mention my earlier phone call. Her white hair is uncombed and messy, as if she's just risen.

"Vous-nous attendais, n'est-ce pas?" I ask, as she runs a hand through errant curls, her large diamond rings sparkling beneath the foyer's track lighting.

"Bien sûr!" she replies, with a look that implies my question is idiotic. "You just called from the lobby!" She hugs me, Diane, and Mom. Then, taking Ian's hands in hers, she asks, "How's med school going?"

"There's a lot of studying."

"Sans aucun doute!" she replies, unaware he likely doesn't understand her. "What a hard worker you are!" Then, turning back to me, she asks, "Did you have trouble finding my apartment?"

"Only at the end," I answer. "Because of the statue, we thought maybe you lived across the hall."

"The guy who lives there's a little strange," she says, forehead furrowed. "I don't know what his story is. Maybe he's a retired priest—or just really old!"

Since Jeanne is ninety, I wonder what age she considers old. "What makes you think he's a priest?" I ask.

"Whenever I run into him, he's either humming a hymn or a tune from a Broadway musical."

I don't react.

"Also, he wears a lot of black," she adds, to bolster her argument. "I've even seen him in a cassock."

"That doesn't prove anything," Mom says, making me wonder if she heard the last of Jeanne's remarks correctly.

"It doesn't," Diane agrees, deadpan. "Maybe he's just trying to be stylish—after all, you can't go wrong in a little black dress!"

Ian and I join Diane in a laugh but Jeanne and Mom are straight-faced.

"We shouldn't make fun of the clergy!" Mom admonishes.

Jeanne, though, breaks into a scowl. "Don't get me started about priests and their deviations from the straight and narrow," she exclaims. "That bunch of hypocrites!" However, perhaps fearing divine retribution, she adds, "Still, they're not all like that."

No one refutes this.

"I'm feeling a little tired," Mom remarks. "I think I need to sit."

"Where are my manners?! Come in! Soyez bienvenue!" Jeanne exclaims and then, in a sweeping gesture of welcome, kisses each of us on both cheeks—the classic bisous that my elderly relatives engage in only on special occasions. "It's so good to see all of you!" Turning to Mom, she says, "Viens t'assoir, Yvette!" With a squeeze of her shoulder, she adds, "We old women have to take care of ourselves!"

Seeming embarrassed, Mom changes the subject. "Quel beau miroir," she remarks of a Venetian mirror in the foyer. "It looks familiar."

"It was Mom's," Jeanne explains. Then she catches sight of herself in it and stops short. "Good Lord! I need a permanent!" she exclaims, fingering her tousled hair. "It probably doesn't matter, though, since I never see anyone who'd notice."

"How about the other residents?" Mom

inquires, as we head toward the living room.

"Most of the people I know are from our old French parish—and they're so ancient they're oblivious!"

"What about the rest?" I ask.

"You mean the out-of-staters?" Jeanne asks. "They act like they're landed gentry just because they saved or stole enough money to retire up here! No thank you—I get enough of the likes of them on my soap operas!"

Suppressing a laugh, I shake my head. "I meant the other people from around here," I say. "You know—like the Yankees."

"You mean all the 'old money' matrons?! I can't understand their Down East accents and they can't understand my French one!" she says with a smirk. Then, more seriously, she adds, "They usually don't talk to anyone they aren't related to or didn't know in grade school! Real snobs! It's funny, considering."

"Considering what?" I ask.

"The way they dress! All they wear are worn-out seersuckers, stripes, and tartans!" she responds. "They must spend their days 'Good Will Hunting,' they're so frumpy looking!"

"Frumpy or dumpy?" Diane asks mischievously.

"Both!" Jeanne answers, and she and Diane start laughing.

"You should be kinder!" Mom scolds.

"I don't know, Mom—seersuckers and tartans!" Diane harrumphs. "It's amazing they can tell themselves apart from their husbands!" She and Jeanne resume their laughter.

"Maybe it isn't always necessary to be able to tell whether someone is a man or a woman," Mom remarks.

"What do you mean?" Diane asks.

"You know, like on that Travel Channel show we saw last week about the gay resorts in Provincetown and Ogunquit," she responds, as if this alone should clarify her meaning.

"I don't follow," Diane says.

"Neither do I," I remark.

"No?" Mom asks, visibly disappointed. "How about the part where drag queens were in a nightclub imitating Barbara Streisand and Judy Garland?"

"What about it?" I ask, as much astounded that she's recalled the term *drag queen* as that she's discussing them.

"Well," she continues in exasperation. "You couldn't tell they weren't women, and everybody in the audience seemed to enjoy watching them. So, maybe it's not all that important what gender someone is."

Her reasoning leaves me speechless. Scanning the foyer for a less controversial topic, I spot a photo of my parents with Jeanne and Uncle Roland, her late husband, on a 1960s

Mediterranean vacation, Mom demure in an ivory sundress and matching hat and Jeanne svelte in a form-fitting black shift, her dark hair tied back and eyes dramatically made up like Liz Taylor's in *Cleopatra*. Or maybe, I suddenly realize, like a female impersonator's—a similarity that, if Mom brought it up, Jeanne would likely not appreciate. I don't mention the photograph.

"Allons-y nous," Jeanne orders, breaking the silence. "I've prepared coffee, tea, and pastry for all of us!"

"You baked?" I ask.

She laughs. "I made the coffee and the tea but the éclairs and Neapolitans are from Keneally's Bakery in Biddeford. I hope you like them!"

Jeanne leads us into her apartment, past a dining room filled with cherry and tiger-maple Hepplewhite furniture—early Americana that testifies to her decades of astute antique collecting as well as to New England's Anglo-Saxon heritage. Once in the living room, however, we encounter examples of an altogether different tradition: a Louis XVII divan and matching fauteuils with delicately carved white woodwork and pale-blue moiré silk upholstery.

"Are these things new?" Diane asks.

Jeanne looks dumbfounded.

"I didn't mean literally," Diane explains, "I meant did you buy them recently?"

"Oh no," Jeanne answers. "They used to be in the library of my house here in town."

"Wherever they're from," Diane continues, "they're lovely."

Jeanne smiles at the compliment and maybe also at the confirmation that Diane, her godchild, isn't a philistine regarding fine furniture. "I either bought them at a Rob Boudreault auction in Portsmouth or at Skinner's in Boston."

"I thought they might've come from your lake house," I tell her. "It's been a while since I've been, so I wasn't certain."

"You should visit me there the next time you're in Maine for Memorial or Labor Day," she answers. "My boys take me up for holiday weekends."

"Is the area the same or has it been developed?" Ian asks, probably, because on the drive from Cleveland, we stayed at a New York friend's place in the Berkshires, a huge summerhouse on a tiny lake so tightly encircled by similarly sized "cottages" that it might as well have been in Darien or Scarsdale.

"It's still the same," my aunt replies. "A miracle of God's and nature's—pristine, lovely, and peaceful."

Mom, having managed to seat herself in a fauteuil without assistance, remarks, "You're lucky you still have your houses, Jeanne."

"You're lucky you're still in yours," Jeanne

counters. "My house in town is going up for sale once the boys have finished clearing it out. Some of my stuff's been moved here and some is being given away or put in storage."

"Aren't your children taking any of it?" Mom asks.

"Sure, but there are things they don't want—like my theater organ."

"You have a theater organ?" Mom asks.

"It's in the sunroom—remember?" Diane asks her. "Aunt Jeanne played holiday carols on it when we visited last New Year's Day."

"I'm the only one who's ever played it," Jeanne laments. "And no one wants to buy it either—not even for a hundred bucks on Craigslist."

"Who's Craig? And what does he list?" Mom asks.

"Craigslist advertises things people want to sell, Mémère," Ian answers. "You know, like 'Angie's List' does with services."

" 'Angie's List'?" Mom repeats.

" 'Craigslist' and 'Angie's List' are directories, Yvette—you know, like the old Yellow Pages," Jeanne explains with a pitying glance. "Anyway," she continues, "the pastor at St. Joseph's found a place that I can give the organ to—a mission church on one of the Indian reservations in 'the County.' "

" 'The County'?" Mom repeats, looking more lost than ever.

"Aroostook County—up north, on the border with New Brunswick," Jeanne informs her.

"What about the lake house," I ask, to refocus us. "Is that going to be sold, too?"

"I'm leaving it to my grandchildren."

"I'm glad," I say. "It'd be a shame to let it pass out of the family—you've owned it for over fifty years."

"It doesn't seem like that long!" my aunt replies with a surprised look. "My, how time flies!"

Mom nods. "Whether or not we notice."

"There's not much that can be done about that," Jeanne says, sounding disconsolate. Then she perks up. "So, let's drink our tea and eat pastry! Just have fun, like in that '80s song, 'Don't Worry, be Happy!' "

"The one by Bobby McFerrin?" I ask.

"Yes, that's it! The one the rabbi mentioned at your wedding!"

"I'm surprised you remember," I tell her.

"Your wedding was the only Jewish service I've ever attended," she explains. "How come you didn't have a priest do the honors?"

"We were supposed to have one as well but he cancelled," I say. "Back then, it was hard to get a rabbi or a priest to perform an interfaith wedding. We had a tough time finding any who'd even consider it. The rabbi that we eventually got only did it because his twin sister was married to an ex-Protestant minister."

"So much bigotry!" my aunt says scornfully. "And what's it got us over the centuries? Nothing but bloodshed."

"C'est epouvantable!" Mom agrees. Then, glancing at Diane and Ian, she translates, "It's appalling."

"Anyway, let's not think about all that," Jeanne admonishes, turning her attention back to the refreshments. "Tea, anyone?"

"Yes, please," Diane answers.

"Milk? Sugar?" Jeanne asks.

"No, thanks," Diane says.

Jeanne lifts a blue-and-white teapot and pours tea into a matching cup.

"Wedgewood?" I remark. "That's English, isn't it? Why not a French tea service to go along with the furniture?"

"This color goes with the furniture," Jeanne replies. "Plus, I don't care much for French porcelain and China. Bisque is pasty looking, and Sèvres is usually too gaudy."

"You?! Not like something French!?" Diane teases.

"You've got me there!" Jeanne admits, with a laugh. "Honestly, though, the English stuff is more elegant. After all, the British had to do something well, didn't they?" she goes on, more characteristically, "I mean other than build an empire and let it fall into rack and ruin!"

This strikes even me, no Anglophile, as an

exaggeration. "It's not as if the French were much better," I protest. "Look at the mess they made of Vietnam and Algeria."

Jeanne glares. "The French are always better! And don't you forget it—not for an instant! Every place the British ever touched went to hell in a handbasket."

"Even this country?" Ian asks.

"Even this one!" Jeanne affirms. "Don't you read the papers? Seigneur! Just about all those crooks and clowns in Washington know how to do is wreak wrack and ruin!" She pauses. "Well, along with 'rape, pillage, and plunder'!"

"Is that from Caesar's *Gallic Wars*?" Diane asks, teasing.

"Jeanne!" Mom exclaims. "We shouldn't say such unkind things about others. Where's your conscience?"

Jeanne smiles. "I don't know, Yvette," she answers, passing Mom a teacup. "Maybe the thieves down in D.C. stole that, too! Just so they could see what one looks like!"

We all burst into laughter. Except Mom.

"Why don't we have our pastries now?" Jeanne asks. "I'll get them from the kitchen," she says, starting to rise from the divan with effort.

Ian jumps up. "Let me bring them in, Aunt Jeanne."

"Would you? They're in the refrigerator," she tells him and then sinks back onto the divan's cushions. "You've got a good grandson," she remarks to Mom as Ian heads to the kitchen. "And you must be a good father," she says to me. "I mean, to raise such a nice young man who's studying to be a doctor!"

"My wife Thea deserves most of the credit," I demur. "I traveled so much for business over the years that she brought up Ian almost single-handedly."

"I know what that's like," Jeanne says. "Roland died when the boys were still in grade school, so I had to raise them and manage our properties by myself. It wasn't easy," she sighs. "At least your wife could call you when you were traveling."

"Provided I wasn't in some place where the time difference was too great—like Asia or Australia," I reply. "On the subject of travel," I continue, "where was that picture in the foyer taken? Malta?" hoping that Mom won't make an unfortunate comment.

Jeanne shakes her head. "Capri," she answers but looks uncertain. "Either there or Amalfi. Do you remember, Yvette?"

"I don't."

"We forget a lot at our age, don't we, Yvette?" Jeanne asks her, sighing.

Mom, though, doesn't answer. She's turned her attention to a cardinal that's landed on the window ledge, a feathered dab of scarlet against the backdrop of Saco's ample treetops, gabled roofs, and prim Protestant steeples and, beyond, neighboring Biddeford's brick textile mills, sagging tenements, and tired-looking Catholic churches. A breeze comes up and the cardinal alights and disappears into the billowing foliage of an adjacent maple.

"What're you thinking?" I ask.

"Not much. Just that most of the Franco-Americans around here used to work and live in Biddeford."

"While every night their Yankee owners came home to pretty Saco?" I prompt, acquainted with the history.

"I don't like to look at it like that—to think the groups were pitted against each other," Mom answers. "Or that one thought itself the better of the two."

"Even if it's true," I press.

"*Was* true," she corrects. "That's in the past."

Returning with the pastry tray, Ian overhears. "Which do you think's more important?" he asks, either just making conversation or because he's truly interested. "The past, present, or future?"

"The future," Jeanne offers.

"Why?"

"Because the past is gone."

"Like we'll be soon," Mom remarks, again looking out the window, where the wind has risen and fast-moving clouds cast patterns of light and shadow across a nearby building, shifting its windows from bright mirrors to opaque panels.

"What about the present?" I ask Jeanne as a burst of raindrops streaks the living room windows with rivulets.

"The present starts in the past," she answers, "yesterday or years ago. There's not much room for change because of that."

"How about the future?" Diane asks.

"Since it hasn't happened, there's more opportunity to influence it," Mom cuts in.

"A sound conclusion based on astute observation," Ian jokes, as if evaluating a diagnosis.

"Were you expecting less?" Jeanne asks. "Your grandmother usually knows what she's talking about." Then, perhaps alluding to Mom's remarks on gender, she adds, "Though sometimes she's surprising."

Mom frowns. "Like sometimes you're incorrigible?"

"Of course." Jeanne replies, placing an eclair on a dessert plate and handing it to Mom. "Whatever else were *you* expecting?"

Outside, a downpour has started. Ian gets up to close the window and prevent the rain from coming in and splattering across the parquet flooring.

"Leave it open," Jeanne tells him. "The shower will soon pass." She turns to Mom. "Like us, right, Yvette?"

Mom sips her tea. "Tu as raison," she replies.

"Pourtant, il nous reste encore du temps pour bavarder—même si ce n'est qu'un peu."

Diane and Ian look to me for translation.

"There's still time yet," I tell them while, just as Jeanne predicted, outside the rain lightens.

"For what?" Ian asks.

"To talk," I reply, not adding, as had Mom, "if only for a little while."

CHAPTER 16

The Bluebird of Happiness
Medium Take

My mother, Diane, and I sit at the kitchen table, drinking tea from mugs decorated with images of Ginger, our long-deceased collie, and eating apricot-filled cookies from a local bakery that has been Mom's favorite since girlhood. The day's mail—some our own, some the neighbors' delivered here in error—is piled before us on the maple tabletop: garish supermarket circulars, glossy apparel catalogs, somber-looking bills, and plaintively designed charity solicitations.

Diane picks up a Metropolitan Museum of Art gift catalog and examines its cover image—a rhinestone "pheasant" brooch, the bird's body a crescent of faux diamonds, its upturned head and inclined tail rendered in opposing arcs of fake blue sapphires, veined turquoise, and translucent opals strewn across a photo backdrop of gray moiré silk.

"The 'Bluebird of Happiness,'" Mom remarks.

"More like the 'Bluebird of Van Cleef & Arpels,'" Diane quips, referring to the famed French jeweler.

Mom looks confused. "Do I know the Van Cleefs?" she asks.

Diane lets this slide. "I doubt it."

"The Arpels?" Mom persists.

Diane arches her eyebrows. "No, Mom—not unless you've been holding out on us and you're really a Parisian socialite."

My mother looks bemused. "You never know."

"How's that?" Diane asks.

"Well, I've lived a long time, and there are periods—whole years—that I don't remember. So, it's possible—I might have been anyone, maybe had a different life, and, now, I wouldn't even know," she continues, not in complaint but simply in sad acknowledgement.

Diane and I exchange glances. To keep the conversation upbeat, I reach across the table and touch Mom's hand. "I'll tell you what you were and are," I say. "You're sweet."

"You can still make me smile," she beams, squeezing the top of my outstretched hand.

"Still?" I tease. "If you can't remember things, how can you be sure that I've made you smile before?"

"I'm not."

"Then, why did you say 'still?'"

"I was being polite," she answers, honestly.

"Like always," I respond.

"As often," she corrects.

"Whenever," Diane offers, joining the game.

"If only," I add, as intent on having the last word as I was in adolescence.

Diane rolls her eyes. "Some things never change."

"Thank goodness," Mom remarks, dead serious.

CHAPTER 17

What a Way to Go

Short Take

Nowadays, Mom falls with increasing and alarming frequency. Late one afternoon, as she, Diane, and I sit in her living room, eating Belgian chocolates from a giftbox I bought while in Brussels on business, I ask her about her most recent fall, which occurred a few weeks back, when I was still in Europe.

"Were you using your walker when it happened?" I ask.

"Of course. I always use my walker." She sounds irritated.

"Well, what were you doing?"

"I was reaching for a piece of candy from the table beside the fireplace and I lost my balance."

"And then?"

"She fell into the brass wood basket," Diane interjects, pointing at it. "She's lucky she didn't hit her head on the brick hearth—she could have had a brain bleed." Diane turns toward Mom. "That would have been the end of you—all for a piece of chocolate," she tells her.

"Well, I would have died happy," Mom says.

"When you die happy, you go straight to heaven."
"I hope so," I say.
"I know so," she replies, reaching for a piece of chocolate.

CHAPTER 18

Home for the Holidays
Long Take

It's a frigid evening in late December, and Ian, Mom, Diane, and I are on the turnpike headed into South Portland to do some quick, last-minute holiday shopping. As we exit the highway for the Maine Mall, however, the traffic slows to a crawl, and we enter a line of cars so long and sluggish it rivals any to be found at this time of year in larger East Coast cities such as New York or Boston. "Merry Christmas," Diane remarks dryly, as she eases her Lexus into the rightmost lane and Karen Carpenter's "Merry Christmas Darling" echoes her on the radio.

Falling snowflakes dot the Lexus's shiny black hood with spots of white that evaporate as soon as they land on it. In the left lane, an orange Hummer with Massachusetts plates tries to wedge its way into the small space between our car and the one ahead, but Diane presses on the horn until the driver, reconsidering, pulls back.

"That's the holiday spirit," I comment.

" 'Tis the season," Diane answers, unsmiling, as she deftly cuts off an Audi with New York plates that's attempting the same gambit. "Screw the God-damned out-of-staters."

"Diane!" Mom exclaims from the back seat. "Watch your language! You shouldn't speak so disparagingly of others!"

"*Disparagingly?* Where'd you pick up that word?" I ask Mom, since it seems beyond the ken of her English vocabulary.

"She's been reading the Jesuit magazine, *America*," Diane answers for her. "You know the Jesuits—social activists but intellectual elitists."

"I knew there was a reason I liked them," I comment.

"Why do you hate out-of-staters so much, Aunt Diane?" asks Ian, who despite being in his mid-twenties and in medical school, can sometimes be naive. "Dad and I are out-of-staters," he adds coyly. "I mean, we live in Ohio."

"That's different," Diane answers. "Except for your father, who seems to have kept his East Coast snobbery," she continues wryly, "Midwesterners are generally polite and mild-mannered. The people from New York, Massachusetts, and D.C. are just plain arrogant—usually without good reason!"

"There's never a good reason to be arrogant," Mom says. "Or to be disdainful either," she adds, doubtless for Diane's benefit. "Do unto others as you would have them do unto you."

Diane ignores this and, gunning the engine,

move us into a space in the breakdown lane, slipping the Lexus into the stream of faster-moving cars so rapidly and seamlessly that not a single irate honk from other drivers occurs in consequence.

"Wow," Ian remarks.

"And *that* is how it's done!" Diane exclaims with satisfaction, as we enter the mall's huge parking lot and head for Macy's.

"Do you think we'll be able to park close enough to the store for Mémère to walk to it?" Ian asks.

"Ha!" my sister laughs, incredulous. "We'll be lucky to find a parking space in this part of the state, let alone one near the store entrance." Then, her tone more serious, she continues. "I'm going to drop all of you off at Macy's, and then park wherever I can and join you afterwards. I've put Dad's old wheelchair in the trunk so that Mémère doesn't have to risk falling on ice."

"I'm not using a wheelchair!" Mom announces fiercely. "I'm not an invalid!"

"No, you're not," my sister agrees, as she slowly cruises the parking lot, watchful for cars with lit brake lights or for people returning to their vehicles after shopping—anything that might indicate a soon-to-be-vacated parking space. "But you *are* in your late eighties and, considering how many 'spills' you've taken in just the past few months, you're also a kind of 'falling artist.'"

My mother frowns. "I think the term is 'trapeze artist,'" she says archly, "and it's also not appropriate."

"Do you mean like in the song, 'The Daring Young Man on the Flying Trapeze?'" Ian asks, trying to defuse the conversation with humor but just adding fuel to the fire.

"Getting out of this car without the wheelchair and trying to walk on this ice would be daring, all right," Diane says, as she pulls up to the curb by a Macy's entrance. "But that's not going to happen, Mom—not tonight, especially not if you want to go shopping."

"I'm the mother and you're the daughter!" Mom declares, reminding Diane of the pecking order. "You should be taking orders from me—not the opposite!"

"I know I'm the daughter, Mom," Diane says, without turning around to look at her. "The very same daughter who watches out for you every day—which is what I'm trying to do right now!"

Mom is silent.

"You don't want to spend another night in the emergency room, do you? That's what usually happens if we don't take precautions." Diane reminds her. "Sometimes, it happens even when we do."

My mother scowls but, eventually, nods in agreement. "It's just that a wheelchair is such an embarrassment," she explains. "People look at me as if I'm not capable—or, if a place is crowded, like the wheelchair and I are a nuisance."

"Nonsense," I remark, while Ian retrieves the chair from the trunk and unfolds it on the sidewalk. "Most people want to be helpful, and, as for the others . . ."

"Like a great a man once said, 'Fuck 'em," Diane interrupts.

Mom winces.

"What great man was that?" I ask.

"Just about any one of them, I'm guessing—especially if they're politicians discussing the voters in private," she deadpans.

"You've got to stop following the news," I tell her.

"I will when all those crooks and clowns stop making it," she counters.

"What she really has to do is something about her language," Mom scolds, as I help her into the wheelchair and close the car door behind her. Diane smiles at us through the Lexus's tinted windshield then waves goodbye and drives off in search of parking.

"It's cold out here," Mom says, lifting her rabbit-fur collar. She's dressed in white, tan, and ivory this evening—from her cream-colored slacks and matching orthopedic shoes to her white Angora wool gloves and beige camelhair coat. Her only concessions to holiday color are a red cashmere scarf, a matching toque, and a long-ago present from my late father, a green-and-gold Christmas brooch of a prancing reindeer, its uplifted antlers a constellation of miniscule rubies and emeralds. Still, a harried-looking, middle-aged woman, weighed down by shopping bags full of gaily wrapped gifts, looks at Mom in her wheelchair and exclaims, "My! Aren't you pretty, decked out with your holiday jewelry! Merry Christmas!" and then keeps going, presumably to her waiting vehicle.

My mother smiles thinly.

"She meant it as a compliment," I tell her.

"I know how she meant it, and I appreciate it," Mom replies, not unkindly. "Sometimes, though, I feel like I'm a baby in a carriage with people cooing over me and saying, 'Oh! Isn't she just darling!'"

"Well, maybe you are," I tease her.

She rolls her eyes.

"I mean, there are worse things than being complimented."

"That's true," she answers sagely, as Ian takes hold of the wheelchair handles. "Let's go inside. I'm freezing."

We enter Macy's through its men's department, which is less busy than I'd expected. "There might be some truth to what I've been reading about the death of retail," I say.

"Or maybe it's because men aren't usually given clothing for the holidays," Ian remarks.

"I've got close to a hundred ties and scarves that disprove that," I retort.

My mother nods in agreement. "In fact, didn't I give you the scarf you've got on right now?"

I'm wearing a Christian Dior scarf that I've owned since before I was married but whose origin has been for me a long-time mystery.

"Yeah, maybe," I answer.

"Not maybe—certainly!" Mom replies. "I gave it to you for Christmas in the late 1970s, not long after you'd graduated from college."

"You have a good memory," I say, despite the ever-increasing evidence to the contrary.

"Only about things that don't matter much," she answers, moving her wheelchair toward Men's Better Suits and Sports Jackets. There, she stops and fingers a sleeve of a blue pin-stripe vest on a mannequin. "Your father liked good clothes. He always dressed so nicely on the weekends."

"Maybe it was because he wore workmen's clothes all week at his plumbing business," I say.

"Yes, maybe." She looks more closely at the tightly cinched vest and the unrealistically narrow contours of the faceless, black-resin mannequin sporting it. "You're nearly as thin as this," she says, commenting on the weight I've recently lost through exercise and diet—and reviving a bone of contention that first arose when, in high school, I took up running. "And just as much of a dummy—someday all your exercise and dieting will catch up with you," she warns.

"I hope so," I reply. "I'm almost back to the weight I was when I graduated."

"From high school or college?" Ian inquires.

"High school," I answer.

Mom shakes her head disapprovingly. "Nobody can stay young forever," she admonishes. "I'm living proof of that."

Ian's iPhone buzzes. "Diane's on her way and wants to know where we are," he announces.

"Tell her to meet us in the food court," Mom says. "I'm feeling weak and would like something to eat."

"Are you sure that you aren't really suggesting this for my benefit?"

"That's my own business," she replies. "But, if I happen to order a cookie and offer to share it with you, you'll accept because I'm your mother—not to mention a sweet old lady."

"Well, that's partly true," I answer, again teasing her.

Looking mortified, Ian quickly interjects, "Dad's just making fun, Mémère. You *are* a sweet and nice old lady—the nicest, in fact!"

Mom smiles. "So, I guess it's true," she responds, glancing first at me and then at him. "Niceness sometimes skips a generation."

"If you say so, Madame ma mère," I say, mugging theatrically.

"I do," she answers. "And, as my son, it's your duty to believe me," she adds, then starts laughing.

Diane appears down the aisle, and Ian calls out to her.

"That didn't take long," I say, as we approach her.

She shrugs. "I was just outside the store's main entrance when I texted."

"What's the fastest way to the food court?" Ian asks. "Mémère's hungry."

"Already?!" Diane asks her with exaggerated astonishment. "What about all those Christmas cookies you ate after dinner?"

"That was then, and this is now," Mom answers, unapologetic.

"There's more to this than she's letting on," I tell my sister without elaborating.

"Whatever," Diane answers. "Let's go find something edible. But remember that we have to do some last-minute Christmas shopping. We still need to find things to give to the rest of the family."

"Which way?" I ask. "I haven't been here in decades."

"Follow me," Diane answers. "The mall entrance is beyond Cosmetics."

We leave Menswear and proceed past Men's Shoes, which is deserted, Women's Shoes and Handbags, which is crowded, and finally arrive in Cosmetics, which is thronged with women intent on enhancing their appearance and clerks eager to help with the project. A heavily made-up blonde saleswoman approaches Diane and offers her a free makeover.

"No, thanks," Diane tells her. "We're kind of in a hurry," she says and gestures toward Mom. "Can't keep her out too late, you know," she continues, only half-joking.

The saleswoman, whose nametag reads, Tiffany, looks at Mom and gushes, "Well, aren't you the sweetest thing? All dolled up for Christmas! You remind me of my Nana—God rest her!" She squeezes Mom's shoulder and adds, "Have a great holiday, hon!"

"Thank you," Mom says in the rarefied, polite tone that signifies, to those who know her well, that she is not at all happy. Still, she adds, "You, too, dear—have a Merry Christmas!"

"You handled that all right," I tell her, as we move away.

"She meant well. I have to respect that," she answers. "Besides, my sensitivity is my own responsibility, no one else's."

"Why didn't you accept the saleslady's offer of a makeover," Ian asks Diane.

"Are you kidding?" my sister replies. "Did you get a load of all that makeup she was wearing? By the time she'd finished with me, I'd have been ready for the Witness Protection Program."

Except for Mom, we start laughing. "She looked nice," Mom says, as often, sacrificing truth in favor of charity. "I thought her makeup brought out her best features."

"And what might those be?" Diane asks her.

"Diane!" Mom exclaims. "It's almost Christmas! For your own good—and everyone else's—try to show some kindness!"

Chastened, we're all quiet as we approach the mall entrance, which is marked by a sparkling and gigantic version of Macy's five-pointed red star logo.

"How nice," Mom says. "They've put up a Star of David in honor of Hanukkah."

"That's the Macy's logo, Mom," I explain gently, as we pass under it and into the mall proper.

"That's right, Mémère," Ian, who was raised Jewish, adds, "Stars of David have six points, not five."

"I'm glad your mother wasn't here to hear that," she tells Ian, sounding embarrassed. "I'd have hated to offend her." She turns to me and asks, "How is Thea?"

"She's fine," I answer. "As it happens, this is the first night of Hanukkah, so she's getting ready to go to a friend's party."

"I wish she'd come with you on this trip," replies Mom. "I miss seeing her."

"I know, but she's afraid of flying and can't bring herself to do it in winter."

The mall area immediately outside of Macy's is not the same as I remember from my adolescence, when it was just an empty, glass-enclosed foyer offering access to the exterior. Now, the space has vendor stalls along the walls and a circular stage at its center, where, according to the signage, an acapella women's group will soon give a performance.

"Look," Diane says, motioning toward a vendor cart with bistro chairs and tables in front of it. "They sell coffee and muffins here. Why don't we stop and get something for you—I mean Mom—to eat. It'll be faster than going to the food court."

"Sure, why not?" I respond. "She's probably not really hungry anyway." Watching the acapella group arrive, I add, "Which makes this all a kind of theater—double entendre, intended."

"Listen!" Diane scolds. "Mom told me she thinks you're too skinny! So be sure you get something!"

"OK." I answer. "Maybe I can have a smoothie."

"Whatever you have, make a show of ordering and eating it! I can't have her being sick with worry. It doesn't take much to set her off these days."

Having received my marching orders, I turn to Mom and Ian, who, because of the crowd gathering for the concert, have fallen a little behind us. "Do you mind if we eat here instead of in the food court?" I ask. "That way, we'll be able to hear the music." Following Diane's direction, I add, "Plus, you were right, Mom—suddenly, I'm hungry!"

My mother looks at me. "Sometimes, Rob, I don't know if you're telling the truth or humoring me. But, I guess it doesn't matter, does it?" she continues with a smile.

I smile back. "What would you like?" I ask, motioning to the posted menu.

"Just coffee."

"No food?"

"You know the elderly—we eat like birds. I'll just share whatever you're having."

"I don't know why you worry so much about me," I say.

"And I don't know why you make me," she replies, sounding aggravated but with a broadening smile, which reveals that—at last—I've made her happy.

I turn to Ian and Diane and ask what they'd like. "Coffee for me," Diane answers. Ian asks for hot chocolate. I place the order at the stall counter. "Do you have a tray for me to carry this to our table?" I ask the vendor.

"I'll walk it over," he informs me.

I return to our table just as a tall, expensively dressed brunette carrying a Gucci purse and shopping bags marked Hermès, Versace, and

Dolce & Gabbana bumps into Mom's wheelchair. Looking down, she exclaims, "Honestly!"

Mom blushes and seems about to apologize, but, before she can, Diane gets up and, in a tone cold enough to freeze her coming coffee, asks the woman, " 'Honestly,' what exactly?"

Flustered, the woman doesn't answer her but instead walks away without ordering. "Bitch!" Diane says, loudly.

"Diane!" Mom chastises. "She might hear you!"

"Who cares if she gets an earful! It'd be a service to humanity—the part that's been unlucky enough to meet her anyway." She harrumphs. "How pretentious!"

"What makes you say she's pretentious?" Ian asks.

"Her purse and high-end shopping bags!" Diane answers. "Those brands don't even have stores north of Boston! She carts those around to make an impression!"

"Well, she made one, all right," I remark.

"You did also, Diane," Mom adds. "And maybe not such a good one."

Diane glares at her.

"But thanks for looking out for me," Mom continues. "That was good of you."

Diane's expression changes. "No problem," she says. "You brought me into this world, and it's my job to take care of you while you're still in it."

Mom winces slightly but only says, "You're a good daughter. Your father always stood up for me like you just did."

"What do you mean?" I ask.

"When people made fun of my French accent."

"Did that happen a lot?" Ian asks.

"More than you'd think," she answers. "Especially back in the fifties, after your grandfather and I were first married."

"I'm surprised," I remark "since there are so many Francophones in Maine and New Hampshire."

"It didn't happen much here. Usually, it was when we went to Boston for a Red Sox game or shopping. Some of the Yankees and Irish down there were pretty closed-minded," she continues. "I wonder if they're still like that."

"The ones you ran into might be dead and buried by now," Diane tells her.

"Probably," Mom answers absently, her attention having shifted to the mall's holiday decorations—the frosted white wreathes at the exits, the glittering snowflakes hanging from the potted ficus and philodendra, the huge Christmas ornaments suspended from the ceiling high above us. "How festive!" she says, as the stall operator serves our beverages. "It reminds me of those old Christmas shopping trips to Boston—everything was always so beautifully decorated."

"How did you get down there?" I ask, both

to encourage this turn in the conversation and because, before the construction of the interstate, the only way to get to Boston was via rail or US Route 1, which was mostly a narrow two-lane highway.

"We drove. Your father never cared for the train. I think it's because as a boy he used to take it to Montréal with his parents. That was a long trip," she says, smiling. "At least nine hours."

"How long did it take to get to Boston on Route 1?"

"Oh, probably four or five hours—and there was nowhere near the traffic there is today. But the speed limit was lower, and there were lots of trucks and buses that slowed things down."

"What were the malls in Boston like back then?" Ian asks her.

She laughs. "There weren't any malls in those days! We used to do our shopping at Jordan Marsh and Filene's downtown. They were beautiful department stores, with mahogany paneling and brass and crystal chandeliers," she says wistfully. "But the best part of the trip was always the finish, when we'd have drinks or dinner at the Hotel Lenox in the Back Bay."

"What was so great about that?" Ian inquires.

"You've never taken him to the piano bar at the Lenox?" Mom asks, looking at me in astonishment.

"The piano bar's closed, Mom," I tell her, "And

you might be wrong about when you and Dad used to go there. The hotel's pretty old but the bar only opened in the 1960s."

"Really?" Mom frowns, nonplussed by this latest evidence of her failing memory. Still, she continues, "Anyway, it was a wonderful place, especially during the holidays—actors from the Theater District and people off the street would come in and sing along to whatever Christmas carol the pianist was playing."

"Sounds chaotic," Diane observes.

"It was charming," I correct her. "Thea and I used to take out-of-town guests there when we were living in Boston, back in the '80s. They always loved it."

"Your father and I certainly did," Mom says. "I remember one night in late December when we were there and an old Irishman with a strong brogue sidled up to the bar and sang, 'I'll be Home for Christmas.' By the time he'd finished, there wasn't a dry eye in the house. Even your father looked like he might start crying." She goes quiet for a moment. "God, how I miss your dad," she murmurs, as tears well up in her own eyes and threaten to spill over.

Diane reaches across the table and places a hand over Mom's gloved fingers. "We all miss him, Mom—it's only natural, particularly at a time like Christmas."

Onstage, a slender, fine-featured woman with

shoulder-length gray hair starts singing Mom's favorite carol, "Silver Bells," about how it's holiday time in the city. She and her fellow carolers begin in a harmony so clear and sweet that it's almost like the pinging sound that crystal makes when it's struck and ringing.

"How lovely," I say to Mom.

"Yes," she concurs, turning away from me to hide her tears. "Even if it makes you feel as if your heart is breaking."

CHAPTER 19

Angels We Have Heard on High
Short Take

One night, on reminiscing about a long-ago trip to the Québécois shrine of Ste. Anne de Beaupré, Mom says to me, "You remember? That was the trip where I was carrying your little brother Michael."

"But Michael hadn't been born yet."

Mom frowns and replies, "I know that—I meant that I was carrying him inside me."

"You mean that you were pregnant?"

She nods. "Yes, and, when I was kneeling at the altar rail, a passing woman bent down and whispered, 'Pray for your new baby,' and I answered, 'I always pray for my babies—even the ones that I miscarried and that were never born.' The woman said, 'They pray for you, too—they are still your babies, your little angels in heaven, cherubs in the clouds, looking down on your head and waiting for the day you join them.' That made me feel less sad about having lost them."

"What did this woman look like?"

My mother is silent for a moment. "I don't remember."

"Was she wearing a veil?"

"Yes, yes, she was—it was a black veil."

"Do you think that maybe she was a nun?" I ask.

Mom smiles. "Yes, that's it—she must have been a nun." She continues, "You're smart sometimes."

"Just sometimes?"

"Well, of course," she replies, "None of us is smart all of the time—only God is smart all the time."

PART II

On Uncharted Waters

CHAPTER 20

Vanity Fair
Medium Take

Mom leans on her walker by one of the living room windows, peering through parted blue-satin drapes at the sodden lawn, deep green from the spring rains and marked with patches of violet clover, yellow ranunculus, and dandelions, the latter of which have already gone to seed and turned into crowns of white fluff. "Pretty," she remarks, while wind-driven clouds cast moving patterns across the grass.

My sister Diane and I take hold of her walker and guide her toward her favorite wing chair. As I help her sit down, she looks at me appraisingly and asks, "What happened to your eyes?"

"What do you mean?" I answer, adjusting the chair's side pillows.

"They look different."

It takes a moment for me to realize what she's talking about. "Oh," I explain, "Remember, awhile back, when my hair turned gray almost overnight?"

"You mean right after the last elections?" she interrupts with a mischievous smile.

"Yes," I reply, surprised that she remembers—

since, on occasion, she even forgets which of her family are living and which dead. "I had an eye exam right about then, and my optometrist suggested that, since my eyes are dark brown, I should try gray contact lenses to match my hair's new color."

Diane smooths her own dark-brown hair and takes a place on the sofa "You're so vain," she says, perhaps because the Carly Simon song by the same name is playing on the radio. "Not to mention gullible—he just wanted to sell you something."

There's an uncomfortable measure of truth to both these observations, so I forego responding.

"A few of my high school friends were vain," Mom says, adjusting her weight in her chair.

"Really?" I ask, thankful for the opportunity to shift away from my personal shortcomings.

"Yes. Mathilde Bissonette, one of my classmates at St. Joseph's, was terribly vain, always buying her clothes in Boston or Montréal and paying hundreds of dollars for a coat or a dress."

"That doesn't sound so bad," I say.

"You don't think so? It was the 1940s! A hundred dollars then was like a thousand today!"

"Aren't you exaggerating a little?"

My mother stares. "Were you alive then?" she asks, her standard response these days when someone questions the accuracy of her childhood or adolescent memories. As I don't answer, she continues, "My point is that Mathilde was too proud for her own good. Seigneur! She even made her boyfriend, Gerard Fleurant, get a hairweave when he started losing his hair! The hair had to be stitched into his scalp by hand!"

"A hairweave? In the 1940s?" I ask skeptically.

"Yes!" she responds, with a firmness that quells further inquiry.

"Did it work?" I ask.

"For a good while—even after they were married, into the 1970s, in fact."

"What happened then?"

"Gerry's hair turned white and started to fall out."

"Did he get another transplant?" I ask.

"No, the doctors said it wouldn't have worked a second time." Mom seems momentarily wistful, maybe because her physician recently advised against her undergoing another knee transplant for the same reason.

"So, what happened?" I persist.

"Mathilde insisted that he style his hair in an Afro."

"An Afro!?" Diane exclaims.

"Remember," I admonish Diane, "This was in the seventies."

"That's right!" Mom says, pleased by my support. "They were all the rage for men then—well, at least for some men." She pauses as if about to elaborate but ultimately doesn't. "Mathilde thought it would make it look as if he had more hair, especially after he got cancer. It was still styled that way when he was laid out in his coffin because she wanted him to look good at the wake." Mom glances at the lawn, whose flowering weed patches remain visible despite the deepening overcast, and sighs, "But it just made him look like a dandelion that had gone to seed."

Diane smirks, "Doesn't his last name have something to do with flowers?"

I nod. "It means 'flowering' in French."

" 'Mourissante,' might have been a better name for him in the end," Mom says.

"Why?" Diane asks.

Mom looks irritated. "Because he was dying and now he's dead!"

"*Mourissante* doesn't mean 'dying,' Mom," I correct her. It means 'deathly boring'—you know, as in 'bored to death' "

"I was half right," she replies, studying her reflection in the window—a tussle of salt-and-pepper curls in place of once-chestnut tresses, a mass of fine lines like a veil over her formerly flawless complexion. "At my age, what more can you expect?"

Trying to console her, Diane says, "And you still don't look half-bad either."

"Maybe on the inside," Mom answers without turning away from her image on the window glass.

CHAPTER 21

Remembering the Dead

Short Take

One morning, after reading a magazine story about the year's celebrity deaths, Mom asks me, "Do you remember when my cousin Simone who lived next door found out that Elvis had died? How she was almost hysterical and yelled across the street to our neighbor, Helene, to tell her?"

"Kind of," I reply. "What about it?"

"Just imagine!" she says, shaking her head in disbelief. "To be so upset about the death of someone you've never met! I wonder if she knows about all the famous people who've died this year."

"Simone is dead, Mom," I remind her.

"Really? Then, she certainly knows."

CHAPTER 22

When the Saints Go Marching In
Long Take

Dressed in slacks and a light sweater despite the warm summer morning, Mom lies on the den sofa, her phlebitis-stricken legs raised and clad in support hose to prevent swelling, while I use the television's remote control to search for French-language channels and Diane studies her iPhone.

Noticing two thrushes who've landed on a shrub outside the window, Mom cries "Look!" Frightened, one of the birds takes flight, but the other lingers for a moment, its head cocked and eyes set on Mom, before following suit.

Diane's iPhone tings, signaling a new text message. "Oh my God!" she exclaims, "Pat Richards died this week!"

"What! Matt Richard died in his sleep?!" Mom asks, misunderstanding as result of her hearing loss, dementia, or both in combination.

Diane corrects her gently. "Not Matt Richard, our snowplow guy," she says, "Pat Richards, your friend from Kennebunkport."

Mom looks shocked. "She died in her sleep?!"

"I'm not sure," Diane answers. "I only know she died a few days back."

"When's the funeral?" I ask.

"Later this morning," Diane replies.

My mother rises shakily from the sofa. "We're going!" she announces.

Diane and I are taken aback. "Are you sure? It's not even in town."

"I don't care!" Mom retorts as she grabs hold of her walker.

While helping her up, I ask Diane. "Where is it?"

"At an Episcopal church in Kennebunkport—the one by the Bush estate at Walker's Point," Diane answers.

This revelation gives Mom, a lifelong Democrat, pause. "Do you think we'll run into the Bushes?" she asks.

"Why? Afraid you'll tear your support hose on them?" Diane quips.

I laugh. "I don't think the Bushes will be at the service, Mom," I reassure her. "It's not as if they knew Pat personally."

"How can you be sure?" Mom replies, heading toward the staircase, presumably to go up to her room and change into more appropriate clothing. "Pat was outgoing and knew all sorts of people! Remember when she threw a surprise anniversary party for your father and me at the Colony Hotel?"

Knowing the story by heart, Diane and I nod. Still, aware of how much Mom likes to tell it, Diane questions her. "Was that the time Pat ran into those summer-stock actors from the Ogunquit Playhouse? Wasn't one famous?"

"That's right!" Mom affirms, delighted, but then, with a frown, adds. "I can't remember his name!"

"Was it Patrick Macnee, the star of *Sleuth*?" I offer, knowing full well that it was.

"Oui, c'était lui! Il était si gentil!" Mom answers excitedly. "He sent champagne to our table!"

"And your point is?" Diane asks.

My mother frowns. "My point is that Pat was very friendly. She even gave the supermarket cashiers and baggers birthday cards! I wish I were so outgoing," she concludes, getting to the heart of the matter.

"Did you envy that about her?" I ask.

Mom, ever precise with language, shakes her head. "No! I appreciated it!"

"She was a wonderful person," I say, partly in appeasement but also because I mean it.

"I understand, Mom," Diane concedes, "but Kennebunkport is a bit of a drive, especially in summer traffic."

"I don't care about the traffic," Mom says dismissively.

"Plus, you've never been to this church," I

remark, hoping she'll recall how she's confused by unfamiliar places.

Mom glares at me. "How can I not go?" she demands. "I traveled to New York to see her off on the *QE2* when she went to France to help her son and his wife with their firstborn! I can certainly manage going to Kennebunkport to see her off now!" She gets on the chairlift and, with a wistful look, adds, "I still remember standing on the dock, waving as the ship's foghorn blew and confetti streamed down." The chairlift ascends, ending the discussion.

"I'd better help her get dressed," Diane says to me.

When Diane and Mom return half an hour later, I've donned the black pin-stripe suit that I always bring with me on my visits in case Mom suddenly passes away.

"You look nice!" Mom exclaims. "Why did you bring a suit with you to Maine?"

"I might have to go to Boston for a business meeting," I lie, with the ease that comes from having an aged and easily perturbed parent.

My mother glances at me sharply. "You're not half as good a liar as you think. And thank God for that!"

"But enough about me," I reply, resolutely nonchalant. "Look at you." Mom is wearing a sleek Givenchy sheath, sheer white wrap, and black patent-leather slingbacks—which, these days, is the most formal shoe style she can wear without risking a fall. "Where does all this come from?" I ask, because, though it looks familiar, it's not what she wore to her cousin Virgil's funeral just a few months ago. "Did you go shopping?"

"Yes," she replies, smiling. "In the '60s!"

"She never throws anything out!" Diane chimes in, rolling her eyes.

"A good thing, too," Mom retorts. "That way, I always have something to wear." She waves a white clutch bag at me by way of illustration. "I bought this in 1955—on my honeymoon!"

"It's lovely," I say to placate her.

"You should see what's inside!" Diane exclaims. "A black-lace veil and matching handkerchief!"

"It never hurts to be prepared," Mom says.

To move things along, I ask Diane which car we'll be taking.

"There's no gas in Dad's old Cadillac, so we'll take my Lexus."

"The black car?" Mom asks.

"That's right," Diane replies.

"Good! It's suitable!"

Diane rolls her eyes again. "It's not like it's a state funeral."

"One should always rise to the occasion," Mom says, deploying a favorite admonishment.

Since this is the last week of May and the summer vacation season has yet to start in earnest, the drive to Kennebunkport is uneventful. On our way through the village, Mom peers out the Lexus's windows at the sailboat-filled harbor, picturesque shops, open-air restaurants, and eighteenth- and nineteenth-century mansions. "A penny for your thoughts," I remark, as the car passes the columned portico of the Colony and starts down the seaside road toward the church.

"Aren't they worth a little more?" Mom responds, without taking her eyes off the ocean and the summer estates rolling by behind the deeply tinted glass.

We both laugh.

"How did you get to know Pat?" I ask. "You don't have any other friends in Kennebunkport."

"She and her late husband were customers of your father's. His company installed the heat in their summer house when they decided to live here year round." She pauses. "Pat was a retired French teacher, and, when she found out your dad and I spoke French, we hit it off."

She turns toward me. "This is making me think of your father and the wonderful times we had. Back when your dad and I were still young, it seemed like friends and family would last forever." Her expression becomes serious. "But, now, everything's past."

"Not everything," I say to console her. "Your children are still alive and a lot of your friends are, too."

She retrieves the handkerchief from her purse and blots a tear. "Poor Pat—dying in her sleep! One moment here, then gone the next!" she says, snapping her fingers.

"Maybe that's the best way to go," I reply and instantly regret my remark.

"You think so?" she asks. "No time to say goodbye or make amends, a disappearing act where you just vanish, like the opposite of a rabbit coming out of a hat—you think that's best?"

"Not really. I just wanted to make you feel better and stop looking back."

She sighs. "I knew that," she says and touches my hand. "Don't worry—I'll be OK. This is not *my* last act—today's about Pat!"

A bird, its species rendered indiscernible in high-speed flight, hurtles toward the windshield then rockets upward into the bright, clear sky. Diane and I watch, breathless, but Mom is unrattled. "Pat loved birds," she says. "She had birdfeeders everywhere—in the backyard, off her patio, on the front lawn, even in her flowerbeds."

"Is that so?"

"Oh yes," she affirms. "She loved birds almost as much as she loved people. In fact, she called them God's little messengers."

"That's poetic," I comment.

"It's a fact."

The car turns into the church drive and pulls into a parking space on the lawn's edge. Diane opens Mom's car door and helps her out onto the uneven grass, while I retrieve her walker from the trunk.

"Can you give me my veil?" Mom asks Diane.

She dutifully retrieves it from Mom's clutch, then drapes it atop her head, making sure it doesn't fall over her face. "Is this all right?"

"C'est parfait!" Mom replies. "I'll lower it if I start to cry. That's what I meant about 'being prepared.'" Glancing at her walker, she adds, "I don't want to make a bigger spectacle of myself than I already am."

Mom's veil billowing in the wind, she, Diane, and I slowly advance up the flagstone walk past briar roses abuzz with bees and yellowjackets and ascend the ramp alongside the granite front steps. Once we're inside the church, an usher greets us. "Friends or family?" he asks.

The first, I tell him. He motions us to the left and, in deference to Mom's age, tells her, "Feel free to remain seated during the service, Ma'am."

"Thank you," she replies, her smile strained.

"The attention embarrasses her," Diane whispers to me. "That's why she's stopped going to Sunday mass."

Diane and I sit beside Mom as she settles into the pew. At the front of the church, Pat's silver-haired son takes his place along the center aisle, where the coffin, adorned with white lilies and blue delphinium, sits amid tall candles. Suddenly, the sound of wings descends upon us as first one and then another starling swoop into the transept and dart back and forth amid its pewter chandeliers so fast that, from below, they are mere streaks of bluish black against the room's white ceiling. Heads turn upward and the congregation's women adjust hats and veils to guard against droppings.

The organist begins a somber Bach prelude while a pair of blond acolytes, their bronze tans testimony to the season, enter the sanctuary, a gilded crucifix held aloft before them. The female celebrant, white-haired and willowy in Pentecostal green vestments, follows.

"Nuns say mass now?!" Mom asks, nudging me.

"No," I reply. "The Episcopalians have women priests."

"Oh," she answers.

Facing the crowd, the priest introduces herself. "Welcome! I'm the Reverend Millicent Ware. Thank you all for joining me in honoring the life of Pat Richards, our sister in Christ." Glancing up at the starlings crisscrossing the transept, she adds, "In my fifteen years as rector here, not one bird has flown into this church. So, I'm guessing that these two, like all Pat's friends, are here today to pay their respects." Laughter follows.

The organ emits the first notes of Fauré's "Pie Jesu," and Pat's funeral officially begins, the familiar opening portions—the Greeting, the Penitential Act, and the Glory to God—proceeding at their immutable, solemn pace. It's unusually hot for May and, as the service proceeds through the Collect, people fan themselves with whatever is at hand—the weekly hymnal, the funeral program, or, in my family's case, hand-painted fans that I bought on a long-ago business trip to Seoul and that Mom, with surprising foresight, has brought in her purse. High above, the starlings, perhaps trying to find their way out, perform loop-the-loops and other aeronautical acrobatics under the peaked ceiling. Fanning herself, Diane frowns. "Someone should open the doors to let those birds out—and let the breeze in!"

I nod, raising a linen handkerchief to my forehead to wipe away forming perspiration.

In the sanctuary, the Reverend Ware, having completed the Gospel readings, takes her place at a lectern emblazoned with the obligatory St. Mark's eagle. "Let us rejoice, for we are assembled this morning not to lament the passing from this earthly realm of Pat Richards but to celebrate her rebirth in the glorious hereafter!" she asserts, the boldness of her proclamation belied by her waiflike appearance yet underscored by the eagle's fierce expression.

Beside me, Mom lowers her veil in anticipation of coming tears.

"All of us gathered here today—Pat's friends, family, neighbors, and fellow parishioners—know she was special!" the priest declares. "Who among us can say that, despite life's tribulations, we greet each morning with joy and bid every evening farewell with gratitude for the love and beauty God has bestowed on us?" she asks rhetorically, and then, as expected, answers the question. "Pat—who was so full of life, love, and appreciation for the gifts of God and others—did exactly that, day in and day out, every day of her life!" The church is silent save for the flutter of waved papers, fans, and birds' wings. "Many were the times she joined us here for sunrise services and evening vespers," she continues, "worked in our community garden, and gave of her time to make and deliver meals for the elderly, infirm, or otherwise incapacitated. May we all strive to follow her example, and, like her, someday reap the reward of eternal peace and repose in the embrace of our Maker!"

As if heeding Reverend Ware's exhortations, the starlings circumnavigate the nave, sweeping low over the altar in concentric arcs, then soaring upward, one landing amid the clerestory windows above the sanctuary and the other racing through the choir loft to exit via the steeple staircase. Startled as the passing bird nearly brushes her top of her head, the elderly organist grabs the keyboard and accidentally activates the automated rhythm function, causing a bass beat to resonate throughout the building.

Gasps arise amid the mourners, but Reverend Ware remains composed at her microphone. "And that," she says dryly, "could be interpreted either as divine endorsement or a coincidence," eliciting chuckles from the congregants. "Whichever, it's a good segue into the eulogy from John Richards," she concludes, motioning to Pat's son, who assumes the lectern.

"Well, this certainly is an unorthodox funeral," he begins, looking up at the choir loft as the automated beat continues unabated.

"Why hasn't that noise stopped?" Mom whispers.

"Beats me!" I reply, my pun eliciting only a weary sigh.

"But that's OK," John continues. "Because, as many of you know, Mom liked commotion." Murmurs of acknowledgement ripple through the crowd. "Wherever she went, she was the life of the party—the person who always introduced herself and brought everyone together. She made more friends in an average year than most of us will make in a lifetime."

My mother nods in agreement.

"In fact," he continues, "Mom acquired friends the way some people collect books or china. She had friends of all ages, kinds, and colors. A few she'd known since childhood, others she'd taught with, and a lot more she'd simply met in the course of her everyday life—while shopping, doing volunteer work, or taking her beloved dance classes. They included the young and the old, artists and professionals, the educated and uneducated. Some of those she met while traveling on vacation speak other languages like Japanese, Spanish, and Italian—I've received condolences from the world over." He surveys the congregation. "I see a number of her friends here today—her neighbor Eileen Snow, her former principal Mary Eaton, and Joe Friedman who taught summer school with her." Then, with a nod to Mom, he adds, "And, of course, Yvette Allaire, with whom Mom liked to talk French, her favorite language."

My mother's expression is inscrutable beneath the folds of her black-lace veil.

"Thank you all—the few of you I've mentioned by name and the many more I couldn't. Thanks for coming to this—Mom's final get together with her friends and family!" Turning toward the choir loft, from which a syncopated jazz beat still emanates, he gestures at the hapless organist. "So, as Mom might have said under the circumstances, 'Go with the flow,' Mrs. Anderson! Play something lively that'll allow Mom to dance her way into heaven!" As he pulls a handkerchief from his blazer's breast pocket to wipe his brow, he adds, "And, for God's sake, will someone open the doors and let some air in here, so that we don't all end up joining Mom on her trip to Paradise?"

Amid peals of laughter, the organist launches into a raucous rendition of "When the Saints Go Marching In," while behind us, the usher opens the door, admitting a shaft of midday light and a strong sea breeze, which blows Mom's veil off her face. Unsettled by the tumult, the remaining starling abandons its clerestory perch, a single feather drifting downward, as the bird shoots through the nave toward the brightness.

My mother turns to me. "I've just seen Pat off for the last time!" she exclaims, tears glistening amid the fine lines and wrinkles of her face, which breaks into a smile. I touch her hand and smile back.

CHAPTER 23

Predictions

Short Take

My mother has finished her favorite holiday breakfast, a maple cream doughnut with coffee and Christmas fudge, and sits at the kitchen table waiting to see me off. Outside, the landscape is blinding white with freshly fallen snow and the sky is the cloud-streaked, brilliant blue that it sometimes is in New England after a major storm.

Gazing out the window at the snow-laden hemlocks in the side yard, Mom says, "They're so pretty—like big sugar candies."

"You like candy, don't you?" I ask.

"I love candy," she gently corrects me and then smiles.

She glances down at the suitcase by my side "Are you going somewhere?"

"Yes. I told you last night—I'm going home today."

She tilts her head slightly. "This is your home."

"Yes, it is," I concur.

"It's your original home," she adds, clarifying her meaning and perhaps covering her tracks.

"That's right," I nod.

"You and Ian are always welcome. And next time, bring Thea."

"I'll be back soon," I promise, bending down to kiss her on each cheek. "You just be here when I come back."

She smiles at me, her eyes glistening beneath thick glasses. "Don't worry—I'll be around for a while. I'll live to be one hundred and ten," she proclaims.

Diane, who's standing nearby, asks, "Doesn't that contradict some of your other predictions?"

"No one's perfect," Mom replies, defensively. She turns back to me, "I love you, Rob. You're my firstborn son."

I hug her. "I love you, too, Mom—you're my only Mom." We both laugh.

In the garage, while my sister backs out the car to drive to the train station, I say, "A hundred and ten?"

She glances at me as she turns the steering wheel. "Let's just focus on the coming year."

CHAPTER 24

The Peaceable Kingdom
Long Take

Early on a Sunday evening, I walk into the sunroom of my suburban Cleveland home, pick up the phone, and call Mom in southern Maine to wish her a happy Mother's Day. It is her sixty-third—I know, since I've just turned sixty-three, and I was born in her first year of marriage. I've waited this late in the day to call because my several siblings and their families typically visit her on holidays, and courtesy precludes her from talking on the phone in the presence of company.

I listen to a succession of unanswered ringtones, put down the phone, and look at my backyard. A daylong rain has broken and, in the fading sunlight, the garden's drenched foliage glistens softly. Emerging from a stand of trees at the lawn's edge, a gray rabbit hops toward the flowerbeds, causing two robins in its path to take flight toward sheltering branches. The rabbit enters the roses and then, likely put off by their thorns, disappears into adjacent shrubbery.

I pick up the phone and once again try Mom's number. This time, I wait until the recorded voice of my sister Diane comes on and requests that callers leave a message. Feeling uncooperative, I don't. Instead, I put the phone back down and wonder—as I usually do when there's no answer at Mom's—if there's been an accident or other crisis, and she and Diane are in an ambulance on their way to the local hospital or maybe there already. Outside, the rabbit's emerged from the shrubbery and is eating dandelions on the lawn, first cutting them at the base and then drawing their stems and fluffy, white seedpods into its mouth as if sipping on a straw.

My cellphone rings. Because the caller's number is unfamiliar and this is my business phone, I answer, "Allaire, Winterholler & Zhao—Rob Allaire speaking."

"Rob?" Diane asks tentatively.

"Yes—I didn't recognize your number," I say to excuse my greeting.

"I'm on Mom's cell," Diane explains. "She doesn't know how to use it, so it's really just for emergencies—"

"Is Mom OK?!" I interrupt.

"Sorry. That was misleading," Diane replies. "Yeah, she's OK—overtired and confused from having company—but, basically, OK. I'm using her phone because mine is charging, and we don't have long distance on the house line." She draws a breath. "Anyway, did you just call?"

"Yes—I didn't leave a message because I planned on trying again in a few minutes," I reply, which is true—even if not entirely. "Where were you guys?"

"Oh, right here—as usual," Diane answers bluntly. "Mom doesn't like me to answer the phone anymore," she continues, her tone exasperated. "She wants the caller to leave a message."

"Why's that?" I ask, trying to mask my own increasing exasperation. "Because of telemarketing?"

"Partly," my sister replies sotto voce, "but mostly it's due to anxiety."

"About what?"

Diane sighs. "Mom's afraid that if one of us answers, and a stranger's calling, he'll figure out that we're alone, and terrible things might happen."

"You mean she thinks people will come over and hurt the two of you?"

"Exactly."

"That's crazy," I respond, although, as I speak, I realize that perhaps it isn't completely.

"Maybe," Diane answers, still whispering, "but she's more and more paranoid. I think it's because, the older she gets, the more helpless she feels. That, and because of television, which can really upset her. We don't even watch the news anymore. Now, it's all *The Weather Channel*, *The Price is Right*, and *Nick at Night*."

Outside, the rabbit and the robins have returned to the lawn—this time, in the company of squirrels and chipmunks, all docilly pursuing their own ends, like figures in a Disney cartoon or in Edward Hicks's painting, *The Peaceable Kingdom*. I turn my attention back to my sister. "She seemed all right when I was there," I remark. "When did things begin going downhill?"

"Not long after your Easter visit." Diane pauses, as if to collect her thoughts. "Actually, I remember precisely when it started. Do you recall when those two murderers escaped from prison a while back?"

"Yes," I answer, wondering where the conversation's going.

"Well, Mom was convinced they were headed here, to Saco. She was so beside herself with worry that I had to change the security code and draw all the drapes each evening."

"But those guys broke out of prison in upstate New York—four hundred miles away from you!" I object.

"I know that, and you know that—even she knows that—but these days logic doesn't always matter to her," Diane answers.

"Who is it?" I hear Mom ask in the background.

"It's Rob," Diane tells her.

"What were you whispering about?" Mom asks suspiciously.

"I wasn't whispering—your hearing aids probably need adjusting," Diane responds—like me moments earlier probably only in part lying.

"Why don't you talk with him? He's called to wish you a Happy Mother's Day."

"He has?" Mom says, sounding more lighthearted as Diane hands her the phone. "Hello, Rob?"

"How are you, Mom?" I respond. "Are you having a good Mother's Day?"

There's a pause, as if she's evaluating her potential answers—or, a more upsetting possibility, simply trying to remember. "It was OK," she replies.

"Did you have a lot of visitors?" I ask, angling for a fuller answer.

"I think so."

As I presume my nieces will have visited, I ask, "Who? Carrie and Melissa?" gaining a newfound appreciation for the old adage that getting information can sometimes be like pulling teeth.

"Yes, maybe," she replies tentatively. Then, brightening, she continues, "Oh, I almost forgot—we drove by your office this morning! We didn't stop, though, because we thought you might be busy."

I've never had an office in Maine, so her remark surprises me. "You did?" I respond, not wanting to complicate matters by contradicting her.

"Yes," she continues excitedly. "And, later, while we were still out, we saw you again at your other job—the part-time one, pumping gas at a filling station." This remark is less surprising, because after I first moved away, Mom would sometimes imagine she'd seen me at a distance—in stores or restaurants or on one of the local beaches. Back then, however, she'd always realized that whomever she'd seen likely wasn't me but only someone I resembled.

"It was probably just a guy I look like," I say gently, trying to bring her back to reality, "because I'm in Cleveland right now."

Another silence follows. "You're in Cleveland?"

"Yes. You know I'd never come to Maine without visiting you, especially not on Mother's Day weekend!"

"You'd never do that, would you?" Mom says at last. "So, it must've only been someone who looked like you," she continues, sadly.

"That's right!" I confirm. "Plus, do you really think I'd work at a filling station?" I say, jokingly. "I'd never do that—just like I'd never work in retail or wait on tables."

"But you did all those things while you were in high school and college!" she protests.

"That was then, and this is now," I reply, still hoping to make light of it. "I'm too much of a snob these days to do anything like that for a living."

"Why?" she demands. "They're honest jobs. You should never be ashamed of doing a hard days' work to provide for your family!"

These words, clearly those of the mother I remember, are heartening. "I know, Mom," I say to reassure her. "I was just trying to get a rise out of you."

"Well, you certainly did!" she exclaims, her tone rueful.

"Don't worry— I'll always do whatever it takes to support my family," I say to placate her. "Just like you and Dad taught me."

Mollified, she murmurs, "I love you, Rob." An alarm rings on her end of the line as Diane tells her it's time for her evening dosage of prescriptions. "Thank you for calling," Mom tells me.

"You bet," I say into the phone, and, before hanging up, add, "I love you, too, Mom— always."

Twilight has descended, and the chipmunks, squirrels, and robins have forsaken the lawn for burrows, treetop nests, and high, hidden perches. Only the rabbit remains, grazing amid clover. After a moment, it hops across the grass, slips through a gap in the fence, and disappears into the woods, low foliage wavering in its wake. I wonder if I will see it tomorrow.

CHAPTER 25

The Windmills of Your Mind
Long Take

It's a sunny morning in late August, the "last hurrah" of coastal Maine's summer-tourist season. On our way back from her weekly hairdressing appointment, Mom and I sit in my Lotus, stuck in a nearly motionless line of traffic heading east from the interstate to the local beaches. "I should have taken a back road to avoid this," I apologize above the sound of the radio, which, set to an easy-listening station, plays Mancini's "Two for the Road."

"Are there any back roads?" Mom asks.

I glance at her to see if she's kidding. "You've lived here most of your life—you tell me!"

"I honestly don't know—it's been so long since I've driven anywhere, I can't remember." She opens the glove compartment, extracts an elegant pair of silver-framed sunglasses with azure lenses, and dons them to shield her eyes from the glare on the car roofs ahead of us. "Whose are these? Your wife's?" she guesses, probably because she can't remember Thea's name.

"No—my girlfriend's," I answer, hoping to evade further discussion of her forgetfulness.

Mom lowers the sunglasses and stares. "Always the joker," she says, then pushes the glasses back up the bridge of her nose and looks out the passenger window. On the brick-paved sidewalk, joggers, dogwalkers, and mothers with toddlers in tow move past the street's Colonial and Greek Revival mansions faster than the nearly motionless cars and trucks before and behind us. "Whatever happened to that friend of yours—the one who had such an eye for women?" she asks.

"Todd Stoppek?"

"I think so," she replies uncertainly.

"He got divorced and moved to Tampa—ran off with another friend's wife," I answer, surprised by my own frankness.

"Good," she answers, still surveying the passing foot traffic. "Not about his cheating or divorce," she clarifies. "About his leaving."

"Why do you say that?!" I ask. "He was one of my best friends!"

"That's exactly why! He was a bad influence—bad business altogether!" She momentarily removes the sunglasses to polish them with a Kleenex from the tissue box I keep in the car for her.

"When did you make his acquaintance?" I ask, not realizing she and Todd had ever met.

"Years ago—the last time I visited you in Cleveland. He joined us for a Bastille Day celebration at the Shaker Heights Country Club."

"I'd forgotten," I say, unwisely adding, "I'm surprised you remember meeting him."

"I remember, all right. He danced with just about every woman present except his wife—la pauvre!" she responds sharply. "Seigneur! He even asked me to dance!"

"Why don't we change the subject?" I suggest so that she doesn't get any more excited.

"Gladly," she responds, removing a black onyx and gold compact from her purse and opening it.

"That's pretty," I remark. "Is it new?"

Mom shakes her head. "Hardly! Your dad gave it to me in the '50s. I found it in my vanity table last week while looking for my support hosiery."

Embarrassed, I don't say anything.

She gazes into the compact's mirror. "Remember a few months back when that customer at the salon said she wanted hair like mine?" she asks. "I can't imagine why—there's way too much of it. That's the reason I have it done each week." Still peering into the compact, she pats the thick, newly set gray waves of her permanent. "Why, I'd be happy to have thin hair like she had," she exclaims. "It's way easier to manage."

"People always want what they can't have," I comment absently, while pulling out my cellphone and checking Google Maps to see if the traffic jam is local or part of something larger.

Mom considers my remark. "Yes, that's true," she says. "Maybe that's why Monique bought the house on the lake, even though she can't afford it."

"Monique? Your hairdresser?"

"Of course! The same hairdresser we just left," Mom replies. "You should remember her name. She's a relation." She rolls her eyes. "And you think I'm forgetful!"

"We have lots of cousins, Mom—and I just met her!" I put my phone down and survey the stationary traffic. "Anyway, what's this about her having bought a place she can't afford?"

Mom closes the compact and replaces it in her purse. "She bought a house on Little Ossipee Lake."

"You mean up in the mountains?"

"Kind of. Ossipee Lake is in the mountains, but Little Ossipee isn't—it's in the foothills," Mom corrects me, "right about where the Ossipee Mountains begin."

"That's a long way from town," I remark.

"She needed a change of scenery, I think. She's taking her divorce hard."

"Why?" I ask.

"Well, it *is* her third."

"Oh," I reply, at a loss for anything more pertinent to say of someone whom, even if a relative, is a stranger to me.

Behind us car horns start blaring. "I see the Massachusetts tourists are just as well-mannered as ever," I comment.

Mom frowns. "For all you know, Maine drivers could be the ones honking."

"That's true," I admit. "They're scarcely any better—almost one and the same, given all the people who've moved up here from Boston."

"You're so critical!"

"It's just the way I am," I tease her. "I can't change that."

"We can all change the way we are," she counters. "What would life be like if we couldn't?"

"Sort of like it is now?"

She grimaces.

The blaring horns fall silent. "So, why did Monique buy this place if she couldn't afford it?"

"It's really beautiful," Mom responds. "It has cathedral ceilings, glass walls, and a terrace overlooking the water."

"You've been there?!" I exclaim. The thought of my all but infirm mother visiting a lake house in the mountains—even if the mountains in question are foothills and Diane likely accompanied her—is alarming.

Mom looks at me as if I've lost my senses. "No! Monique showed me pictures while I was having my hair set."

I'm relieved.

"She got a good deal," Mom goes on. "The house came furnished—right down to the flatware, linens, and clothes in the closets."

"The clothes in the closets?" I repeat, never having heard of such a thing, not even for "turnkey" condo sales in Florida or Arizona.

"Yes," Mom replies, nonchalantly. "The previous owners were from Chicago and only used the house in summer so they didn't think it was worth their while to remove what they'd left in it."

"Must be nice to be that rich," I say, stepping lightly on the gas pedal as the traffic starts to move forward and then pressing down on the brakes as it stops again moments later.

"Yes, but Monique isn't. That's the problem. She could barely afford to heat the place last winter!"

"Wow, sounds rough," I remark, wondering how many more banalities I'll mouth before the conversation's over.

Mom nods in agreement. "She told me she's had to cut all unnecessary expenses."

"For example?" I ask, since Monique's dubious home purchase makes me wonder what she considers frivolous.

"Like, instead of buying a new summer wardrobe," Mom answers, "she's just been wearing clothes she finds in the house's closets." She pauses. "Good thing she and the previous owner's wife were the same size."

I frown. "From the looks of Monique today, I'm not sure they are."

"What do you mean?" Mom asks sternly, doubtless thinking I'm being too critical.

"Monique's blouse and slacks looked way too big for her," I answer.

"You think so?" she asks. "Maybe she's lost weight—her divorce has been very stressful."

I'm about to question this theory when "The Girl from Ipanema" begins on the radio.

"I love this song! It makes me want to go to the beach!" Mom exclaims as she turns up the volume.

Staring at the immobile beachbound traffic ahead, I mutter, "Maybe everybody else heard it also."

"What's that?" she asks.

"I like it a lot, too," I lie so as not to agitate her.

"Didn't the orchestra play it at your wedding?"

"Yes—while Thea and I greeted guests in the receiving line," I reply, astonished that she can recall details from decades past but can't remember how to get around a town in which she's lived for over half a century.

"That was a lovely wedding reception," she says with a smile. After only a moment, though, her smile fades, and, lowering her sunglasses, she asks me in a near whisper, "What were we talking about earlier?"

"Monique, your hairdresser," I respond, "and how the clothes from her new house fit her."

"Of course!" Mom answers. "They looked pretty good on her, I thought."

"À chacun son goût," I respond noncommittally. "I thought they seemed a little loose."

"You think so?" Mom considers this. "Well, frankly, Monique never was a sharp dresser. It wasn't her fault. Her Dad died when she was a baby and her mother didn't have much money, so Monique had to wear a lot of hand-me-downs growing up. Not that it matters how anyone dresses."

"It doesn't?" I ask in a neutral tone.

My mother glances at me sharply. "Of course, not! I brought you up to know better—it's how you are on the inside, not the outside, that counts," she says. "Though, of course, everyone doesn't always see it like that."

Mom studies her hands as the music on the radio once again changes—this time, to "The Windmills of Your Mind," performed by an unidentifiable singer and a similarly obscure, though lush, string orchestra.

"I don't think that I could do what Monique did," she says.

"What do you mean?" I ask.

"Move into someone else's house, latch onto the odds and ends of the person's life and start using them as if they were my own."

"But they actually are Monique's, aren't they?" I respond. "Since she bought them?"

Mom grimaces. "That's not what I meant. I mean that they don't reflect who Monique is as a person. They're the previous owners' things that they bought according to their own preferences, not hers."

I agree with this but, fearing it might eventually upset her, feign cluelessness. "Do you think you might overcomplicate things?" I ask, scratching my head theatrically for emphasis.

This engenders a hard look. "Life's complicated," she answers flatly.

I backtrack. "So you don't think you could do something like that—latch onto the bits and pieces of someone else's life and use them?"

"I don't."

"Why? Monique's not pretending to be the wife of the house's original owner. She's not an actress in character who's stealing something!"

"That's true," Mom agrees half-heartedly. "But she's wearing his wife's old clothes, living in rooms she decorated, eating dinner on dishes she bought—using her belongings like stage props." Mom pauses. "She's assuming this woman's identity and going through the motions of her life like it's the one she wanted."

"Do you think that's true?" I ask.

"Maybe," she answers. "After all, Monique didn't have the best marriages."

"No?" I say, hoping my exaggerated air of surprise isn't too transparent.

"No," Mom confirms. "They were awful—her first husband was abusive, the second one was an alcoholic, and the third one decided he was a woman."

"You're kidding?!"

She shakes her head no.

"That's quite a track record!"

"Track record?" she asks, seeming perplexed. "Why're we talking about sports?"

This catches me off guard. English is Mom's second language, but she's been speaking it since adolescence, so she's usually familiar with its idiomatic expressions.

"It's a turn of phrase, Mom," I say, as on the radio, the singer intones a lyric about the circles of our lives ceaselessly unwinding like windmills in the mind. "You've heard it before, haven't you?" I add gently.

"Yes, I think so," she answers, still sounding confused. "What were we talking about anyway?" she asks again.

"How your hairdresser's house came fully equipped with furniture and clothing—which you didn't seem to approve of."

A look of recognition passes across Mom's face like a cloud lifting. "It isn't so much that," she explains with a shake of her head. "Monique can live her life as she pleases. Play acting and pretending just aren't for me—they're not 'my cup of tea.' "

I note her renewed familiarity with colloquial English, but say only, "It isn't?"

"No. I've had my own life, and I choose to keep on living it—even with all its warts and blemishes."

"Warts and blemishes?" I repeat.

My mother pushes the silver-and-azure sunglasses up off her face and onto the top of her head, where they sit amid her gray curls like a translucent tiara. "Yes," she answers gravely. "Even with my faded looks and all my aches and pains—even with my dementia!" she concludes, her voice going low at the last.

As this is the first time she's mentioned her illness I'm astounded. "Why?" I ask unthinkingly.

She gives me a long, sad look. "Because it's usually better to face life's challenges than to try to hide from them." Lowering the sunglasses, she turns towards the window. "Honestly, Rob," she says with a sigh, "sometimes I wonder how you'll get by when I'm not here to state the obvious."

CHAPTER 26
English as a Second Language
Medium Take

Mom, Diane, and I are sitting in Mom's seldom-used formal living room, on blue damask and moiré-silk upholstered furniture that has been covered in these fabrics and colors, or others much like them, for nearly as long as I can remember. Across from me, a gilt-framed oil painting of a luminous dawn at sea hangs above the sofa, an elegant evocation of a view that, on most days, can be experienced in fact on the nearby bay rather than, as now, through skillfully wrought artifice. We are waiting for my son Ian and niece Carrie to serve the afternoon's snack—or, as Mom refers to it, a goûter, which today consists of iced tea and bite-sized chocolate chip cookies.

"I love that picture," I remark, attempting to distract Mom while we wait for the food to arrive from the kitchen, since, as her dementia worsens, she occasionally becomes impatient.

"You do?" Mom responds, absent-mindedly pulling tiny tufts of wool off her gray, summer-weight sweater.

"Yes. It really captures the feeling of the ocean

on a calm, still morning—the majesty and peace of it."

"The ocean isn't always like that," Diane says, seeming to have decided that the satisfaction of contradicting me warrants stating the obvious. "Even on beautiful, placid days, it can be dangerous—what with the undertow and hidden currents."

"Sometimes, appearances can be deceiving," Mom observes, as she removes another piece of errant wool from her sweater. "And, other times, revealing."

Diane nods in agreement. "A professor once said that in a philosophy class I took in college."

"Did he?" I ask, with as much politeness as I can muster.

"Yes," Diane continues. "He explained that in the former case, we should view appearances with skepticism whereas, in the latter, we need to heed them."

Mom stops picking at her sweater. "What did he mean by 'former'?" she asks. "Was he talking about something he'd said in another lecture?"

"No, Mom," Diane answers. "He just meant in 'the first example.'"

My mother looks perplexed.

"In English," I explain, "Sometimes 'former' means 'first' and 'latter' means 'second.'"

Ian and Carrie carry the refreshments into the room on Georgian-style silver salvers. "I've always liked these," I remark. "I can't recall—are they period?" I ask my sister.

"Almost nothing we own is," Diane answers. "Mom and Dad had so many of us kids they could only afford reproductions. Plus, Aunt Jeanne took most of the heirlooms when Mémère passed away, years back—remember?" she asks, referring to my late father's mother.

Carrie pours the iced tea, while Ian doles out the cookies. "What you were saying when we came into the living room was kind of confusing," Carrie says, passing a glass to me. "I mean, I thought 'latté' was a kind of coffee."

My mother sighs. "English is so funny at times. I'll most likely have died and gone to heaven by the time I really get the hang of it. Then, what good will it do me?"

"You never know," Diane replies playfully. "Maybe they speak English in heaven."

Mom stares at her. "If they do, I'm going to request seating in the French section."

"Why?" I ask.

"Well," Mom says, "I've spent my whole life trying to learn English, and I still don't completely understand it—I think I deserve a break when I move on to paradise!"

"You mean you want to 'rest in peace' in the

hereafter?" Ian proposes, smiling, as he passes the tray of cookies before her.

"You're smart," Mom says to him, eyeing the cookies with appetite. "No wonder you're going to be a doctor."

CHAPTER 27

Amen

Medium Take

Dressed in a flowery summer shift, Mom enters the kitchen, her walker before her. Noticing the vase of tulips and hyacinths on the table, she seems taken aback—as often these days when confronted by the unexpected. "How lovely! Which one of you bought these?" she asks me and Diane.

"Neither of us," Diane replies. "Thea, Rob's wife, sent them to you yesterday, for your birthday. Remember?" she asks, as she deposits the morning's first round of pills by the toast and juice that she's set on the table beside Mom's white-and-gold prayerbook.

"She did?" Mom asks, looking confused. "Oh, yes, I remember now," she says at length. Then, perhaps to draw attention away from her forgetfulness, she adds, "I love flowers."

Turning her walker in the direction of the table, I pull out her chair so that she can sit down without incident. "I love everything that's beautiful," she continues, as she grasps my arm and lowers herself.

The opening theme of "Le Jour du Seigneur," a

Québec-based religious program that broadcasts the Catholic mass, blares from the countertop television. Diane lowers the volume. "Is beauty what's most important?" she asks flatly, parting the lace curtains over the sink to reveal a backyard half obscured by morning fog and drizzle.

Diane's question and tone catch me by surprise. However, I suspect that both result from her disappointment with the weather, which has likely scuttled her plan to pick blueberries this morning.

"Certainly not!" Mom replies. "Love is the most important thing!"

To support her argument, I ask, "You mean that love triumphs over beauty?"

"Of course," she answers.

"So, everyone should be loved, whether or not they're beautiful?" I continue, to further bolster her line of reasoning.

"Certainly," Mom answers. "Because everyone and everything is beautiful to God," she continues as she opens her prayerbook.

"Even sin and sinners?" asks Diane, gazing through the rivulets running down the window glass.

"Yes, of course—because they're part of God's creation!" Mom replies.

"Even murderers and war?" Diane persists, frowning as she surveys the sodden landscape.

My mother scowls. "They're all part of part of His great plan!" she affirms.

Ill-advisedly, I ask, "So, evil and suffering are part of the divine scheme of things?"

My mother is silent for a moment. "Yes, we have to believe that they are," she answers at length, "and that, in the end, they have a purpose and that the purpose is good!"

"Why do we have to believe that?" Diane asks, turning toward us, the rain now beating hard against the window behind her.

"Because faith is blind—like love—and like me!" Mom declares agitatedly, while adjusting her bifocals and reaching for her prayerbook. "And, today, all this is good news for the two of you!"

"Bien sûr," I reply, touching her hand to stay its trembling.

"Well, at least you admit it!" she replies, somewhat mollified, "Admitting you have a problem is the first step to recovery."

On television, a priest, completing the sign of the cross, intones, "Ainsi soit-il."

"What does that mean?" Diane asks.

"So be it," I explain.

"Amen!" Mom adds, either in affirmation or correction.

CHAPTER 28

As Close as It Gets

Short Take

We sit at a table in Mom's knotty-pine kitchen, by a window hung with white-lace curtains. She is performing her morning devotions, reading from an array of prayer books—some somber-looking black missals, others, pamphlets whose brightly colored covers depict saints with eyes turned upward towards heaven or, at least, a semblance of deliverance.

I ask, "Do you recall how, when I was little and we'd spend summer at the cottage, you'd take me to the beach on sunny afternoons and tell me about God—how he was eternal and had existed before the world was made and would still exist after it was gone?"

Glancing up from her reading, she replies. "Yes, why?" She sounds apprehensive, perhaps fearful that, her morning prayers interrupted, she might forget to resume them, which has happened before.

"You'd say that God was like a ball—a circle with no beginning and no end." I paused. "That used to make my head hurt."

She smiles, the wrinkles on her face crinkling. "It makes mine hurt now."

"Remember that one day I asked if the ocean was like God and had no beginning and no end?"

"I do," she replies, laughing. "I answered, 'No,' that it had an end on the other side, which was heaven."

"What did you mean, exactly?"

A tireless student of geography, Mom laughs again, this time harder. "Well," she answers with the same hint of surprise with which she'd so often explained the obvious to me in childhood, "If you'd launched a boat from that beach and sailed it right across the Atlantic, you'd have landed in France."

"France is heaven?"

Her smile broadens. "As close as it gets."

CHAPTER 29

Under Paris Skies
Medium Take

Climbing la rue du Mont-Cenis to le basilique du Sacré Coeur, I attempt to call Diane and Mom on my cellphone but cannot get a signal even here, on la butte Montmartre, the highest point in Paris. I've been trying to reach them all day because this morning in my hotel room, awoken as usual by the cars, buses, and motorbikes swirling through la place de la Republique, I discovered that Diane had dialed me from Maine overnight. Now, holding the cell to my ear while I approach Montmartre's summit, I listen in vain for a ringtone but get only a no-service message.

I put away the phone and cross la place du Tertre, which, lined by artists' stalls and sidewalk cafés, could be an Utrillo watercolor—except for the tourists, street performers, and patrols of black-bereted soldiers with machine guns slung over their shoulders. A curly-haired, long-skirted girl emerges from a gang of Roma on the far end of the square and approaches me, a beggar's cup and tattered leaflet in one hand and a red-paper poppy proffered for sale in the other. "Une fleur pour les pauvres!" she proclaims, holding up the leaflet from the charity she supposedly represents. "Votre don sera bien apprécié!"

"Non, merci," I respond, shaking my head. As I brush past her up the steep incline of la rue du Chevalier de la Barre toward the basilica, a young man from her group follows. Mindful of my passport and wallet, I turn around and ward him off by shouting, "Va-t-en!" so loudly that one of the soldiers on the square moves in our direction, causing the young man to flee into an alley. I shout "Merci!" to the soldier, who simply looks at me blank-faced and returns to his fellow patrol members.

At the top of the hill, I cross Sacré Coeur's parvis and, ignoring the sweeping view of Paris, enter the basilica, a white Romano-Byzantine building whose teardrop domes and towers evoke both Rome and Constantinople, church and mosque, minarets and steeples.

Inside, a queue of sightseers snakes along the perimeter from the narthex to the sanctuary and back again, virtually ensnaring the few faithful at prayer amid the sea of empty pews in the nave. I join the line as it slowly passes the shrines full of marble statuary and votive candles along the side aisles, half listening to a guide a few yards ahead while he extols—in French, German, Italian, and English—the beauty of the church's interior.

Approaching the apse, he adopts an almost reverential tone as he informs us that the blue, white and gold tilework image of Christ spanning its ceiling is among the world's largest religious mosaics.

My phone beeps, and the guide frowns. "Soyez respectueux! C'est un lieu de prière ici!" he exclaims. For the benefit of the non-Francophones among us, he translates, "Be respectful! This is a place of prayer!"

"Et ce que vous faites maintenant—c'est quoi, ça? La prière?" I retort and, following his example, also provide a translation, "And what're you doing right now?! Praying?!"

He glares.

My phone beeps again. It's a text from Carrie, who's currently in Seattle, telling me that she's concerned because she can't get in touch with Diane or Mom.

"Bonne journée," I dismissively bid the guide as I break out of the queue to respond to Carrie. Sitting down in an empty pew, I type, Don't worry—I'll find out what's happening! I then text Diane, Where are you?! She doesn't answer.

Deciding not to rejoin the column of tourists inching along the wall toward the altar, I cut across my pew to the main aisle and head back to the narthex. There, I go into the poorly lit gift shop, where—amid rotating stands of medals, rosaries, prayer books, and saints' hagiographies—I hope to buy Mom a present for her approaching birthday. Scanning a rack beside the entrance, I come across a paperback on one of Mom's namesakes, St. Rita, the patron saint of hopeless cases.

My phone beeps again. Across the way, a dark-haired, young woman in a white summer shift, voile scarf, and straw sunhat, closes the missal she'd been examining and looks at me. I mouth, "Desolé," in apology.

"Pas de problème," she responds, as I hurry from the shop and leave the basilica.

On the front steps, I pull out the phone, see that Diane is the caller, and say "Hello?" but don't receive an answer. Evading yet more Roma beggars, I cross the parvis, hoping to get a signal at its far end, by the drop-off overlooking the city, when once more, my phone starts beeping. It's Diane—however, on answering, I again hear nothing. I'm about to return the phone to my pocket, when Diane texts me. I heard you pick up and say, 'Hello' but then the call failed.

I don't know why I can't get a voice signal, I text back. I'm on one of the highest points in Paris.

Where? The Eiffel Tower? she asks.

No—by Sacré Coeur, at the top of the hill in Montmartre.

Maybe instead of the phone you should say a prayer—God's lines are always open, she replies drolly.

Ha-ha, I type, even though the situation doesn't strike me as funny. I've been trying to reach you ever since you called last night, I continue. What's going on?

Nothing much. Mom knows you're traveling and wanted me to check on you. I forgot about the time difference. Sorry.

No problem, I write back, not meaning it. But Carrie and I tried to get through to you all day and couldn't. Was there an emergency? Did Mom fall again?

Carrie's with you? Diane texts back.

Of course not! She wrote me on Facebook! I dash off and then regret the exclamation point. So, everything's all right there? I continue, hoping this sounds calmer.

We're fine, Diane replies after a moment. We were out running errands—at mass, the doctor's, and the pharmacy. Then, suddenly and despite the poor signal quality, the phone starts streaming live video of Diane and Mom sitting in Mom's Maine kitchen, the familiar flowered wallpaper and knotty-pine cabinets behind them. "I'm proving to you that Mom is fine," Diane says, by way of greeting, "because you seemed skeptical."

"Did I?" I ask innocently.

"Yeah, you did," she affirms. "Now, though, you look shocked."

"I'm just surprised the signal's strong enough for video."

"Well, you are by a basilica," Diane replies, smirking, "plus, sometimes, against the odds, miracles happen."

Mom nods. "That's true! Like yesterday when we got a handicapped parking space outside Macy's in South Portland!"

"It's not quite the same, Mom," Diane says patiently. "We're on a video call with Rob, who's on the other side of the Atlantic."

My mother frowns. "People make video calls every day," she retorts, "but it's not every day that you can find handicapped parking by Macy's."

Diane simply looks at her, and then changes the topic. "Why are you visiting the basilica?" she asks me.

"I've never been here before," I reply. "And I wanted to buy Mom a religious souvenir."

"You did?" Mom asks, breaking into a childlike smile. "What is it?"

"I haven't bought it yet but it's a book about one of your patron saints—it's called *Saint Rita, Protectress and Help of Hopeless Cases*."

My mother's smile is replaced by a look of confusion. "Saint Rita isn't my patron saint."

"Sure she is—Rita's one of your middle names, remember?"

Mom doesn't answer. "Well, whether or not she is, don't bother to buy the book!" she tells me.

"Why?" I ask.

"Because it sounds depressing," she replies,

"and I have enough to be depressed about already."

I want to ask what she has to be depressed about but don't as I know the probable answers—old age, illness, and the feeling that she's been abandoned by deceased friends and family. Instead, I ask, "What would you like me to get you?"

"How about a picture?"

"Of what?"

"Of the basilica and its grounds."

"I can take one from here," I say, pointing beyond the parvis's balustrade to the panoramic view of Paris, where street and window lights are coming on and the setting sun has cast a roseate glow on the Eiffel Tower, which looks tiny and toy-like in the distance.

"No, I want you in the picture," Mom objects just as her image fades and the call breaks.

Diane texts that she's trying to get a new connection but that, every time she calls, all she hears is a ringtone. On my end, the phone remains silent. After a minute, she texts anew, Why don't you have someone take a picture of you like Mom asked and send it to me. That'll probably be faster.

This makes sense, so I look around for someone to ask other than the Roma when I notice the young woman from the giftshop peering out over the balustrade not far away, her broad-brimmed hat pushed back by the updraft rising over the precipice. Seeing me, she lowers her sunglasses and smiles faintly. I walk up to her and call, "Bonjour!" over the clamor of an approaching Chinese tour group.

"Allô, ça va, monsieur?" she inquires, as she turns to face me, placing her right foot forward and grasping the railing with her left hand like a ballerina at the practice bar. Or, it strikes me, like Mom, similarly scarfed and hatted, standing on a Montréal balcony in an old photo I've installed as my iPhone wallpaper to honor her birthday.

"Trés bien, merci," I reply politely. "Et vous, mademoiselle, ça va?"

"Ça va, monsieur," she responds, with equal politeness. Next, doubtless due to my accent, she less courteously inquires, "Êtes-vous Canadien ou Americain?"

"Americain mais d'une famille Quebécoise," I reply, describing my Franco-American background and add, "Si vous me permettiez, je voudrais vous demander une petite faveur," explaining that I'd like to ask her a small favor.

"D'accord," she agrees. "But I have a small favor to ask you for, too," she continues in a strong accent. "That we speak in English." Maybe afraid that she's offended me, she continues, "I don't get much chance to practice."

"No problem," I assure her.

"And your favor?" she asks, smiling.

"Could you take a picture of me and the view?

I want to send it to my mom." Unexpectedly embarrassed, I add, "She's very old, and it's the only thing she wants from my visit."

"Bien sûr," she answers in French then quickly corrects herself, "Sure thing! Will right here be OK?"

I nod my assent. "And can you take one of me after?" she asks.

"Agreed." I hand her my phone and lean back against the banister as she takes the photo.

Studying my phone before returning it, she inquires, "Is the screen picture of your mother?"

"A long time ago," I reply, nodding.

"She was pretty," she comments and adds, "She looked a little like me," her tone hesitant and accent stronger.

"Yes," I reply, "Only even prettier."

Her expression is impassive behind her sunglasses.

Flustered by my blunder, I revert to French. "Désolé!" I exclaim and throw in, "Je m'excuse" for good measure.

"You're a good son," she says at last.

"Thanks," I respond, "though she's a better mother."

She touches my arm then hands me her camera and steps back against the railing, the late afternoon sun and Paris vista a backdrop of changing light and color against her white-clad figure. The wind catches a length of her voile scarf and draws it skyward and, lifting a hand, she pulls it back toward her. Then she faces me and smiles.

I take her picture.

CHAPTER 30

Cousin André

Short Take

Mom sits in a blue brocade armchair in her living room, itself a study in blue, white, and gold—blue satin drapes, blue-and-white objets d'art, paintings streaked or dappled with blue, all against a champagne-colored wallpaper unchanged in forty years. She is looking at a photo album taken from the secretary desk, intently studying each page in turn. She stops to look at a particular picture.

"What are you looking at?" I ask.

"A photo of my cousin André right after he came home from the Korean War."

"Was he the one who wrote poetry and taught high-school English?"

"Yes, that's the one." She pauses for a moment. "It's funny that he taught English. He had a strong French accent."

I smile.

"Yes, I know," she says, with a hint of irritation. "I have one, too, but his was even stronger than mine. Still, they say that he wrote English very well."

"You never read his poems?"

"I tried, but they were too depressing," she replies, contemplating the picture of André—an expressionless, dark-haired man, surrounded by relatives at a family function, yet somehow seeming alone. "He wasn't very happy."

"Didn't he die young?" I ask.

She nods, grimacing. "He was only thirty-nine. He killed himself."

"Was he married?"

"He had been, but it didn't work out. When he died, he was single and living in San Francisco." She seems at a loss for words. "He saw too much. Smart people always see too much. Maybe it's better not to be so smart. Life hurts less."

"You think so?"

"Yes, it's like being in a messy room with the lights out—you don't notice the mess."

"Not until you trip and fall," I say.

She sighs, then grasps the arms of her chair as if on a roller coaster heading down. "Isn't that the truth," she observes.

CHAPTER 31

Garden Party

Long Take

"See you tonight, Mémère," my niece Carrie calls, while backing her car out and waving goodbye.

Mom waves back.

"How have things been with Carrie living here?" I ask her.

"She's been a real Godsend," Mom says, smoothing her aqua sundress. She draws her yellow shawl more tightly around her shoulders, despite the mid-July heat. "Diane needs capable help," she continues, as she repositions herself in her wheelchair. "It's a lot of work to take care of me."

"Is it?" I ask, pushing her wheelchair down the sloping back lawn.

"Oh, yes," she affirms, as the chair sticks in the grass, which is long and lush from a week of rain. "You see?"

I pull the chair free, unintentionally jostling her.

"This thing is such a nuisance," she says.

"It was my fault," I say. "Sorry—I didn't think this would be such a bumpy ride!"

Mom shrugs. "That's life—from start to finish."

"You're right about that!" I say with a laugh, as we resume our descent.

"If nothing else," she responds. Before I can contradict her, she goes on, "I haven't been this far down the lawn in ages."

"Really?"

She nods. "It's been at least five years—maybe ten. It got hard after I started using a cane, and now that I'm mostly on the walker it's nearly impossible."

"Then, you're saying the chair serves a useful purpose?" I tease.

Mom turns her head so that I can see her frown. "That's a matter of opinion."

"So, I should focus on my driving?"

"You got it, mister!"

Passing the row of pines and maples at the lawn's bottom, we enter a seldom visited part of the property where the house of our former neighbor, Mrs. Sawyer, once stood.

I stop Mom's wheelchair in the shade of an oak that's gradually smothering the remains of Mrs. Sawyer's perennial garden—late-blooming narcissi, dormant peonies, and old purple-and-yellow irises. A dragonfly, deep blue and iridescent, hovers above the blossoms and then vanishes. "Flora Sawyer was aptly named," Mom says, bending down to touch one of the irises, before brushing pollen off her fingers. "She planted so many flowers."

"I don't remember much about her."

"She was a lovely person," Mom replies, her favorite description for people of whom she has no reason to think otherwise. "A real old Yankee."

"From Down East or upcountry?"

Mom seems surprised I remember the distinction. "The second," she answers. "Flora was raised up the road a bit—though, she probably would have said, 'a piece.'"

"In Goodwin Mills or Hollis?"

"In Hollis—which is where she returned to live with a nephew when she sold the place to us."

"She didn't have children?"

"She couldn't," Mom replies, raising hand to cheek and reflecting. "Back then, that was the only way Baptists—or just about anybody else—ended up childless."

"Mrs. Sawyer was a Baptist?"

"Strict and strait-laced as they come," Mom responds. "Your father used to mow her lawn, and once when he cut it on a Sunday, she came out onto the front porch and called, 'Mr. Allaire, isn't this the Sabbath?' She thought that, since it was the Lord's Day, he shouldn't be working."

"How did he respond?"

"He kept on mowing. He didn't understand what she meant because he'd never heard the word 'Sabbath' before, just the French 'Sabbat.'"

"What was her reaction?"

"She let him get on with it. Flora was a realist. She had to be after her husband died, and she was left alone here." A breeze rustles the oak leaves overhead and blows through the boughs of the ailanthus trees along the Sawyer house's former foundation. We look in the trees' direction.

"Our Pekingese died under those trees," Mom says, as I push her toward them.

"I found him," I respond. "He was stretched out in the shade like he'd settled down to take a nap but never got up."

"It was appropriate," Mom says quietly. "Ailanthus means 'Tree-of-Heaven' in China, where the trees come from."

"You know a lot about Mrs. Sawyer and her place," I reply, pulling her chair up beside the trees.

My mother nods. "I met Flora when she sold us the land for our house, and I got to know her better afterward. I'd bring her blueberry muffins or leftover birthday cake from one of the children's parties, and we'd talk." Mom peers into Mrs. Sawyer's old cellar, which is filled with brambles, fallen masonry, and less easily identified objects. Two squirrels emerge from the morass, chase each other in circles, and then disappear back into it. "Flora was a survivor," Mom continues, "she kept on going, whatever life threw at her."

"What do you mean by 'whatever life threw at her?'"

"She was in her eighties, a widow, and childless!" Mom exclaims, as if the answer should have been obvious. "I don't know how she hung on here. The place had no central heating or real plumbing—only a woodstove in the parlor, a handpump in the kitchen, and an outhouse by the barn, which was ready to fall over. Don't you remember?"

"Kind of."

"Maybe these will refresh your memory." Taking an envelope from the folds of her shawl, she pulls out a stack of black-and-white photos of the property and hands them to me.

"So, this is why you wanted to come here," I say, as I look at the pictures. "Where'd you get these?"

"Carrie and I found them this morning in an old photo album."

"Wow—there used to be a gazebo over there by the oak and the garden!" I remark, studying a snapshot of a tilting, latticework structure entangled in vines. "At least, that's what it looks like—it's hard to tell because of the creepers."

"It was pretty run down," Mom admits. "Habit and the vines were probably all that kept it standing."

I laugh. "How many other pictures do you have in there?"

"Just a few," she replies, pulling more out of the envelope and passing them to me. "Carrie thought these were the most interesting because they include you, Diane, and the other children."

The photos depict events I've either forgotten or barely remember. Among them are a picture of me and my father pruning the wild roses along the house's front entrance, another of my brothers building a snowman beside the sagging woodshed, and yet another of my sisters dressed in old lace they'd found in the attic—lengths of yellowed fabric draped over their heads, arms, and torsos as in a Victorian illustration of the Three Graces. The most arresting, though, is of all of us wearing party hats and sitting at a low table in the ruined garden while my harried mother, young and pretty in a floral shift, cuts the cake with one hand while holding down her windblown hair with the other.

"What was the occasion?" I ask Mom.

She squints and studies the picture. "I'm not sure," she answers. "Your sisters always wanted to celebrate something or other—a good report card, a birthday, the start of summer vacation."

I look at the picture more closely. "It probably wasn't any of those things," I say, giving it back to her.

"Why do you say that?"

"All our birthdays are in spring or winter but this picture was taken in summer, probably a while after school had ended. See how overgrown the garden is," I continue, pointing out the clumps of tall plants at the photo's borders. "What's that stuff, anyway?"

"Bamboo," Mom answers. "Japanese knotweed, actually—at least, I think that's what Flora called it. She told me her mother-in-law planted it behind the barn in the 1920s. By the time we had everything torn down in the '60s, the stuff had spread all over—there was so much that you and the other children cleared a trail to play hide and seek in it."

"I remember," I remark. "Isn't that some bamboo over there?" I ask, pointing to a mass of plants not far from us.

"Yes," Mom answers. "And children still use the trail you kids cut through it."

As my nieces and nephews are now adults, I ask, "What children?"

"Mostly your cousins' children, after they've finished blueberry picking."

"I see," I reply. "By the way, how are the blueberries this season?"

"The wild ones are doing all right—or so I'm told. I haven't gone into the field to see. It's too hard for me on my walker."

"Would you like to go now?"

She looks at me as if I'm crazy.

"It wouldn't be a problem with this wheelchair," I say. "I could push it out there without much trouble."

"You think so?" she asks. "The field grass is

pretty long. The wheels could get stuck like they did on the lawn."

"I'm skinny, but I'm strong," I joke.

"Like your father when we first met," she says wistfully.

"I'm a lot older than he was then," I respond, hoping to stave off further nostalgia.

"Aren't we all?" she says and looks toward the field.

"You're sure you don't want to go?" I ask.

She doesn't reply right away but finally signals her agreement. "Et pourquoi pas? It could be the last time I'll see it."

"Bien non!" I protest, though I realize she might be right. "What's the best way to get there? Should we start from the lawn?"

Mom considers this. "The trail through the bamboo would be faster."

Recalling how rough it was in my childhood, I hesitate but then move her wheelchair toward the trail. "Here goes nothing," I remark, guiding the chair onto its bumpy surface.

"What do you mean?" Mom asks.

"That this should be easy," I answer.

She looks skeptical. "You need to be more honest or spend more time practicing your lying."

"That depends on the circumstances," I reply, as I push her wheelchair forward.

"If you say so," Mom responds. "But right is

right and wrong is wrong and a lie is always the second."

"You're a holy innocent," I remark with a sigh.

"Far from holy," she answers. "And, as for being 'innocent,' I should be so lucky."

A cardinal flies out of the bamboo and shoots upward, a streak of red against the blue sky.

"Speaking of innocence," Mom says.

"You mean this particular bird or birds in general?" I ask, as we proceed down the ever-narrowing path.

"Don't be silly," Mom admonishes.

"I wasn't being silly, just obtuse," I answer.

"Whichever—neither suits you!" she counters. Suddenly, the trail gives way to a clearing where mourning doves mill amid recently felled vegetation. At the clearing's center, Diane and Carrie stand beside the same miniature chairs and table from the long-ago children's party, and, now, as then, a cake and a pitcher of lemonade sit in its middle.

"Surprise!" Carrie cries. "Happy belated and early birthdays, Uncle Rob and Mémère!"

"Respectively, anyway," Diane adds archly.

"What does this mean?" Mom asks her.

"Yes—why the celebration?" I join in. "Mom's birthday is a month away, and mine was in April."

My mother stares. "I was asking Diane why she said *respectively,*" she informs me. "It wasn't necessary—I already know she respects me."

I can't tell if Mom's confusion results from her sometimes shaky grasp of English or her dementia. "Not *respectfully* but *respectively*," I reply, "which means something else." I turn my attention back to my sister and my niece. "So, what's the deal with the party?" I ask Diane, and, addressing Carrie, say, "I thought you were at work in Portland."

"I called in sick," she answers, smiling. "When I saw how happy the picture of the children's party made Mémère, I thought it would be fun to re-enact it—especially since you weren't here for your birthday and won't be for hers either."

"I don't see what my birthday has to do with it," I reply, hoping to evade the topic of missing Mom's. "I haven't been here for my birthday in ages."

"Eons is more like it," Diane observes.

"Weren't you supposed to be taking a nap while Mom and I were outside?" I respond accusatorially.

Diane frowns. "Don't blame me—I got roped into this when Carrie couldn't find the kids' chairs and table," Diane complains. "Nobody seems to know where to find anything around this place anymore," she says, nodding toward Carrie and Mom. "At least, not anyone who's here regularly," she continues, looking directly at me.

"I think this is a lovely surprise!" Mom declares

to stave off further discussion. She turns to me. "And don't you be an old grouch!"

"It's settled then!" Carrie declares. "Let's all sit down and have cake and lemonade!" she continues, gesturing toward the children's table, with its pink plastic tablecloth, blue paper plates, and yellow party favors.

"Where'd you get all this on such short notice?" I ask her, moving Mom's wheelchair up to the table.

"They're left over from the birthday parties Mémère gave for me and my brothers and sisters when we were little," she explains. "She doesn't throw much away. We used to call this place 'Mémère's store,' there are so many things in the barn, attic, and basement! You can't imagine!"

"He won't have to," Diane says sardonically. "Because he's going to help with the inventory when we vacate and hold the final clearance sale."

"Which won't be anytime soon," Mom says.

Chastened, Diane quickly responds, "No, of course not!"

"Let the festivities begin," Carrie proclaims, pulling out one of the children's chairs for either Diane or me to sit in.

"Ladies first," I tell my sister.

"Ever the gentleman," she replies with a smirk. "But, since 'age comes before beauty,' you and Mom have priority. Plus, I need to help Carrie serve the refreshments."

"Whatever you say," I respond curtly, which causes Mom to glance up at me. Pretending not to notice, I position her wheelchair at the table and start to sit beside her. "God, these things are tiny," I lament, lowering myself onto a chair no taller nor wider than a child's stepstool.

Mom sighs. "Stop complaining," she says under her breath, "and try to enjoy the party. Diane and Carrie went to a lot of trouble—show a little appreciation."

"For this ordeal?" I reply, as I try not to knock the chair over.

"Life's an ordeal," she mutters. "The sooner you accept that, the sooner you'll be able to get on with it."

"Get on with it?" I repeat.

"That's the general idea," Mom asserts.

Unable to dispute the accuracy of this, I watch Diane and Carrie pour the lemonade, cut the cake, and take their places around the table. "Oh, wow," Carrie says, seating herself, "the legs on these chairs are so short my knees reach up nearly to my shoulders."

"I know," Diane agrees. "Good thing we wore slacks, not skirts today."

"What do you mean?" Mom asks. "Rob and I aren't wearing slacks—I'm in a dress and he's in shorts."

Diane frowns. "Yes—but you're not sitting in one of these little chairs," she says. "And since it's not likely Rob would be wearing a skirt, the need for slacks—or pants—doesn't apply to either of you, does it?"

Mom's face reddens. "No, of course, not," she murmurs. "Sometimes, I'm so dizzy-minded."

"That's one of the things we love about you," I say and pat her hand.

"Yes," Carrie echoes. Keeping things moving, she cuts a piece of cake, places it on a spatula, and turns to Diane. "Would you like some?"

"Yes, thanks," Diane replies. However, as she bends forward to accept the proffered piece, one of the legs on her chair cracks, and she falls forward, knocking the table off kilter and sending food, party accoutrements, and mourning doves flying.

Carrie shrieks, and Diane and I curse, but Mom is convulsed with laughter.

"What's so funny?" Diane asks crossly, rising from her knees as Carrie and I wipe splattered lemonade from our feet and sandals.

"It reminds me of parties when you were children," Mom says, trying to contain her laughter. "My God, sometimes you were a bunch of little hellions!" she exclaims gripping her wheelchair's arms to keep from falling.

"That doesn't explain why you're laughing," Diane says testily.

"It doesn't?" Mom gasps, between more peals of laughter.

"Not really," I respond while helping Carrie

recover the party paraphernalia strewn around the clearing. "I find the whole thing unsettling."

"Oh, don't be so negative," Mom admonishes.

Diane, brushing cake crumbs off her arms and blouse, glares at her.

"Or you either," Mom says to her. "Sometimes you're such a grump!"

"Me! A grump!?" Diane retorts, her patience exhausted. "Would a grump go to the trouble of helping Carrie pull this together to surprise you?! Would a grump make your breakfast every morning, put you to bed every night, and help you go to the bathroom every freaking hour on the hour?!" she demands.

My mother doesn't answer.

"Would she?" Diane insists, her face bright red. "I'm curious!" she nearly shouts. "I want to know if you're so disconnected from reality you think a 'grump' would keep on going and plugging away when things seem hopeless!"

Utter stillness follows. Even the mourning doves, who've returned to pick and peck at the scattered refreshments, stop cooing.

Carrie, her expression pained, says, "Mémère, Aunt Diane didn't mean to sound so harsh, she's just . . . ," but Mom raises a hand and stops her in mid-sentence.

"There's something I have to say," Mom begins, looking past Carrie at the bamboo and the open field beyond. "I didn't mean to upset you,

Diane," she says quietly. "I know how much you do every day to keep things running here." Her voice cracks. "I also know I couldn't manage without you," she continues more softly. "It's just that sometimes my illness and old age make me foolish! I'm sorry," she concludes, as tears start to stream down her cheeks.

Again, silence prevails. "No, Mom," Diane begins, looking like she too might start crying. "I'm the one who's been foolish! I'm so sorry! Sometimes I'm an imbecile!" She bends and kisses Mom on her forehead.

"It's all right. I know I'm a lot of work," she reassures Diane, who hugs her.

"Why don't we all go to the field and inspect the blueberries?" Carrie proposes, to put the ruined party and its quarrels behind us, both literally and figuratively. "That's where you and Mémère were headed, isn't it?" she goes on, turning to me.

"How did you know?"

"Where else would you've been going?" Diane responds. "We guessed that after the two of you'd gone to Mrs. Sawyer's you'd probably offer to take Mom to the blueberries."

"That's right!" Carrie chimes in as she leads the way out of the clearing past paper plates, cups, and other bits of party detritus. "It wasn't like we needed a fortune teller to figure out what would happen."

"I don't know," Mom demurs, as I take hold of her wheelchair and follow. "Sometimes things around here are predictable and other times not."

Diane and I exchange glances but don't comment. Instead, we follow Carrie down the remaining stretch of trail to the field. At the path's end, the bamboo stops abruptly, like land at the water's edge, its dense green close in our wake and the bright wildflower-filled field ahead, welcoming as a sunlit cove, inviting as a windswept bay. "Wow," I whisper, struck both by the speed of the transition and by the field's unspoiled beauty, which I'd almost forgotten.

Mom nods. "C'est tellement beau ici," she agrees. I guide her wheelchair past patches of meadowsweet and yarrow toward the blueberry barrens, when a cloud of starlings takes flight before us. She gasps delightedly. "Les oiseaux sont comme des anges terrestres!" she exclaims, while the birds rise.

"What's that, Mémère?" asks Carrie, who doesn't speak French.

Diane chimes in, "Yeah. I'd like to know, too."

"Birds are like earthly angels," I translate, as the starlings fly over the woods at the field's end and then disappear altogether.

"Where do you think they're going?" Carrie asks.

"To heaven," Mom answers. "Like I'll be, one day soon."

"Mom!" Diane and I exclaim, while Carrie cries, "Mémère!"

My mother is unfazed. "Heaven—or hell—is the final destination," she continues. "At least, for people—maybe even for animals and insects."

"Maybe for people and animals," Carrie concedes. "But probably not for insects." We laugh.

I push Mom's wheelchair toward the spot the starlings have forsaken—green bushes strewn with blueberries, striking as light thread in dark fabric or bright mica amid sand's duller silica. "What bounty!" Mom exclaims.

"Bounty?" I repeat.

"Yes! Remember when you and your brothers and sisters were children? Some years, the blueberries were plentiful and others not. 'Bountiful' was how you described the good years."

"What did I call the bad years?" I ask. "The famines?"

She shakes her head. "You didn't call them anything. I did, though—'the time of bickering.' "

"Why?" I ask.

"Your memory must be even worse than mine," Mom replies. "When the blueberry crop was light, you kids became very competitive. You'd fight over who'd picked the most, fastest, and cleanest."

" 'The cleanest'?" Carrie repeats.

"The cleanest batches have the fewest leaves and twigs in them," Diane explains. "I picked the cleanest."

"Not always," I say.

"Who else did? Not you!" Diane retorts, reviving a childhood disagreement. "You picked the fastest, but your batches were like messes the cat dragged in—all that was missing were dead mice and birds' wings," she mocks.

Mom frowns. "Just like the old days—arguing over nothing!" she exclaims. "Who cares who picked the cleanest or fastest! All that pointless quarreling exhausted me back then and it still does now," she goes on, her voice beginning to tremble. "It's awful."

"You're right, Mémère!" interjects Carrie, ever the peacemaker. "Instead of arguing, why don't we focus on how beautiful it is here," she says, as with a sweep of her arms, she gestures at our surroundings.

"From the mouths of babes," I say to Diane, who nods.

"I'm sorry," Diane says to Mom. "Sometimes we're childish."

"Especially me," I add, not wanting to be upstaged by Diane and also unwittingly demonstrating the validity of my assertion. "I should know better, being in my sixties."

"Age doesn't always bring wisdom," Mom responds, "except maybe to King Solomon and the Old Testament prophets." She sighs. "I'm living evidence. I shouldn't have gotten so upset about your arguing or mentioned how exhausting it was for me when you were children. It was my fault that I was tired."

"How could it have been your fault?" I ask.

She stares at me, apparently astounded that once again I'm missing the obvious. "It's like Mom used to tell me—I wasn't strong enough to handle it."

"Your mother was a sweet lady," I respond, "but judgmental."

"I loved Mom," Mom states flatly.

"I did too," I respond. "She was always good to me though . . ."

"She could be harsh," Diane says with characteristic bluntness.

"Even if she didn't mean to be," I add, so as not to offend Mom further. "Anyway, whatever she did or didn't say doesn't matter. The fact is you *were* strong enough or you wouldn't be here now talking with us."

"Maybe," Mom replies. "Still, I should know better than to complain."

"Don't worry about it," Diane says. "What's life without a little grousing?"

"Like a bag of chips without crab dip?" I joke.

"Or nachos without guacamole," Carrie contributes.

"I don't know what those two last things are," Mom says absently. "But I know one should bear one's crosses in silence."

"Whether or not that's true," I respond, "Why

don't we follow Carrie's suggestion and focus on the moment?"

"Yes, see how pretty everything is, Mémère!" Carrie reiterates, pointing to a cluster of blue asters from which, seemingly on cue, two monarch butterflies emerge in interwoven flight as if contra dancing. "Let's go look at the flowers!"

"Rob, why don't you and I walk to the spot where we used to do our best picking?" Diane says, lending support to Carrie. "It's not much further."

Worried that handling Mom's wheelchair in the field might be a challenge for Carrie, I hesitate. Then, though, I half-heartedly reply OK at the very moment that Mom responds to Carrie in exactly the same fashion.

Diane and Carrie laugh. "You'd think you two were related."

"I am her firstborn son, after all," I reply defensively. "We're bound to think alike on occasion."

"That's right," Mom says. "It's only natural."

"Yes—just like the flowers we're going to go look at," quips Carrie, not to be deterred.

"The wheelchair won't be too hard for to you push through the field grass?" I ask, unable to refrain from voicing my concern.

"I've pushed it over rougher ground," she assures me.

I don a skeptical expression. However, Mom,

looking toward the asters, says, "Everything will be fine."

"Just be careful," I caution Carrie.

Diane nods in agreement. "Because when the grass gets tall like this in mid-summer it's hard to see what's ahead."

Not just then, I reflect but don't say.

"You two worry too much," Mom says dismissively, her mood changing. "Like I said earlier, Carrie's very capable. Nothing bad can happen."

I want to contest the last, but again, think it best to keep my mouth shut.

"Just don't go too fast," Diane admonishes.

"Sure thing," Carrie replies, as she turns the wheelchair in the direction of the asters, and Mom waves goodbye.

Diane and I start off toward the blueberry patch that she's indicated—an irregularly shaped swath of shrubbery half-hidden in the lighter field grass like a shadowy archipelago on a bright ocean. We haven't gone far, when we hear Carrie shriek, and turning, see Mom's wheelchair upended amid the asters and Mom lying on the ground with Carrie bent over her. "Mémère! Mémère!" she cries in a panic-stricken voice. "Are you all right?"

"What happened?" Diane yells as we run back.

"We hit a rabbit hole and the chair tipped over!" Carrie, near tears, answers.

Mom lies amid the asters, her aqua dress and

yellow shawl starkly differentiated from the plants' pale-blue blossoms and green foliage. "Are you OK, Mom?" Diane asks, touching her arm. "Did you break anything?" Mom shakes her head no but starts to shiver.

"Are you sure?" Diane persists, gathering Mom's shawl around her to stay the shivering. "Do you have a sharp pain like you did last year when you cracked your pelvis?"

"No," Mom replies, sounding a bit dazed.

"OK. That's good," Diane reassures her. "Now, let's get you off the ground and back to the house," she continues, positioning herself behind Mom and slipping her forearms under Mom's shoulders to lift her.

Mom draws a short breath.

"Do you hurt anywhere?!" Diane asks, alarmed.

"No more than usual," Mom answers unconvincingly.

Carrie, watching, struggles to keep tears from falling. "Are you sure, Mémère?"

"Don't fret," Mom answers, her voice small and frail-sounding. "I wouldn't be the first person this place has killed." Then, with a gesture toward Diane, she continues, "And I won't be the last either."

"What do you mean—this property and me?!" Diane asks Mom, as Carrie starts crying.

"I mean the world and everyone in it," Mom answers.

The hard truth of this leaves all of us at a loss for a response. After a moment, however, I compose myself. "Be that as it may, Mom," I tell her, "there's only one thing to be done right now, and you know what it is, don't you?"

She looks at me. "Get on with it?" she replies.

I nod yes. Then, she lifts her hands and, as I pull her up and Diane pushes her forward, she begins anew, again resurgent, once more ascendant.

CHAPTER 32
A Life of Sacrifice
Short Take

One afternoon, sitting in the den, drinking tea, Mom notices a picture of Syrian refugee children on the cover of a magazine and says, "When I was young, for a while, I wanted to be a missionary nun."

Entering the room, Ian, who was raised Jewish, looks surprised.

"Really—why?" he asks her.

"So that I could live a life of sacrifice and work with the little children. But, then, I got married and had children of my own." She pauses for a moment, then, with a bemused laugh adds, "I guess that was a kind of sacrifice."

CHAPTER 33

Merry Christmas Darkly

Long Take

Mom lies on the blue living-room sofa, legs raised to reduce the swelling from phlebitis, eyes closed while she naps to reduce the fatigue from dementia. In the bay window, a Christmas tree glistens with heirloom decorations that will fill her younger vielle de Noël guests with innocent wonder and the older ones with wistful nostalgia.

At Diane's request, I water the room's poinsettias and paper white narcissi, set out plates of Christmas cookies and foil-wrapped chocolates, and tune the radio to the local easy-listening station, which is playing "White Christmas."

"How's that for good timing?" I ask Diane as she enters the room with Mom's afternoon doses of medicine. "It just started snowing again."

Diane shrugs. "It's not much of a coincidence. From Thanksgiving to New Year's, this station only broadcasts Christmas carols, the news, and the weather." As if to prove her point, the song ends and is followed by an account of Christmas preparations in Israeli-occupied Bethlehem and a brief meteorological report of the obvious—that it's currently and will likely continue snowing.

"Why do you listen to it then?" I ask her.

"For the same reason that all we watch on TV are '40s and '50s classic movies. The predictability calms Mom." She walks over to the sofa and touches Mom on a shoulder. "Wake up—I've brought you your 'appetizers.'"

"Appetizers?" Mom asks, yawning. "Is it already dinner time? Is anyone coming?"

Diane smiles. "I was kidding—it's too early for dinner. But we will be having company later. In fact, we have some already," she says, gesturing to me.

"We do?" Mom responds and turns in my direction, but because her glasses are pushed up onto her forehead, looks right through me. Diane pushes Mom's glasses downward, and Mom, focusing, says, "Ah."

"Comment ça va?" I ask her.

"Trés bien," Mom replies, seeming groggy.

I look at Diane with concern. "She's on painkillers for the joint inflammation she gets in winter," she explains in a whisper. "They can make her a little disconnected."

To help ground Mom in the present, I say, "Look! It's lovely, isn't it?" and point to the window through which feathery snowflakes can be seen falling straight down, covering the lawn and the woods in a thick white blanket.

"Yes," she says, blinking, as her eyes adjust

to the brightness pouring into the room between the window's satin drapes. "It reminds me of when the children were younger," she continues, presumably referring to me, Diane, and our five other brothers and sisters. "We had all sorts of presents—so many that even when I stayed up until dawn on Christmas morning there wasn't enough time to wrap all of them."

"I remember that they couldn't all fit under the tree," I say.

Mom looks at me oddly.

"That was true even when we had two trees—one in each bay window," says Diane, placing a coaster and waterglass etched with iridescent icicles on the coffee table in front of Mom. "The presents covered the living-room floor from one end to the other." She places a number of multicolored capsules next to the waterglass, then helps Mom sit up on the sofa. "Time for your two o'clock pills," she tells her.

"Already?" Mom asks, still looking sleepy.

"Already," Diane echoes. "Your meds schedule doesn't change just because today's a holiday."

"It's a holiday?"

"Almost," I say. "It's Christmas Eve—soon people will be arriving to wish you a Merry Christmas."

"You seem to know more than I do," Mom says with a smile before swallowing the pills and water Diane has handed her. "I'm glad you're visiting. When did you get here?"

"Early this afternoon, while you were sleeping."

"How were the roads?" she asks.

"Pretty good," I answer. "It wasn't snowing when I landed."

My mother once again looks at me strangely. "Where did you fly in from?"

The question only surprises me a little, because though I'm now pretty much retired, I traveled a lot in my career and often visited her on the way back from one or another far-flung location. "Cleveland," I answer, as she sits back against the sofa cushions.

Mom raises an eyebrow. "What a coincidence," she says politely, "My son, Rob, lives in Cleveland."

Trying hard to keep my worry from showing, I say, "I know."

"You do?"

"Yes, he does," Diane says, as she takes away Mom's waterglass. "And why do you think that is?" she coaches her.

Unsettled, Mom takes a harder look at me. "Because he is Rob," she replies uncertainly.

"Exactly," Diane answers, while she puts the waterglass down on a table.

Mom smiles broadly, first at Diane and then at me. "I was just teasing," she says to cover her error. "And the two of you are easily fooled, I must say," she adds for good measure.

To change the subject, I walk over to the Christmas tree and examine a few of its ornaments—plumed larks and tufted sparrows, silken gold pears and apples, a miniature piano in gilt, tortoise shell, and enamel. "Where're the tiny harp and violin that matched the piano?" I ask. "Did they break?"

"They're probably in the attic or the barn." Diane answers. "Ever since we cut back to a single tree, we don't have room to display all the ornaments, so I rotate them from one year to another. I'll try to remember to bring those out next Christmas."

"Don't make a special effort," I call after her as she returns to the kitchen. "You've got enough going on to keep you busy."

The doorbell rings.

My son, Ian, who's been in his room studying, comes downstairs. "I'll get it," he tells me on his way into the foyer.

"Who's here?" Mom asks as she picks up a holiday cookie coated with white-and-green sprinkles.

"We don't know yet," I answer, "but we will in a minute."

Mom bites into the cookie, causing crumbs and sprinkles to fall into her lap and onto the sofa and cream-colored oriental carpet, but she doesn't appear to notice. "How can you be sure?"

"Because I'm a prophet," I tease.

She looks at me sidelong. "Since you're in business," she says, gathering her wits about her, "shouldn't you be more interested in turning a profit than in being prophetic?"

"One can lead to the other—if you're lucky."

"Are you?" she asks.

"I'm lucky to be here with you today."

Mom grins. "Ever the charmer and always the right answer—at least, when it matters."

I grin back at her. "And who do you think I take after?"

She breaks into girlish laughter. "Flatterer!" she exclaims before turning to the doorway while Ian, Carrie, and her sister, Melissa, enter the living room and Diane comes back pushing a serving cart laden with more refreshments.

"Merry Christmas, Mémère!" Carrie and Melissa exclaim as they hug Mom each in turn. "Hi, Aunt Diane and Uncle Rob," Carrie says, smiling at Diane and walking across the room to shake my hand. Melissa, who's already seated herself on the sofa, waves at me and my sister. "Yeah, hi Aunt Diane and Uncle Rob! How was your flight?" she asks me. "Was Cleveland's airport busy?"

"Not especially."

"Is it ever?" she inquires, most likely simply to bait me, which is consistent with her personality.

"On occasion."

"What kind of occasions?" Carrie asks politely, probably to undercut Melissa.

"Occasions like this one," I explain. "Around holidays."

"And during medical conferences," adds Ian.

"Spoken like a doctor in the making," Diane says.

"Are there a lot of medical conferences in Cleveland?" Carrie asks.

"Enough, but there are even more doctors," I answer.

"How's that?"

"Because of the Cleveland Clinic," Ian replies.

"Oh," says Melissa. "Is it big?"

"More people work there than live in Maine's capital," I say to repay her for her earlier ribbing.

"How many are there in Augusta?" Carrie asks.

"About 35,000," I say.

"That's not so many," says Melissa.

"Certainly not for a state capital," I reply. "But for a hospital system, it's significant."

"Maine is small," Mom says. "That's why I like it."

"Maybe you also like it because you've lived here for the better part of a century," Diane observes, using a holiday napkin to pick up the errant crumbs and sprinkles surrounding Mom on the sofa.

Carrie, a sociology major, nods. "Familiarity has a lot to do with preference. It influences why we like some people more than others—which doesn't always have happy consequences," she adds, maybe because, on the radio John Lennon and the Harlem Community Choir are singing "Happy Xmas (War is Over)" and chanting about stopping fighting among the races.

"Anyway, Mom, as much as you love Maine," Diane continues, bending down to scoop up the crumbs on the carpet, "I think you'd like Cleveland, too—God knows, all those doctors would come in handy for you."

My mother scoffs. "Don't make me out to be a sick old lady!"

"I didn't call you that, but all your prescriptions and doctors' appointments don't say you're the picture of health," Diane counters.

"Those are routine prescriptions and appointments," Mom protests primly. "It's not as if I'm always in the ER or the ICU!"

"That's true," Diane concedes, taking bowls of walnuts and cashews from the serving tray and handing them to Carrie to place on the room's occasional tables. "But you've got to admit you need frequent medical attention."

Mom scowls. "It doesn't matter how well or sick I am—I might like living in Cleveland, even if I don't need all those doctors."

"What makes you say that?" Carrie asks, knowing how much Mom is attached to New England.

"It's not the place that's important, but the people who live there," Mom replies, "and most are nice enough."

Melissa shakes her head. "I don't know, Mémère—for years, Cleveland's been called 'the mistake on the lake.' Those old Rust Belt cities are depressing!"

"I've never understood what 'Rust Belt' means," Mom responds. "It's not like metal only rusts in one place—it rusts here, too, doesn't it?"

Diane frowns. "Yes, it rusts everywhere, Mom," she confirms. "But 'Rust Belt' means places whose fame and fortune were made in manufacturing."

My mother takes a bite out of another cookie, again causing crumbs and sprinkles to fall onto her lap and the sofa.

Diane grimaces.

"I still don't understand," Mom tells her. "What's wrong with manufacturing? Making things is a better way to earn a living than by just talking or lying about everything like all those people on television."

"You mean the actors?" Ian asks.

"Yes," she affirms, taking a second bite of the cookie and sending yet more crumbs flying. "Along with the politicians and the Wall Streeters."

Melissa laughs. "You've got a point, Mémère, but it doesn't change the fact that most of those old Rust Belt towns are awful."

"Nonsense!" Mom exclaims. "Glorifying some places versus others is just a way for people to lord it over one another and feel superior. I've never met anyone who believed that who wasn't wrong! Thinking you, your country, or your religion are best is the taproot of the world's troubles!"

Likely to keep from further upsetting Mom, Melissa doesn't respond. Instead, she picks up a holiday cookie and takes a bite, dispersing additional crumbs and sprinkles.

This is too much for Diane. "Enough of these exploding sugar cookies," she declares as she picks up the cookie platter and heads back to the kitchen. "I'll bring out the chocolate-chip ones I baked yesterday! They aren't decorated for the holiday but they don't detonate!"

"Detonate! Was there gunfire?!" Mom asks apprehensively. "Maybe deer-hunting season's been extended," she ventures.

"We're talking about the holiday cookies," I reassure her. "Diane's replacing them with some that don't crumble," I add, gesturing to the cookie particles surrounding Melissa.

Mom adjusts her glasses to take a closer look. "Melissa! You should be neater when you're eating," she reproaches her. "Here!" she says and hands her a napkin from the pile on the coffee table.

Melissa and Carrie exchange glances.

Diane returns from kitchen, the serving tray laden not only with the promised chocolate-chip cookies but also with swirl-frosted cupcakes, carafes of soda water and eggnog, and a holly-themed China tea service that belonged to one of our great-grandmothers.

"Wow!" Ian exclaims. "Who're you expecting?"

"Relatives, mostly," Diane answers. "Plus a few friends and neighbors."

"There must be quite a few," Ian, an only child, says.

Diane nods her head in confirmation. "Remember, there're a lot of us even in the immediate family."

"Yes," Mom concurs, smiling at Ian. "Not as many as there used to be, though, now that my siblings and most of your grandfather's have passed on," she continues. "In the old days, every house we'd visit on Christmas or New Year's was filled with cousins, aunts, and uncles—usually dozens."

"Things must have been crowded," says Ian.

"They were–and a little crazy, too, with the caroling and piano playing, and your great-aunts Jeanne's and Clémence's poodles always barking."

"Caroling and piano playing?" inquires Carrie, who sings in a community chorale.

"That was Jeanne's doing," Mom says. "She sang in the church choir but loved to sing just about any time. I think she saw holidays as a way to get more practice in," Mom jokes, "and to do music education with the family. She'd usually try to teach the children to play simple tunes like 'Twinkle, Twinkle,' 'Für Elise,' and 'Frère Jacques' on the piano."

"How are aunts Clémence and Jeanne?" I ask Diane, about my father's last surviving siblings.

"Hanging on," Diane replies, in a tone that makes me suspect I shouldn't have inquired.

This suspicion is confirmed when Mom asks, "Are they coming over later?" and Diane frowns at me.

"Probably not," she responds, transforming her frown into a smile as she turns toward Mom. "Clémence won't go anywhere in this kind of weather, and Jeanne doesn't much like to either."

"I knew that about Clémence," Mom replies, "but I thought the snow wasn't a problem for Jeanne. Didn't she used to ski in Vermont and New Hampshire and go skating with her grandchildren?"

"Years ago," Diane responds. "I doubt she does much skiing or skating these days." Turning to me, Diane says, "Speaking of skating, can you help me get the ice-rink music box from the basement? I'd like to put it out on the hearth before we get more company."

"Sure," I answer and leave the living room with her. On our way to the basement, she says,

"About our aunts—Clémence isn't coming because she broke a hip, and Jeanne can't make it because she has an inoperable aneurism and is in hospice."

"When did this happen?" I ask, pulling the music box down from a high shelf and handing it to her.

"This week," she answers. "I haven't told Mom yet. Lately, she's been obsessed with the fact that she, Clémence, and Jeanne are the only surviving family members of their generation. She'll be really upset if she finds out the ranks might be getting thinner."

"Sorry I asked about them visiting," I reply as we climb back up to the main floor.

Diane shrugs. "So am I, honestly. But, even if you hadn't, Mom would probably have asked about them sooner or later. Maybe we can have a FaceTime call with Jeanne to make things seem more normal."

"Won't seeing Jeanne in a hospital room tip off Mom?"

"Jeanne's not in the hospital," Diane replies, as we pass through the back hall. "She's moved in with her son, Ed. He and his wife decided she'd be better off in home hospice."

We put the music box on the hearth and connect it to the power panel that sources the room's electronic decorations—the lights on the tree, the candles in the windows, the garland above the fireplace mantel and the iridescent angels at each end. "Do you want me to switch on the rink," I ask after I've plugged it into a socket.

Diane shakes her head. "Don't bother—sensors turn everything on when it gets dark outside."

"That's up to date," I remark. "I remember when everything depended on timers."

"Get with the program, Rob. It's the twenty-first century."

"Don't remind me," I reply, as Melissa re-enters the living room from the foyer, where she'd been hanging her coat as well as Carrie's in the closet.

"Why not?" she asks me. "Afraid it will bring more tough times for Cleveland?"

My mother, who's standing in the bay window with Carrie and Ian watching the snow accumulate, turns and stares at Melissa. "Don't be rude!" she scolds as they help her back to the sofa.

"I was kidding," Melissa objects.

"You're old enough to know better," Mom responds, seating herself with Carrie's assistance. "So behave yourself and be good!" she warns, while on the radio, the lyrics from "Santa Claus is Coming to Town" admonish more or less the same.

Melissa is quiet for a moment. "I was only saying what's true, Mémère—some places are better to live in than others."

Mom gives Melissa a sharp look. "Just like

some people think they're better than others?" she demands.

"I never said that," Melissa protests.

"No—but it's the same line of reasoning," Mom replies. " 'I live in a better place than you do, so I'm better,' " she says in a mocking tone. "Believe me, I heard that plenty of times growing up on the wrong side of the tracks before I married your grandfather and moved here into this more 'desirable' neighborhood," she continues. "And, considering the people I've met in each place, it seems like delusional thinking!"

Diane, who's expert at distracting Mom when she grows too agitated, picks up a bowl of chocolates, takes one for herself, and passes the rest to her. "Don't these look good?" she asks. "Why don't you have one?"

Mom looks at the gold-, silver-, and green-wrapped chocolates, and after a moment, says, "Yes, I think I will, thanks," and takes one.

Probably to make up for Mom's harshness, Diane asks Melissa, "Would you like some too?" Melissa nods, and Diane hands her the bowl.

The phone rings in the family room.

"I'll get it," Carrie offers, walking off to answer it. "It's one of your cousins," she calls out. "He wants to know if Mémère is ready for the FaceTime call with Aunt Jeanne."

"That's a coincidence," I say to Diane, sotto voce.

"Not really," Diane whispers. "I texted Ed while we were coming up from the basement."

Mom, her chocolate finished, asks, "Is Jeanne coming to visit?"

"Well, here goes," Diane says to me. Turning to Mom, she says more loudly, "Not today. She isn't feeling well enough, so she and Edmond are having a FaceTime call with us instead."

"What's Edmond got to do with it?" Mom asks her.

Diane is silent, likely preparing herself for the interrogation that will follow her answer. "Jeanne's moved in with Edmond."

My mother looks shocked. "I knew she wasn't crazy about her independent-living apartment but I didn't think she'd move out of it."

Because Diane, blank-faced, doesn't answer, I do for her. "Maybe she missed Elise," I suggest, referring to Jeanne's miniature poodle. "She hated leaving her with Ed when she moved into that apartment," I continue, a deliberately misleading statement of the sort that's become a staple of my interactions with Mom as her dementia worsens.

"Maybe," Mom says, sounding unconvinced. "Or maybe there's something you're not sharing—one way or the other, truth will tell eventually."

"I don't know what you mean," I answer, taking a chocolate.

She watches me unwrap the candy. "That

settles it—you're lying. You never eat sweets unless you're hiding something."

"Maybe it's the present I brought you," I answer gamely, though I realize that I've likely already lost this round of cat and mouse.

Mom turns to Diane. "So, what's going on?"

"What's going on is that we're about to have a FaceTime call with Jeanne," Diane answers, as she props her iPad up against a bowl on the coffee table. "Anything you want to know beyond that you'll have to find out on your own."

The video call goes through, and Jeanne's and Ed's faces appear on the iPad's screen in overlarge format, like family photographs mistakenly shot in extreme close up. "Oh!" Ed exclaims, catching sight of their images in the playback window. "Let me fix the perspective—and Merry Christmas everybody!" he continues, as he repositions his phone.

"Yes, Joyeux Noël á tous et toute!" Jeanne adds, pushing disheveled bangs off her forehead and wrapping a red-velour bathrobe more tightly around herself.

"Bonne fêtes á toi et ta famille entiêre!" Mom responds, and then, with disquieting indiscretion, inquires of Jeanne, "You're not dressed yet?"

Jeanne scowls. "So, what did you want to know before, Yvette?" she responds bluntly. "The sound came on before the picture, so Ed and I heard you and Diane talking."

"I wanted to know why you moved out of that independent living place," replies Mom, unfazed.

" 'Independent'?!" Jeanne snorts. "It's called 'independent' but that's just marketing malarkey. I gave up my independence when I let my kids talk me into getting rid of my house," she says abjectly. "Well, then—and when old age stole everything else from me!"

"Bien sûr," Mom acknowledges sadly. "That's a robber who's hard to escape."

Jeanne's face is immobile, as if the iPad's screen has frozen. "I'm dying, Yvette," she blurts out. "I have a pulmonary embolism that's like a time bomb waiting to detonate inside me."

"Someone said 'detonate' a while ago," Mom says, "but I can't remember why."

"We were taking about crumbs and sprinkles," Melissa volunteers.

"Sprinkles!?" Jeanne repeats, incredulous.

"Yeah, as in cookie crumbs and sprinkles," Melissa clarifies.

Jeanne frowns. "Whatever! This is how the cookie's crumbling for me!"

"I'm so sorry!" Mom exclaims, looking disconsolate.

"We all have an expiration date," Jeanne replies. "Mine'll just turn out to be sooner than expected."

Elise starts to yip in the background.

"Can you quiet that dog down?" Jeanne says to Ed.

"Sure thing, Mom—I'll give her something to make her stop barking."

"Do that, please," Jeanne entreats, and, then smiling, adds, "Get something 'Für Elise.' "

We all start laughing, including Ed and Jeanne. However, when everyone else's laughter subsides, Jeanne's doesn't but instead turns into coughing—at first light and then harder.

"What's wrong, Mom?" Ed asks in alarm. "Are you choking?"

"Not choking," she manages to say between coughs. "I just need a moment," she wheezes. Ed helps her sip from a glass of water. After what seems like minutes but is only seconds, Jeanne's coughing abates, leaving only the sound of her labored breathing. "Pardonnez-moi! I don't know what happened," she pants, in a hoarser voice than earlier. "Yvette, I'm sorry—I need to go," she continues. "I'm not supposed to get excited, and if I don't rest right away, this could trigger something bigger."

"Forcément," Mom dolefully concurs. "Take care of yourself Á la prochaine!" she concludes.

"Later," Jeanne agrees, blotting her eyes. Ed waves as the call ends, and he and Jeanne's faces vanish.

"I'd like a drink," Mom says to Diane.

225

"Sure," my sister answers. "Sparkling water or eggnog?"

"No, I mean a 'drink,'" Mom explains, "as in a martini or a Manhattan."

Diane gapes. "You haven't had that kind of drink in years—not since before Dad died."

"After that call, I need one."

"I'm not sure we have any liquor," Diane protests. "I haven't bought any in ages."

"I saw some champagne in the rec-room refrigerator a couple of weeks back," Melissa says. "Maybe someone gave it to one of you for a holiday or birthday present."

"Well, it's a holiday today," Mom responds, "so it's appropriate to open it."

"Just like it's always five o'clock somewhere in the world, right, Mémère?" Melissa laughs as Diane and Ian go off to get the champagne.

"What are you talking about?" Mom asks her.

"Happy hour doesn't start until five o'clock, so people say that when they want to drink earlier," she explains. "It's an English expression."

"Which must be why I don't understand it," Mom responds tersely.

"You seem upset, Mémère," says Carrie.

"I am," Mom answers. "Jeanne's news shocked me. But maybe it shouldn't have," she continues. "Like she said, we all have an expiration date and—surgeries and treatments aside—it's not all that adjustable."

None of us comment.

Ian returns with the open champagne bottle in an urn-shaped ice bucket with a big gold bow tied around it.

"Why so fancy?" Melissa asks as Diane enters carrying a tray of stemware.

"If we're going to drink champagne we might as well do it in a festive fashion," Diane answers. She sets the tray down on the coffee table, and Ian takes the champagne bottle out of the ice bucket and wraps it in a red napkin.

"Just say when, Mémère," he says, as he begins to fill a crystal flute for Mom.

"Excuse me?" she replies.

"Tell me when the glass is full enough, and I'll stop pouring."

"Oh, I don't want any, thanks."

"What?!" Diane exclaims. "The champagne was your idea to begin with!"

"Was it?" Mom asks. "I don't know what I was thinking." She looks at the flute, which Ian is still holding. "Please give my glass to someone else—I never drink champagne except on holidays, and Christmas Eve doesn't really count."

We're all dumbstruck.

"I'll have a glass," Carrie says, breaking the silence, and looks at Melissa to prompt her to do the same.

"Yes, I will, too," Melissa complies.

"And one for me," I tell Ian.

"But you don't drink," he objects.

"We should all take a glass and toast Christmas—whether or not we're going to drink the contents."

Mom is expressionless.

"Also, it's fun to watch champagne bubbles rise to the surface," I add, unable to think of anything more persuasive.

"OK," Mom says and takes her glass from Ian.

"À tous les Noëls passés et à ceux à venir," I announce once Ian has filled everybody's glasses.

"Aux ceux passés—sans aucun doute," Mom responds.

"To Christmas past and present," I say, translating my toast. With some trepidation, I also translate Mom's addendum, "Certainly to past ones."

We raise our glasses. "To Christmas," everyone proclaims. I lower my glass without drinking, and Ian and Mom do likewise.

"This champagne is bitter," Melissa says, as she puts her glass down on a coaster. "It must be pretty old."

"As a matter of fact, it isn't champagne," Diane retorts, irritated. "The label says it's 'brut sparkling wine.'"

"How's that different?"

Diane frowns. "Real champagne comes from the Champagne region of France—I'd think you'd know that."

"So, where's this wine from?" Carrie asks.

"Upstate New York," I tell her, hoping this bland fact might defuse the situation.

To my mortification, Melissa says, "I hate upstate New York."

"But you graduated from the Rochester Institute of Technology!" Ian exclaims.

"That's why I hate it. Other than studying, there's nothing to do there but watch the snow fall in winter and wish you were across the lake in Toronto during summer."

"Rochester has the Eastman School of Music," Ian, who is an amateur violinist, counters. "It must have a lot of concerts."

"Classical music! Boring!" Melissa pronounces, and gleefully adds, "Like most of the people stuck living in Rochester!"

"Melissa!" Carrie exclaims. "Remember, Mémère was just talking about not stereotyping people and places!" she scolds. "Try to show a little more kindness!"

"Sorry," Melissa apologizes to Mom, who's now facing downward, studying the pattern in the oriental carpet.

"What are you sorry about?" Mom asks, looking up. "I wasn't paying attention,"

"Making fun of people and where they come from."

"No need for apologies," Mom replies, "We're all entitled to our opinions." Then, lifting her champagne flute, she runs a finger along its perimeter. "You're right!" she says to me. "It's fun to watch the bubbles rise to the surface!"

I smile but say nothing. No one else does either.

"A child is born on Christmas Day in the morning," the refrain of a carol, emanates from the radio.

"A timeless story," Carrie says, making conversation. "A baby, fresh and innocent, enters the world."

"While an old woman, sick and tired, prepares to leave it for another," Mom responds.

"Mom!" I reprove her.

"Quoi?" Mom asks, her voice emotionless. "At least, that's fair— this world for the fresh soul and another for the fading one."

"What if there isn't another world?" asks Ian, his medical and Jewish background having made him both pragmatic and skeptical.

I'm discomfited by his question, but Mom looks unperturbed. "We have to believe there is and that it's better."

"Why believe in something that might not be real," Melissa thoughtlessly joins in, "and that probably isn't any better than where we are now—if, like you said, no place is better than another?"

"Not here on Earth," Mom replies, looking like she's been assailed by a stranger. "But up above things must be better."

"How can you be sure?" Melissa perseveres, as if tactlessness is her vocation.

Diane glares at her. "If believing offers people hope, that's enough," she says from her seat by the fireplace.

"Hope springs eternal," I say to underscore her argument.

Mom turns to me. "It's probably the only thing that does," she says quietly.

"I can think of something else," Diane says, reaching for the electrical panel on the floor by the hearth. "Light! Which is what we need right now—something light and entertaining!" she continues as she begins to turn on the room's holiday lighting and animated decorations.

"Isn't everything supposed to come on automatically at nightfall?" Carrie asks.

Diane frowns. "Night seems to be falling early, so we might as well start," she replies, flicking switches, while around us, the tree lights, window candles, and mantel garland illuminate like flowers blooming and the room's myriad mechanized ornaments—from waving elves and snowmen to cooing partridges and fluttery winged angels—spring to life like toys in a children's fantasy.

"Wow!" exclaims Ian, accustomed to the typically less elaborate décor of Hanukkah.

" 'You ain't seen nothing yet!' " Melissa says, turning on the ice-rink music box, which

231

launches into a tinkling iteration of "Silent Night" and propels its tiny skaters into assorted circles, pirouettes, and figure eights.

"How pretty!" Carrie exclaims as she watches the figures and their reflections twirl across the rink's mirrored surface. "Don't you think so, Mémère?"

Mom, observing twilight's descent outside, doesn't answer.

"Mémère?" Carrie repeats, gesturing at the music box. "Isn't it really something?!"

"Yes, dear," Mom replies, watching her reflection brighten and the lawn, trees, and sky beyond blacken then disappear into the dark yet gleaming glass.

CHAPTER 34

A Winter's Tale
Medium Take

In contrast to her broad political and social perspectives, Mom's view of the physical world beyond the walls of her house is narrow, constrained by her growing immobility and declining vision. Still, every morning, she awakens to the same lovely and reassuring sight—the chintz canopy of her four-poster bed, a jumble of lavender roses, pink peonies, and golden yarrow floating overhead, like Baroque cherubim in tumultuous flight.

Today, as every day, Diane is getting Mom up and out of bed. Although Mom is small and light, I'm helping, as Mom's never-ending needs increasingly wear on Diane. Together, we pull Mom up, turn her body sideways, and place her feet squarely on the floor. Then we slip her arms into the sleeves of her favorite velour bathrobe and make sure that she has a firm grasp on her walker.

"I'm useless," Mom says into the air. "It's not fair to the two of you that you have to help me with even the simplest tâches."

"Tasks," I amend, the former editor in me

unable to keep from correcting her unconscious slip into French.

She looks me full in the face. "What are you doing here, Lucien?" she asks, mistaking me for her long-deceased eldest brother. Turning to Diane, she asks, "And, you, what are *you* doing here? I should be able to do this myself! My brother and sister shouldn't have to help me out of my own bed!"

Diane ties Mom's robe around her waist. "You seem a little scattered this morning, so we thought you could use some help," she responds. "And I'm not your sister—you don't have one," she adds, perhaps hoping the bald-faced truth will snap Mom out of her confusion and return her to the present.

"Did she die?!" Mom asks, astounded. "When did it happen?! Why didn't anyone tell me?!"

"You *never* had a sister," Diane clarifies.

"Non?!"

"No! Not unless you're even better at keeping family secrets than I thought," Diane says. Pointing to me. she continues, "And this isn't your brother—Lucien died years ago."

My mother, her glasses slightly askew and hair uncombed, cocks her head quizzically. "Then, who are you two?" she asks. "My servants?"

Diane frowns. "Sometimes, I feel like one! I'm your daughter, remember? I live here and help you with everything." Pointing to me, she adds,

"And this is Rob, your eldest son—the one who moved far away and who you talk about almost every day."

My mother starts to tremble. To distract her, I ask, "Why don't we walk to the window and look outside?"

Mom nods. "I'd like that." She seems about to say my name but, perhaps afraid that she'll get it wrong, doesn't.

We cross the cold floor, its carpets long ago removed to accommodate the walker, and parting satin drapes, peer through the window at a landscape of treetops and spires. Pine, birch, and maple boughs in the woods across the way reach skyward as if in supplication—a view as changeless as a painting save for seasonal variations: summer's verdant foliage, autumn's bright colors, springtime's budding branches, and now winter's softly falling snow.

"I love snow," Mom says, touching a frost swirl on the window. "It turns everything into something beautiful."

Behind us, Diane is making up the bed. "You wouldn't love it so much if you had to shovel it like I do," she says, smoothing the chintz coverlet.

"I know," Mom answers. "Thank you for your help with everything."

"You're welcome," my sister replies curtly, plumping a pillow.

"You're a good daughter, Diane," Mom continues, looking at her own reflection in the glass and at the snow falling behind it. "You were a good little girl, and now you're a good woman. I'm lucky to have you taking care of me," she adds.

I turn toward Diane, who's stopped working in mid-gesture, the look of surprise on her face matching my own. Mom is back with us. For how long, however, is anyone's guess.

CHAPTER 35

In the Middle Kingdom

Long Take

I check my cellphone to make sure it's in airplane mode, and then reread the message I earlier received from Diane. Mom seems really out of it today, she texted. She's even more forgetful and shaky than usual. This worried me when I first read it, as the boarding door closed and the crew ordered everyone to stow their electronic devices, and it worries me now, as I reread it several hours later. However, since I'm thousands of miles away and can't do anything to help Diane or Mom, I sigh and return the phone to my pocket.

On the airline seatback in front of me, a monitor tracks the external temperature's drop from -200F° to -205F° to -210F° as the plane traverses the Arctic Circle, making me wonder at how many degrees below zero jet engines stop working. Halfway through this US-to-China flight, I've exhausted nearly every diversion, from the mediocre dinner to the darkly disturbing James Bond movie after. Yet, unlike my fellow passengers, most of whom are asleep, I remain awake. Tired of contemplating the frozen blackness beyond my portal window, I decide to occupy myself with work, so I flick on the overhead lamp and take out my computer.

The long-haired young woman asleep in the seat to the right of me groans softly and moves her head away from the light. Hoping I haven't woken her up, I turn on my notebook and open a sales spreadsheet entitled, Opportunities, Won and Lost, which strikes me as an apt name for a life inventory, a summary of all the chances we take that pan out or don't. Skipping over the spreadsheet's "Won" column to focus on the longer "Lost," I think of the many things my client's local marketing people could have done differently to shorten the latter and of the difficult conversations I'll now need to have with them because they didn't.

To take my mind off this prospect, I start an email message to my wife Thea, since, despite this airline's reputation for few amenities, it offers wi-fi access.

How are you? I write and push the return key.

To my surprise, she responds right away. I'm fine. How are you?

OK but coming down with something, I type. I feel achy.

You didn't seem sick when you left this morning, she writes back.

I know, but while we were over Canada a man two rows behind me sneezed so hard his spittle landed on my shoulders.

Gross!
To put it mildly.
Have you taken medicine?
I forgot to bring any.
Just ask a flight attendant.

Fat chance they'd give me some, I think ruefully while typing, Yes, maybe, which I assume she'll correctly take to mean that I won't.

Have it your way, she writes back, confirming she's understood me. Still, you'd be better off asking now than regretting you didn't later.

What do you mean?

Haven't you heard about the avian flu outbreak in Southeast Asia? The Chinese are afraid it might become an epidemic and are quarantining people who could be carriers. You don't want to get to China looking sick.

Her news startles me, but because this is the start of a two-week business trip and worrying won't help me any, I don't want to discuss it further. What do you say we change the subject? I type back.

Whatever, she responds. How was boarding at Newark?

The usual rehearsal for the end of the world, I reply, punctuating my remark with a scowling emoji.

What do you mean?

There was a security breach, so they evacuated the terminal and re-ran everyone—thousands of us—through X-ray and bag inspection. We were herded down corridors and escalators and sent back through the scanners—it was like a scene from a Busby Berkeley musical, only with carry-on luggage and clumsy dancers.

You're exaggerating, Thea types.

It took three hours! I respond. I felt like dropping this trip altogether and flying back to Cleveland.

There's a pause. Are you still there? I write.

Sorry, she replies after a minute. I'm in the kitchen watching a cooking show. What were we talking about?

The mess at Newark! I answer.

You always overreact and get too worked up, she replies, returning to her earlier theme and a long-standing point of contention between us.

Not always, I protest. A lot of the time, my reactions are warranted.

Thea doesn't respond. It's no use debating this, she finally answers. Where are you, anyway?

Still on the plane, I reply, checking the flight path for an exact location. Over the Bering Strait, at the moment.

OMG! I saw a documentary about the Pacific Ring of Fire and the Bering Strait! The high seas, howling wind, and sudden snow squalls! Aren't you afraid!?

Not especially—none of that affects you much at 35,000 feet.

Well, be careful!

I want to ask her how, under the circumstances, I should go about doing this but instead only write, Now, who's overreacting?

Another pause follows. Well, I've got to go, Thea replies. I need to make dinner, and I have a meeting after.

Although I wonder what meeting, I don't inquire. OK. Talk with you later.

Yes, later, she responds. Happy landing!

Thanks. Happy meeting, I reply.

I'm about to return my attention to the spreadsheet when an instant message arrives from my sister.

Mom fell half an hour ago, it reads.

She did!? I type back rapidly.

Yes—she lost her balance and fell straight backwards while I was talking to her! It was frightening!

How is she now? I ask, typing even faster.

In a lot of pain—the EMS techs think she might have broken a femur, I read with alarm. I'm in an ambulance on my way to the hospital with her, Diane continues.

My breath catches. My God! I type. Keep me posted!

Will do, my sister responds. I'll phone you as soon I find out what's the matter!

Make sure to call my cell, not the house, I advise her. I'm traveling.

Figures! Where to this time?!

Asia—please don't tell Mom.

You think I'm crazy? Diane fires back. Mom worries when you just travel to Detroit or Chicago.

I want to reply that Mom's worries in respect to those two places might be well founded, but Diane writes again before I can do so. I've got to go—we're pulling up to the ER entrance. I'll get back to you.

Thanks, I type back, despite her having already dropped out of the conversation.

The achiness I mentioned to Thea is increasing and, since the news about Mom has also made my head start hurting, my need for medicine has become more urgent. I close my notebook, pull my computer bag up onto my lap, and rummage through it in the half light, hoping to find aspirin left over from a previous flight. Eventually, I pull a package of nighttime Advil out of the bag's deepest recesses and tear it open.

The noise disrupts the sleep of the young woman to my right, who after a few fitful movements, turns to face me and, eyes still closed, drops her head on my shoulder. This makes me abandon my plan to climb over her and the guy beside her to go to the restroom, so instead I drink down the pills with what little remains of the water I bought before boarding. Hoping the Advil will soon take effect, I close my eyes, and after a while, succeed in falling into a restless sleep.

Upon awaking, I discover that the young woman and her seatmate—perhaps her husband—are up and stretching in the aisle ahead, as if in a fitness center. This is a surprise but, glad of the opportunity to leave my seat, I get up and head toward the toilets behind me.

When I return, finding my two row mates reseated, I gingerly climb over them while they either feign or in fact sleep. Once sitting, I open my notebook and check my email messages for more news about Mom. Not seeing any, I reclose it and once more consult the flight monitor. It indicates we're over Mongolia, a country whose windswept steppes I hope never to visit, emergency landings notwithstanding. Looking away with a shudder, I take out Madame de Sévigné's *Lettres* to distract myself. However, my throat begins to tighten. "Damn!" I think, and, closing my book, begin to worry. When a flight attendant comes down the darkened aisle with the nighttime water service, I gesture to her, since I've decided to take Thea's advice and ask about getting some medicine.

"Water sir?" she initially asks, but then noting the French book in my lap, translates, "De l'eau, monsieur?" while pouring a cup of water.

"Non, merci," I reply, because it seems easier to go along with her presumption that French is my primary language. "Mais pourriez-vous me fournir quelque chose pour un mal de gorge?

Malheureusement, je n'ai pas apporté aucun remède," I continue, describing my predicament and explaining that I forgot to bring medicine.

"Attendez s'il vous plaît—je verrai," she murmurs, her sympathetic smile illuminated by the soft glow of my reading light as she assures me that she will see what medicine she can find.

I return to Madame de Sévigné's *Lettres*, which though they recount the thoughts and actions of the long departed, ring truer to me than the majority of my business interactions. The flight attendant reappears and hands me a snifter of deep brown liquid. "Du cognac," she whispers. "Je n'ai pas pu vous obtenir des médicaments, mais ceci, c'est encore plus efficace pour un mal de gorge à mon avis," explaining that she couldn't find aspirin, but that she believes cognac is even more effective than painkillers for soothing a sore throat.

"Bien sûr!" I reply, as astonished as I am grateful. Unable to contain my curiosity, I ask where the brandy came from.

"De la première—from first class," she answers.

"Vous êtes vraiment gentille!" I compliment her.

"J'ai été formé par Air France—ou le confort du passager est toujours la priorité," she answers, explaining with justified pride that she trained at Air France, where customer service is paramount.

"Je vous remercie infiniment," I thank her.

"De rien." She smiles and then disappears down the aisle.

Awoken by our conversation, the young woman at my side turns towards me. "Étes-vous français?" she asks in a flat, unmistakably American accent, wanting to know if I am French.

"Of French-Canadian descent," I inform her.

"Oh, wow! You speak French pretty well, considering!" she remarks offhand.

"You think so?" I respond, unduly polite.

"Yeah—I took French all through high school and majored in it at college, but I never understand French-Canadians," she continues, nonchalantly pushing her long hair back off the sides of her face like an actress in a shampoo commercial.

"Don't worry," I say, not meaning it. "French can be a real challenge for people without much experience."

Raising her eyebrows in surprise and then grimacing, she seems about to reply, but in the end, only blushes deeply and turns away.

I take a sip of cognac and consider resuming Madame de Sévigné's *Lettres*, but having just lived through a moment worthy of them, instead return to my computer to check for further news of Mom. There's nothing, which disturbs me, since the maxim, "No news is good news" doesn't promise to hold true in this instance.

I reopen my spreadsheet to do more work, but, unfortunately, the cabin lights come up, signaling the start of breakfast. As it's likely to consist of watery eggs and rubbery sausages—or, since we're bound for Asia, soggy noodles and dry fried rice—I don't plan on having any. In contrast, the young woman beside me, probably hungry and maybe less traveled, raises her head in anticipation, careful not to look in my direction. As the serving cart proceeds down the aisle, the flight attendant asks whether each passenger prefers an American or Asian breakfast. When she arrives at our row, my seatmate requests the former whereas I indicate that I'm not interested in either.

"Êtes-vous sûr, monsieur?" the flight attendant inquires.

"Bien sûr, merci," I reply.

The young woman beside me gives a long, exasperated sigh—accompanied, I imagine, by a rolling of her eyes or comparable expression of disdain, though I'm not certain as she continues to look straight forward.

The flight attendant turns to her. "Is something the matter, miss?" she asks, with practiced solicitude, her brow furrowed and English faultless. "Can I do anything else for you?"

Perhaps guessing that her behavior has been judged and found wanting, the young woman seems embarrassed. "No, thank you—nothing," she answers, energetically shaking her head.

"Well, if you think of anything, don't hesitate to press the call button."

This elicits another enthusiastic nod and thank you from my seatmate.

The flight attendant turns back to me. "Et vous aussi, monsieur, n'hésitez pas!" she adds, with a complicit smile.

I smile at her in kind, then look out the portal window. Beneath us, the bleak Mongolian landscape has been replaced by great swaths of green and yellow fields while, in the distance, cloud- and smog-enshrouded low hills and mountains portend our impending arrival in Beijing, our destination. Thinking again of the discussions I will need to have with the marketing staff once I get there, my headache worsens, so I close my eyes in hope of respite.

When I reopen them, the flight attendants, having already cleared away breakfast and passed out the arrival cards, are busy selling liquor, perfume, cigarettes, and other duty-free items. Taking out a pen, I fill in my card with information on my length of stay, hotel name, and trip purpose—all of which must be squeezed into spaces too tiny to accommodate it. Done, I check my computer to see if Diane has sent an update on Mom but once again find nothing. As the fasten-seatbelt signs come on, Chinese, Japanese,

Korean, and English recordings successively announce the plane's descent into the Beijing area and request that all electronic devices be put away, seatbacks set upright, and tray tables lifted. I comply, hoping that, when we're on the ground and I can check my phone, I'll find further news about Mom among my text messages.

The plane drops into a cloud bank, and the cabin lights dim in advance of our landing. Though nothing is visible, I turn toward the window, and as always when arriving in a country where I'd prefer not to perish, cross myself and silently say the Lord's Prayer, Hail Mary, and Act of Contrition in French. The window clears as the plane makes its final approach, revealing a huge airport with multiple control towers and an adjacent army base, replete with troops marching and military vehicles either parked or in transit. Once the plane touches down, this aerial perspective gives way to a ground-bound, fast-moving view of the runway and the landscape beyond it until the retro-jets kick in—jolting us all forwards and backwards—and the scenery's rate of passage lessens.

While we taxi toward the terminal, I turn on my cellphone. Its screen displays an array of Chinese Kanji characters, followed by an English-language enjoinder to connect to a China telecom carrier. I do this, then check my text messages. They include several from the local office as well as advertisements for ground transportation but nothing about Mom, so I return the phone to my pocket.

When the plane arrives at the gate and the end-of-flight chimes sound, the rush to retrieve items from storage bins erupts—resulting in the usual crossed paths, shoving, cold stares, and impatient glances. As soon as the woman beside me and her companion vacate their seats to join the melee, I enter the aisle, collect my carry-on bag from the overhead bin, and wait for everyone to start toward the exit. After only a moment, however, hearing someone behind me swearing softly, I turn around and see my erstwhile seatmate struggling to remove a bulky bag from the overhead, her traveling companion having disappeared down the aisle, presumably to retrieve their other suitcases. "I can't do this," she complains to no one in particular, as she tries to free her luggage.

Improbably gallant, I say, "Please—allow me," and, before she has time to refuse or I to reconsider, I reach up and pull her bag down for her. She looks at me coldly for a second and then, her expression changing, says, "Merci, monsieur—c'est gentil," her accent as flat and jarring as ever but her tone neither offended nor offensive and devoid of condescension.

"Je vous en prie, madame," I respond, relieved, and reciprocally polite add, "My pleasure." Then, since the exit line has started stirring, I turn around and move forward.

It's a long way from the plane to Chinese Immigration, and, although getting through Entry and Customs proves no worse than usual, by the time I'm done and reach the exit ramp that leads into the main terminal, I feel like I'm running a fever. I hope I can get some medicine soon. My carry-on luggage in tow behind me, I pass through the Arrival area's final exit checkpoint and descend the long, cordoned ramp into the general airport and China proper, scanning the crowd of waiting limo, taxi, and hotel-bus drivers for one holding a placard with my name. At last, I spot my chauffeur, a spiky-haired young man who, in skin-tight jeans and sharp-angled sunglasses, looks like a rockstar or drug dealer, and who I soon discover, speaks no English whatsoever. So much for his helping me find medicine, I think, while smiling broadly, he takes charge of my bag and motions me to follow him to a car parked by the curb.

On the hour's drive into the city, I check my phone repeatedly for more news about Mom but, each time, I'm disappointed. Since Diane is usually good at keeping me current, this isn't what I'd expected, and, probably from anxiety, my headache worsens—sharp pains shoot through my temple and my eyes begin watering. Taking out a tissue and dabbing at them, I reflect that, in contrast, my young chauffeur's driving is pretty much what I'd anticipated: daredevil maneuvers undertaken at breakneck speed to the accompaniment of blaring music. "Do you think that maybe you could go more slowly?" I shout above the racket, hoping that, even though he doesn't speak English, my tone of voice might convey my message. However, all he does is nod and—alarmingly—lift one hand from the steering wheel and give me the OK signal.

To calm myself, I look out the window, but the barrier walls and poplar trees that line the roadway and camouflage the peasant villages behind them are going by so rapidly I find the view equally unnerving. I decide to text Thea. Have you heard anything more from my sister about Mom? I write. Minutes pass before the phone alerts me to an answer.

Sorry, Thea responds. I was just finishing a stitch in the scarf that I'm knitting.

Knitting for whom? I type, while the driver brakes and then accelerates so recklessly that if I weren't wearing a seatbelt I'd fly onto the floor in front of me.

For charity. My knitting group, the Naughty Knitters, is donating them to inner-city schoolchildren.

I wince, both at the group's name and at its—in my opinion—misguided social mission: providing knitted scarves and mittens to inner city schoolchildren who likely have little interest in wearing handicrafts donated by white suburban matrons. However, I merely text, Oh—so you haven't heard anything?

Not from Diane.

Irritated by what seems like a cagy answer, I respond, Nothing from anyone else either?

Of course, not—I would have said so, wouldn't I?

Since I don't answer, after a minute, she texts, Maybe Diane wrote Ian.

God, I hope not, I type back rapidly.

Me also, Thea replies just as quickly. He has an internal medicine exam on Friday. None of us should be telling him anything that might upset him.

Absolutely, I text back. I'll let Diane know that—and maybe she'll have news for me.

Agreed on both counts, Thea responds. I have to start dinner. Good luck finding out something.

Thanks, I reply. I'm about to start writing Diane when the car suddenly changes lanes and I'm tossed from one end of the back seat to the other, and my phone goes flying. "Merde—vous allez nous faire tuer!" I exclaim, lapsing into French, which sometimes happens when I'm angry or frightened. "You'll get us killed!" I translate, forgetting that he doesn't speak English.

"Desolé!" the driver haltingly replies, slowing down the car. "Une voiture a changé de voi devant nous!" he apologizes explaining that a driver ahead cut into our lane.

"Vous parlez français?!" I ask, while searching for my phone, astounded he speaks French.

"Un petit peu!"

"Tant mieux!" I pull my phone out of the crevice between the door and the car seat. "Au nom du bon Dieu, je vous prie de conduisez plus lentement," I continue, entreating him to drive more slowly.

"Bien sûr!" he answers, chastened.

My phone pings and, to my relief, I discover Diane's just written me.

Sorry it took so long to get back to you—I've been at the hospital all day.

No problem, I write, obviously lying. How's Mom?

Out of surgery.

Surgery??!! I type, my punctuation atypically emphatic.

Yes, I thought you knew—I told Ian earlier.

You told Ian??!!!

Has your phone been hacked? Your texts are full of exclamation points and question marks, she responds. Nonplussed, I don't answer. I told him, Diane continues, because he asked how Mom was doing, and I didn't want to lie.

Unwilling to contest this line of reasoning, I ask, So, how's Mom right now? Was the operation successful?

The doctors thought it went well. They put the fractured femur back together without significant complications.

Without 'significant' complications?! I type back. Were there other kinds?

Not really, Diane answers. Except that, during the operation, Mom started to come to and they had to increase her dose of anesthesia.

So?!

It could cause her dementia to increase. We'll know better as we move forward.

My sore throat and headache begin again to worsen. What a situation!

Yeah, it's business as usual here—just one fun-filled event after another, Diane replies, caustically. That's why I have to go now—I need to get some sleep before I go back to the hospital for Mom's release from Recovery.

Sleep well!

You too, she answers, then asks, It's already evening there, isn't it?

It is, but I'm supposed to meet the local marketing staff for drinks after checking into my hotel. I'm not feeling great, though—so I'm going to try to get out of it.

Good luck with that!

Thanks, I reply as she goes offline. Since now seems as good a time as any, I write the marketing department's manager to beg off meeting, not mentioning my illness but rather citing fatigue.

He responds almost instantly, welcoming me to China and expressing his regret at my need to cancel. However, he doesn't attempt to dissuade me, which leads me to believe he's probably pleased to have the evening free, despite the short notice.

Glancing out my window, I notice that the highway signs, written in both Chinese and English, indicate we've entered Beijing's city limits. I watch while we pass through outlying sectors of traditional buildings, then neighborhoods of run-down apartment towers with laundry fluttering from balconies, and eventually, near Tiananmen Square, an area of sleek skyscrapers surrounded by marble-bordered canals and parks filled with ornamental trees and shrubbery. Finally, at an exit for the diplomatic district, the car leaves the highway and descends into the stop-and-go traffic that even now, early on a Sunday evening, engulfs the city's broad avenues, winding streets, and narrow alleys.

Again forgetting that the driver speaks no English, I ask, "How long will it take to get to the hotel from here," and then, catching myself, switch languages. "C'est loin d'ici, l'hôtel? Combien de temps pour y arriver?" I ask, wishing I spoke at least a smattering of Mandarin.

The young man lifts his right hand and splays three fingers, presumably to communicate that we'll get there in as many minutes. Because of heavy traffic, though, a half an hour passes before we arrive at the hotel, a soaring blue-glass monolith, and by that time my head is pounding and fever rising. "Désolé pour le retard!" the driver apologizes for the delay as he guides the car under the building's porte-cochére.

"Pas de problème," I answer and tip him with an uncounted handful of Chinese currency.

He flashes me a wide grin. "Adieu monsieur!"

I reply in kind while watching him jump back into the car, which then disappears into the traffic.

A liveried bellhop approaches. Taking my luggage, he leads me into a teak-paneled lobby as cavernous as a canyon, with a water wall on one end, a fountain at the other, and clusters of oddly shaped furniture strewn across its multi-hued terrazzo floor like malformed islands on a kaleidoscopic ocean. Dizzy and starting to sweat from my fever, I stop and sit down on a trapezoidal sofa.

The bellhop, looking puzzled, stops beside me. "Is everything all right, sir?"

"I'm just tired from my flight," I reply insouciantly, concerned about being quarantined as a potential flu carrier.

The bellhop's expression seems skeptical.

"I only need to rest a bit," I assure him as my cellphone starts pinging. "One moment, please," I add and, taking out my phone, discover that Ian is texting me.

Have you heard anything more about Mémère, he writes. She should be out of Recovery by now.

Maybe she should be, I text back, but so far I haven't heard.

You haven't?

Not a thing, I confirm and, because the bellhop is watching, refrain from wiping the perspiration off my forehead.

That's strange, Ian says.

No news is good news, I reply, contradicting my earlier reflection on the matter.

Not in medicine! he cautions.

Be that as it may, I write back, annoyed by his bluntness, an unexpected consequence of his medical education. I'll let you know as soon as I hear one way or the other.

A pause follows, which makes me realize that my own bluntness has probably made him equally uncomfortable. Yes, do that, please, he texts me.

Sure thing. Talk with you later.

OK, he concludes.

I put my cellphone back in my pocket, nod at the bellhop, get up, and follow him toward the check-in desk. As we cross the lobby, side-stepping more groupings of misshapen furniture, we pass a placard announcing the start of a Belgian consular reception on the hotel mezzanine and, moments later, encounter a group of associated guests arriving—men in summer suits and women in cocktail dresses, conversing in French, Dutch, or Walloon.

Thinking it better to ask them than the Chinese hotel staff about where I can get medicine, I say, "Bonsoir, madame," to one of the Francophones, a thin, silver-haired woman in a green shift with a matching wrap draped over her tanned shoulders.

"Bonsoir, monsieur," she responds. Given my travel-rumpled clothes, she likely presumes that I'm not on my way to the reception, and so guesses at the next-best possibility. "Étes-vous Belge? Puis-je vous rendre d'assistance?" she asks, inquiring if I am Belgian and then politely asking if she can help me.

"Pas Belge—d'orgine Québécois," I reply, only mildly bending the truth, because, although I'm not Québécois, my family is originally from Québec province. "Je vien juste d'arrivé, et j'ai attrapé un rhume—pouvez-vous me diriger vers un magasin qui vend des médicaments, même à cette heure tardive?" I say, explaining that I just arrived, have a cold, and am trying to find a place to buy medicine.

"Vous avez de la chance!" she says and informs me that I'm in luck as there are many stores at the back of the hotel lobby. "Cet hôtel-ci a de nombreux magasins à l'arrière de la sale."

The bellhop, one hand poised on the handle of my carry-on bag and smiling tightly, asks, "May I help, sir?" not sounding the least bit exasperated, which doubtless attests to his having undergone rigorous hospitality training.

"No, thanks," I answer. "This nice lady was just pointing out where I can do some shopping later—in the shops at the back of the lobby."

"Ah, yes," he replies, his expression lightening. "You can find anything there—gifts and also personal items, like toiletries, aspirin, and cold medicine. What are looking for, sir? I'll have the concierge send it to your room while you check in."

"A present for my wife," I lie. "So, it's probably best that I buy it myself."

I turn back to the Belgian woman and thank her. "Merci, et bonne soirée, madame."

"Je vous en prie, monsieur," she replies, and wishing me a good evening, hurries off to catch up with her companions, who've moved on without her.

Looking at the bellhop, I gesture toward the hotel's check-in desk. "Shall we?" I ask and start in its direction. When we arrive, I take out my wallet, extract another sheaf of uncounted Chinese RMB notes, and hand them to him.

He smiles broadly and says, "Thank you, sir," while bowing. As I watch him head back to the hotel entrance, I hope my tip was large enough to keep him from giving a second thought as to whether I have a fever.

Behind a long reception desk adorned with carvings of red dragons in flight across a skyscape of hammered silver, a pony-tailed young man signals me to approach and register while his colleagues attend to other arriving visitors—mostly businesspeople and retired couples as well as a few families with children. "Good evening sir," he says, "May I have your passport?" I hand it over.

As he runs it through a scanner, I pick up a leaflet on the counter promoting a museum exhibition, "China: The Middle Kingdom—Art Through the Millennia." The adolescent daughter of a blonde checking in beside me picks one up also. "Why do they call China 'The Middle Kingdom?' " she asks her mother.

"What?" the woman answers, rummaging through her handbag for her identification or other documentation.

The girl thrusts the leaflet in front of her.

"Oh this," her mother says, studying the piece of paper. "If I remember right from college, it's because in ancient times the Chinese thought China was the center of the world and closer to Heaven than all other places," she says.

Her explanation strikes me as accurate and a reasonably good description of Chinese attitudes in the present—if one removes the reference to Heaven.

"Sounds like an interesting exhibition," I

comment, breaking my rule of not engaging strangers in unnecessary conversation.

"We'll probably go," she responds, smiling. "You?"

I shake my head. "No time. Here on business."

"Too bad!" she says with a laugh, then adds, "Well, have a good trip anyway!" and returns to searching her purse.

The desk clerk, done with my passport, hands it back. Adjusting his glasses with one hand and typing with the other, he peers into a monitor to confirm my reservation.

"Your suite is on the thirty-seventh floor in the executive section," he announces and picks up the room's keycards to give them to me.

I must look surprised because he pauses in mid-gesture. "Will that be satisfactory?"

"I'd asked for a double room on a regular floor," I say. "Will this be more expensive?"

Blank-faced, he studies his screen again. "Not this time," he replies, breaking into a smile. "It seems that the hotel is out of double rooms, so as a courtesy you've been assigned the suite at the same rate as a double—there will be no additional charges."

"That's great," I respond, likewise smiling. Considering the scrutiny to which my client's accounting department subjects expense reports, this is good news for me. As the cost is not an issue, I start to speculate about the potential benefits of my upgraded accommodations. "Do you know if the executive lounge offers food?" I ask. The burning in my throat is growing, and I hope that maybe I can soothe it with some sherbet, ice cream, or one of the pureed fruit soups that I've sometimes been served on my trips to China.

"It does, sir—mostly small things, dim sum and soups, but very good!" he assures me, his already attentive manner growing more so. "Is there anything else I can do for you this evening?" he asks, handing me my room's keycards.

"Actually, there is," I tell him. "I'd like to visit the hotel shops before going up and unpacking. Can you have my bags sent to my room ahead of me?"

"Of course, sir. I'll make sure that they are in your suite by the time you enter."

"Thanks. I appreciate it," then add, "The shops are where, exactly?" because, despite the Belgian woman's assistance, I'm not certain.

"Right over there, sir." He points discreetly. "Past the fountain and the sign that says, 'Boutiques et Autres Divertissements,'" he continues, pronouncing the French words with surprising accuracy.

The French signage, which I've previously encountered in Chinese establishments of this caliber, seems to me absurd and pretentious, but as it would be unforgivably rude to say such,

I just thank him and take off in the indicated direction.

Due to the late hour, only one of the hotel shops is open—a high-end jewelry and objets d'art outlet whose entrance is adorned with elaborate Chinese paper lanterns in deference to the approaching lunar New Year celebration. Hoping the staff or customers might suggest a place to buy medicine, I enter the store but am disappointed when—amid its painted fans, cloisonné vases, and ebony sculptures of celestial, spiritual, and other classical Chinese dragons—I find only an elderly Western couple shopping and an Asian saleslady in a red silk dress behind a counter. Presuming the salesperson to be my best prospect, I approach her. "Good evening, miss," I say, "I have a question."

She looks up from the rows of jade, quartz, and onyx bracelets she's been straightening, and for a moment, I'm astounded. White skinned with high cheek bones and long, dark hair in a topknot tied with a scarlet ribbon, she's striking—indeed, as beautiful as a woman in a Qing dynasty court painting. "How can I help you, sir?" she asks, with the habitual poise of a great beauty while I try to keep from gaping. "Is there something I can get for you?" she inquires, motioning toward the bracelets in the showcase and the necklaces displayed on velvet forms along the countertop.

"I'm looking for a present for my wife," I

answer. I don't want to bring up the subject of medicine and my illness too quickly.

"Are you looking for anything in particular?" she asks.

"Something elegant," I reply and, improvising, add, "Maybe a piece like the one on your shoulder," referring to her brooch, a subtle slip of silver inlaid with gray nacre.

"We're out of these, unfortunately," she responds, looking authentically, albeit professionally, dismayed. "But we have other pieces by the same jeweler." She holds up a slender silver chain from which hangs a freshwater pearl pendant.

"Is the jeweler local?" I ask.

She gives me a questioning look.

"My wife usually prefers things that have been made by local artisans," I explain before realizing that, since local sourcing is not much of a selling point in China, I've done little to shed light on my ostensible motivation.

"No, he isn't," she replies. "He's American, from Boston."

"My wife and I used to live there—maybe that will be local enough!" I joke. Her answering smile—as bright, white, and blank as any model's in a toothpaste commercial—indicates she doesn't get it.

The old couple overhears me. "Did you say you once lived in Boston?" the woman asks, pushing her walker towards me, as her companion, on a cane, follows. "Ed and I are originally from Massachusetts—from Canton, by the Blue Hills Reservation."

"My wife and I used to picnic there," I tell her, "a long time ago—before we moved to Cleveland."

"We left years ago, too—a little after we were married—but we moved further away than you. We came to Guangzhou right after Nixon opened up China."

"That was early on," I say. "Did you come on business?"

"Sort of," she says, with a smile that, despite her gray hair and wrinkles, is so mischievous it makes her look nearly girlish. "God's business—we're missionaries," she explains. "At least, that's what we *were*—we're just starting our retirement."

"Going back to the States?" I ask to show interest.

"As a matter of fact, we're going home to Canton." Her expression is still mischievous. "But not the one in Massachusetts—the one here in China." I don't respond so she elaborates. "Canton is Guangzhou's name in English—Westerners named it that when they established a concession there in the eighteenth century, during the Old China Trade."

I'm astonished, not because of the information

about Guangzhou's English name being Canton, which I knew, but because she and her husband, who look as old and frail as Mom, have elected to remain in China. "So, you like this country enough to stay here in retirement," I remark neutrally, careful not to betray my amazement.

She smiles. "It's really our home now—not Massachusetts, or anywhere else in the US. Plus, we've bought a condominium right by the church and school we founded so that we can keep helping out there."

"That's dedicated of you," I say, genuinely impressed.

"It's our duty and pleasure," she answers candidly.

I don't doubt her sincerity.

The saleslady coughs, reminding me that I've yet to decide about the pendant. "Sorry," I apologize. Partly from guilt, I add, "I'll take it."

"Certainly, sir," she replies, flashing her flawless smile, and opens a velvet-lined jewel case in which to place the pendant. While I reach for my wallet, my cellphone pings, which I hope means Diane is contacting me. Checking, though, I discover it's a news alert about North Korea conducting missile tests over the Sea of Japan. This worries me, as I'll be flying to Seoul the day after tomorrow. Since I have more than enough to deal with already, however, I try not to think about it.

I hand the saleslady my credit card and turn

back to the woman and her husband, who are now examining painted porcelains—tiny pagodas, seated lions, yet more dragons, and other icons of Chinese culture. "Do you know where I could buy medicine this time of evening?" I ask. "I caught a cold on the trip over, and my throat's aching," I explain, careful to depict myself as the victim of a minor malady rather than as a potential virus carrier.

The woman frowns. "That could be a challenge—can you think of a place?" she asks her husband, who is also frowning.

He shakes his head discouragingly. "There's a Carrefour not far from here but it closes soon, and it could take you a while to get there."

"I have some aspirin in my purse," the woman offers, pulling out a packet of aspirin and handing it to me. "It won't do much for your sore throat but it might help you feel a little better—you look peaked!"

"Thank you," I gratefully reply.

"Maybe the hotel restaurants serve sherbet or ice cream that could soothe your throat," she says, trying to be helpful.

"I hope so," I reply. The clerk hands me my purchase. "I'll check after I've gone up to my room and rested."

"You probably don't want to wait that long," the woman advises me, her frown returning. "The restaurants will start closing soon."

"That's too bad!" I respond—now frowning myself. "I was hoping to get the puréed soups they serve here between courses—the ones made of peaches, pears, and other fruits." I sigh. "Maybe room service offers them."

"You shouldn't wait too long to order from room service either," she advises. "Even though it's open all night things run out, especially soups and side dishes—we've had that happen," she adds in final warning.

As I turn toward the door, she touches my arm in a bashful gesture of farewell. "It was nice to meet you," she says. "I'm Mary and this is Ed," she concludes, motioning to her husband, who takes my hand and shakes it.

"Rob Allaire," I respond, giving my full name, a habit formed from years of business introductions. "Nice to have met you both," I tell them. We all smile at one another awkwardly, until I say, "I guess I'd better go try to find some medicine."

"Good luck! Feel better soon!" Mary calls after me as I leave. I hope her good wishes prove effective because, after crossing the lobby's vast expanse to get to an elevator, I'm dizzy. In fact, when the elevator finally comes, ringing a three-tone chime as it opens its doors to let me enter, I'm so lightheaded I have to hold onto the walls for fear of fainting and falling while rising.

On the thirty-seventh floor, I step into the hall,

gingerly test my balance, and convince myself that I feel steady enough to keep going. Scanning the wall directions to determine my room's location, I start down a long corridor lined in sienna-colored shantung and hung with brightly painted Chinese watercolors of flying, seaborne, and landbound dragons so intricate and disparate that, were I feeling better, I'd stop and study them more closely. As I pass the floor's hospitality lounge, I glance inside to see if the buffet offers anything to make my throat feel better but, as it appears to be already shut for the evening, I just keep walking.

When I reach my suite and open the door, I discover a carry-on and a computer bag in the foyer and momentarily think the suite's already occupied. Then, recognizing the luggage as mine, I realize I must be very sick indeed to have forgotten I'd sent it up ahead of me. Hurrying into the bathroom to take the aspirin I received from Mary, I press a switch to turn on the lights but instead inadvertently make the mini-blinds behind the room's glass walls begin to float upwards. "Where the hell are the lights?" I ask—which, because they're voice-activated, flash on, intensifying my headache beyond measure. Desperate, I alternately pull, push, and twist the lavatory's mysteriously designed contemporary faucet until it fills my glass with water. I'm just about to swallow my aspirin when I notice the

"Water Not Good to Drink" sign on the counter and I remember that Chinese tap water is seldom potable. "Christ!" I exclaim. "When is this freaking day going to be over?"

Leaving the bathroom, I enter the suite's sleeping area, where I find Evian water bottles set out on a console beneath a large, flat-panel television. I open one and swallow my aspirin, after which, even dizzier than before, I grab the remote, fall onto the bed, and start the television. It turns on with the same three-tone chime that the elevator made earlier, and so with my eyes closed, for one exhausted moment, I have the strangely calming thought that perhaps I'm ascendant and on my way to Heaven. Then, though, I start to fear that this might be a premonition about Mom.

A knock at the suite door startles me out of both my reverie and worry. "Yes?" I call out.

"Room service," a sing-song male voice replies. As I've yet to place an order, I'm puzzled and walk over to the suite's entrance to investigate. Peering through the peephole, I see a uniformed and diffident-looking adolescent standing behind a serving tray and smiling.

"Are you sure you have the right room?" I ask through the closed door.

"The order ticket says, 'Room 3782, for Mr. Robert-Étienne Allaire,'" he answers, in an accent so strong it's barely comprehensible.

Thinking it might be part of the executive-floor's standard service, I let him enter.

"Good evening, sir," he says and pushes the cart into the room. "Where would you like this?"

"More to the point, *what* is it?" I ask.

"Excuse me, sir?"

"I didn't order this," I explain.

"But this is the room on the ticket," he protests, looking confused, as he reexamines it. In a moment, though, he brightens. "Ah, wait!" he exclaims, removing a card from the serving tray and handing it to me.

The card reads, "We wanted to be sure you got something to eat before room service closes. Feel better and enjoy your stay in China!" It's signed, "The Reverends Ed and Mary Sanborn." Touched by their thoughtfulness, I reflect that, evidently, some people live their espoused values.

The waiter asks, "All right to leave this with you, sir?"

"Yes—please put it over there," I reply and point to a space between the bed and the window.

He rolls the cart there and lifts one after another of its serving covers, revealing the very entrees I'd planned to order—pureed soups of pulverized pears, plantains, and bananas mixed with cherries, apricots, and blueberries. Dipping a spoon into one, I taste the velvet-textured blend of finely shredded fruit pulp, which slides down my burning throat and begins to soothe it. I'm just about to swallow a second spoonful when my cellphone starts ringing.

I answer it, pleased to see my sister's image appear on the phone screen. "Diane? Where are you?" I ask stupidly, given the array of blinking and beeping medical equipment behind her.

"At the hospital, with Mom," she says to humor me.

"How is she?"

"Why don't you ask her yourself? She's right here." Diane disappears, presumably handing her iPhone or iPad to Mom. There's a thud and clatter as my phone's screen first goes awry and then dark altogether. After a few seconds, Diane's face reappears.

"Mom's still weak, so it's hard for her to hold the iPad. I'll have to prop it up," she says, as her face disappears again and this time is replaced by tilting views of hospital furniture, laminate flooring, and then nothing.

"Damn!" I mutter and, feeling more tired by the minute, sit back down on the bed. "I can't see a thing!"

The room-service waiter misunderstands me. "You can use the TV for your call, sir—the picture will be bigger."

I suppress a look of exasperation. "That's not the problem," I start, then stop. "Wait—are you saying that I can take my call on the television?" I ask, buoyed by the thought that this would permit me to lie down while talking with Diane and Mom.

He nods enthusiastically. "Yes—please allow me," he says, as he reaches for my phone and points it and the remote at the television, which he turns off and back on again. Emitting the same three-tone chime as before, the set displays the manufacturer's name in both Roman type and Kanji characters, and next brings up images of Diane and Mom—the latter lying in a hospital bed, her hair disheveled and arms attached to IV dispensers and medical instruments via a jungle of translucent tubes and colored wires.

To hide my shock, I turn to the waiter and thank him.

"My pleasure, sir," he replies, smiling. "Is there anything else I can do for you this evening?"

"No thanks—you've been a great help already," I reply and tip him with a handful of Chinese coins and bills that, once again, I don't bother counting.

His smile broadens. "Have a good evening, sir!"

"You too," I answer, as, with a bow, he makes his exit.

"How much did you tip him, anyway?" Diane asks, smirking.

"No idea," I reply. "I don't have a good handle on the value of Chinese currency."

"Big spender," she teases.

"When I don't know how much I'm spending," I concur and lie back against the headrest to keep my dizziness from increasing. "How're you?" I ask and then to my dismay, start coughing.

"Tired but OK," Diane frowns. "You don't look so good, though—have you got a cold?"

I manage to contain my coughing momentarily. "Yeah, I think I caught it on the plane. A guy a couple of rows behind me sneezed, and his spittle landed on my arms."

"Ewww . . . ," Diane exclaims.

"Precisely—but it isn't worth discussing," I reply, since I don't want to worry Mom. "How are you doing, Mom?" I ask.

"OK, I guess," she replies with a sigh. "All things considered."

Diane raises an eyebrow. "Maybe we should go into a little more detail," she suggests gently. "Rob's been worried."

"All right," Mom answers. "I'm not sure where to start though." She sounds fragile.

"Why don't you start at the beginning?" Diane says, touching one of Mom's shoulders.

"OK," Mom replies hesitantly. "But maybe you could get things going for me."

"I'll be happy to," Diane tells her and then turns back to me. "Like I texted you, last night Mom fell and broke a femur and the EMS guys brought us here to the hospital."

I already know all this, I think irritably, as my

headache worsens. "I remember," I say as calmly as possible. "And then Mom went into surgery so they could reset the femur," I prompt my sister.

"Right—and the surgery was successful, but after that things got interesting."

"Interesting?"

"To put it mildly," Mom remarks, once more sighing.

"What do you mean?"

"The anesthesia hit Mom pretty hard," Diane explains.

"That isn't unusual for someone her age," I respond.

"Right," Diane concurs. "Anyway, she was under for a long time and, since we'd been here all night and I was pretty tired, I decided to go home and rest before she came to."

"And?" I ask, feeling as if I'm playing Twenty Questions.

"She came out of the anesthesia early while I was at home, which led to confusion."

"On the hospital's part?!" I ask, no longer able to conceal my impatience.

"No—on Mom's!" Diane responds, as if the question were imbecilic.

"I'm the one who didn't know what was happening," Mom concurs, sheepishly. "When I woke up, an orderly was pushing my stretcher down a corridor. He didn't speak to me and then he left me alone in a freezing-cold room. It was terrifying!" she concludes, trembling. "I thought they were going to experiment on me!"

"Experiment on you?!" I repeat.

"She watched a clip from *Coma* a few months back, while I was busy with the laundry and didn't know what she was up to," Diane explains. "Anyway, she thought that what happened to the patients in that movie was going to happen to her here in the hospital."

"How awful, Mom!" I say.

"It was—especially since I was alone!" she replies. "I was by a window, so I could see our house in the distance. I kept hoping Diane would come out of it and make her way here to save me!"

This surprises me. Though the hospital is tall—from its upper stories, one can see church steeples, the widows' walks of the Old China Trade sea captains' mansions, and boats on the river as they head to the harbor—Mom's house is too far away to be visible from it. My bewilderment must be apparent, because Diane elaborates. "There's a house by the hospital that kind of looks like ours, and Mom mixed up the two," she explains to me, before turning back to Mom. "Anyway, it's not important that you were a little confused," she says, again touching her on a shoulder. "What's important is that I came and found you."

"That's true," Mom agrees, her voice calmer. "And then everything got better."

"It did," Diane confirms. "I wished I'd arrived

sooner, though, so you wouldn't have been so upset."

"Or caused so much trouble," Mom adds, contritely.

"What do you mean?"

My mother doesn't answer.

"Mom was so frightened," Diane says, "she decided to make things difficult for her captors—she pulled out her IVs, took off her ID bracelet, and stuffed everything under the stretcher blankets."

"Did it fool them?"

My mother looks embarrassed. "No—I bled all over the stretcher, so a nurse figured out what I'd done—plus, she found my ID bracelet."

"Yeah," Diane says, her tone ironic. "The nurse told Mom she was glad she'd found the bracelet because now she knew who to charge for the cleanup."

"Funny lady," I remark.

"Not especially," Diane responds.

Blushing, Mom looks downward and suddenly notices herself on the iPad's playback video. "Seigneur! Comme j'ai l'air ébouriffé!" she says, raising her hands to her hair in an expression of horror. "Look at my hair! It's horrible!"

Diane examines Mom's messy gray curls. "I'll work on it tomorrow when you're feeling better. Honestly, it's not that bad," she says to console her.

"Don't lie! People could mistake me for a washerwoman," she complains abjectly.

"Pas du tout, ma tante," disagrees a nurse's aide, a plump and familiar-looking middle-aged blonde, who enters the room, writing on a clipboard. "I've known you since I was little, and you've always been a lady, Aunt Yvette!"

"You remember Claudine, don't you?" Diane asks me. "Dad's cousin who moved here from Saint-Georges de Beauce when we were in high school?" Turning to Claudine, she points at me and tells her, "We're talking with Rob—he's in China."

Claudine, beaming, places her clipboard on the bedtable and turns toward me. "Bonjour, Robbie! China! That's far away! Is it safe?" she asks, as sans cérémonie now as when we were teenagers.

"Quite safe," I answer, hoping Mom hasn't heard her question. "How are you?"

"Ça va," Claudine confirms. Turning to Mom, she says, "I've been off for a few days, so I was surprised to find you here this morning—I hope you're recovering from your surgery!"

Mom smiles weakly. "J'ai déjà commencé à récupérer, mais lentement," she says, explaining that her recovery's slowly beginning.

"Good news, quand même!" Claudine responds. "I'll pray for you, and maybe it'll go even faster," she adds, placing a hand on one of Mom's arms.

"Tu es tellement gentille," Mom says in thanks, as Claudine prepares to move onto the next patient's room.

"Mom always enjoys talking French with her," Diane tells me, perhaps because, largely unable to understand French herself, it's the only comment she can think of.

"À bientôt," Claudine calls to Mom while leaving. "You'll see! You'll get better! It's easy here, where we're safe and sound—not like where your son is in China!"

Once Claudine has left, Mom turns back to me. "Where are you right now?" she asks, more alert than at any time since the conversation started. "Aux États Unis ou au Québec?" wanting to know whether I'm in the States or Canada.

"En ni un ni l'autre," I say with a sinking heart, as I admit that I'm in neither. "I'm in China."

Mom purses her lips. "That's what I thought you told Claudine! China's so far away—and so dangerous!" she declares, unhappily. "What are you doing there?"

"I had to come."

"You had to?!" she says in palpable disbelief. "No one *has* to go to China—except maybe the Chinese!" she concludes, as self-satisfied as a child who's caught an elder in an error.

"My visit's work related."

Since, in our family, work has always taken precedence over just about everything, Mom knows she's been trumped and goes silent. "That's different," she reluctantly acknowledges. "Your father took risks to support us. Sometimes, we just do what we have to."

"Most times, maybe," I say to her.

"Well, aren't all of you gloomy?!" says Claudine, who's returned to retrieve her clipboard, which she'd forgotten on the bedside table.

"Or realistic," Diane answers, putting a more positive spin on it for Mom's benefit. "Whatever we call it, it's about duty—you start something, you keep at it, despite the challenges."

"That describes life," I comment.

Leaning against the doorframe, Claudine nods. "It's what my life's been like," she says. "My husband, Ray—may he rest in peace—had problems, but I stuck with him, and together we raised our children. I mean, it's not like anybody else was going to step in and do it."

"Exactly," Diane concurs, as Claudine, clipboard in hand, again passes through the doorway and into the corridor.

"Claudine's life hasn't been easy," Mom reflects, "but that's true of most people."

I start coughing again.

"Not only are you in China, but you're sick on top of it!" Mom declares with a look of alarm. "Just don't die before me!" she entreats. "My children preceding me in death is one tragedy I hope life spares me!"

"Rob's only got a cold," Diane reassures her, as I try to stop coughing. "Plus, life's not all that horrible. You need to stop and think about all the good stuff!" she cajoles. "We should enjoy life—remember, we pass this way but once!"

Mom casts a melancholy glance around the hospital room as if to suggest that once might be enough. Then, her expression changing, she turns back toward the iPad camera and looks straight at me. "But where you are, maybe it's different," she says, more in question than in statement.

"How?" I gasp, just managing to suppress my coughing.

"You're in Asia," she goes on. "Don't Asians believe in reincarnation?"

"Only if they're Buddhists," I answer. "And reincarnation isn't a guaranteed or even the preferred outcome!"

Mom's gaze pierces through her pain killers and my illness and sleep deprivation, her upset apparent and implacable across the continents and oceans that separate us. "I guess we're both out of luck, then," she states grimly.

"Not really," I protest. "You're already on the mend, and my cold won't last forever—it'll be gone by the time I come home from China," I conclude as I try to stave off a renewed bout of coughing.

My mother keeps staring. "We all find our way home sooner or later."

"Maybe even if home is where we are already," I counter, rallying. "For example, earlier this evening, I met an elderly missionary couple . . ."

"Missionaries?" Mom echoes, looking amazed.

"Where on earth did you meet missionaries?" Diane asks me.

"In a giftshop, off the hotel lobby," I reply. "They sent this to me," I continue, repositioning the phone so that she and Mom can see the serving tray by the window.

"They sent you dinner!" Mom exclaims. "Why?"

"It's too involved a story to go into," I answer, uncertain how long I can keep from coughing again. "What I can tell you about, though," I continue, "is that, years ago, this couple came to China to start a school in a town with the same name as the one they'd left in Massachusetts and that, now, in their retirement, they're staying on so they can continue to help run it." I look hard at Mom. "It's the right thing for them to do, don't you think? I mean, they've spent their lives here, in China, helping others." I pause for emphasis. "Just like you and Dad did in Maine, raising me, my sisters, and brothers."

My mother doesn't respond.

"Rob's got a good point," Diane says, turning toward her.

"Which is?"

Diane raises her eyebrows as if the answer

should be apparent. "Home is whatever place we're surrounded by the people we've lived our lives for. At worst, heaven's just a concept—at best, an unknown destination."

"The final destination," Mom corrects her, "if we're lucky."

"You don't need to worry about that, Mom," Diane replies with a sigh. "You've led a good life—which is only one of the reasons you shouldn't want to leave it."

Mom looks at her. "I shouldn't?"

"No, you shouldn't!" Diane repeats impatiently. "Everyone wants you to stay!"

"You do?" Mom responds, surprised or goading her, the aftereffects of the anesthesia making both seem possible.

Diane is taken aback. "Of course, Mom," she continues, more softly, "We want you here, in the thick of it, alongside the rest of us!"

"Plus, no one knows what things will be like afterwards," I say in support of my sister's argument. To be clear, I add, "I mean in the hereafter."

Mom doesn't dispute this but doesn't say anything else either.

"Why, it might be even stranger than it is here in China," I continue with a laugh, trying to take the edge off my comment.

Mom seems intrigued. "What are things like in China?" she asks, maybe because she's truly curious or—once again—due to the anesthesia.

"Well, it's certainly nothing like the States," I answer.

"How is it different?" she persists.

"In a lot of ways," I reply, feeling so weak and dizzy I'm not sure I'm up to explaining. "It's hard to call out anything especially."

Mom looks unconvinced.

"Wait!" I exclaim, against all odds, suddenly inspired. "Maybe it's best that you see for yourself." I turn my phone toward the window and, pushing a bedside button, open the drapes to reveal Beijing's traffic-laden thoroughfares, boulevards, and streets, a light-encrusted meshwork that reaches to the horizon, where still more lights shine in the surrounding mountains and on the river before them.

My mother raises her hand to her chest in awed reaction. "It's so big, and you're so high up," she says, then falls silent. "Each place is different but the same, isn't it?" she presently observes.

"What do you mean?" Diane asks.

"Over there," she says, gesturing toward the view displayed on Diane's iPad, "like here, there are cars and trucks, hills and water, lights and darkness."

Her unexpected comparison of rural Maine and urban China leaves me speechless, but Diane, unfazed, articulates Mom's meaning. "That's right, Mom, there are people everywhere—and most are just trying to go on living."

My mother continues to contemplate the city, which, from my hotel room's elevation, shimmers like a sheathe of sequined black silk or satin. She clears her throat. "So far, I've been lucky enough not to outlive any of my children," she says thoughtfully, "but, maybe, for a little while back there, I lost sight of how much life itself is simply worth living."

"It's easy to do when you're sick, Mom," I tell her. "I understand, and all I've got is a bad cold."

"Thank God for that," she says, smiling, and true to her religious beliefs, adds, "for everything, actually."

"You sound better already, Mom," I tell her.

"You do," Diane affirms. "And you do, too, Rob—you've stopped coughing!"

"I'll be fine," I respond, because, my anxiety about Mom having been lessened, I know that eventually I will be.

A nurse enters Mom's room pushing a cart full of medical instruments. "Time to test your blood levels," she tells Mom.

Diane walks toward her iPad. "Wave goodbye to Rob now," she says to Mom. "We have to let this lady go about her business."

"Couldn't she come back later?" Mom asks.

"Not really," Diane answers. "These tests probably need to be taken at regular intervals."

"They do—sorry," the nurse apologizes.

"We'll talk again soon," I tell Mom. "It's late

here, and I need to get some sleep before my meetings tomorrow."

"Good luck," she says and, in the same way that she ends all our phone calls, closes with, "I love you, Rob."

"I know—I love you too, Mom," I answer.

When Diane turns off her iPad, she and Mom disappear from the television screen and are replaced by a channel directory. I scan it, lower the volume, and choose the international broadcaster *TV5 Monde* from the available selections. *Telematin*, the Paris morning show, comes on, filling the room with murmured French conversation.

Too tired even for a sip of soup or water, I sink further into the bed covers and reflect on the singularity of my being comforted by the sound of my first language as I lie sick in a Beijing skyscraper, within the Great Wall's long-shattered locus of protection, at the center of the Middle Kingdom, suspended halfway between Earth and Heaven. I think of Mom's comparison of this ever-evolving ancient city with the placid New England coastal town where she raised me and where now, precipitously infirm, she awaits whatever might transpire once her life is over. Turning my head on the pillow, I look at the glowing urban landscape and the outline of the mountains beyond, darkly curved or jagged forms suffused with points of light and reaching upward into the night sky's greater blackness like shadowy Chinese lanterns, the Ring of Fire around the Pacific, or a serpentine celestial dragon, its armored, argentate wings encircling and sheltering an old but brightly beating heart.

CHAPTER 36

Mirror, Mirror on the Wall

Medium Take

Mom stands before the mirror in her bathroom, one hand grasping the pink lavatory vanity, the other touching a sunken cheek. She peers into the oval mirror, her expression pained.

"What happened to my face?" she murmurs, fingering a fold of wrinkled flesh. Though never having been much aware of it, Mom was beautiful in her youth. Now, following her beauty's disappearance, she seems borne down by its loss.

"What's wrong?" I ask from the bathroom doorway, hoping, against the odds, that I can somehow make her feel better.

"I'm like an old sweater with a loose thread that's been pulled," she replies, still staring into the mirror. "And now everything is skewed and sagging," she goes on, her voice breaking as if tears might be forthcoming.

Mom is in fact wearing an old sweater at the moment, its white wool complementing the cream and rose of the bathroom's floral wallpaper. Through the bullseye window at her back, sunlight streams in, illuminating her silver hair.

"There's nothing wrong with old sweaters," I assert. "You have one on right now."

She looks away from the mirror to face me. "You're right," she replies. "After all, they're still useful. Plus, it's not the way people look that's important but what they are inside that counts—n'est ce pas?" she continues, asking for verification of one of her own teachings from my childhood.

"Yes—and you're still beautiful inside," I assure her.

She lets go of the sink and grabs my hand, probably as much to keep her balance as from affection. "You're a good influence," she says, her eyes beginning to well and voice to quaver. "A steadying one, at any rate," she adds and unexpectedly laughs.

"Let's go downstairs and have some coffee," I say, hoping to prolong this change of mood.

She nods and whispers, "I love coffee," as if sharing a secret rather than stating the long apparent.

"I know," I reply and help her through the bathroom door to the waiting walker.

"I love you too, Rob," she declares emotionally.

"I know that also, Mom," I say, as I place her hands on the walker's handlebar.

"What don't you know?" she asks playfully, her sense of humor once more resurfacing.

"Just about everything," I reply.

Now, she again looks disconsolate. "Welcome to the club."

CHAPTER 37

A View over the River
Long Take

After Ian and I place Mom's wheelchair in the Cadillac's trunk, we get into the back seat, and Diane maneuvers the large car out of the garage and down the long drive, avoiding the jeeps, four-wheelers, and convertibles of relatives picking blueberries in our field and of guests at the neighbors' pool party, which has run out of parking.

"It's busy here today," Ian says, lowering his window. "And hot, too—almost like Florida."

"Par for the course," Diane responds. "It's Labor Day in Maine—summer's last hurrah."

"How come we're not using your Lexus?" I ask her, as with one hand she opens the Caddy's glove compartment.

"It needs maintenance and new tires," she replies, donning her sunglasses. "Since that'll cost a couple of thousand dollars, I'm storing it in the barn and using Dad's old car instead."

"I don't know why he never uses it," Mom says from the front passenger seat, adjusting her own sunglasses against the slanted August light.

None of us comment.

"He wanted it so much that I didn't complain about the cost," Mom goes on. "But now he doesn't even drive it!"

"I think maybe you're using the wrong tense," I say, in case she's misspoken rather than forgotten Dad's passing.

Diane, who regularly deals with Mom's spotty memory, is not so lenient. "It's been four years since Dad died," she tells her. "Plus, because of his stroke, he stopped driving a decade ago."

"I know that!" Mom snaps, her indignation almost believable. Latching onto the excuse I unwittingly provided her, she exclaims, "English! I'll never master it!"

"It's not your first language," I say sympathetically.

"It's not yours either but you've got the hang of it," she replies in a discouraged tone, further evincing either her acting ability or confusion.

"That's to be expected," I answer. "I'm younger, and I've been speaking English longer. What's more, my French is nowhere near as fluent as yours."

"How could it be?!" she responds. "I'm an old lady who's had lots of practice—you're just a youngster!"

"Rob's not so young anymore," Diane says, taking the car around a corner. "He's already eligible for Social Security."

"Really?!" Mom looks at me.

"I'm eligible for *early* Social Security," I correct my sister. "I'm only sixty-four—these days, you have to be sixty-seven to qualify for full benefits."

"I can't believe you're already in your sixties!" Mom exclaims. "How old am I then?!"

"You'll be ninety soon," says Ian, who's reading a textbook from one of his med school classes.

This might be a higher number than Mom expected because she moves us on to a different topic. "Where are we going?"

"To visit Aunt Jeanne," Diane replies. Jeanne is one of my father's two sole surviving siblings, the only other living family members of Mom's generation.

"Jeanne?!" Mom repeats, with such surprise that for a minute I wonder if she's forgotten who Jeanne is.

"Yes, we talked about this at breakfast—remember?" Diane says.

"But won't Jeanne be busy at the real-estate office helping Roland?" Mom answers.

Diane sighs. "She sold off some of the business after Roland died, so she's not as busy as she used to be. Anyway, it's Saturday, so she should have time for company."

"Roland died?!" Mom exclaims. "Why didn't anyone tell me?!"

"He passed away thirty years ago, Mom,"

Diane says, wearily. "You went to his funeral—maybe it slipped your mind."

My mother says nothing.

"Is Jeanne still in the independent-living wing at the Goodall Home?" I ask.

After a pause, Diane replies, "She's living at Ocean Crest now."

"Ocean Crest? Where's that?"

"You've been there," Diane says, making a face. "It's the retirement community on Surf Street—the one Porpoise Point is part of."

"Porpoise Point? The nursing home Pépère lived in after he got sick?" Ian asks.

"Yes," Diane answers hesitantly, probably because Mom hasn't been back there since my father's passing. "At first Jeanne was in the assisted-living section," she continues, "but because she's getting more confused, she's been moved to long-term care." We stop for a red light. "God only knows what it's costing—that place's prices were already sky-high back when Dad was there."

Looking out the window, Mom doesn't appear to hear.

When the light changes to green, we turn onto North Street and enter a slow-moving line of beachbound cars, SUVs, and minivans. "The traffic is fierce this summer," I remark. "I should have brought my bicycle from home to get around town more quickly."

"A bicycle wouldn't be much help right now," Diane says, with a nod toward Mom.

"I meant my bike would have come in handy if you needed me to run errands." I explain. A little too proudly, I add, "I'm cycling twenty-five miles a day now back in Ohio."

"You're nuts!" Diane says, braking, as the traffic comes to a full stop. "How do you even find the time for that?"

"It only takes two hours," I retort, shielding my eyes from the sun glare reflecting off the motionless line of vehicles ahead. "Which is probably how long we'll be stuck in this mess."

Diane scowls as car horns begin honking. "Everything will start to move faster in a few minutes—this is just a backup from the Route 1 intersection."

"All these cars are noisy!" Mom complains, amid the rising din of engines idling and more horns blaring.

Diane pushes a button to close the Caddy's windows. "I'll switch on the radio," she says, turning a knob on the dash.

"In local news," a broadcaster announces, "a great white shark was spotted off the Biddeford Pool and Cape Porpoise beaches."

"A shark!" Mom repeats, alarmed, as Diane quickly switches off the radio.

"Don't worry, Mom," I reassure her. "We're not driving all the way to the ocean."

"But you said we're going to a place called Porpoise Point," she protests, revealing she'd previously heard us. "Aren't sharks attracted to porpoises?"

"They are," I admit, "but there aren't any porpoises at Porpoise Point."

"There aren't! Did they die!?"

"There've never been any, Mom," Diane tells her, as the traffic starts to pick up again. "It's called Porpoise Point because it's on property that used to belong to the Porpoise Biscuit Company."

Mom smiles. "I love Porpoise Biscuits!" she declares. "Can I have one while we're there?"

Though the Porpoise Biscuit Company went under long ago, Diane replies, "I don't know. Maybe. We'll have to see if they have any."

The car moves into the town square, first passing the Veterans' Memorial, a World War I cannon and a soldier's statue on a geranium-bordered traffic island, and then the First Congregational Church, a postmodern replacement for the original, high-spired nineteenth-century structure destroyed in a fire caused by a contractor.

"Sad what happened to that place," I say.

"Lots of things are sad," Mom sighs, making me regret my remark.

"But lots of things are happy, too," I counter. "Just look at the day we're having—the bright sun, the blue sky, the flowers blooming."

"I guess you're right," Mom concedes. "Everything is relative."

"And speaking of relatives," I go on, hoping to distract her further, "when was the last time you saw Jeanne?"

"Jeanne?! It's been quite a while," she replies. "Maybe around the time Diane was born—I'm pretty sure Jeanne came to the baby shower," she continues, not sounding at all certain.

This is more than Diane can stand. "You saw her last Christmas—right before she moved into Seal Lion Point," she states bluntly.

"I did?" Mom asks.

"Yes!" Diane answers. "She lived with Cousin Edmond for a bit after she moved out of the Goodall Home. He and his wife, Evelyn, asked us over for eggnog and holiday cookies. Don't you remember?"

"Cousin Edmond," Mom repeats. "Who's he?" she asks timidly.

Diane is expressionless. "He's Jeanne's middle son—the one who looks after her. Just like, I—your middle daughter—look after you!"

"You *do* look after me," Mom acknowledges. "It will be nice to see Edmond," she adds, though it's far from clear that she remembers him.

"We're not seeing Edmond—only Jeanne," Diane explains, frowning. "Edmond doesn't live at Porpoise Point."

"He doesn't?" Mom asks. "Why not?"

"Because he's too young for a rest home—though, like me, he could probably use a rest!" Diane exclaims in exasperation.

We drive by the colonial- and ranch-style houses of Valleyview Circle, which is neither in a valley nor circular—an incongruity that, to break the tension, I mention.

"Maybe the developer visited Long Island one time too often," Diane says, redirecting her ire.

Pleased that my tactic worked, I continue in the same vein and say, "One time probably would have been sufficient."

"Sufficient for what?" Mom asks.

"To figure out that giving average properties fancy names will get out-of-staters to pay top dollar for them," I answer, as the Caddy enters Ocean Crest. "This place, which is full of Massachusetts retirees, is a case in point: it sits on a riverbank—not a hilltop—and it's miles from the ocean."

Ian looks up from his textbook, smiling. "You're good at pointing out contradictions."

"It's his strong suit," Diane says dryly. "That, and excessive cycling."

We pass a tanned, white-haired man and woman walking in the street, presumably to avoid being sprayed by lawn sprinklers. "They remind me of Andy and Maureen McManus," Mom says, referring to high school friends of hers and my father's who long-ago moved to Boston and then to Florida. "I wonder how they're doing?"

"Are they still living in St. Pete?" I ask my sister.

"They're dead," she whispers.

"What did you say?" Mom asks.

"I said we haven't heard from them in ages," Diane lies.

My mother is momentarily silent. "That doesn't sound like what you said," she replies.

"It is, though," my sister answers.

Turning a corner, Diane drives us toward Porpoise Point, a gabled, vinyl-clad structure surrounded by picturesque independent-living cottages like a large rhinestone at the center of a paste tiara—an observation that, Diane's remark about my "strong suit" notwithstanding, I can't resist expressing.

"Are we going to shop for jewelry?" Mom asks, again misunderstanding. "I don't need any but I like window shopping!"

"We're visiting Jeanne," Diane tells her, and, perhaps hoping more information will jog her memory, adds, "Dad's middle sister and your sister-law. We just discussed this, remember?"

"Did we?" Mom responds, sounding unhappy. "But I was looking forward to window shopping."

"Visiting Jeanne will be fun, too," I assure her.

She turns and looks at me skeptically from the front seat. "If you say so."

"I do, indeed," I say with a smile. As the car

comes to a stop under Porpoise Point's porte-cochère, she smiles back.

Ian and I get out, retrieve Mom's wheelchair from the trunk, and help her into it. Approaching the building's front door, we pass a middle-aged man on a bench, a newspaper and drink on the tray of a walker beside him. "Good morning," he says, "Nice to see you again."

"Yes, good morning," I answer, pushing Mom's wheelchair forward. "Nice to see you, too," I add, though I don't recall having met him before.

Once we've entered the building and are safely out of earshot, Mom says, "He looks familiar."

"He was here when Pépère was," Ian tells us.

"Your father lived here?" Mom asks me.

"For years, Mom," Diane answers. "After he had his first stroke."

"Oh, yes," Mom says sadly, as we come up to the front desk.

The gray-haired receptionist smiles at us. "Haven't seen all of you in a while," she says, tactfully not mentioning my father's passing. She gestures toward a Victorian tea trolley by the lobby sofa. "Help yourself to some pastries—they're for guests and residents."

"No, thanks. We're here to see our aunt," Diane says, giving her Jeanne's name. "Do you know where we can find her?"

"Just a second," the receptionist replies and, ignoring the ringing phone, pores through the resident directory in front of her, turning pages with one hand and holding down the rest with the other so that her desktop fan doesn't make them flutter. "Room 216—on the second floor," she finally announces. "Sorry for the wait, but this fan blows stuff around if I'm not careful."

"No problem," I assure her. "A little breeze is a good thing on a hot day like this one."

"You said it!" she replies with a smile. She turns toward Ian, who at twenty-five still looks so boyish that he sometimes triggers maternal instincts in older women. "Are you sure you won't have a donut or a cookie?" she asks him.

"No, thanks," he answers, but then reconsiders. "Maybe I'll take one for my aunt and another in case I'm hungry later."

The woman beams as he walks over to the tea tray, grabs a napkin, and picks up two chocolate-glazed cupcakes. "Good thinking," she says. "The elevator is that way," she adds, pointing in its direction.

"Dad loved those pastries," I remark while we start down the hallway, which is warmer than I'd expected.

"Yeah," says Diane. "He put on so much weight from eating them it killed him."

My mother shakes her head. "Life killed him," she corrects Diane, as we step into the overly warm elevator. "Like it does everyone." None of us reacts.

On the second floor, the elevator doors open to the sight of an elderly patient in a pink robe and bunny slippers, busily dusting the gilded frames of Winslow Homer reproductions on the wall across from us. "She was here when Pépère was, too," Ian whispers, as we step into the airless corridor and make our way toward the nursing station. "She used to come into his room and dust the bureaus while we were visiting."

"That's probably because this place is short-staffed," Diane says.

"Really?" Ian asks. "How do you know?"

"Online complaints. There aren't enough employees in housekeeping and maintenance. That's why residents like Simone—the woman we just saw—have been pressed into service."

I stare at my sister. "You're joking, right?"

"Not about the short-staffing," she replies grimly. "But, yes, I'm joking about residents being forced to work—Simone's Alzheimer's is the reason she's always cleaning."

"I don't understand."

"Alzheimer sufferers do things compulsively," Ian explains.

"Bingo!" Diane says, turning to him. "All that tuition money your parents are forking out for med school is paying off."

He smirks at her, and she smiles in response. "Simone's Alzheimer's is also why she was always going into Dad's room," Diane goes on. "She thought she was married to him."

Mom overhears. "I remember her now!" she says, peering back down the hallway at Simone. "So, she outlived my Henri—her imaginary husband!" she continues with a sigh. "I hope she outlives me, too!"

"You do?" Ian says, surprised

"Of course! If I die first, I'll be the one who goes into the grave beside your grandfather, not that imposter," Mom says, glaring in Simone's direction.

"Mom!" Diane admonishers her. "That's crazy!"

"It's not crazy—it's the truth!" Mom objects.

Mercifully, before the discussion goes further, we arrive at the nursing station, a square-columned pavilion meant to evoke "New England" architecture. I walk up to the counter and ask a young, orange-haired attendant about Jeanne's room location. "Down the hall to your left," she says, lifting a tattooed arm and pointing. "Past the seating area with the fireplace and electric organ."

I thank her and proceed down the corridor, pushing Mom's wheelchair ahead of me, while Diane and Ian follow. "Do you think Aunt Jeanne will remember us?" asks Ian, when we arrive at Jeanne's room.

"We'll know in a second," Diane replies, as I pass through the doorway.

Sitting in a wing chair by the window, Jeanne, her hair blowing in a river-borne breeze, looks up as soon as we enter. "Bonjour!" she exclaims and lets go of her book, a white-and-gold missal, which drops onto the carpet. She smiles as I pick it up and hand it to her. "How nice of you to come, Robbie—and of you both, too!" she declares, pointing at Diane and Ian, perhaps unable to recall the names of either. "No one ever visits!" she continues, an assertion I know to be false because Edmond has told me that he or his brothers, Pierre and Yannick, visit her daily. "Will you be in town long?"

"Not long—Ian needs to get back to med school in Ohio." I motion toward him to make sure she knows who I'm talking about. "But Mom wanted to see you," I explain, bending the truth only a little, since even if Mom didn't initiate this visit, she's long wanted to see Jeanne—at any rate, when she's recalled knowing her.

Jeanne turns to Mom. "Yvette!" she exclaims, holding her hands up to her face, "I didn't see you there, in your wheelchair! Comment ça va, ma chère belle-soeur?" she asks, wanting to know how Mom, or as she phrases it, her dear sister-in-law, is faring.

Unsettled either by Jeanne's outsized greeting or by her mention of the wheelchair, Mom responds curtly. "Trés bien! Et vous, madame?" she inquires, using the formal "vous" instead of the more casual "tu" typically employed with family.

"Assez bien, merci!" Jeanne replies, apparently not noticing Mom's break with linguistic convention. In a confidential tone, she adds, "Mais, en vérité, this hotel is strange!"

Diane, Ian, and I exchange glances. Mom, though, merely asks, "How?"

"It's kind of hard to say," she replies. "The staff's attentive and the rooms are OK, but the air-conditioning doesn't work, and there's no room service!"

"No room service?!" Mom echoes, clearly astonished. "Maybe there's not enough help in the kitchen—you know, because of summer vacations," she speculates.

"Maybe," Jeanne responds. "Or maybe not."

"Why do you say that?" Mom asks.

Jeanne shrugs. "Because whenever I ask about room service, everyone looks at me like I'm crazy and tells me not to worry about it."

A young nurse's aide in pink scrubs, her long hair drawn back and woven into a single braid, enters the room. "Hello," she says to us.

"Are you one of my granddaughters?" Jeanne asks her.

"Not that I'm aware of," she replies playfully, suggesting this isn't the first time she's been asked. "But you can certainly adopt me." We all laugh. "Now that you know who I'm not," she continues as our laughter diminishes, "I wonder if you'd mind closing the window."

"Why?" Jeanne inquires.

"When the windows are open, it screws up the building's air-conditioning."

"Maybe there're other windows open," Diane says, "because it's kind of warm already."

"It *is* warm in here," the young woman admits. "But it's always like this during a heatwave," she confides, insouciant, "and it's almost ninety degrees outside, even though it's still morning!"

As Diane doesn't respond, our visitor continues more soberly. "Anyway, like the saying goes, 'I don't make the rules, I just follow them.' Sorry!"

"No need to apologize," my aunt assures her. "We know you're only doing your job."

"Thanks for understanding!" the nurse's aide answers, her cheeriness resurgent. "I appreciate it."

After she's left, Ian walks toward the window to close it, but Diane raises a hand to stop him. "Do you want the window shut?" she asks Jeanne.

"Not really," my aunt replies, after pondering the question. "It's awfully warm in this room, which must be why I opened the window to begin with."

"It *is* hot in here," Mom concurs.

"That settles it," Diane tells Ian. "Leave the window open."

"Are you sure?" he asks, as he generally likes to adhere to policy.

"Couldn't be surer," Diane answers. "We're the guests, and what we want is what matters. At the rates this place charges, management ought to accommodate us, not the opposite!"

Ian looks at me to see if I agree. I do, but fearing the topic might upset Mom, don't say so. Instead, I walk over to the mahogany night table, which, like the wing chair, I recognize from one of Jeanne's old houses, and pick up a stuffed black poodle. "Is this supposed to be your Zoey?" I ask.

"Ah, yes—that's my souvenir of her!" my aunt exclaims, beaming. "Zoey's living at Edmond's these days—or is it at Pierre's or Yannick's? I can't remember. Anyway, one of them brings her here now and then, and she's always excited to see me!"

"You must be happy to see her, too," Ian says.

"Oh, I am! I love that dog almost as much as my own children!" Jeanne responds, laughing. "And she probably loves me more than they do! She'd come see me on her own if she could!" she continues. "But she has to rely on the boys, and they never visit!"

I decide to contest this statement, however gently. "When was the last time one of them stopped by?"

Jeanne doesn't immediately answer. "To be honest, I can't remember."

"Edmond told us that he or his brothers visit you every day," Diane tells her.

"Every day?!" Jeanne looks astounded. "I don't think so."

"Are you sure?" Diane asks, with a plainspokenness she usually reserves for Mom. Taking this morning's *Portland Press Herald* from the top of a bureau, she waves it at Jeanne. "Who else could have brought you today's paper?" she goes on, as doggedly as a television detective.

"Sometimes the hotel staff drops it off," my aunt replies unflustered.

"And do they bring you flowers?" Diane asks, removing a small card from a floral arrangement that's also on the bureau. "With notes that read, 'Have a wonderful day, Mom!' and are signed Edmond?"

Jeanne is quiet. "Maybe you're right," she concedes. "Edmond and his wife might have dropped by this morning." She sighs. "I forget things."

"Don't worry, Jeanne," Mom consoles her. "Sometimes I do, too."

"Don't you mean you do 'often'?" Diane asks Mom.

I try to distract Mom before she gets Diane's drift. "You have a little dog like this also," I tell her, indicating Jeanne's plush poodle, which I'm still holding.

"I do?" Mom asks.

"Yes. Melissa gave it to you on your last birthday," I say, as I hand her the poodle.

"Is it black like this one?"

"No, it's blond, like Ginger and Skippy," I reply, referring to pets we had when she was raising us. "And it's not a poodle either—it's a golden retriever."

Mom frowns. "Then how are the two alike?"

"They're both stuffed," Diane says unceremoniously.

"Plus, yours keeps you company—just like this one does Jeanne," I add to mitigate Diane's answer. "You call it Winnie."

"Winnie?" Mom repeats. She seems bewildered.

"After the A.A. Milne character," I prompt her.

To make sure she's understood me, Ian adds, "From *Winnie the Pooh*."

My mother continues to study the stuffed poodle.

"You were petting Winnie just before we left the house this morning!" Diane chides.

A look of recognition crosses Mom's face. "Of course! Now I remember!" she exclaims happily. "I said I was glad Winnie couldn't have puppies that I'd have to care for like I did Ginger's!" She starts to pet the plush poodle. "That was hard!"

"You're right, Yvette!" Jeanne agrees. "If a pet had a litter, it was just more work for us! When my first poodles, Fi-Fi and Frou-Frou, had puppies, it was a lot of trouble—almost as much as raising my own children!"

Mom gives Diane and me an appraising look. "Maybe not quite that much," she says, seriously.

Jeanne bursts into laughter, and whether or not she understands why, Mom joins her. The two laugh longer and harder, than I—and, since her face reddens, maybe Diane—consider warranted.

"We weren't that much trouble," I object, inducing more laughter on my aunt's part, which Mom again mirrors.

"I was only trying to get a rise out of you, Robbie!" Jeanne confesses between bouts of laughter. "But children really are a lot of trouble," she adds, growing more serious, "even if it's usually best not to admit it."

Though it's unlikely she's kept up with the turns in the conversation, Mom nods in agreement.

Jeanne smiles. "You're a good sport, Yvette," she tells her. "You always humor me—whatever crazy thing I'm going on about!" Taking a piece of paper from the night table, she starts to fan herself, and says, "It's getting even hotter in here!"

"It *is* warm," Mom concurs.

"The 'air-conditioning' in this place is a joke," Diane says with a scowl. "And not a good one!"

"At least there's a breeze," Ian says, indicating the billowing draperies at the open window by which Jeanne's sitting.

"True," Diane says. "So maybe we should let in

more of it." She walks over to the room's second window and starts to move its sash upward.

Just then, a middle-aged brunette in a white lab coat enters from the corridor. "Hello," she says, smiling brightly as she gives us all the once over. Before anyone can respond, she turns to Diane. "Close that window and the other one, too, please," she tells her in an oversweet, mellifluous tone of voice more suited to singing a lullaby or a Broadway ballad than to giving an order.

"I beg your pardon?" Diane replies so politely it's plain that's not her meaning.

"I'm sorry," the woman responds, not sounding sincere. "I should have introduced myself—I'm Lara Petersen, the new director of patient care and resident services." She pauses, apparently to let us fully appreciate her status. "And I need you to close these windows."

"Why?" Diane asks.

Ms. Petersen looks as if she hadn't expected to be questioned. "Let me explain," she begins with a sigh, as patronizingly as if she were a bad teacher and Diane a slow student, "the way our building is constructed all our windows have to be kept closed for the air-conditioning to work properly."

"And if it doesn't work?" my sister asks.

"What do you mean?"

Afraid of how Diane might reply, I answer. "It seems warm in here."

"I hadn't noticed," Ms. Petersen says unconvincingly and walks over to the room's thermostat. "The temperature is seventy-four—that's acceptable according to the facility's operating manual," she announces smugly.

Diane's complexion darkens. "Interesting information," she says, her arm still poised on the window sash. "I've got something interesting to share, too."

"Do you?" Ms. Petersen responds in an even more melodious and condescending tone than previously. "What?"

"That I don't care who you are or what you consider 'acceptable,' " Diane says, as she lifts the window sash higher. "All I care about is that you're the seller and we're the customers. So, since the air-conditioning isn't working, the windows are staying open."

Though Ms. Petersen's eyes widen, she keeps smiling. "Let me explain," she says, less musically. "Open windows drive up the temperature across the building, which makes the other residents uncomfortable." Mistaking Diane's stare for acquiescence, she continues. "I'm glad you understand because . . ."

"What I understand," Diane interrupts, "is that your company cut corners building this place and now it expects the residents to suffer the consequences."

"That's pretty cynical," Ms. Petersen responds, her smile finally vanishing.

Diane shakes her head and looking at her pityingly, replies, "Businesses sacrifice quality for profit every day. That's not so when they're upfront about it—like discount airlines—because customers adjust their expectations. But nursing homes are different." Diane asserts. "You promise high-quality care for the sick and elderly and get well compensated whether or not you deliver."

Ms. Petersen blanches. "We do our best for our residents!" She objects. "And our rates are standard!"

"Ha!" Diane snorts. "When your monthly is broken down to a daily rate, the people here might as well be living at the Ritz! At least there they'd get real service, not lip service!"

"Has a Ritz opened here?" Mom asks, excited. "That would be great for Jeanne!"

"Yes!" Jeanne agrees. "I love their 'high teas'—plus they have room service!"

"Diane was talking figuratively," Ian explains.

"Are you sure?" Mom asks. "This is a small town but sometimes good hotels pop up in out-of-the-way places." Mom turns to me. "Didn't you once stay in a Ritz in Augusta?"

"Saco's smaller than Augusta," I answer, "Besides, that hotel was in Seoul, Korea."

Meanwhile, Ms. Petersen's face has gone from white to scarlet. "Be that as it may," she tells Diane, "keeping the windows closed is a rule, and our residents and their guests have to respect it!"

"Says who?" Jeanne inquires, trying to rise from her chair.

Ms. Petersen turns to her, surprised. "It's in the contract, ma'am," she replies, not combatively but mawkishly, as if addressing a toddler.

"Next time let me know before you drop by, and bring the contract and your in-house counsel." She grabs hold of her walker. "I'll have my attorney here so we can get to the bottom of this."

Ms. Petersen looks shocked. "Ma'am, I never . . ."

"No, I presume you haven't," Jeanne interjects. "But maybe it's time you started."

Her face crimson, Ms. Petersen, speechless, rushes out of the room and into the corridor.

"Time she started what?" Mom asks Jeanne.

"I've no idea," Jeanne replies, pushing her walker to the doorway. "But I liked her reaction."

My mother laughs.

Jeanne looks down the hall in the direction Ms. Petersen headed. "I'd say I'm looking forward to her next visit but I've given up lying," she informs us as she turns away from the door. "Now that I'm older," she concludes, with a wicked smile, "I figure I might take a shot at being wiser."

Diane, Ian, and I burst into laughter. Mom,

however, doesn't join us. "Even when we have to lie, there's nothing funny about it."

"Right on both counts," Jeanne responds. "There're times you can't avoid lying," She pushes her walker back toward the wing chair. "But I try to avoid it. When Roland and I ran the property business, we were as honest as possible with our suppliers and tenants."

"Dad and Aunt Diane mentioned on the drive over that you and Uncle Roland used to have a property business," Ian says. "I didn't know."

"You didn't?!"

"Ian was born after Roland passed," I remind her.

"Why, you're a youngster!" Jeanne teases Ian, with a look of mock wonder. "You would've liked Roland," she says, letting go of the walker and sinking back into her chair. "He was a great father! It was hard raising three boys without him—and even harder running the business as a single woman!"

"How?" Ian asks.

Jeanne looks astounded. "Back then—even now, maybe—men thought women were pushovers!"

"Really?"

"Sure!" she exclaims. "Especially small-town businessmen! It was like Mayberry on the *Andy Griffith Show* here—some hayseed was always hoping to get the better of me."

"They didn't often succeed, as I recall," I comment.

"What do you mean?"

"You put up a good defense—sometimes, even an offense."

"Like when?"

"Like when you interrupted a city council meeting by proving the council members were lying," Diane tells her.

"I never interrupted a council meeting," Jeanne protests.

"Actually, you did," I say.

"How do you know?" she asks.

"I read it in the paper."

"They write all kinds of things in newspapers!"

"That they do," I admit, "But I was with you on multiple occasions when you called people out because you thought they weren't being above board."

"Like when?" she challenges me.

"Like the time you stopped an antiques auction in Kennebunk by questioning the authenticity of an 'eighteenth century' banjo clock on the bidding block."

"It *was* a fake!" she replies emphatically and starts laughing. "That clock was younger than I am!"

"But you bought it anyway," Diane reminds her.

"Of course!" she recalls, still laughing. "It was

a nice reproduction and after I pointed that out, I got it for what it was worth!"

"Isn't that it?" Diane asks, motioning to a clock hanging on the wall by the dresser.

Jeanne looks. "Seigneur, it is—I'd forgotten I still have it!" she exclaims.

"Don't worry about it," Mom consoles her. "At our age, we're always forgetting—I even forgot that we were coming here this morning."

"Among other things," Diane remarks.

"What did you say?" Jeanne asks. "I don't hear so well anymore."

"She said we all forget things as we get older," I answer, hoping Mom didn't hear Diane either.

"True enough," Jeanne responds. "But I also forgot a lot when I was younger. Roland never did, though. I counted on him for that and to keep the company up and running."

"I counted on Henri also," Mom says. "His HVAC business provided for us."

"Dad told me you worked in the business, too, Mémère," Ian says to Mom.

"Mémère kept the books, but Pépère managed it and also did a lot of hands-on work," I clarify.

"Il a beaucoup travaillé," Mom says, "way too much."

"I'll say," Diane adds. "He was on construction sites moving two-ton boilers right up to his retirement."

"Wow!" Ian says.

"He was a good man," Mom says.

"A good man and a good husband. 'L'homme de ta vie,' en fait," Jeanne summarizes. "Like Roland was mine." She sighs. "I think of Roland every day, even now, thirty years since he passed."

"I think of Henri, too," Mom responds. "He did everything else while I cared for the house and children."

"And, now, I do everything," Diane teases.

My mother looks at her. "The business is gone, Diane," she replies. "Plus, these days, there are no children."

"Except maybe you," Diane says, again teasing.

"What do you mean?"

"Aunt Diane was just joking," says Ian, coming to the rescue.

Mom smiles at him and turns toward Diane. "You *do* take good care of me, Diane. I'm lucky to have you."

"Just like we're lucky to have you," I tell Mom.

"You really are lucky, Yvette," Jeanne chimes in. "Your kids are devoted to you—not like my three boys, who never come to see me!"

Diane, Ian, and I exchange glances. "Didn't we just discuss how Edmond and his wife were here this morning?" Diane says.

"Did we?" Jeanne asks, looking startled. "Do you recall, Yvette?"

Mom frowns. "I'm not sure."

"We certainly did," Diane insists.

Jeanne turns toward the window. "If you say so," she says, the breeze blowing strands of hair off her forehead. "You know, these days I forget things."

"I do, too—everyone our age does," Mom offers, poised to retrace the very conversational ground we've just covered.

"This is like the movie *Groundhog Day*," Diane declares in exasperation.

"How?" Mom looks perplexed. "We're not talking about when winter will end."

"*Groundhog Day* is a movie," Ian explains. "In it, the same day keeps repeating itself, so it's hard to tell the difference between the present and the past."

Mom grimaces. "My days are nothing like that," she says to Diane. "Sometimes I'm reminded of other times and places, but, mostly things seem new and fresh."

"It's that way for me, too," Jeanne chimes in. "Every day here is different, which is what I like about it—even if no one ever visits."

Diane winces but doesn't comment.

"What do you like best?" Ian asks.

"There's usually a lot going on."

"Do you mean games like bridge and bingo?" I inquire—like Ian, trying to keep the conversation tethered to the present, "and activities like concerts and crafts?"

Jeanne nods. "There are other diversions, too."

"Like what?" I ask.

"Well, every time someone smokes inside or burns their toast, alarms go off and the next thing you know, sirens are screeching outside and firemen come running down the hallways."

Mom, who looks disquieted, nonetheless says, "How exciting."

"That's a nice way of putting it," Diane says archly.

"It passes the time," Jeanne explains.

Mom frowns. "I thought time passed on its own."

We all look at her.

"It does," I assure her. "But distractions help when a day seems to be going by slowly," I continue, before realizing I've probably just described a typical housebound day of hers.

"That's why I don't mind memories," Mom says. "They break the monotony—life can get boring when you only go out occasionally."

"Would you like to go out more often?" Ian asks her.

"Yes."

Diane looks irritated. "So why do you usually refuse when I suggest we do just that?"

Mom looks at her in amazement. "For starters, my walker and wheelchair—not to mention how hard it is for me to keep from falling."

Ian, who's just finished a geriatrics rotation, tries to mediate. "It must be worth the effort sometimes, though," he suggests to Mom. "Like now, visiting Jeanne."

"Certainly," Mom replies. Her good manners unfailing, she turns to Jeanne, "It's always a pleasure to visit you, ma chère belle sœur," she tells her.

"Comme de te recevoir, ma chère Yvette," my aunt duly replies, more or less in kind. "Especially since no one ever visits."

Having reached the limits of her tolerance, Diane moves toward the doorway. "It's been nice seeing you, Jeanne," she announces, "but we've got to get going."

"You just got here!" my aunt objects.

"Actually, we've been here quite a while already," Diane says, bending the truth, since neither Jeanne nor Mom could contradict her with certainty. "Besides, we have to stop at the supermarket on our way home."

"You didn't tell me that!" Mom says.

"I did," Diane responds, now outright lying.

"When?"

"Right before we got in the car," Diane replies and, to make her lie more convincing, adds, "We need to buy groceries for lunch and dinner."

Mom furrows her brow. "I looked in the fridge this morning," she says, now also apparently lying, as she isn't strong enough to open the refrigerator door without assistance. "It's full—what do we need?!"

"I have to buy a couple of things for myself and Ian," I tell her, hoping to prevent more conflict even if it means joining Diane's deception. "With all the cycling I've been doing back home, I need a lot of protein and natural sugars, and we're out of nuts and berries."

"We might not be out of nuts," Diane says looking at me.

"You aren't cycling while you're here," Mom objects.

"That's true," I admit, "but my diet has to be consistent for me to keep up my performance."

" 'Your performance?' " Mom repeats. "Have you taken up acting?" she asks seriously.

"Yeah," Diane mutters, "in the 'theater of the absurd.' "

Suddenly looking helpless, Mom asks, "What were we talking about? I've forgotten."

"You don't remember?" Diane asks, her irritation giving way to worry.

"Not really."

"We were just saying it's time we get going," I tell her.

Mom stares at me, Ian, Diane, and Jeanne as if she's never met us. "Yes, of course," she says, without conviction, and perhaps from habit adds, "That sounds like a good idea." She turns to Jeanne. "As always, it was great seeing you, but now, unfortunately, it seems it's time to go."

"You're so kind, Yvette!" Jeanne replies with a smile as she grasps Mom's hand. "I'm glad you came by today," she continues, and then gliding effortlessly from appreciation to indignation, concludes, "You're the only one who ever does—even my own sons and their families never visit!"

"Enough already!" Diane snaps, possibly as much to her surprise as ours since she blushes afterwards.

"Enough of what?" Mom asks.

"Enough of the 'long goodbyes,'" my sister replies, her tone contrite, "we'll be late if we keep on talking."

My mother looks at her yet again, it seems, not understanding.

"For lunch," I volunteer.

"Oh," Mom replies docilely and then says, "Au revoir," to Jeanne.

"À bientôt," Jeanne answers.

I push Mom's wheelchair into the corridor while Diane follows, and Ian turns to wave goodbye to our aunt.

"Bye-bye," Jeanne cries. She adds a plaintive, "Come back soon," for good measure.

Diane rolls her eyes.

"It's not Aunt Jeanne's fault," I say.

"No, it isn't," Mom says, "but it might be her responsibility."

Surprised, I ask, "How's that?"

"Most things are someone's responsibility."

"Even loneliness?" Ian asks.

I dread Mom's answer, as it seems does Diane, since her gait falters. Luckily, however, Mom's attention is drawn to the seating area we passed on entering, where residents in wheelchairs or mobile beds, IV stands beside them, are listening to a Salvation Army officer struggle through "Nearer My God to Thee" on the organ while a colleague provides an off-key delivery of the hymn's lyrics.

"'Throw Out the Lifeline' might have been a better selection," Diane quips.

Shocked by her callous, if accurate, description of the residents' condition, I say, "At least, the entertainment is a distraction for them!"

"I was talking about the entertainment!" Diane explains, glaring.

Mom looks at her and then at the Salvation Army officers and their audience. "I wish everyone would stop stating the obvious," she says. Accordingly, we proceed down the remaining length of corridor in silence.

At the nursing station, the orange-haired attendant who was sitting there earlier has been replaced by the pretty young woman we met while visiting Jeanne. "You guys have a good day," she admonishes over the hum of a clip-on fan attached to her computer monitor.

"You, too," Mom responds. "And visit your

grandmother," she adds, without irony, "She's lonely."

The young woman looks puzzled, but then, realizing that Mom's referring to Jeanne, says, "Of course, ma'am—I'll visit her as soon as I finish filling out this form."

"You're a good granddaughter," Mom says. The young woman smiles.

On the elevator landing, Simone is still dusting the furniture and pictures.

"Aren't you tired, Simone?" Diane asks her gently. Motioning to a stuffed chair Simone has just dusted, she says, "Why don't you sit down and rest for a while?"

Simone neither looks at her nor stops dusting.

We get into the elevator and when its doors have closed behind us, Mom says, "It must be horrible to be that confused and to still be working! I forgive her for trying to steal my husband!"

I flinch.

"Simone didn't try to 'steal' Dad from you!" Diane corrects her. "She couldn't have because most of the time she doesn't know what she's doing!"

"She doesn't?" Mom asks.

"No!" Diane retorts, as the elevator reaches the first floor and its doors open. "Not any more than you . . ." she continues but catches herself, "than any of us do."

"God help her then," Mom responds.

I push her wheelchair into the lobby and past two whirring floor fans intended to compensate for the inadequate air-conditioning.

The receptionist smiles as we approach but seems surprised on noticing that Ian is carrying the napkin-wrapped cupcakes she'd persuaded him to take earlier. "You and your aunt weren't hungry?" she asks.

"I forgot to offer her one, and I guess I lost my appetite," he mumbles sheepishly.

"You certainly don't take after your grandfather then," she says and promptly blushes at her mention of my late father.

"No, he doesn't," Mom says sadly. Glancing at me and Diane, she continues, "None of them do, and none of them can replace him."

"I'm sorry," the receptionist replies, embarrassed.

My mother nods in acknowledgement. As I move her wheelchair toward the entrance, she whispers, "Not as much as I am," so softly that I barely hear her.

Once we've passed out the entrance and onto the front walk, the airless and inescapable late-morning heat envelops us. The disabled man who'd been sitting on the bench under the porte-cochere has been replaced by the white-haired couple we passed in the driveway. Holding hands, they look—in their coordinated green-and-tan golf shirts, slacks, and sneakers—like matched collectibles, a winsome pair of fabric dolls on display at a craft fair or in a giftshop. They smile at us.

"Beautiful weather—even if it's a scorcher!" the man remarks, his Massachusetts accent unmistakable.

"For sure," Diane replies, "and better than the snow we'll get this winter."

"True," the man agrees, "which is why we spend the season in Florida."

"When do you go down?" Diane asks to show polite interest.

"This year we're leaving right after Labor Day," the woman answers in the same Massachusetts accent as her companion, "so we can celebrate our anniversary there."

"Is it a big one?" my sister asks.

"Yes," the wife responds, her smile broadening. "And we want to spend it somewhere that's special to us."

Despite their accents, Diane asks, "Are you originally from Florida?"

"No!" the woman replies, laughing, "but we met on spring break in Daytona—nearly forty years ago! Can you imagine!"

"My husband and I were married over sixty years," Mom announces.

"How wonderful!" the wife says. "Has your husband been gone long?" she asks, tempering her smile.

"Four years now," Diane answers for her.

"I'm so sorry," the woman says and plainly means it.

"Thank you," Mom replies. "I still miss him."

"I'm sure you do. How couldn't you?"

"It would be impossible," Mom replies without emotion.

The woman nods empathically. "Of course!"

"Some days are worse than others," Mom elaborates.

Since the woman seems uncertain how to react, Ian steps in. "Really?"

"Yes," Mom responds. "Especially when something reminds me of him as much as this place does."

The wife and husband look at each other.

"My grandfather lived here before he passed away," Ian explains.

Despite their deep tans, the couple's faces redden. "Oh," the woman remarks, the man echoing her.

A humid wind rises up off the river, rustling the black-eyed Susans and echinacea along the entrance walkway, and then dies away, leaving the plants and air still again.

"Well, we have to be on our way," Diane states, pulling her keys out of her handbag. "Nice to have met you," she says to the couple and, with Ian, heads toward the parking lot to retrieve the Caddy.

"Nice to meet you, too," the woman calls out after them, reclaiming her cheerful demeanor. "Yes, nice," her husband repeats.

"You have a great day," the woman says to Mom while I push the wheelchair forward.

My mother gives her a strange look. "Yes, thanks," she replies courteously, and then, turning away, mutters, "but my best days are behind me."

As we move down the walk, Mom looks up and over the sloping lawn, perennial beds, and trees between us and the river as if watching a bird in flight. I follow her gaze but see only a clear, azure sky—brilliant as a sunstruck mirror, featureless as the future, and pervasive as the past.

PART III

In a Field of Dreams

CHAPTER 38

Disconnected

Medium Take

It's a hot, sunny afternoon in mid-August, on the eve of Mom's eighty-ninth birthday, the reason for my visit. She and I are sitting in folding chairs on the blacktopped drive just outside the back door. At the bottom of the sloping yard, the barn's long shadow promises dim coolness. The incline, however, is too steep for Mom to navigate with her walker, so we stay in the drive, the asphalt radiating heat beneath our sandaled feet, Mom wearing a white summer shawl over her frail shoulders and I using a paper napkin to blot beads of perspiration from my brow.

I peer through my sunglasses at my smartphone's barely discernible screen, while Mom sips iced tea from a bar glass frosted with a pattern of silver garlands. "What are you looking at?" she asks.

"Email," I answer.

"Who from?"

"Business contacts in Cleveland and Chicago."

"Really? You know a lot of people in Cleveland and Chicago?" she asks, eyebrows arched. "I'd have thought that most of the people you know would be from Maine and Boston—or maybe even Paris," she adds, laughing, before taking another sip from her glass.

"I've lived in the Midwest a long time," I explain, no longer surprised by anything that she might forget, at least for a bit.

She thinks about this. "You've lived there too long," she pronounces, her voice unexpectedly serious.

"Why do you say that?"

"I mean, it's not like you went to Arizona for a few weeks or to Florida for the winter, is it?" she says, irritated by my obtuseness. "You've been gone for decades!"

"But I come back to visit," I protest. "Plus, you always know where I am and how to reach me."

"Not always." She shakes her head. "You travel too much. Sometimes you're in China or Japan, and other times, in Munich or Genève. I'm never sure where you are!"

"I don't travel as much now that I've started my own business—remember?" I protest.

"There are a lot of things I don't remember," she replies, glaring. "Honestly, some nights when I dream about you, it seems as if you're just gone—like a coin that rolled beneath the sofa or disappeared into a crack in the floor."

This remark startles me until I recall that she recently misplaced her engagement ring and that it has yet to be found. "But I've never actually disappeared, have I?" I ask her calmly.

"No," she admits with a sigh, "You haven't, because you're here right now." She looks as if she might start to cry. Instead, though, she touches my hand. "It's nice that you're here with me."

"I'm glad you think so," I answer. "Being here with you is one of my favorite things."

"Good!" she replies, her mood improving just as suddenly as it had soured. "How did we start talking about this, anyway? It's too sad!"

"It is," I agree, nurturing the positive shift in the conversation. "And it's not relevant—since, like you said, I'm here."

"But how did we get on the topic?" she insists, forcing me to retrace our steps and risk returning to the maudlin.

"I told you that most of my connections are elsewhere," I admitted.

"That's right!" she says triumphantly, pleased by her recollection and my concession. Then, she adds, "All mine are here." She pauses. "I used to have connections elsewhere—friends in Montréal and Boston—but they're mostly dead or senile now."

"I know," I agree.

Mom turns her gaze toward the lawn's end, where beyond a border of pines and maples, the field grass undulates in the sea breeze like the waves on the nearby bay. "So, now I guess I'm disconnected," she concludes.

CHAPTER 39

Abandoned

Medium Take

"My parents abandoned me," Mom says, anguished, as we sit on the sofa in her den, the television off because there are few programs that don't upset her, the only sounds the hum of a far-off lawn mower and the brush of the wind as it passes through the trees along the yard's edge.

"Why do you say that?" I ask.

"Because it's true!" she replies. "They left me when I was little! I've been searching for them ever since but haven't found them!" She stares straight ahead, as if hoping to find them at this very moment.

Diane looks at me. "A few weeks back," she begins, sotto voce, "she started dreaming that all of her family who've died over the years—her parents, brothers, Dad—left her when she was younger."

"I was just a little girl," Mom continues, "when I woke up one morning and discovered they were gone." She winces as if the memory physically hurts her. "I was all alone in the house without them. It was terrifying!"

Diane turns to Mom. "Like I keep saying,"

she tells her. "You and your parents lived under the same roof until you turned twenty-five and got married—your father gave you away at the wedding."

My mother continues to stare into the distance. "How can I be sure that's true?" she asks her.

"Because, since I take care of you day in and day out, 24/7, maybe you should trust me," Diane says caustically.

Mom doesn't respond, antagonizing Diane further. "OK, ask Rob, then!" she tells Mom. "He's your firstborn—maybe you'll believe him!"

Mom turns in my direction, wide-eyed, as if she hadn't previously noticed me.

"Diane's telling the truth," I say. "You and your parents were always in touch with one another. You talked with your mother every day of her life, right up until the day she passed away in her eighties." I pause here, wondering whether I should add that she was with my grandmother at the very moment of her passing but decide against it. "Maybe that's why you miss her so much," I conclude reassuringly.

Mom considers this. "That's a good story," she at last announces.

"Those are the facts, Mom," I reply in a neutral tone. "I didn't make anything up—why would I?"

She's silent for a moment. "You work in

marketing, right?" she asks skeptically. "Isn't telling tales part of what you do for a living?"

Her patience exhausted, Diane jumps up, pulls a photo album from a bookshelf, opens it, and places it in front of Mom.

"Here—look at this! And this! And this!" she orders Mom, pointing out photo after photo of Mom with her parents at christenings, weddings, backyard barbecues, and other family gatherings that took place over the course of decades.

Mom studies each wordlessly until her eyes well up with tears and she starts quietly crying.

CHAPTER 40

Deaths in the Family

Medium Take

It's late on a Saturday afternoon and I'm at home in suburban Cleveland. Outside, it's snowing—a fluffy lake-effect snow falling so hard that it rapidly blankets the landscape, making driving treacherous and causing me to forego a planned trip to the supermarket.

Instead, as often at this time of day, I decide to give Mom a call. My sister Diane answers.

"Hi," I say.

"Rob?" Diane asks. I hadn't identified myself because, like Mom, I have a distinctive voice, which I expected Diane to recognize.

"Yes, it's Rob."

"Oh, hi. I thought it was you," my sister responds.

I want to ask why she didn't just say as much to begin with but, presuming there's a reason that I might not want to know, instead I ask, "How's Mom?" and the reason reveals itself.

"Both she and I have had better days," Diane announces, sounding exasperated.

"Did she fall again?"

"No, thank God," she replies.

"Then, what?"

Diane sighs. "She's very confused this afternoon."

"How?"

"You'll see," Diane answers, with an air of exhausted satisfaction. "Mom's just come into the room and wants to talk to you."

I hear Diane hand the phone to Mom, whose voice, scratchy and tentative, comes on the line. "Hello, Rob?" she asks.

"Yes, Mom, it's me." I reflect that questioning my identity seems to be a familial theme today.

"Where are you?"

Because my career entailed a lot of travel, Mom has sometimes lost track of my whereabouts. Once, back when she was still able to use her mobile phone unassisted, she called me at midnight in Beijing and, another time, when I was in Bangalore, she phoned me at daybreak, thinking it was evening. Still, since I've been semi-retired for some years now, her question surprises me.

"I'm at home in Ohio."

"Ohio?" I know she considers Ohio desolate, nothing but windswept cornfields beneath boundless skies, an inaccurate impression to which she clings despite past visits to Cleveland, Cincinnati, and Columbus. "How did you end up there?"

"I married Thea. She's from here, remember?" I ask her, referring to my wife of more than thirty years.

"Of course! I love Thea!" she answers to cover her tracks. Then she changes the topic. "What's the weather like there?"

"It's snowing," I respond, watching the snow outside the kitchen window gradually transform the black, wrought-iron patio furniture into an ensemble of white-coated curves and angles of nearly indiscernible purpose.

"It's snowing here, too," Mom replies, disconsolately. "It's like it's snowing all over the world."

"Why do you say that?"

She doesn't answer, but instead proclaims, "I've made a discovery," as if she's just found a rare archeological artifact or geologic specimen.

"What's that?" I inquire.

"Anna's dead."

"Aunt Anna died forty years ago," I respond, deciding to confront the matter head on.

"That long?"

"Almost to the day."

"Really?" Her voice is mournful.

"Anna was your favorite aunt, n'est ce pas?" I ask in the hope of re-focusing her on the positive.

"Yes. She doted on me when I was a girl— even brought me along on her trips to Boston and Montréal." Mom pauses. "I can't believe I forgot she'd died!"

I try to cast the matter less severely. "I'm sure you didn't really forget."

"Yes I did," she responds, as always, unwilling to forgive herself for her memory lapse. "When I woke up from my nap, I asked your sister where Anna was living these days, and she told me she wasn't living anywhere because she was dead! I'd completely forgotten until she said that!"

"Did you dream about Anna during your nap?" I ask, attempting to forestall the visibly approaching tears. "If you did, maybe you were just confused when you woke up."

"Maybe," she answers anxiously. "But napping and dreaming don't explain all the other things I've been forgetting."

Reluctantly, I ask, "Like what?"

"Like how everyone died," she says quietly.

"Everyone?" I say into the phone.

"Everyone who meant anything to me," she responds, her voice trembling. "My father and mother, my brothers, my in-laws." She starts to sob. "I'm the only one left alive, and I don't even remember how they all died. Diane's told me, but I can't remember." Her sobbing increases.

I've learned the best way to pull her out of such despair is to deploy logic. "Not everyone is dead," I say calmly. "I'm here, your other kids are, and most of your sisters-in-law and brothers-in-law are, too."

The sobbing lessens. "Really?"

"Yes."

"How did the others die, though?"

I run through the litany of the dead and the disparate causes of their departures: one brother's demise from cancer, another's by stroke, yet another's from kidney failure, and, then, her mother's passing from cardiac arrest—not mentioning that this occurred while Mom cradled her in her arms, waiting for the ambulance.

Mom draws a deep breath, either newly mindful of the past or simply resigned to it. "I guess death runs in my family."

"In all families," I amend.

Ever the egalitarian, she replies, "Well, at least that's fair."

"What do you mean?"

"There's no preferential treatment," she says with a sigh.

CHAPTER 41

Occupational Therapy

Short Take

One evening, on overhearing Diane say the word "she," Mom asks, "She who?" her tone suspicious.

To put her mind at ease, Diane answers, "Not you, Mom—we're not talking about you. You're not our preoccupation."

My mother sighs. "That's right, I'm your occupation," she corrects her.

"Touché, Mom," Diane concedes, sounding disheartened.

CHAPTER 42

A Case of Mistaken Identity

Short Take

Waking up from an afternoon nap in the den, Mom adjusts her glasses and squints at me, seemingly mystified. "Who are you?" she inquires from where she lies on the long, brown-leather sofa.

"Why do you ask?" I tease.

"Because this is my house and I want to know," she declares with authority as she pushes back the blanket that Diane placed over her, a woven throw depicting scenes of nearby Portland harbor.

"Your eldest," I answer to keep from further agitating her.

"My eldest brother?!" She exclaims, shocked. "Why, I haven't seen you in ages, Lucien! You should be ashamed of yourself—never visiting your baby sister!"

"I'm Rob, your eldest son," I gently correct her.

She pushes her glasses up the bridge of her nose and takes a long, close look at me. "Well, what I said goes for you, too, sonny," she chastises me.

CHAPTER 43
A Member of the Wedding
Long Take

Thrushes chirp at a feeder outside the window in Mom's Maine kitchen as sunshine pours in through lace curtains, casting a fretwork of light and shadow across pine cabinets and accenting the knots in their woodgrain like ripples on a lake surface or tufts in a chenille blanket. Groggy after a late-night flight from Cleveland, my son Ian and I sit at the table, having coffee and muffins, while Mom eats a chocolate-chip cookie and reads her morning prayers from a missal whose cover depicts a glowing crucifix flanked by less resplendent angels.

"How are the muffins?" I ask Ian.

He looks up from his medical textbook. "Great—they taste like they were just baked."

"That's because they were," says Diane, as she enters the kitchen, limping from an arthritic knee. "I made them and the cookies this morning, with blueberries Carrie picked in the field and chocolate chips she bought on her way home yesterday." Diane pushes aside one of the French history books I'd planned on reading and places a couple of leather-bound photo albums on the table in front of me and Mom.

Mom looks up from her missal. "Oh good! You found them!" she exclaims, smiling.

"It wasn't easy," Diane replies. "Carrie hid them behind some file folders in the den bookcases, even though I've told her never to double-shelf stuff."

"I'm sure she didn't do it on purpose," Mom says.

"We all forget things," I add, since Diane earlier complained about my having left the downstairs lights on last night.

"Some more than others," Diane replies, looking in my direction.

"Don't pick on Lucien—or on Carrie either!" Mom admonishes her, mistaking me for her long-deceased elder brother, whom I don't in the least resemble.

"That's Rob, your oldest son, not Lucien," Diane corrects her. "And don't excuse Carrie just because she's your favorite granddaughter."

"I love all my grandchildren equally," Mom retorts, "just like I do my children!" Outside, the bird chatter grows louder as sparrows and swallows join the thrushes.

"The birds are having a party!" Mom exclaims happily.

"If you want to call it that," Diane says.

"I do," Mom tells her.

I open a white photo album whose cover reads, *A Wedding*. "Maybe we should look at pictures," I say, hoping to circumvent an argument.

"That'd be good," Ian concurs, either because he's guessed what I'm up to or because he's actually interested. He turns a page in the album and gestures to a photograph of women in furs and top-coated men standing on the steps of a clapboard church, its roofline dripping with icicles. "Was this taken the day you married Pépère?" he asks Mom.

Mom studies the photo. "I'm not sure."

Diane looks over Mom's shoulder. "Your anniversary is in May. Unless winter lasted into spring the year you and Dad got married, this isn't from your wedding. Besides, the church looks like Notre Dame in Saco," Diane continues. "You got married at St. Joseph's in Biddeford."

Mom studies the photo more closely. "How can you tell it's not St. Joseph's?"

Diane suppresses a sigh. "St. Joseph's is brick, and this church is wooden."

"Then, you must be right about the picture," Mom says. "What a relief! It would upset me not to remember the guests from my own wedding!"

Carrie, who's living with Diane and Mom while finishing her master's degree, enters the kitchen and overhears. "I think that picture's from Aunt Jeanne's wedding," she says, referring to my father's sister. "I found it in an album with her name on it."

Diane looks surprised. "You took this photo from another album and placed it in this one?"

"Yes," Carrie answers. "Mémère asked me to put all the family's wedding pictures in one album. She thought they'd be easier to find if they were all together."

"And you didn't label any," Diane observes, scanning the other unidentified pictures on the page.

"Mémère didn't tell me to," Carrie says defensively and begins to fiddle with her iPhone.

Diane's expression speaks volumes.

"I guess it might have been a good idea to label them," Carrie admits, after a moment.

Diane remains stony faced.

"Not necessarily," Mom volunteers. "It might be fun to guess who's in each picture."

"Yes," Diane says to her. "And maybe, while we're at it, you could point out your favorites—not that you need to," she continues, eyeing Carrie.

"Why don't we get back to the pictures?" I suggest.

"Good idea," Mom replies, as Diane looks up at the ceiling in aggravation.

I turn a page to a photo of a different bridal party posed before a studio curtain, the tuxedoed groom and ushers bearing carnation boutonnières, the satin-gowned bridesmaids rose corsages, and the silk-clad bride a bouquet of lilies and verbena, her train gathered in a lustrous swirl before her.

"That's some dress!" Carrie exclaims. "Especially the train!"

"It's long, all right," Ian observes.

"Not as long as the ceremony was," Mom says.

"You remember Jeanne's wedding?" Carrie asks.

"As clearly as yesterday."

Diane and I look at each other. "Are you certain?" I ask.

"Of course," Mom responds. "You should remember, too, Lucien. You were with me."

"He's not Lucien," Diane reminds her.

My mother studies me. "I'm sorry. I was confused but now I see that you aren't Lucien—in fact, you're probably one of my children."

I don't ask which one she thinks I am but simply respond, "No problem."

She smiles, as do I. "Are you sure you attended Jeanne's wedding?" I ask again. "I thought she was already married when you and Dad started dating." I let her weigh this information. "Did you know her earlier?"

Mom hesitates before answering. "I can't recall," she admits, sounding dispirited.

"Don't worry, Mémère," Carrie says. "This isn't a memory test—no one's evaluating you."

Mom looks at Ian. "Not even him?" she asks,

apparently recalling that he's a medical student.

"Not even me," Ian reassures her and motions in my direction. "Like Dad, I'm only here to visit."

"That's all?" Mom asks suspiciously.

"And to look at pictures," I answer, joking.

"To look at pictures?" she repeats.

"Of course," Ian responds with a grin. He directs Mom's attention to another photo—this one of a broad-shouldered bride in a bouffant wedding dress and a slender groom—a mere cipher by comparison—in a long-tailed morning coat and striped trousers. "Who are they?" he asks her.

"The bride's name is Dorothy and the groom's is Alan," Carrie answers for Mom. "At least, I think that's what Mémère told me."

"Do you mean Dorothée and Alain?" I ask her.

"Maybe. I don't always understand Mémère when she speaks French," Carrie says.

"Or when anybody does," Diane says, though she herself understands only a little.

"I want to learn," Carrie objects. "I'm taking French 101 this semester," she says and, holding up her iPhone, displays the course's web page.

I don't react to either my niece or sister. "It's probably Dorothée and Alain Beaudoin," I tell Mom, who's puzzling over the photo. "Our relatives from Madawaska."

"My grandmother's cousins!" she exclaims.

"And yours, too," Diane reminds her.

"Of course," Mom replies. "We weren't very close, though."

Diane frowns. "You told me that when you and Dad were first married, you'd go to the beach with them."

"Yes," Mom admits, "but we went to the beach with any relatives from up north who came to visit. They all lived so far inland they appreciated time by the ocean."

Diane studies Dorothée and Alain's picture. "Those two must have been a real sight in bathing suits."

"Don't be unkind!" Mom scolds.

"I call them like I see them," Diane parries. "You've got to admit they weren't balanced physically."

"True," Mom allows, "but they were compatible."

"You always described Dorothée as outgoing," I protest, "and Alain as timid."

"Did I?"

"You did," Diane confirms. "You also told us Dorothée liked golf and bowling while all Alain cared about was collecting antique silver and China."

My mother's expression brightens. "That's what I meant! What one liked, the other didn't! They complemented each other!"

Diane rolls her eyes. "Like mismatched salt and pepper shakers!"

"Diane!" Mom exclaims.

Ian mediates. "Maybe what they had in common wasn't obvious."

"That's right," chimes in Carrie. "People sometimes seem different but share a lot beneath the surface."

"Care to be more specific?" Diane challenges.

"Like my med-school classmate who married a musician," Ian offers. "She and her husband are each committed to their professions but also to each other."

"I know an agnostic guy who's married to a devout Roman Catholic, and he and his wife seem to have the same sense of ethics," I comment.

"How about straight men who marry transgender or gender-fluid women?" offers Carrie, some of whose friends are such.

Diane stares at her.

"They love their wives because of who they are and what they have in common," Carrie continues, oblivious to Diane's reaction.

Mom turns away from the photo album. "What's 'transgender'?"

"Never mind," Diane tells Mom while glaring at Carrie.

Cowed, Carrie backpedals. "Or when a gay man marries a lesbian—maybe that's a better example," she says hopefully.

Diane's glare turns into a glower. "Just what

353

might a couple like that have in common?!" she demands of Carrie.

"They could be devoted to their family and to each other," Mom interjects.

Though this surprises me, I say, "Agreed," both because I believe it but also to keep Diane from upsetting her by continuing to dissect Alain and Dorothée. "Commitment is what's most important."

"Even without a physical connection?" Ian asks.

"Sex isn't everything in marriage," Mom responds. "Love and faithfulness are the ingredients that bind a couple—like eggs and chocolate chips in cookie dough." She pauses, and as no one says anything, adds, "Or blueberries and flour in muffin batter."

"Chocolate chips and blueberries aren't binding agents," Diane tells her.

"You can't be sure of that—or of what keeps two people together," Mom declares, standing her ground. "Both baking and marriage are more art than science."

Diane looks at Mom in wonder. "Why are we talking about this anyway?!" she demands irritably.

"Because *you* criticized Alain and Dorothée," Mom announces with relish.

Before Diane can reply, the birds at the feeder erupt in a furor of frantic trills and flutters.

"What's going on?" I ask, looking out the window as the birds vanish into nearby foliage.

"A hawk or gull must have flown over," Diane answers.

"A hawk!" Mom cries. "Why can't the hawks stay away from here!"

"Don't worry, Mémère," Carrie says. "The hawks won't hurt us."

"They won't?" Mom asks.

"Absolutely not," Carrie reassures her.

"But what about the little birds!?"

"I wouldn't be concerned about them, Mom. They're faster than the hawks," I say, though I suspect this isn't true.

Probably because Mom looks unconvinced, Ian says, "Let's keep looking at pictures, Mémère," but to my dismay adds, "Maybe you can tell us more about Alain and Dorothée."

Mom nods, and Ian turns the album's pages to yet more pictures of the young Alain and Dorothée—most taken in city parks, on busy streets, or in crowded restaurants.

"Madawaska looks bigger that I expected," I say. "I thought it was just a village up on the Canadian border."

"It is," Diane confirms. "I wonder where these pictures were taken."

"Probably in Lewiston," Mom says. "There wasn't much to do or any steady work in Madawaska back then . . ."

"Or now," Diane interrupts.

Ignoring this, Mom continues, "So, eventually Alain and Dorothée moved to Lewiston."

"Did Alain work in the textile mills there?" I ask.

"Dorothée did," Mom replies. "After the war, the mills were moving jobs south to get cheap labor, but they were still hiring seamstresses in Maine for specialized work like making salesmen's samples."

"Dorothée was a seamstress?!" Diane exclaims. "That doesn't jibe with your other descriptions of her. You told us she was a tomboy as a kid and mannish as she got older."

"She was," Mom says. "But, in those days, every woman had to learn to sew. Dorothée turned out to be really good at it."

"What did Alain do in Lewiston?" Ian asks.

"He sold menswear at Peck's."

"Peck's?" Carrie repeats, over the chatter of the birds, who've returned to the feeder.

"Peck's was a department store. It closed years ago," I tell her, as she turns to her iPhone, probably to research this.

"That job suited Alain," Mom continues. "From the time he was a teenager, he was nattily dressed."

"Nattily dressed?" Diane repeats, "In Madawaska?!"

"Like I said," Mom reminds her, "he and Dorothée moved to Lewiston."

"That's the 'big city,' all right," Diane replies facetiously. "A natty dresser must have fit in well there."

"People can be who they are, wherever they are," Mom asserts as soberly as if quoting from the Bill of Rights, which she might believe she's in fact doing.

"You think that's the moral of Alain and Dorothée's story?" Diane asks. "I think it's just the opposite."

Mom stares.

Once again, Ian comes to the rescue. "Look at this picture," he says, drawing Mom's attention to a photograph of Dorothée and several uniformed, dark-lip-sticked young women in a factory workroom, their permanents flattened under tight hairnets and eyes obscured by thick safety glasses. Pointing to another photo of the same women, this time sans glasses and dressed in slacks and jerseys at a bowling alley, he says, "Here they are again. Were they Dorothée's co-workers?"

Mom grows animated. "They must have been!" she exclaims. "Dorothée told me she bowled with the other seamstresses!" Ian turns to a different page and image—this one of a smiling, suit-jacketed Alain and several similarly garbed young men standing behind a glass display case full of bowlers, Panama hats, and fedoras. As the shortest, Alain is at the group's center, the others flanking him in order of ascending height, all grinning, with their arms draped over one another's shoulders.

"Alain looked happy," I observe.

"He made good friends at Peck's," Mom responds. "In Madawaska, he'd been a loner, but in Lewiston, he met other guys like himself," she pauses. "You know, careful dressers." I smile at this expression. "He palled around with them until he and Dorothée had children," she concludes.

Diane looks surprised. "Alain and Dorothée had children?"

"Two—a girl and a boy. The girl was a still-birth."

"That's awful!" Carrie exclaims as her iPhone falls from her hands and lands on the floor before her.

Mom nods in agreement. "Dorothée and Alain were grief stricken. She quit her job, and both of them stopped socializing."

"How did they manage without Dorothée's income?" Ian asks.

"Store clerks like Alain were paid enough to live on back then," Mom replies. "And Dorothée had saved the money she'd made at the mill, figuring it would come in handy when she and Alain started a family."

"When was their son born?" I ask.

"Not long after their daughter," Mom answers,

probably unable to be more precise. "That was Jocelyn."

"What was the son's name?" Diane asks.

Mom looks at her. "Like I said, Jocelyn."

"Diane's asking about their boy, not their girl," Ian tells Mom gently.

"Jocelyn was the boy's name," Mom maintains.

Ian and Carrie look at each other. "They gave their boy a girl's name?" Carrie asks.

"*Jocelyn* is the masculine version of *Jocelyne*," I inform them.

Carrie sighs. "I'll never be any good at French."

"It's not all that hard," I say.

Ian appears skeptical. "Doesn't it have dozens of tenses and hundreds of irregular verbs?" he objects, as Carrie checks her phone for confirmation.

"That's because French's roots are a mix of regional dialects and Latin," I explain.

"Did you learn that from one of those?" Diane asks me, pointing to the French history books that she earlier pushed aside to make room for the photo albums.

I shake my head. Then since they don't seem much impressed by my explanation for French's complexity, I paraphrase an old maxim. "Besides, when it comes to grammar, ours is not to reason why but only to comply."

Carrie looks at me as if I'm speaking another language at this very moment. "I don't know," she demurs. "French isn't always logical—it even assigns genders to inanimate objects like lamps and tables!"

"How's that a problem?" Diane asks her.

"It's confusing," Carrie replies, in a tone that suggests this should be apparent.

"English can be pretty confusing, too, though," Diane remarks. I wonder what her angle is.

Ian nods. "The foreign med students have a hard time with it."

"Does the medical jargon trip them up?" I ask.

He shakes his head. "It's more the inconsistencies."

"What do you mean?" Carrie asks.

"Like when a professor refers to a hospital as 'it' if he's talking about an institution and 'they' if he's talking about its staff."

"The Brits do the same sort of thing," I comment. "They say stuff like, 'Macy's has a good selection,' but also, 'Macy's aren't very good at customer service'—sometimes in the same sentence."

"I guess that can be confusing if English isn't your first language," Carrie concedes.

"And maybe even if it is," Diane says, studying Carrie as intently as a cat does a clueless mouse.

Carrie seems perplexed. "What do you mean?"

"You know," Diane elaborates, her eyes narrowing as she closes in for the kill, "like when a trans person insists on being referred to in the plural, as if he or she were several individuals."

Carrie blushes. "As Mémère said, we've all got the right to be who we are," she asserts.

"Even when that confuses people?"

"Life isn't just about meeting everyone's expectations," Carrie counters, turning redder.

Diane sighs. "True, but it's also not about coming up with awkward solutions that can cause misunderstandings."

Carrie doesn't respond immediately. "Maybe it's more important to be understanding of people than to worry about somehow causing confusion," she replies.

I see both Diane's and Carrie's perspectives, but it's Mom who settles the matter. "Understanding others is certainly the most important thing," she says, reiterating a lifelong sentiment of hers. "Everything else is just window dressing."

Coincidentally, at that very moment, the birds around the window feeder again burst into a ball of motion then scatter in every direction.

"Is the hawk back?" Ian asks.

"Probably," Diane answers, going to the window.

Because Mom looks worried, I try to draw her attention back to the photo album. "How long was it before Dorothée and Alain had Jocelyn?" I ask, waving a hand at one of their pictures.

"Seven or eight years," she says, uncertainly.

"They must have been happy when he came along," I comment.

"They were—even though, as a baby, he didn't resemble either of them."

"Was he adopted?" Carrie asks.

"At first, some people thought so," Mom answers, "because Dorothée hadn't looked pregnant."

Diane turns from the window. "That's the answer, right there!" she proclaims.

"Not necessarily," Mom retorts, sounding annoyed. "Big women don't always show when their pregnant."

Diane rolls her eyes, and Mom grimaces. "Anyway, as Jocelyn grew older," Mom continues, "he started to look like both Alain and Dorothée."

"How's that possible?!" Diane demands.

"It's common," Ian responds. "Kids sometimes don't look much like either parent until they get older."

"Thank you, Dr. Ian," says Diane, wryly. "Still, the story sounds fishy to me."

Scowling, Mom flips through the photo album's pages. When she finds the one she wants, she pushes the album towards my sister. "Look at this picture!"

"This one?" Diane says, placing her finger on a photo of a trim young man in his late teens or early twenties.

"Yes!" Mom says. "That's Jocelyn! Notice the resemblance to Alain when he was younger?"

Diane blushes but concedes nothing. "Lots of

guys that age look like one another," she rejoins, which is so patently false no one responds. "Who's the guy with Jocelyn here?" she asks, pointing to a photo of him and another young man, both dressed in summer whites and striped bow ties and standing arm in arm on a garden terrace, the San Francisco skyline behind them. "Looks like it was a special occasion."

Mom hesitates. "It's Jocelyn and his husband at their wedding," she answers.

"Aha!" Diane exclaims, exultant.

"Aha, what?" Mom asks.

"Like father, like son!" my sister pronounces triumphantly.

"Good God, Diane!" Mom mutters. "I'm sick and tired of how hard you are on people!"

In an instant, Diane goes from looking gleeful to indignant. "You think you're tired?!" she asks Mom. "Who got out of bed at 6 A.M. to do your laundry, make your breakfast, and get you up, dressed, and bathed?!" Mom doesn't reply, which makes Diane angrier. "And, speaking of being tired," she continues wrathfully, "I'm kind of tired of you right now. Isn't it about time for you to take your morning nap?"

Mom doesn't react.

"Didn't you hear me?" Diane demands. "I said, it's time for your nap!"

"I think someone's throwing a temper tantrum," Mom responds.

Diane's expression tightens. "Or maybe someone else's lost touch with reality."

"To whom are you referring?" Mom asks in a tone of mock innocence yet marked formality.

"Come on!" Diane orders, starting to pull Mom's chair away from the table.

"Why the rush?" Mom asks.

"Because, as always, you need to go to the bathroom before lying down on the sofa!"

"I don't need to today!" Mom objects.

"Are you sure?" Diane asks. "Remember what happened yesterday, before Rob and Ian got here?"

My mother looks unsure. "I don't," she admits.

"You wet yourself," Diane declares unceremoniously.

Mom's face blanches. "You're embarrassing me!"

"Whatever," Diane replies.

Mom turns away from her.

"OK, so, you had a little 'accident,'" Diane amends, "and we don't want that to happen again." She moves so that she and Mom are again face to face. "Do you like this version of the story better?" she asks. "I do—because it'll mean less work for me!"

"Comme tu es bête!" Mom replies coldly.

They glare at each other, while I reflect that it's fortunate Diane doesn't understand that Mom has just told her she's awful.

"You know, Mémère," Carrie intervenes, "even if you don't need to use the bathroom right away, if you go now, you probably won't have to interrupt your nap later."

Mom considers this. "OK," she says at length and lets Carrie help her out of her chair and onto her walker, after which Diane takes over and, limping, leads her to the bathroom. Along the way, neither speaks to the other.

When the bathroom door closes behind them, I ask Carrie, "Do they bicker like this a lot?"

"Not a lot," she answers. "But when they do, it can be brutal."

The term's harshness unnerves me. "Brutal? How?"

"Like now," Carrie answers. "If Mémère doesn't do as she's told, Diane calls her on the carpet, and then Mémère gets short with her."

"My mother's stubborn, and Diane comes on strong," I remark, trying to be even handed.

"About Aunt Diane—sometimes, for sure," says Ian. "I don't understand why she's worked up about those distant cousins. Not to mention why she's so upset about personal pronouns," he adds, looking at Carrie.

"Diane can be a handful," Carrie says. "I've learned that since moving in."

"What do you mean?" Ian asks.

Carrie looks down at her lap and, for once, refrains from consulting her iPhone. "Taking care of Mémère day in and day out has made Aunt Diane pretty time conscious," she explains. "If she thinks you're wasting her time by beating around the bush, she'll be blunt about it—even about things that aren't her business."

"She's always been like that—it's her personality," I say. "But she means well and is usually just trying to help you."

"I know," Carrie replies. "Lately, though, she's been terribly short-tempered—especially when Mémère says the same things over and over."

"Does Mom repeat herself much?"

"Enough," Carrie answers delicately.

"That means her dementia's increasing," Ian remarks.

I know he's right but don't want to acknowledge this.

"It's a little worse than that," Carrie says carefully. "The last time Mémère saw her doctor, he diagnosed Alzheimer's." My dismay must be apparent because she hastens to add, "But it's just in the beginning stages."

The bathroom door swings open, and Mom appears in the back hallway with Diane directly behind her. Mom peers at us as if we are at a great distance instead of only steps away at the kitchen table. Carrie waves to her, and as Mom waves back, her walker begins to totter.

"Don't get distracted, Mom!" Diane cautions. "Pay attention to where you're headed!"

As if to antagonize Diane, Mom looks to the right and starts turning in that direction instead of moving forward.

"Watch where you're going!" Diane orders.

"I am!" Mom protests.

"You're not!" Diane disagrees. "You're turning toward the broom closet—not walking into the kitchen!"

"If I'm looking at the broom closet and headed toward it," Mom says in an icy tone, "what's the problem?"

Diane's face reddens. "You're the problem!"

"The problem's that you're impatient," Mom retorts.

"Is that so?!" Diane exclaims, growing wide-eyed. "You'd try the patience of a saint!"

"Which you aren't!" Mom shoots back.

Diane takes hold of Mom's walker from behind her, turns it toward the kitchen and pushes her in that direction. "Hey! You're going to make me fall!" Mom cries in alarm as she starts to wobble. Diane leans forward and reaches out for her, but suddenly, her bad knee gives way and she, too, begins to lose her balance.

Carrie and Ian jump from their chairs, Ian taking hold of Mom and the walker and Carrie grabbing Diane's arms to steady her. For an instant, all stand as still as actors in a tableau vivant or figures in a diorama. Her face ashen, Diane says, "Thank you," to Carrie and Ian.

Mom looks disoriented. "Where are we going?" she inquires.

"Where do you want to go?" Carrie asks.

"I don't know."

"Maybe you'd like to sit down at the kitchen table again?" Ian suggests, but Mom doesn't respond.

"Bring her into the den and help me get the sofa ready," Diane says. "That's where she'll be napping."

"Follow me, Mémère," Carrie encourages. "It's just a little way."

"Why are we going to the den?" Mom asks.

"So that you can take a nap. Remember?" I tell her.

"I do feel tired," Mom admits without moving forward.

"That makes a nap sound good, doesn't it?" Carrie coaxes.

"Maybe," Mom says tentatively and lets Carrie guide her down the back hall and into the den, with Diane behind them.

As Ian and I follow, Diane turns to me and mutters, "Thank God for favorites," sounding at once relieved and exasperated.

I respond, "I guess."

Because the den is bright with morning light, I walk to the bay window to draw the drapes.

"What are you doing?" Mom calls out from by the sofa, where, one hand on her walker and the other on Carrie, she waits while Ian arranges pillows.

"Closing the curtains so you'll sleep better," I respond.

"Don't! I'm going to look out," Mom says and shakily begins to turn toward me.

"Mom! Be careful!" Diane cautions. "You'll start to fall again!"

"I want to see outside," she responds.

"You'll regret it later," Diane admonishes, "when you're in the ER lying on a stretcher."

"I want to see out," Mom reiterates, as single-mindedly as a two-year-old contradicting its parents. "Please help me to the window," she implores Ian and Carrie, who in turn look to Diane for direction.

"Whatever!" Diane says, surrendering to Mom's obstinance.

Ian and Carrie turn Mom around and slowly proceed toward where I'm standing.

On reaching me and stepping into the bay window, Mom first looks to one side and then to the other. "Draw the drapes farther apart and open the sheers, please. I'd like to see nature in all her glory," she announces.

As I do this and she leans in to get a better view, a flock of sparrows explodes out of the shrubbery beneath the window and rockets upward. Startled, Mom gasps and lurches toward the window glass. I grab her arms, and we start to fall together but don't, since Ian and Carrie lunge forward and somehow manage to grab hold of each of us.

Diane rushes over. "Seen enough yet or do you actually need to keel over?" she demands of Mom.

Mom ignores her.

"You should rest now, Mom," I say, turning her away from the window.

"You might be right," she answers, her face devoid of color.

Diane and I lead Mom back to the sofa and help her lie down. I place a blanket over her and draw it up nearly to her chin. Nestled amid the large sofa cushions beneath the blanket, she looks as small and fragile as a China doll. Her eyes begin to water.

Diane frowns. "What's wrong now?"

Her voice breaking, Mom answers, "You were mean to me!"

"I'm sorry, Mom," Diane says, "but when you don't listen and put yourself in danger, it's upsetting!"

"Still, you shouldn't yell at me," Mom insists, as the tears in her eyes well higher and threaten to spill over. "I'm the mother, and you're the daughter," she reminds her.

"Please don't cry, Mom!" Diane says, no longer frowning. She touches Mom on the shoulder. "I'm only trying to do what's best for you."

Mom doesn't answer.

"Let's think about something else, Mémère," Carrie suggests trying to defuse the situation.

"What?" Mom asks.

Carrie seems stymied. Then she exclaims, "I know—the wedding pictures! Weren't those fun to look at, with all the well-dressed men and women?!"

Mom breaks into a smile. "Weddings make me happy."

"Just like you make us," Ian says and, bending forward, kisses her on the forehead.

Mom's smile grows larger.

"Try to sleep now," I tell her. "You'll feel better after."

"You're right, Lucien," she says, again mistaking me for her eldest brother.

I don't correct her. "Sleep well," I say.

"Sweet dreams!" adds Carrie.

As we head for the den door, Carrie hands Diane a small, white object that looks like an old transistor radio.

"What's that?" I ask.

"A baby monitor," Diane answers. "So that we can hear what happens in here while we're on the patio."

"The patio?"

Diane nods. "We're going outdoors. Mom's a light sleeper—I don't want to risk waking her."

"I'll bring some lemonade and cookies," Carrie tells us.

"I'll help you," Ian says, and the two go into the kitchen.

Outside, Diane places the baby monitor on the patio table, part of a set of wrought-iron garden furniture that my parents bought while I was in high school. "I can't believe these have lasted so long, and that you're still using them," I say as I pull one of the chairs away from the table.

"I hire a handyman to paint the whole set with Rustoleum each fall, and I have him put it away for the winter afterwards."

"You take good care of it," I say.

"Waste not, want not."

I touch one of my chair's leaf-scrolled arms, which glistens as if painted yesterday rather than last autumn. "At this rate," I say to Diane, "these things could last forever." We hear Mom cough on the baby monitor, and I add, "Just like our mother."

Diane looks at me. "Or not. Mom's declined since summer started."

"She seems to be holding her own, though," I say, while realizing this isn't the whole truth of the matter.

"With a lot of help," Diane replies. "It's not the first time I've almost fallen along with her when she loses her balance. Just now, you nearly did yourself." Diane looks away. "I'm not sure how much longer I'll able to manage everything alone."

"What about Carrie?" I ask.

Diane looks at me quizzically. "What about her?"

"Doesn't she help?"

"She's busy with her studies—plus, honestly, she's kind of scatter-brained," Diane replies with a sigh. "You saw how she combined the photos from the different albums. What if she mixed up Mom's medications?" Diane makes a face. "Anyway, she graduates in December, and after that she starts a job in Boston."

"Have you thought about getting a home health aide?" I ask.

Diane shakes her head. "Mom doesn't want a stranger in the house. Also, with the taxes, food, insurance, and utilities, it already costs so much to keep this place going that hiring an aide is out of the question."

"I could stay for a while and help with Mom and the expenses," I offer. "I do most of my consulting remotely—and anyway I've been thinking of retiring."

"You can't leave Thea alone in Cleveland indefinitely. Plus, you probably don't have all that much money to spare after paying for Ian's medical education."

I don't dispute this.

Carrie and Ian emerge from the house, the first carrying a platter of cookies and the second a pitcher and tumblers from an old crystal bar set of my father's.

"How come such fancy glasses?" Diane asks Ian.

"I told him to use them," Carrie answers, setting the plate of cookies down on the table. "This is a special occasion—what with him and Uncle Rob visiting."

Diane frowns anew, which I hope Carrie doesn't notice.

"These are beautiful," Ian remarks, as he pours the lemonade into the tumblers and hands one to me.

"They're Baccarat," I tell him. "You don't see glasses like these much anymore."

"Not outside of antique shops or museums," Diane says archly, holding a tumbler up to the light to examine it. "Maybe I'll try to sell them on eBay this winter."

"You wouldn't!" Carrie exclaims in alarm.

Diane smirks. "You're so gullible you could have been born yesterday."

"I'm not as skeptical as you," Carrie acknowledges. "But that isn't bad. Sometimes you have to take things at face value."

Diane regards her scornfully.

"You don't agree?" I ask my sister.

"I don't," Diane confirms. "I think we have to evaluate everything and question whatever's suspect."

"Even things like Mom insisting that people who seemed mismatched were, in point of fact, happily married?" I ask daringly.

Diane eyes widen. "Listen! I don't give a rat's ass about Alain and Dorothée—or freaking Jocelyn either!" She looks away. "I just want Mom to stay focused on the present and understand her limitations. Things are tough enough already without her mistaking you for Lucien, thinking that hawks are attacking us, or almost falling out of windows!"

I say nothing further.

Carrie unfurls the parasol at the table's center.

"Does that really need to be open?" Diane asks. "It's not very hot today."

"But it's pretty bright. I can close it, though," she offers, "if you think it'd be better."

Diane shakes her head. "Leave it open. It might keep this from overheating," she says, pushing the baby monitor into the shade of the umbrella. A gust of wind ripples the parasol's scalloped edge and rustles the branches of the alder trees along the lawn's border, causing a hawk to emerge from their branches. Unsettled, countless thrushes, sparrows, and jays arise as one from the adjacent field, fly overhead in multiple formations, then disappear over the house's roof line behind us. Without a moment's hesitation, the hawk follows.

"Mom might be right about that hawk attacking

us," I say to Diane, jokingly. "It's relentless."

"That hawk's not focused on anything but those other birds," Diane says, looking at me. "Everything else is irrelevant to it, like the hawk should be to us." As if to underscore her point, bees and butterflies hover unperturbed amid the marigolds at the patio's edge as, high above, the mass of songbirds flies back across the roofline like a boomerang, streams along the lawn's perimeter, and then vanishes into the blueberry bushes by the barn at the backyard's far end.

"What do you think's happened to the hawk?" I ask Diane.

"Looks like the songbirds gave it the slip," she answers. "They've probably learned a thing or two from seeing speeders outsmart the police on the turnpike," she concludes drolly.

We all laugh. "Are there many speeders?" I ask.

"It's mostly the tourists," Carrie answers. "On my way home from Portland last night, the cars with Massachusetts and Connecticut plates were going really fast and doing some interesting maneuvers."

"You could see the turnpike from the train?" Diane asks.

There's a pause. "I didn't take the train to school yesterday," Carrie admits. "I drove."

"Why?" Diane asks. "I thought you'd figured out that the train's cheaper."

Carrie looks sheepish. "Last week, I missed

the Saco stop while looking up something on my phone. I had to stay on until the train got to Wells and then wait at the station there for four hours before I could board a train headed back in this direction."

"That's why you got home so late on Tuesday!"

Looking even more sheepish, Carrie nods. "I don't want that to happen again, so I'm driving."

"Here's another possible solution," Diane posits. "Instead of driving, you could put your phone away while you're on the train and use the travel time to study."

Carrie doesn't answer.

"What sorts of 'maneuvers' did you see on the turnpike yesterday?" Ian asks, likely to get us through the moment.

"Cars passing on the right, cutting others off, and weaving in out of traffic," she replies, visibly relieved to return to the original topic. "The worst was a pickup truck that made an illegal U-turn across the median strip."

"At one of the plow turnarounds?" Diane asks.

Carrie shakes her head. "Over a concrete embankment."

Ian, who learned to drive on comparatively tame midwestern highways looks shocked. "Why would people do anything that dangerous?!"

Carrie shrugs. "Maybe they missed their exit."

"Or forgot something they needed," I suggest.

"What could be that important?" Ian asks.

"Their brains, maybe?" Diane guesses while she pours herself a glass of lemonade. "They'll need a lot of luck to find them, considering how long they've likely been missing," she continues, winking at him.

I suppress a laugh and wonder if, as Diane's older brother, I should assume Mom's role and chide her for her unkindness. Instead I turn my attention to the bottom of the lawn, where, in the hawk's continued absence, the thrushes have come out of the blueberry bushes to peck for seed amid the grass and clover. Cardinals, blue jays, yellow wrens, and orange songbirds soon descend from the alders and join them, speckling the far end of the lawn with bobbing bits of color.

"What kinds of birds are the orange ones?" Ian asks, following my gaze.

Carrie Googles the answer on her iPhone. "Either orioles or warblers."

"They're pretty," he remarks.

I'm about to agree when, to my surprise, his words are echoed by Mom's voice on the baby monitor. "Can she hear us?" I ask my sister.

"Keep your voice down!" Diane whispers as she grabs the baby monitor. "This must be running in both microphone and speaker mode," she says and quickly switches its settings. Still holding the monitor, she turns to Carrie. "Why did you set it this way?"

"Sometimes, I talk to Mémère when she's

sleeping—I think it comforts her," she replies, without offering any evidence for why she believes this.

Diane glances at me pointedly.

On the monitor, Mom keeps talking. "You look lovely!" she says, her voice excited.

"Maybe she has visitors," Ian speculates.

I shake my head. "We would have heard the front doorbell ring or seen anyone who came up to the backdoor through the driveway."

"She's probably dreaming," Carrie explains. "Her dreams are vivid."

"Don't worry—our dresses look great!" Mom assures her phantom listeners. "Besides, no one will be looking at us bridesmaids—the bride's the center of attention!" A pause follows. "Of course, I'm sure!" she insists, as if someone's objected. "And anyway most guests won't remember much after all the toasts and other drinking. That's why I don't care that my dress shows too much cleavage."

Carrie discreetly adjusts her blouse's low, scoop neckline. Diane and I smile at each other.

"Should we wake her?" Ian asks.

"No. Mom loves weddings," Diane replies.

"D'accord!" Mom says on the monitor, "the ceremony was perfect, and the bride's wedding gown is almost as beautiful as she is!"

"Aussi polie dans ses rêves que dans sa vie," I comment.

"Which means?" Diane asks.

"That Mom is as polite in her dreams as when she's awake."

"Except if she doesn't want to do something," Diane says.

"Lots of people are a little irritable when they're tired," Carrie says as she grabs a napkin that's about to blow off the table.

"'A little irritable'?" Diane responds. "Is that how you'd describe her telling me I'm too bossy!"

"When did she say that?" I ask my sister.

"Last night," Diane answers. "She didn't want to go to bed, and when I insisted, she told me she was moving to a new hotel where the staff was less bossy."

"Sometimes you are bossy," Carrie says.

Diane's face turns red.

"Maybe impatient's a better word," I offer, as more small orange birds appear on the lawn, heads darting and eyes cocked for whatever predator—the hawk, a cat, or a fox—might be lurking amid the alders.

My sister stares at me.

"Impatient is a better word," Ian concurs, seeming to be aware that we're skating on thin ice. "How could you not be, with all the cooking and cleaning you have to do?" he asks Diane. "Not to mention, helping Mémère from dawn until dark."

Though Diane is silent, I fear the proverbial ice might soon fracture.

"Sometimes, though," Carrie responds. "Mémère's so confused she doesn't know what's happening." She looks directly at my sister. "Or really think about what she's saying—that's why we have to be understanding."

A lump arises in my throat as the ice gives way beneath us.

"'Understanding'?" Diane repeats heatedly. "Do you mean about the crap she says to me or about the actual crap that I wipe off the floor when she doesn't get to the bathroom?!" she continues, her face flush with anger. "Or have you been too busy playing with your phone to notice?!"

Before Carrie can answer, Mom's voice once again issues from the baby monitor. "Bien sûr, ma tante Agathe!" she says, addressing a long-dead relative through marriage. "The bride's gown is beautiful!" Mom pauses. "And, yes, this is the best-dressed wedding party I've ever been part of!"

"She's laying it on kind of thick!" Diane criticizes.

"She's just overcompensating," I say in Mom's defense. "Mom never much cared for Aunt Agathe because she broke up Uncle Denis's first marriage."

Carrie looks surprised. "I didn't know Mémère could be like that."

"Well, now you do," Diane says, with an air of vindication.

"We're talking about a dream," Ian reminds us.

On the baby monitor, Mom keeps talking, her dream's narrative steadily unfolding. "The bride's about to throw the bouquet!" she says to Aunt Agathe or some other likely long-deceased relation. "I'll try to catch it!"

A half-hearted cry follows. "Dommage! Je n'ai pas pu l'accrocher!" Mom exclaims, "Quand même, c'est peut-être allé à quelqu'un qui le mérite plus!"

"What did she say?" Ian asks.

"Yes, translation, please," adds Carrie.

"She said she didn't catch the flowers but maybe they went to someone more deserving."

"That's Mémère," Carrie responds. "Kind-hearted even in her dreams."

Diane, glowering, seems about to contradict her, when a loud bump and a crash resound over the baby monitor. Listing to one side because of her bad knee, she scrambles out of her chair and rushes toward the backdoor. "Did Mémère fall off the couch?" Carrie calls out, as we hurry after Diane.

"We'll know in a minute!" Diane answers grimly, while we pass through the back hallway.

Entering the den, we find Mom reclining where we left her, staring at nothing in particular, like a fish floating while asleep, neither rising to the surface nor sinking to the bottom. Her walker lies askew on the floor beside the sofa.

Diane touches her shoulder. "Are you all right?"

"I'm fine," Mom protests, though her tone suggests the opposite.

"What happened?" I ask her, motioning toward her walker.

Mom glances in its direction. "I tried to get up, but I guess I'm worn out from the wedding."

"Did you dance too much during the reception?" Ian asks her gently.

"No, I got tired running to catch the bride's flowers."

"That's too bad," Carrie says. "But, overall, was the wedding fun?"

Mom looks surprised. "Why ask me?! You were there!"

"I was?" Carrie responds.

"Yes!" Mom exclaims. "You were part of the wedding party—like me and your sister!"

"You mean Melissa?"

Mom frowns. "No—Diane, your older sister!"

"Diane isn't my sister, Mémère," Carrie replies kindly. "She's my aunt—your daughter."

"My daughter?!"

"Yes," Diane attests, helping Mom sit up. "I live here and take care of you. Remember?"

Mom takes a closer look at her. "I'm not sure," she answers. Then, breaking into a smile, she adds, "But I do remember that you had the most beautiful dress at the wedding."

"How could that be?" Diane asks, beginning to sound irritated again. "Aren't bridesmaids dressed identically?"

"You were the maid of honor, so your dress was different," Mom corrects her.

"How?" Diane asks.

"The bridesmaids' dresses were puffy and ruffled," Mom explains, "but yours was simple and elegant—like the bride's! She looked like a queen—and you were as pretty as a princess!"

Ian, Carrie, and I smile. "That sounds wonderful, Mémère," Carrie says.

"Yes," Mom agrees. "Diane was lucky."

"Why do you say that?" Diane asks curtly.

"Every young man wanted to dance with you, and all the single women were jealous!" Mom answers. "I'm amazed you don't remember!"

"How could I remember, Mom? It was your dream, not mine!" Diane retorts, now even more agitated. "And why would anyone be jealous of me? I'm in my fifties and don't have any social life to speak of!"

My mother seems surprised. "Why don't you go out more? I'm always telling you to!"

Diane grimaces. "Maybe because I spend my every waking hour taking care of you!"

Mom looks at her. "That's exactly why the others envy you."

"What do you mean?!" Diane replies, incredulous.

"It shows how good you are."

"They envy me for that?!"

Mom nods. "Yes. And because, like I said, you're the lucky one."

"How's Aunt Diane the lucky one, Mémère?" Ian asks.

"She caught the bouquet," Mom explains.

"That just goes to show that I'm a good catcher," Diane says dismissively.

Mom shakes her head. "No—it means that you're a good catch and that you'll get married soon."

Diane looks shocked. "Me?! Get married?! Why would on earth would I even want to?!"

"We all need somebody, Diane—either to care about or to care for us," Mom responds, as Ian and Carrie help her up off the sofa. "I won't be around all that much longer," she concludes bluntly.

My sister ignores Mom's last remark. "At my age, Mom," she replies, "Marriage isn't in the picture."

"Anyone can get married, dear," Mom says, taking hold of her walker. "You don't need to be anointed. What's more," she concludes, "you're smarter and bigger-hearted than the competition—much more so than the others in the wedding party." Then, recalling that Carrie was also in the bride's entourage, she adds, "With the possible exception of your sister."

"What about you? Can't you get married?" I ask Mom, mostly to keep Diane and Carrie from reminding her that they aren't sisters. "After all, you were a member of the wedding."

Mom looks as if she can't tell whether or not I'm teasing. "I'm out of the running," she says.

"Why?"

"As the eldest, you should know already," she replies, either recognizing me for her son or again mistaking me for her older brother.

"Maybe I should but I don't—so tell me."

"Because it's not good to marry in absentia," she responds dryly.

"It's worked for some," I insist, hoping I can get her to envision a future wherein she's among the living.

"Who?"

I think about this. "Like royalty. In the old days, lots of kings and queens got engaged and married by proxy before they'd ever met."

Mom looks at me skeptically. "Name some."

"Louis XVI and Marie-Antoinette," I reply before I realize this probably isn't the best example and start to wrack my brain for another. "Or Napoleon and his second wife—the one whose name I can never remember."

"Josephine?" Carrie offers.

I shake my head. "The woman he married after

her," I say. "Maybe Marie-Louise of Austria," I speculate, though I'm not sure a person so named ever existed.

Carrie Googles my answer on her iPhone. "That's right!" she exclaims, looking as amazed as I am that I guessed correctly.

"It doesn't matter," Mom says, her expression indicating she thinks we've taken leave of our senses.

"Why not?"

"Because, even if I'm historic," she replies archly. "I'm not royal."

"You are to me."

The look she gives me is piercing. "Of course, I am, Rob," she replies. "I'm your mother."

Suddenly, the sound of throbbing wingbeats and high-pitched avian cries fills the room as outside the hawk reappears and dives for the songbirds, who, flaring into flight, escape into the closest trees and bushes. Thwarted, it levels its trajectory, sweeps low and fast over the lawn and then, in one fluid movement, tilts its head upward and streaks into the sky, disappearing from the yard and our field of vision.

CHAPTER 44

By the Sea, by the Sea, by the Beautiful Sea

Long Take

"What's that?" Ian asks, pointing toward the horizon and a triangular white speck that's almost indistinguishable from the sparkling water before it and the bright morning sky beyond.

"A sailboat," I reply.

"Man!" he exclaims. "The crew must have set sail at dawn to be that far out this early!"

As it's already eighty degrees and, unusual for September in Maine, the forecast calls for ninety, I respond, "You almost have to when it's this warm."

"What do you mean?"

"On hot days, the weather sometimes changes around noon and thunderstorms come up fast. Then the swells can be huge and the sailing rough, so the earlier a boat sets out and returns, the better."

Sandpipers race ahead of us as we walk just beyond the reach of the waves. Nearby, a pretty woman in an aquamarine windbreaker, her silver hair whipped by the breeze, throws a ball over the sand. Her white Samoyed runs to retrieve it, and a flock of squatting gulls takes to the air. Otherwise, the beach is empty.

"Where is everybody?" Ian asks.

"At work," I answer. "In Boston, Montréal, and all the other places they come from."

"I didn't realize it would be this empty after Labor Day," he responds. "I don't often get a break from med school in the fall, so we've never come in September."

"No, we haven't," I agree, "and we wouldn't be here now, if Mémère hadn't insisted I visit."

"I thought she wanted Lucien to visit," he jokes, referring to Mom's increasing tendency to confuse me, her oldest son, with Lucien, her long-deceased and eldest brother.

"Of the two, I was the one who could make it—not that I'll be much help," I say, since, more and more, I feel powerless before Mom's growing disorientation.

"You do what you can," Ian replies, "which is all anyone can do."

A large, slow-moving Navy plane passes low over us. "I haven't seen anything like that here before!" Ian exclaims.

I watch the plane move up the beach then disappear over an outcrop. "I've never seen a plane like it here either," I respond. "But when I was a kid and we were living in our cottage at Hills Beach, we used to see fighter jets from the Pease Air Force base in New Hampshire all the time. We'd hear them, too—at least, when they broke the sound barrier. The sonic booms rattled the windows and shook the walls."

"Why did your parents sell the cottage?" Ian asks.

"Erosion," I reply. "Every year during hurricane season, part of its lot would be swept out to sea. Eventually, the waterline got so close to the house my father decided to get rid of the place. He sold it to a Massachusetts couple who spent a fortune moving it closer to the street and building a seawall. It's been sold a couple of times since—always for a lot more money than your pépère got for it!"

I look at my watch, a gold Bulova that was once my father's and find that, as often, it has stopped. "I need to take this to a jeweler when we get back to Cleveland," I tell Ian. "What time is it?" I ask. "I want to go to the bakery and pick up maple-cream donuts for your mémère on the way back."

Ian looks at his iPhone. "Almost seven."

"We'd better get going," I respond. "Those donuts sell out fast."

We leave the water's edge and cross the upper beach, which, unraked since Labor Day, is dotted with pebbles, shells, and bits of seaweed—the last blackened and brittle from being washed up onto the dry sand and exposed to the sun's heat.

Reaching the dune grass, we start down the

path to the road. The silver-haired woman and her Samoyed come up behind us. "Beautiful morning," she remarks.

"Sure is," I reply. "Nice dog."

"Thanks," she replies, looking at me. "You live around here?"

"Not now, but I was born in Biddeford, and grew up in Saco, the next town over."

"I grew up in Saco, too. Did you graduate from Thornton Academy?"

I nod. "Class of '73."

"Class of '74," she responds.

"Rob Allaire," I say.

"Antoinette Robertson," she replies, and we shake hands. "I knew I'd seen you before."

"I thought you looked familiar, too," I lie and add, "You haven't changed a bit," my standard remark with long-unseen schoolmates, regardless of gender. Ian looks askance.

"Were you such a charmer at Thornton?" Antoinette asks, smiling. "If you were, I'm sorry we didn't know each other better."

Embarrassed, I laugh. "Actually, I had a classmate whose last name was Robertson. She married a cousin of mine—Éric Fournier," I say. "Her first name was Esmée. Any relation?"

"Esmée is my sister!" Antoinette exclaims. "Were you at the wedding?! It was, here, on this beach, and I was the maid of honor!"

"Wasn't invited," I reply, shaking my head.

"I'm Éric's second cousin—only first cousins made the A-list."

Antoinette smiles wryly. "Too bad! If you'd been at the wedding, maybe you wouldn't have had to lie about remembering me," she chides, once more embarrassing me.

Her Samoyed nuzzles Ian's legs as we walk toward the road. I bend down to pet it. "Like I said before," I say, to change the subject, "he's a good-looking dog!"

"He's a 'she,'" Antoinette responds, still smiling, though now her smile is broad and unnuanced. "Her name's Pirta—'blizzard' in Inuit—for her white fur."

"My mistake," I apologize. "We had a male Pom with white fur. I guess that's why I thought she was male." I know this is a poor excuse but am unable to think of a better one. "We also had a female Shih-Tzu whose hair was black," I go on, hoping to build my case, though likely only digging myself in deeper. "They had nice coats," I conclude, "but not as nice as hers."

Pirta rises on her hind legs and licks Ian's face. Antoinette takes out a dog biscuit. "Look! A treat!" she coaxes. The dog leaves Ian's side, and Antoinette turns her attention back to me. "Pirta's brother was black but he passed away a while ago."

"That's too bad," Ian responds. "Both of our dogs died over the last few months."

"One in the spring and the other at the start of summer," I elaborate.

Antoinette gives me a pained look. "I'm so sorry!" she says sympathetically.

"Thanks," I reply. "It was hard, but what can you do?"

"Appreciate them while they're still with us," she replies, taking me aback by answering my rhetorical question.

"That's the only option, all right," I concur. Pirta noses around the granite boulders and the species roses that separate the dune grass from the roadside, the sea breeze ruffling her fur like gossamer. Antoinette motions to the dog, which returns and heels beside her. We're quiet for a few seconds, the sole sounds Pirta's panting, the wind blowing, and the waves crashing.

"Well, I should be on my way," Antoinette says and bends to leash Pirta. "Nice meeting you."

"Nice to meet you, also," I reply, abandoning all pretense of having remembered her from high school.

"Likewise," Ian says as he pets Pirta.

Antoinette smiles anew and, after shaking our hands, leaves the path and heads down the road, Pirta leading the way. At her vehicle, a bronze Jeep Cherokee, she turns and waves. "You guys have a lovely day!"

"You, too!" I respond.

As Ian and I arrive at our own car—my father's

1970s turquoise Cadillac convertible—Antoinette drives by and calls out, "Love the color!"

"Thanks!" I yell back.

Pirta barks.

Opening the car door, Ian says, "I miss our dogs."

"So do I. But that's life."

"Or its opposite," he responds, taking hold of the steering wheel.

I open the passenger door—surprised, as always, by its length and weight—and settle into the bucket seat, its cream-colored leather already hot to the touch from the sun.

"Want the top down?" Ian asks.

I consider the car's age. "What if we can't get it to close later? Start the air-conditioning instead."

"Will do," he says, turning a silver knob on the mahogany dash. "Which way to the bakery?"

"Up Pool Road to Main Street," I answer. "I'll show you."

He turns the key in the ignition. "You're the navigator."

"Right now, anyway," I say, again thinking of my inability to truly help Mom.

Biddeford's Main Street is not as busy as in summer, so we're able to park before the bakery's nineteenth-century storefront. "Do you want to come in?" I ask Ian, carefully opening the car door to keep it from hitting a planter of past-season flowers at curbside.

"No, thanks. I need to study," he answers and retrieves a medical textbook from the back seat.

"Up to you," I say.

A bell attached to the bakery's front door rings as I enter, and a few old men drinking coffee at a café table by the window glance my way. Then, in a mix of French and English, they resume a conversation about friends, former co-workers, and one-time classmates who are seriously ill or have recently passed.

Despite the multiple fans whirring under the room's stamped-tin ceiling, the place is hot because of the ovens, and perspiration rises on my forehead. As I wipe it away, a tan, middle-aged woman in a yellow halter top, her blond hair pulled into a ponytail by a matching scarf, emerges from the backroom. "What can I get for you?" she asks.

"Maple-cream donuts, if you have any," I reply, taking in the empty display cases.

She follows my gaze. "You're in luck—we just finished a batch," she informs me as seemingly on cue, a tow-headed adolescent pushes a cartful out of the kitchen. "How many would you like?" she asks, while he puts the donuts in the display case.

"A dozen, please," I tell her. Hearing, the young man places a carton on the counter and fills it with the requested number. He looks so much like her I ask if they're related.

She nods. "He's my son—we're all family here," she says, gesturing to an assortment of photos on the wall behind her, the largest of a man who also resembles her.

I point at it. "Your grandfather?" I ask, though I suspect she's too old for this to be the case.

Flattered, she smiles. "Actually, it's my dad, Bill Healy—he took over from my grandfather after the war, in the '40s." She closes the carton of donuts and ties a string around it. "Will there be anything else?" she asks. I shake my head. "That'll be nine dollars."

I hand her my credit card while studying the picture of her father, who looks familiar. "I think my dad might have known yours," I say.

"What was your dad's name?"

"Henri Allaire."

A look of recognition crosses her face. "Our dads did know each other."

"I thought so," I say. "I'm Rob."

"Maeve here," she replies. "I remember your father," she continues. "He'd drop by our beach house sometimes, and he and my dad would go for a swim or reminisce about their Navy days." She looks out the window at the Caddy. "Is that your dad's old car?"

I nod. "How'd you know?"

"From his visits," she answers, still smiling. "You don't see a lot of turquoise Cadillacs nowadays."

"There weren't all that many in the old days either," I comment. "Dad bought it because turquoise is my mom's favorite color."

Maeve's expression changes. "How is your mother? I haven't seen her in a while," she explains, swiping my credit card.

"She's doing all right," I say dishonestly while my receipt prints out. "But she forgets a lot of things and isn't always aware of what's going on around her."

Maeve looks at me knowingly. "My father's like that, too," she remarks. "Sometimes, he doesn't know what day it is or he mistakes me for my sister."

"Sounds familiar."

"Funny way to put it," Maeve responds, wrinkling her forehead. "Because these days there's not much Dad finds familiar." She sighs. "Some mornings he doesn't know where he is."

"My mom's getting to be like that—it's tough to watch," I admit, as Maeve returns my credit card and hands me my receipt. "But maybe it's not important that they know where they are or even who we are—not as important as knowing that we're there for them, anyway."

Maeve's smile returns. "And that we love them," she adds, as I sign the receipt and return it to her.

I signal my agreement and pick up the box of

donuts. "Nice to meet you," I say, turning away. "Have a good day."

"You, too," she responds. "Tell your mom that Maeve Healy says 'hi'!" she continues. "Whether or not she remembers me."

"Sure thing!"

I'm about to step out the door when one of the old men from the café table walks over to me. "Did you say your last name is Allaire?" he asks in heavily accented English.

"I did," I answer, wondering if he's a distant relation or another friend of my father's.

"Is your mother's first name Yvette and her maiden name Hébert?" he adds, sounding as if he knows the answer.

I nod.

He grins and says, "You look a lot like her!" This surprises me, because I resembled her in my youth but don't now, especially since my hair has thinned and gone gray.

"I'm Julien Grenier," he continues cheerfully. "Your mom was a friend of Madeleine's, my older sister, when they were at l'Academie Marie-Joseph. They'd go to the beach together," he pauses before adding. "Your mother was a real looker! I had a crush on her!"

I ignore the last. "Of course—Madeleine!" I respond with a smile, though I don't recall Mom often mentioning her. "How's she doing?"

"She died five years ago," he says, his grin gone.

"Desolé!" I reply, mortified. "Mes condoléances."

"Your mother didn't tell you?"

"I live in the Midwest and don't get here often," I explain. "She must've told me, and I forgot. Sorry."

"Pas de problême," he says, excusing my faux pas. "It happens to the best of us."

"To all of us," one of the other old men pipes up. Everybody laughs.

"I'll tell my mom I saw you. I know she'll be pleased," I say to Julien. "Bonne journée," I conclude, wishing him a good day.

"Et à vous aussi," he replies in kind, as I step out the door.

When I get in the car, Ian asks, "What took you so long?"

"A couple of people in there knew my parents, so we got to talking."

"This really is a small town—everybody knows everybody else," he says, guiding the Caddy away from the curb. "It's like a Russian novel."

"By Tolstoy?" I ask.

"Chekov," he counters.

Despite the light traffic, the trip back to Mom's takes longer than expected, in part because we get stuck behind a backhoe going below the speed limit. After a mile, Ian sighs. "It's illegal to drive heavy equipment down a public road! Why aren't the police doing something about this?"

"Like you said, it's a small town," I reply, teasing. "Maybe the police are back at the bakery eating donuts."

Ian rolls his eyes. "Where do you think that thing's headed?" he asks.

"Your Aunt Diane told me there's a subdevelopment being built a half mile or so away," I answer. "That must be its destination."

As we approach Mom's, he asks, "Should I put the car in the barn or will we be going out again?"

"Better put it away. It might rain later so we probably won't go anywhere," I answer and add, "And you know how particular your Aunt Diane can be."

On turning into the drive, however, we find two unfamiliar cars blocking the barn entrance. For an instant, I think they might belong to guests at another of the neighbors' pool parties, but, glancing next door, I see the pool is closed and covered for winter. "I wonder whose cars these are?" I say to Ian.

"Blueberry pickers?"

"Too late in the season," I reply, looking out at the field, where the fall grass has turned champagne yellow, a color interrupted only by the autumnal scarlet of an occasional sapling maple.

"Blackberry pickers?" he offers.

"Too late for those, too," I reply. "All that's left

by now is windfall, which only the birds harvest." As I say this, a swoop of swifts rises from the field grass, disturbed by a man and woman at the field's end, before the narrow band of woods that separates it from an adjacent subdivision. The man is writing on a clipboard and, incongruously, given the heat and setting, dressed in a suit. The woman—wearing khakis, a plaid shirt, and a construction helmet—is peering into a device on a tripod. After a moment, she, too, writes on a clipboard. I assume the cars in front of the barn are theirs.

Ian asks, "Who are they?"

"Maybe your Aunt Diane knows," I reply. "Whoever they are, she probably won't be happy about their parking in front of the barn, so we'll likely get an earful in a minute."

"No doubt about that," he says, as we leave the Caddy and enter the house, where the air-conditioning is already set low and the drapes drawn against the coming midday sun. Neither Diane nor Mom are around, so I set the baker's box on the kitchen counter and ask Ian to put the donuts on a platter.

"Where are the platters?" he asks.

"In the sideboard. Please use an everyday one."

As I cut the string on the baker's carton, Ian returns from the dining room and places a banquet-sized crystal platter on the counter. "I asked for an everyday platter," I remind him.

"This was the only one in the sideboard."

"Are you sure?" I ask. "There used to be a dozen formal and plain ones in it."

Diane enters the kitchen. "A dozen formal and plain what?"

"Platters," I answer. "Did you move them to a new place?"

"Sort of," she replies. "The neighbors borrowed the plain ones for their Labor Day pool party, and I sold most of the Waterford on eBay."

As the Waterford platters had been our grandmother's, I'm too shocked to respond. "Except for that one," she continues, referring to the large platter. "I couldn't find a big enough packing crate and, even if I had, it would have cost a fortune to ship it."

"Why are you selling stuff?" I ask, while Ian, placing the donuts on the platter, pretends not to listen.

"I'm only unloading things we don't use," she says, defensively. "It'll make it easier to empty the house after Mom passes." She sighs. "Anyway, like I explained the last time you visited, Mom doesn't have the kind of money she used to. And now that Carrie's taken a job in Boston, I need to hire people to help with the housework, yard, and shopping. The costs add up."

"Wasn't Carrie supposed to get some of her high-school friends to help you? That's what she told me she was going to do back in August."

"None of them were interested. It turns out that helping a middle-aged woman care for her ninety-one-year-old mother isn't an exciting job option for a young person," Diane replies caustically.

"So, Carrie just left you in the lurch?"

"You could say that, though I don't think that's quite how she saw it," Diane answers, blank-faced.

"What do you mean?"

"She offered to help me place Mom in a nursing home."

Though I'm deeply dismayed, I try not to show it. "And?" I ask to get a better take on Diane's reaction.

My sister looks at me as if I'm obtuse. "That might have to happen eventually," she says, "but you know how confused Mom is already! Why, some mornings, when she wakes up, she doesn't even recognize me or realize she's in her own bedroom! She'd go downhill fast in an institution!"

"I agree," I say with relief. "Staying put is best for her. But there's still the question of how to keep this place up and running. I told you in August if you and Mom need money to let me know, and I'll help."

Diane stares. "I appreciate the offer, but—like I said then—how much can you afford? I mean, you're partly retired and paying Ian's med school tuition."

I shrug uncomfortably. "I'll give as much as I can."

"I know, but you have enough expenses already," she replies. "Anyway, I've come up with a better solution than selling the family crystal on eBay."

"What's that?" I ask. "Have you discovered the picture in the upstairs hall is an original Monet, so you're auctioning it at Sotheby's?"

"Very funny," Diane replies. "I'm going to borrow money on the property—not the house and barn, just the field."

"So that's what those people in the field are doing!"

"What people?!" Diane asks.

"A lady surveyor and a guy in a suit," Ian answers, returning from the dining room, where he's placed the donuts on the table.

"The bank must have sent them!" Diane says. "I didn't know there'd be a site inspection today! I applied for the loan only last week!"

"Maybe it's because of all the local construction," Ian offers. "The real-estate market here seems like it's really hot!"

"It is," Diane replies. "But I'm not trying to get a mortgage, just an equity loan."

"Makes no difference," I tell her. "The higher the appraisal, the more the bank will pressure you to borrow. Maybe you should just sell the field outright. That would generate more cash, and you and Mom wouldn't have to pay interest."

Diane gives me a hard look. "You know Mom would go ballistic if the field were developed. Besides, we only need enough money to carry us through the rest of it."

"The rest of what?" Ian asks, then blushes, realizing the answer is the remainder of Mom's life. The back doorbell rings, and he looks out the window. "It's the people from the field."

"I'll find out what they want," Diane says. She turns to me. "Can you guys go upstairs to see if Mom's awake?"

"Of course," I reply.

As Ian and I go upstairs, he points to the picture in the second-floor hallway and asks, "Is that the original Monet?"

"More like a barely reasonable facsimile," I answer.

He smirks.

We go into Mom's bedroom, which remains, as ever, an exercise in chintz and Chippendale, its unlined drapes tightly but ineffectually drawn against the bright outdoor light.

Hearing me open the door, Mom, almost invisible amid the folds and billows of the comforter, stirs and asks, "Yes?"

"Good morning," I say, walking across the room with Ian behind me.

"Who is it?" she inquires.

I bend beside the bed so that she can see me clearly. "Oh my!" she exclaims. "I forgot you were visiting, Lucien!" Before I can correct her, she gestures at Ian and asks, "Who's this?"

"My son, Ian."

"Isn't your son's name David?" she replies. Not waiting for an answer, she continues, "It doesn't matter—I always enjoy seeing my nieces and nephews."

I ignore her confusion. "How are you feeling?"

"Tired."

"Didn't you sleep well?"

Still supine among the bedclothes, she gives me a strange look. "Sleep?! I'm worn out! I just got back from the beach!"

I'm not entirely surprised by this response because Diane has warned me that Mom's dreams have become so true-to-life that, on waking, she sometimes doesn't realize she's been dreaming. "Why was the beach tiring?" I ask, playing along. "It's usually relaxing."

"The beach was fine!" she responds. "It was getting home that was exhausting. We missed the last bus and had to walk the five miles back!"

"Who's 'we'?" Ian asks.

"Why, Madeleine, of course!"

As this is her first mention of Madeleine in decades, now, I'm truly surprised. "I just ran into her younger brother, Julien, in town!" I inform her.

"How could you have?! He was at the beach, too!" Mom exclaims. "He must have caught the bus without us—le petit niaiseux!" Raising her eyebrows, she adds, "He's so annoying—always undressing me with his eyes."

Ian turns red, as do I.

"What are you guys talking about?" Diane asks, entering the room.

"I was telling Lucien about my day at the beach," Mom replies. "And how tired I am because of walking home with Madeleine."

"That's a long walk," Diane allows, unfazed. "But you must feel refreshed after a good night's sleep," she continues, approaching the bed and motioning to me to help Mom sit up.

"Sleep?!" Mom asks, with a frown, while we turn her on the mattress and position her on the edge of the bed. "What are you talking about?! I told you—Madeleine and I just walked all the way back here from the beach!" she exclaims, while Ian puts slippers on her feet.

"Why'd you do that?" Diane asks, still nonplussed, as I slowly stand Mom up, and she helps her don her bathrobe.

"Because we missed the bus!" Mom replies, growing more agitated. "Why else?!"

Diane pulls the robe's sleeves down to Mom's wrists. "You were dreaming, Mom. There hasn't been bus service to the beach since the 1940s and you've hardly seen Madeleine since then."

My mother looks astonished. "I haven't? Why?!"

"I don't know," Diane replies, holding onto Mom while we turn her yet again so that she faces her walker. "Maybe because after you got married you were both too busy raising your families."

"That's terrible!" Mom declares. "Help me find Madeleine's number! I'm going to call her today!"

"You can't do that," Diane says, as we move Mom onto the walker.

Mom looks at her sternly. "Of course, I can!"

"No, you can't."

"Why not?" Mom demands, taking hold of the walker and starting to move forward.

"Because Madeleine died five years ago," Diane announces flatly.

Mom stops advancing and, wide-eyed, looks at my sister. "That isn't true!"

"Yes, it is."

"It can't be!" Mom insists. "I just went to the beach with her!"

"Listen, Mom," Diane begins patiently. "I told you a minute ago that you didn't go to the beach. You had a dream. It only seems real because you're just waking up."

"It wasn't a dream!" Mom responds. "And I can prove it! I took pictures!"

"You brought a camera to the beach?"

Mom shakes her head. "No! I used my phone!"

408

Diane and I smile, knowing that Mom has no idea how to answer a cellphone let alone take a picture with one.

"Let's not talk about this anymore, OK, Mom?" Diane says. "Rob—I mean, Lucien—bought your favorite maple-cream donuts."

"He did?" Mom asks with delight, as easily diverted as a child.

"Yes," Diane answers. "So, let's go into the bathroom and get you dressed for breakfast."

"All right," Mom replies docilely, letting Diane lead her out of the room.

As Ian and I return downstairs, he asks, "Should I start the coffee and tea, and take out the orange juice?"

"You'd better wait. Sometimes it takes Diane a while to dress your mémère."

"Aunt Diane has a lot to keep up with around here," Ian remarks as we enter the foyer.

"That's an understatement."

He looks at me thoughtfully. "I think I'll start getting breakfast ready, so she won't have to if she and Mémère come down early."

"On second thought," I say, "that's probably a good idea. Need help?"

He shakes his head. "I can handle it."

"OK," I say and walk into the study to check email messages on my laptop.

Half an hour later, hearing the rumble of the chairlift, Ian and I return to the front hall. There, we find Diane helping Mom, who's wearing a lilac-and-blue floral sundress, off the lift and onto her walker. "Sorry it took so long," Diane apologizes. "Mom wanted to look nice for you and Ian, so we had to go through all of her closets and choose just the right outfit for a muggy day in September." I half expect Diane to raise her eyebrows sardonically but, perhaps because she knows how important the proper attire is to Mom, she doesn't.

"How do I look, Lucien?" Mom asks me, while we start across the foyer.

"As pretty as a picture," I answer.

"You've always been charming."

"Maybe not always," Diane says.

"Now, Diane, be nice to Lucien," Mom scolds. "He and his son are our guests."

"I'm not talking about Lucien," Diane says, apparently tired of humoring her.

"What do you mean?" Mom asks.

"Never mind," Diane says, backing down.

We enter the dining room, and, seeing the platter of donuts, Mom gasps. "My favorites! Comme tu es gentil, Lucien!" she says thankfully.

"De rien," I reply, helping her into a chair while Ian lays down linen placemats and napkins and, since we're at the dining-room rather than the kitchen table, some sterling flatware and Lenox plates, which I'm pleased to discover Diane has yet to dispose of.

On her way to the refrigerator, Diane asks Mom, "What would you like to drink—milk or orange juice?"

Mom mulls this over. "Coffee."

"OK," Diane responds, "but just a demitasse so you don't get an upset stomach."

Mom doesn't reply. Instead, she turns to me. "The staff people at this hotel can be bossy but they set a nice table," she confides as she studies her place setting. "It's to my taste," she says and, examining the floral-patterned flatware and gold-trimmed China, adds, "and also somehow familiar."

I debate whether to let her go on thinking she's in a hotel or to tell her she's in her own house. I decide to do the latter. "That's because you're at home and all this is yours," I remark, as mildly as possible.

She looks at me. "How can you say such a thing, Lucien? You were with me when we checked in yesterday."

"He's not Lucien, Mom," Diane tells her, entering the dining room. "He's Rob, your oldest son. And this isn't a hotel. It's your home, where you've lived for almost sixty years," she says as she crosses the room to get the sugar from the sideboard.

Mom turns to me. "See what I mean about the staff?" she murmurs. "You have to keep these people busy so they don't become overfamiliar."

Raising a hand, she calls out to Diane as if to a waitress. "Oh, Miss—we'd like to move to a table by the pool," she informs her.

"OK, Mom," Diane begins firmly, "I'm telling you for the last time—you're not in a hotel restaurant." She places the sugar bowl on the table. "Also, there's no pool. This is the dining room of the house you and I live in. We have a patio, but we can't move out there right now because, Emmett, the landscape guy, is coming to mow the lawn and it'll be too noisy."

Mom stares, uncomprehending. However, when Ian enters from the kitchen, her puzzlement turns to surprise. "Ian! What are you doing here?!"

"I came with Dad," he says, gesturing in my direction.

Mom turns toward me. "Why didn't you tell me you'd brought him home to visit, Rob?!"

Caught off guard by the unexpected recognition, I stammer, "I thought I had—I must have forgotten!"

"You're getting so absent-minded I worry about you, Rob," she says with an indulgent smile.

After Diane has served Mom her coffee, she and Ian sit down across from us. "Well, Mom," Diane begins, as Mom sips her coffee. "Are you rested from your long walk home with Madeleine?"

Mom nods but looks embarrassed.

"Weren't you going to show us some beach pictures?" Diane asks.

"Maybe later," Mom responds evasively. "I left my phone in my room."

"I'll get it for you," Diane replies, rising.

"Don't bother," Mom tells her. "I know now that my trip to the beach was a dream," she says sheepishly. "Even if it hadn't been, I can't take pictures with my phone—I'm not sure I even have a phone," she admits. "I'm sorry I lied."

"You weren't lying, Mom," Diane reassures her. "You were confused, and I'm just trying to help you get back to reality."

My mother looks down. "I also know that, like most of the people I grew up with, Madeleine's gone," she adds, sadly. "I miss them all so much that now and then I imagine they're still around."

"That's understandable, Mom," Diane replies. "But isn't it better to live in the present than the past? In the here and now, you still have us."

Mom looks up at her, me, and Ian. "Of course, you're right," she says, without much conviction. "I have all of you." Her eyes well with tears, which roll down her cheeks.

I wipe the tears away with a napkin. "What would cheer you up, Mom?" I ask. "Would you like to go outside after Emmett's done mowing? He shouldn't be too long," I say, though, since the lawn is enormous, I know this isn't true. "We can sit on the patio for a bit and take in the sun."

Mom shrugs. "Instead, maybe we could drive out to Hills Beach and up Fort Hill to look at the ocean," she suggests. "That would take us by the cottage your dad and I lived in when we were first married, and you and Diane were toddlers."

Diane puts her cup down and, probably thinking of all that's entailed in taking Mom on an outing, looks at me. However, to my surprise, she says, "That's a great idea, Mom! You always like driving by our old house. But first you should eat your donut. You haven't even touched it."

Mom shakes her head. "I'm not hungry."

"Maple-cream donuts are your favorites, Mémère," Ian reminds her.

Mom regards her plate and the clear-glazed donut, the dollop of beige maple cream atop it perfectly swirled as a nautilus. "It's so pretty—it seems a shame to eat it."

"But that's its destiny," I coax her. "You'll disappoint it if you don't."

Her face breaks into a smile. "That's silly," she says with a chuckle. "But since you bought these, and I don't want to offend you, I'll try one." Picking up her knife and fork, she begins to cut and eat the donut in small bites.

Across the table, Diane breathes a sigh of relief. "If we're going to the beach, we need to put Mom's walker and wheelchair in the car," she says, standing up. "Ian, you stay here with Mémère. Rob, you come out and help me. I want to leave as soon as Mom finishes."

"Sure," I reply. Ian, who's wiping maple cream off Mom's face, nods his assent.

After Diane and I have retrieved the walker and wheelchair and gone out the backdoor, I see that the convertible's top is down. "Who lowered it?" I ask as a chime of house wrens rises from the field and flies above us.

"I did," she answers. "The bank guy is interested in buying the Caddy, so I lowered the top. But I didn't want him to know it's broken and has to be raised by hand, so I left it down, figuring we could close it after he left."

"That was risky," I say, as yet more house wrens pass low overhead and release droppings—which, fortunately, miss both us and the car. "We could have had a real mess to clean up," I remark, gesturing to the Caddy's interior.

"Life's full of risks," Diane answers. "This one was manageable—at least, with Windex."

"I wish every problem could be solved that simply," I reply, thinking of Mom's fractured memory. "Are you really going to sell it?" I ask, as I hoist the wheelchair and walker into the trunk.

"Like I told you in August, it costs $6,000 a month to keep this place going. While you were upstairs, I researched the Caddy's value. It would cover a quarter's expenses. If the bank guy doesn't want to pay that, I'll sell it at an antique car auction."

"But, after you've sold it, won't you just have to spend a lot to get the Lexus back on the road?"

"Fixing the Lexus will cost a fraction of what this car will net. It's simple arithmetic."

Our conversation's cut short when a 4x4 pickup truck with a trailer full of lawn equipment pulls into the drive. A scraggly haired man in overalls steps out of the truck's cab and waves at Diane, who waves back. "Hi Emmett," she says. "You're early."

"Couldn't wait to see you," he replies, as he walks up to us.

"Such a flirt," Diane responds, mugging.

Emmett smiles awkwardly then looks at me. "I don't think I've had the pleasure," he says as I shake his hand.

"This is my brother, Rob. He lives in Cleveland," Diane explains. "That's why you've never met him."

He sizes me up. "You two don't look a bit alike," he tells my sister.

"Because we're not," Diane replies unceremoniously.

"You're from Cleveland, huh?" Emmett says to me, running a hand through his unkempt hair. "How do you like living there?"

"It's OK," I reply, long inured to this question. "And nicer than you'd probably think. There're beautiful parks and suburbs, and a real sense of community. It's kind of a big small town."

Diane looks doubtful. "How can that be? Millions of people live in and around Cleveland—three times as many as in Maine! They can't all know one another!"

"Trust me," I say. "Just like here, in certain circles, everybody seems to know everybody else and everybody else's business, too! It's gotten worse with social media!"

"Lots of things have," Diane remarks. "When Carrie lived with us, I couldn't get her to stop checking her phone's Twitter and Instagram feeds long enough for her to take out the garbage."

"Maybe in a way that's what she was doing," I joke.

Emmett laughs while Diane frowns. "What really gets to me is . . ." she begins.

"Let me guess," I respond, "the distraction?"

"No!" she retorts. "The disconnection! Social media's almost as bad as dementia—half the time you don't know where you are and the other half you're focused on something that's probably not even real!"

"That's why, if I'm elected governor, I'll regulate social media," Emmett interjects. "What people see online needs to be credible."

"You're running for governor?" I ask, hoping my astonishment isn't apparent. "As a Democrat or Republican?"

"As an independent," Emmett replies.

"More like an eccentric," Diane mutters.

417

"What's that?" Emmett asks, cupping an ear.

"I said, 'It's a short ticket,' " she lies.

"Well, it's the guy at the top who matters," Emmett says and turns his attention back to me. "Too bad you're an out-of-stater and can't vote for governor. Maybe you can vote for me when I run for president."

"Maybe," I reply, since almost anything, no matter how implausible, is possible.

"Really?!" he asks.

"You can bet on it," I respond, not specifying whether the bet would be winning.

My mother emerges from the house in a floral sunhat that matches her dress, Ian holding her by the arm as they descend the back steps. "Need help?" Diane asks.

Mom shakes her head, no, but Ian mouths, yes, so we hurry to them.

"Hi there, Mrs. Allaire!" Emmett calls cheerily. "How are you doing?"

Mom peers in his direction and replies, "Fine, thank you," in the formal tone she employs with acquaintances she mistakes for strangers.

"It's Emmett," Diane tells her.

Though Mom's expression betrays no hint of recognition, she exclaims, "Oh, Emmett!" and turns to Diane. "You didn't tell me we were having company!"

"He's the lawn guy, Mom!" Diane hisses. "Both Rob and I mentioned he was coming."

"Rob? Is he visiting us like Lucien?"

"I meant Lucien," Diane amends, rolling with the punches.

"Oh," Mom says then smiles at me. "I'm so glad you're here, Lucien. When did you arrive?"

"Last night, after you'd gone to sleep," I say, though I arrived yesterday morning and had lunch and dinner with her.

Walking toward his equipment trailer, Emmett waves goodbye. "Glad to see you're doing all right, Mrs. Allaire!" he shouts. "Have a good day, OK?"

"You, too," Mom replies, as gaily as a schoolgirl to her latest crush.

"And don't forget to vote for me for governor!" he adds, climbing onto the mower.

"Of course!" she responds.

He starts the mower and, over the roar of its engine, yells, "Because I'll need every vote I can get!"

Mom laughs. "Such a nice, ambitious young man! You should get to know him better," she advises Diane.

Diane makes a face. "You mean like you think I ought to know Amos better?"

"Who's Amos?" Ian asks me in a whisper.

"A cousin who kept his racehorses in our field," I answer. "He's a Eucharistic minister who brought Communion to Mémère every Sunday until Diane told him to stop."

"Why?" Ian asks.

"He upset Mémère by telling her we're in the End Time and that the Second Coming is around the corner."

Ian, who was raised a Reform Jew, is shocked. "Why would he say a thing like that?"

"Probably because the local track is closing," I say with a laugh.

Ian shrugs. "Like I said before—this place is right out of a Russian novel."

"Chekov again?"

"More like Dostoevsky," he answers.

I wince but, since we've fallen behind Mom and sister, only say, "We'd better hurry."

Catching up with them, I hear Mom tell Diane, "Remember what I said to you the last time Lucien visited!"

"What was that?" Diane asks crossly, as we all head to the car.

"I won't be around forever, and someday you'll need someone to share this big house with," Mom answers. "Someone to care about and to care about you—like Emmett!" Looking at me, she adds, "You must recall my saying that, Lucien—you were in the room!"

Without comment, Diane opens one of the Caddy's doors for Mom. While she helps her into her seat, Ian turns to me. "Did that guy say he was running for public office?" he asks. "Does he have any political experience?"

"Not to my knowledge," Diane responds. "Probably not to his either."

"That isn't the whole story," I tell Ian. "He's also planning to run for president."

Ian gives me a sidelong glance, while Diane closes Mom's door with a decided thump.

"You can't fault a man for initiative! Especially not one you have a good chance of landing!" she tells Diane. "You should consider him as a potential beau!"

Diane harrumphs. "The only kinds of 'bows' I'm considering right now are the ones on a straitjacket."

"Diane!" Mom exclaims in horror, probably thinking Diane is alluding to plans for her.

"Seriously, Mom—I'm about fit to be tied!" Diane continues, walking to her side of the car and sitting in the driver's seat. "I'm sick of hearing about Emmett! Just drop it!"

Mom goes quiet. Then, either to show her compliance or because she's already forgotten the subject, she regards the Caddy's long, polished hood and declares, "Turquoise! My favorite color!"

"We know, Mom," Diane replies, starting the car and beginning to back it out. "That's why Dad bought it."

"That was so sweet of Henri!"

"Even though you've always complained it's way too big to drive?" Diane asks.

"It's the thought that counts," Mom replies blithely but then turns more serious. "It's been a long time since we visited your father in the nursing home," she says to Diane. "Is that where we're headed now?"

"We're going to the beach, Mémère," Ian says to be helpful.

"Oh," Mom responds. "But, since the nursing home is in the same direction, maybe we could drop in and see him on the way."

"Dad's dead, Mom," Diane says bluntly. "He passed away four years ago."

"He did?!" Mom cries, blanching. "Why wasn't I told! I didn't attend his funeral!"

"You were told," I explain. "And you were at his funeral—you just don't recall."

Mom grimaces. "I should remember!" she says, sounding confounded. "Why don't I?!"

" 'God works in mysterious ways,' " I remark. "Sometimes, He lets us forget things that are too upsetting."

This seems to calm her. "You're right, Lucien," she sayst. "Instead of complaining, I should be grateful for His graces, whatever their form."

Diane decelerates.

"What's wrong?" Mom asks.

"Traffic," Diane replies, as we pull up behind a bulldozer and an excavator—again, both crawling along at a snail's pace.

"Construction equipment!" Mom exclaims. "Is something being built nearby?"

"A new subdivision is going in a couple of miles up the road from us," Diane says, stretching both the distance and the truth.

Mom frowns. "So long as it isn't too close. We don't need more houses alongside our field."

Maybe because she's driving and can't face me to say, "I told you so," Diane turns her head in my direction and remarks, "Like I said."

" 'Like you said' what?" Mom asks.

"The subdivision is far away," Diane replies, prevaricating anew.

This seems to appease Mom, as she again goes silent. To change the topic, I comment on the weather. "Awfully hot out," I remark. "It's only mid-morning, and the day's already a scorcher."

"You think so, Lucien?" Mom responds. "Since I'm always cold, I can't judge." She turns to Diane, "Maybe you should bring the top up so your uncle's more comfortable."

The back of Diane's neck reddens. "The top's not easy to close right now, Mom."

"It doesn't close?!"

"Of course it does," Diane reassures her. "But I'd have to pull over and close it manually, which might make us late for the beach."

"So, the top's broken?" Mom asks worriedly.

"Not really," Diane replies. "The gears just

need grease—that's how Dad used to fix the problem," she adds, lying.

Mom reflects on this. "OK," she replies. "But what will we do about your Uncle Lucien being too hot?"

"I'm sure he won't melt!" Diane responds, her neck stiffening.

Grateful that I can't see Diane's expression, I say to Mom, "Don't worry about me," and almost add, "Mom," but, fortunately, remember not to.

"Don't be crazy, Lucien!" Mom replies. "I'll always worry about you! Anyway, I have the solution!" she declares brightly, opening the Caddy's glovebox, from which she retrieves a straw boater banded in blue and crimson. "You can wear a hat like I am!" she tells me, and then takes out two more—one a mangled yellow Panama, and the other a battered and broad-brimmed women's hat with an ivory satin ribbon. She gives me the boater and the Panama to Ian and attempts to put the third on Diane, who bristles.

"Please, Mom!" she exclaims, trying to push Mom's hand away. "We'll have an accident!"

"Oh, just try to have some fun, Diane!" Mom chides. "This might be the last day of good weather, and we're on our way to the beach—we should be having a party, not worrying!" she continues, placing the hat on Diane's head at a rakish angle. "There!" she exclaims, with satisfaction. "You look like Audrey Hepburn in *Breakfast at Tiffany's*!"

Diane peers into her visor's mirror. "Maybe if she'd spent the night in a dumpster!"

Mom giggles.

"I can't believe we're going downtown dressed like this!" Diane complains.

"We're going downtown?" Mom asks happily.

"We have to—it's on our way," Diane explains, without enthusiasm.

"I love downtown!" Mom announces. "Maybe we can do something exciting!"

"We're talking about downtown Saco!" Diane exclaims. "The last exciting thing that happened there was when the First Congregational Church burnt to the ground twenty years ago, and it wasn't any fun at all!"

"Don't be negative, Diane!" Mom cajoles. "I had lots of fun times downtown!"

"Name one!" Diane challenges.

Pondering the question, Mom replies, "VE-Day! The streets were full of soldiers and sailors on leave with their wives or girlfriends, all singing and dancing. That's how I met your father! He jumped out of a jeep and swept me off my feet."

Diane tilts her head in a signal of disbelief. "So, basically, you're saying he assaulted you," she observes, probing the thin veil of what sounds like a fantasy.

"Honestly, Diane!" Mom responds. "Sometimes you're so sour it takes my breath away!"

"If only that'd keep you from making up these wild stories," my sister mutters.

"How's that?" Mom asks.

To avert a response from Diane, I ask Mom. "Are you sure you aren't thinking of a scene from a movie?"

Beside me, Ian says, "One of my high-school history books had a picture of something like that happening in Times Square."

Mom shakes her head. "It happened right here, to your grandfather and me!" she tells him. "Your pépère took me by the hand, started to swing me this way and that, and the next thing I knew, I was putting one foot before the other and dancing with him as naturally as a bird takes flight."

This description, though dubious, is so joyful, that none of us contests it. Instead, Ian asks, "Was Pépère a soldier or a sailor?"

"Neither. He was an airman—one of those tall, good-looking 'boys in blue' who flew off 'into the wild blue yonder,' " she answers with a smile, referring to the US Air Force anthem.

"The 'boys in blue' are policemen, not airmen," Diane corrects her, "and Dad was only five-foot seven."

"Height's a matter of perspective!" Mom sniffs. "I'm five-foot four, so he seemed tall to me!"

"And Dad was in the Navy, not the Air Force," Diane continues, accurately.

Mom frowns. "I know what branch of the Armed Forces he was in better than you do," she responds. "I was alive then—you weren't!"

Sticking to my role as Lucien, I ask Mom, "Remember how when Rob was little and you were living at the beach, you taught him the Air Force anthem?"

"Do I remember?" she replies, beaming. "I could never forget, with the open sea and sky, and Rob looking so much like his father," she continues, causing Diane to harrumph since, of the two of us, she more strongly resembles him.

"Did you know you'd marry Pépère when you first met him?" Ian asks, to move the talk in a less volatile direction.

"No," Mom answers. "I realized that one evening when he took me to the ballroom on the Old Orchard Beach pier. The place was crowded, full of decommissioned servicemen and their dates dancing—so many that the building was swaying on its pilings." She pauses and looks out the car window. "I should've been afraid, but your grandfather led me across the dance floor so surely and firmly that, as we weaved in and out of the other dancers, I felt safe and protected. That's when I knew that if he proposed I'd accept." Mom stops talking.

"Did he ask you that night?" Ian inquires.

"Ask me what?" she asks, seeming to have lost the thread of the conversation.

"To marry him."

"Not then but a few months later," she replies, gathering her wits about her, "after a beautiful day at the beach. That afternoon, he looked so tan and handsome playing volleyball in his bathing suit and sunglasses that when he proposed in the evening, I said 'yes' on the spot."

Diane harrumphs again. "You and your obsession with sunglasses!" she tells Mom. "You've got so many, in so many different colors I'm surprised you aren't wearing any right now!"

"I'm not?!" Mom exclaims, as she lowers the windshield visor to view herself in its mirror. "You should have mentioned that earlier!" she scolds Diane, opening the glovebox and putting on a pair that match the blue of her floral hat. "It's so bright today, we should all be wearing sunglasses," she says and, without further ado, extracts a coral-pink pair that goes with Diane's blouse, a lemon-hued set that matches Ian's yellow tee, and another in shade of red that complements my claret-colored polo shirt. "I hate to make you two guys wear women's sunglasses," she complains, as she rummages through the glovebox, "but I can't seem to find your grandfather's Ray-Bans® in here."

"That's because you've squeezed so much other stuff into it," Diane tells her, as we put on our sunglasses. "Plus, you gave most of Dad's things to Goodwill a year after he passed."

Mom looks startled then melancholy, my father's death appearing to have again slipped her mind.

Continuing his effort to keep her focused on happy topics, Ian asks, "What dances did you and Pépère do back in the '40s?"

"Foxtrots and waltzes," she replies, "and, of course, the jitterbug!"

"That's a hard one," Ian says.

"Not really," Mom responds. "You just keep in step with your partner and in time with the music. Dancing's like swimming! You have to go with the flow. Sometimes, you move farther out with the tide and other times come back toward the shore. Life's the same!" she says, suddenly inspired. "You can fight the current and risk getting drowned by the undertow or let yourself be swept away and be happy wherever you end up!"

"You've got to be a good swimmer to beat the tides around here," Diane wisecracks.

Mom looks at her.

"It can be done, though," I say, conciliatorily. "And more easily than those old dances with their fancy footwork."

"What are you talking about, Lucien?!" Mom asks. "You did all those dances! You must remember what it's like to just let yourself go and be led!"

Diane snorts. "He's a man, Mom! Men lead, they don't follow!" she corrects her. "Whether or not women like it!"

"Bossy women tried to lead back then, just like they do now," Mom replies pointedly.

Diane glares at her but Mom's attention remains fixed on me. "Haven't you ever been led, Lucien?" she asks.

"While dancing or in life?"

"Your pick," she answers coyly.

Dancing seems the simpler choice. "Just once—at a dinner dance with a client's staff in Boston."

"Was your partner nice and pretty?" Mom asks.

I weigh my response. "She was pleasant enough—but tall with broad shoulders and muscular calves. She pulled me through the bossa nova like a quarterback trying to make a pass."

"Did she make a pass?" Mom asks, aghast.

"Fortunately, no."

"That's good!" Mom replies in relief. "Women shouldn't make passes at . . ." she begins before coming up with, "men who've got spouses."

Diane snorts again. "Are you sure you don't mean 'at men wearing sunglasses'?"

"Sometimes, Diane, you make no sense whatsoever!" Mom answers. "Why would Lucien have worn sunglasses while doing the bossa nova?! He could have tripped and hurt himself!"

Diane doesn't answer but her face reddens.

"Wasn't that the woman you later found out was trans?" Ian asks softly, so Diane and Mom won't hear.

I nod.

"Talk about letting life lead you where it might," he remarks.

"Or taking from you what it will," I say back.

He flinches.

"What's that?" Diane asks.

Because we're approaching an intersection, I ask, "Shouldn't we be taking a right up ahead?"

"I've lived here all my life—I think I know the best way into town!" she reproaches me.

"Don't be so sure," Mom cautions. "Lucien's been alive longer than you—he might know better. Plus, one must respect one's elders!"

"Luckily for you!" Diane retorts but to my surprise, follows my suggestion and turns the car right. As she does, some kids on the corner point and wave, which sometimes happens because of the Caddy's age and color, but that I suspect today is more likely due to our silly hats and sunglasses.

Mom, serene as the Queen being chauffeured from Buckingham Palace to Windsor Castle, waves back and says, "What nice young people."

"More like hecklers," Diane contradicts.

"Pardon?" Mom asks.

"She said, 'This car draws a lot of attention,'" I lie.

"That's true, I guess," Mom allows. "I'm just glad it seems to make people happy."

"If only!" Diane murmurs as we enter downtown Saco where—the summer's tourists gone and fall foliage tours yet to arrive—it's quiet, with little foot or car traffic passing before its old Colonial and Federal mansions.

"I remember this place when it was full of music and people singing and dancing," Mom says.

"So you've mentioned," Diane reminds her, sounding irritated.

A horn honks in the opposing lane. I turn to discover Antoinette Robertson waving with one hand and holding onto her Jeep's steering wheel with the other, Pirta wagging her tail beside her.

"You know her?" Diane asks, grimacing.

Before I can reply, Antoinette stops the Jeep, and seriously or joking, calls out, "Love the hat—and the sunglasses that match your shirt!"

"An accident!" I call back.

"Yeah—of biology or fate," Diane says wryly, braking the Caddy.

"Sorry?" Antoinette asks.

"She said, 'you've got good taste,'" I explain, not sure that in her place I'd believe this.

Regardless, she smiles broadly. "Be that as it may, I love the getups and the car!" she says to all of us, and as Pirta barks, waves goodbye and drives away.

"Such a pleasant young woman," Mom remarks, "and what a beautiful white dog!"

"Young?! That chick's at least as old as Rob!" Diane responds. "And that dog probably went white from fright!"

"What do you mean?" Mom demands.

"When it saw these crazy colors you made us wear!" Diane responds.

"Don't be foolish, Diane—dogs are colorblind! Besides, what's this got to do with Rob?"

"I meant Lucien," Diane says, amending her previous statement.

At the end of Saco's Main Street, we drive downhill, past the town's Victorian mills, long-since converted into boutiques, restaurants, and condominiums, and go over the river into neighboring Biddeford, whose mills of the same era remain decrepit and abandoned—as if we'd crossed the Styx and gone from the bright surface world into dim Hades.

I say something to this effect, and Mom turns, scowling. "Come on, Lucien—it's not that bad! There are stores and places to eat here, too—anyway, when we were young, these mills offered people a good living! Those were the days!"

"You think so, huh?" Diane asks her. "Actually, most of the folks who worked in the mills back then made so little they had to live in rundown and pretty cramped tenements—even when they had more kids than days in the week. Honestly,

Mom, you've got to stop confusing what you cook up with what really happened!"

"Like I said before," Mom replies curtly, "I was alive then, you weren't!" Suddenly, however, her mood changes. "Aren't we near the bakery where Lucien bought the donuts?" she asks Diane brightly.

Diane nods, stony faced.

"I'd like to go by it," Mom continues. Diane frowns but drives the car toward the bakery. As we approach, Mom says, "Let's drop in and get more donuts!"

Diane turns and looks at her so long and hard it's a small miracle we don't have an accident. "In case you haven't noticed, Mom, getting you in and out of this ocean liner of a car isn't exactly easy! Anyway, we've got plenty of donuts at home already!"

"But I want to see Madeleine's brother, Julien!" Mom protests. "Lucien ran into him there this morning!" By chance, at that moment, a dark-haired young man clad in black emerges from the bakery and walks briskly down the sidewalk in the opposite direction from us. "There he is!" Mom exclaims. "Julien, you stinker!" she calls. "Why'd you make me and Madeleine walk home alone from the beach!" Fortunately, the young man, already a block away, doesn't hear.

"Mom!" Diane shouts. "Julien is almost your

age! That guy's young enough to be your grandson—maybe even your great-grandson!"

Mom turns toward Diane with an agility that belies her feeble condition. "If I say he's Madeleine's brother, he's Madeleine's brother!" she retorts. "I knew Julien, you didn't! I was alive then, you weren't!"

"Keep this up, and you might not be alive much longer!" Diane replies fiercely, again taking her eyes off the road to face her, which makes me think that, if their argument goes on much longer, none of us might be either.

"Follow him!" Mom commands.

"What?!" Diane asks.

"You heard me!" Mom declares, her voice cold enough to freeze bathwater.

Diane relents and follows him, but because we have to stop for a red light, the young man outdistances us. When the light changes and we catch up with him at l'Église St. Joseph, the church where Mom was baptized and married, he climbs its granite steps, opens the arched main doors, and disappears behind them.

"Was Julien a priest, by chance?" Diane asks Mom dryly.

"He was an altar boy but I don't think he went to seminary," Mom replies, raising a hand to her chin. "Oh well, what does it matter? Even if that young man isn't Julien, let's go inside!" she continues. "This church is where my life began!

And it's practically as breathtaking as the Sistine Chapel!"

This is more than Diane can stand. "First of all," she starts, "your life began when you were born—which wasn't here—and, secondly, this church is nothing special!"

"Yes, it is!" Mom protests. "It's got beautiful, vaulted ceilings decorated with images of the Holy Trinity and the saints reaching out to one another amid clouds of angels."

"None of which Michelangelo painted!" Diane retorts. "St. Joseph's was built in the late nineteenth century, so that stuff is just stencil work from a factory!"

"Whatever it was, it's not there now because the church was renovated in the '70s," I tell them. Then, to end their discussion, I ask, "Don't we need to take the next left to get to the beach?" which is indeed the case. Neither reply but Diane activates the left-turn signal, taking the corner sharply.

Mom turns around and looks at me. "On second thought, even though those red sunglasses match your shirt, you look ridiculous in them, Lucien," she says, and after rummaging through her purse, hands me a pair of large black ones.

"Aren't these yours?" I ask. "I think you wore them the day we drove out to the breakwater at Camp Ellis a few years back." Then, recalling that this was where she and my father were first engaged, I regret my words. However, as her demeanor doesn't change, I presume she no longer remembers.

"They're mine," Mom confirms. "But, since I'm not in the habit of carrying men's sunglasses with me, they'll have to do. Go ahead—put them on! I want to see how they fit!"

I comply, but in the process dislodge my tribanded straw boater, which flies out of the car and onto the street, where it lies like a piece of brightly striped roadkill.

"Those sunglasses make you look a little like Jackie O!" Mom exclaims.

"Don't you mean Clark Gable or Cary Grant?" I respond but realize that, given my average looks and now disheveled gray hair, this is unlikely.

"For sure not!" Diane declares, laughing. "But you don't look much like Jackie O either!"

"You don't think so?" Mom asks her.

"No," Diane responds.

"Why not?"

"For one, Jackie's hair was brown and usually so lacquered a hurricane couldn't have moved it!" Diane answers. "More importantly, though, he's not wearing a pillbox hat!" she adds with another laugh.

"Or any kind of hat," I amend, as I try to keep my hair out of my face.

Mom peers into the glovebox. "We're out of hats, but this should do the trick," she says, retrieving a sheer red scarf. "Wear it like a kerchief," she directs. "It'll keep your hair down and help with the Jackie O look."

Far from pleased, I nonetheless humor her and try to wrap the scarf around my head and tie it under my chin. But because of the wind I can't, so it falls to my neck, its far ends caught in a cross draft and spiraling upward like swirls of smoke then slipping sleekly back like streamline marks.

Mom looks astounded. "That reminds me of the scene in *Funny Face* where Audrey Hepburn comes down the stairs in front of the Louvre's Winged Victory statue!"

At the steering wheel, nearly large enough for a cabin cruiser, Diane scoffs. "Enough with the celebrity references, OK?!"

"Sure," Mom replies, not sounding like she means it. "You have to wear this, though," she tells her and removes a pink chiffon scarf from the glovebox. I can't see Diane's face but presume she's grimacing. Still, she takes the scarf and, with one hand, somehow manages to get it around her neck.

As deftly as a magician pulling handkerchiefs from her sleeve, Mom next takes a purple polyester and then a rainbow-colored silk scarf from the glovebox, giving the first to Ian and putting on the second herself. As she does, more scarves of various hues slip out of the box and pool at her feet like a puddle of polychromatic paint. "How come you have so many?" I ask.

"You ought to know," Diane responds. "Remember all the ones you brought home from business trips and gave to me and Mom as presents? This is their summer home."

"You're telling me that the Gucci and Hermès scarves I gave you spend the summer in a hot glovebox?! That's 'cruel and unusual punishment!' " I tease. "Especially for works of art."

"Works of art?!" Diane retorts. "Most of these are tourist souvenirs or tradeshow giveaways! I mean yours reads, 'Semicon China 2011' and Ian's is decorated with a sequined Eiffel Tower that's more sparkly than the real one on Bastille Day!"

I start laughing, and then everyone does—Mom, the most avidly.

Diane turns and looks at her. "The things we have to do to make you happy!"

"How grumpy you can be!" Mom retaliates. "I just want everybody to have fun!"

"And make us look like a bunch of clowns in a toy car!" Diane responds.

"The Caddy's way too big for anyone to think that!" Mom counters with another laugh.

We turn onto the road to the beach and two teenage girls at a crosswalk wave. "Way to go!" one yells.

"See?" Mom says to Diane. "People know we're just having a good time!"

"Or think we've escaped from a loony bin," Diane grumbles in reply.

"What did you say?"

Diane doesn't answer but instead steps on the gas, causing our scarves to ripple backwards like ship pennants in a headwind.

"Maybe we should play some music," Ian says nervously.

"Great suggestion!" I say and reach over the front seat to switch on the radio. Mom, however, stops me.

"Quelle bonne idée!" she exclaims, praising Ian's suggestion as she turns the knob herself and causes Bobby Darin's rendition of "Beyond the Sea" to emanate from the speakers.

"This is too much of a coincidence!" Ian exclaims.

"It's not one at all," Diane calls back to him over the music. "It's a cassette your grandmother likes to listen to when we drive to the beach."

Mom turns up the volume. Somewhere, someone he loves waits on a far shore and watches the ships set sail, Darin croons, to swelling violins so strong and lush they break through the sound of the wind as we speed toward the ocean.

Since we're approaching a speed trap, Diane decelerates and lowers the volume.

"Why did you do that?!" Mom asks.

"The cops have the next intersection staked out—I don't want to draw their attention!" Then, glancing at her scarf and Mom's blowing wildly upward, she frowns and adds, "At least, any more than we will already!"

"You worry too much!" Mom responds, extending her hand toward the volume control.

"Don't you dare!" Diane growls at her and clicks off the cassette player.

"Spoilsport!" Mom retorts, pursing her lips. "I want to hear the song!"

Before Diane can reply, I interject, "And you will—I'll sing it!"

"Would you, Lucien?!" Mom replies sprightly.

I nod.

"Could you sing the French version by Charles Trenet? The one we used to listen to on the record player when we were in high school?" she asks, as eagerly as if still a swooning adolescent.

"Bien sûr!" I reply.

Ian, incredulous, asks me, "You know the words?!"

"I bought the CD a while back," I whisper. "Maybe I'll remember them. Even if I have to fudge a few, she might not notice."

To my amazement, when I start, I easily recall the first couple of verses about the silvered, dancing sea but after that I switch the lines about the water's shifting reflections beneath the rain and the summer sky's infinite expanse of azure and, to my dismay, skip others altogether. Thankfully, I manage to end the song on the correct final lyric about the ocean penetrating one's heart forever.

Mom clasps her hands happily. "The ocean really did pierce my heart forever," she announces. "And you still carry a tune as well as you did at our réveillons de Noël, Lucien!" she tells me—though, to my recollection, Lucien was usually too tipsy to stand straight, let alone sing, at our Christmas Eve gatherings. "C'etait merveilleux—truly marvelous!"

"I'll tell you what might not be so merveilleux," Diane says as we arrive at the intersection and make a left turn toward the beach. "When the azure of this summer sky darkens with rain."

"You understood the song's lyrics?!" Ian exclaims, gaping. "I thought you couldn't speak French!"

"If you hear it enough, you pick up a few words," Diane replies.

"I always thought you understood more than you let on," I tell her.

"I need a few tricks up my sleeve to deal with you two," she answers, gesturing to me and Mom.

"Very funny—but why're you talking about rain?" I ask, since the sky above us is an unblemished robin's egg blue—flawless as the vault of a bell jar and bright as the firmament in a Botticelli painting.

Diane laughs. "Those thunderheads—you

dunderhead!" she replies, pointing to a cloudbank in the distance, where the sky has indeed gone from beryl to indigo blue.

"Looks like the weather's changing," I concur.

"I thought it would," Diane replies. "That's why I wanted to get out early—the forecast calls for midday squalls."

"Really!" Mom cries. "But the car top's broken!" she cries, now as alarmed as only moments earlier she'd been carefree. "We'll be soaked and get pneumonia! How could you've let this happen?!"

"Let what happen?" Diane asks.

"The top get broken!"

Diane frowns. "Of everything I tell you that you conveniently 'forget,' this is the one thing you remember?!"

"What if we're hit by lightning?!" Mom continues hysterically. "We could be fried to a crisp, with only our burnt-out skeletons left of us!"

"That only happens in cartoons!" Diane replies impatiently. "Anyway, rubber doesn't conduct electricity and, since the Caddy's tires are big enough for a semi, there's zero chance we'll be electrocuted!"

My mother looks unconvinced.

"Don't worry, Mom!" I reassure her. "If it looks like rain, we'll bring the top down manually. Nobody'll be killed—we won't even get wet!"

This calms her, and she is quiet as we pass

the University of New England and proceed to Hills Beach, a taper of land nearly as thin as the horizon between sky and water, with a salt marsh to one side and an ocean bay to the other. While we drive head-on into the approaching darkness, fast-moving clouds intermittently hide and reveal the sun, rendering the landscape dim then bright, like theater lights flashing before the start of a performance.

To distract Mom, Diane switches on the radio and tunes it to an all-standards station. Between spates of static, "Somewhere Over the Rainbow" surges from the speakers as Judy Garland sings about wishing on stars and flying high above the rooftops to land someplace where troubles melt like sugary treats and storm clouds fade behind her. Scattered raindrops blot the windshield, while in plaintive, increasingly tremulous tones Judy asks why she can't happily fly, birdlike, over the rainbow to its other side.

"I can't answer that," Diane says. "But I'm pretty sure we won't be seeing rainbows today." No one contradicts her.

When we near our old house, a gust of wind blows into the car, bringing a fresh volley of raindrops, but neither deters Mom. "Pull into the drive! I want to visit the place!"

"What?!" Diane exclaims, "Don't you want to go to Fort Hill and look at the Atlantic? If there's a cloudburst, we won't be able to see a thing! It won't even be worth going!"

Mom shrugs off Diane's concern. "The storm is still a ways off. These guys are just advance scouts," she pronounces, brushing raindrops from her arms.

This throws Diane into a tizzy. "OK, so even if that's true—which it's not—what if the owners of our old house are home!?"

"They won't be," Mom says dismissively. "Summer people never stay past August—that's why they're called 'summer people.'"

Diane flushes red but turns into our old drive and parks on a sandy patch of ground by the garage. Mom asks Diane, "Remember when you and Rob pretended to be pirates and buried my turquoise necklace and earrings here? We never found them afterward."

"Rob played the pirate, and he buried them!" Diane snorts. "I just played the princess he stole them from!"

"You were each to blame!" Mom replies. She looks back at me. "Isn't that right, Lucien—didn't they both bury them?"

I shrug my shoulders. "Not sure," I reply, since I truly can't recall.

"That's understandable," Mom says to me kindly. "You bought me a lot of jewelry in the Mediterranean during the war. I can't expect you to remember what happened to every last piece."

She turns back to Diane, her tone once more accusatory. "You and Rob were always playing with my things! You, pretending to be a socialite and your brother, a jewel thief! So many of the beautiful enamel bracelets and cabochon necklaces Lucien gave me got lost or ruined!" she concludes dolefully.

"That was cheap Turkish market crap that probably deserved to be broken!" Diane declares. "I know! I was a professional jewelry buyer!" she goes on. "And, besides, Lucien didn't give you those! You got them from your youngest brother, Arnaud—the first of your family to pass and the one with the worst taste!"

"Say nothing but good of the dead," Mom replies.

"I'll keep that in mind when you've moved on to the great Turkish bazaar in the sky!" Diane replies acidly.

"What makes you think I'll leave this Earth before you do," Mom retorts.

Diane glowers. "Really, Mom, sometimes . . ."

"Sometimes what?"

Unexpectedly, Diane's expression brightens. "Sometimes, I get lucky!" she exclaims, breaking into a smile. "I just remembered—we found your jewelry a week after we'd buried it!"

My mother shakes her head. "That isn't true! If you did, where is it now?!"

Diane reaches over Mom's knees and removes

yet more scarves and sunglasses from the glovebox. Then she pulls out a tangle of jewelry—some made of resin studded with faux pearls and some of gold set with semiprecious gemstones—in the middle of which are the turquoise earrings and necklace.

Mom gasps.

"That glovebox is like Ali Baba's cave!" I say.

"Or a magician's top hat," Ian says. "What'll come out of it next—a rabbit or a dove?"

"The rabbit hopped away," Diane deadpans. "And the dove's in the field eating the last of the blueberries and blackberries."

Mom turns over the morass of jewelry and, with surprisingly little effort, extracts the turquoise necklace. "Are you sure this is the same piece?" she asks, holding it up. "It isn't how I remember it."

"Not much is," Diane says.

"I've never pretended to be perfect," Mom says with a sigh.

"Good thing," Diane says.

Mom's face reddens. "No one's right all the time."

"Some of us, not even much of the time," Diane gibes.

"Don't be so hard on yourself," Mom responds, as she attempts to put on the necklace.

"Let me do that," I offer.

"C'est gentil, Lucien," she says, pulling the

two ends of the necklace towards the back of her neck and lowering her head so I can help clasp it.

"Pas de problème, Mom," I reply reflexively, dismissing her praise before I realize I shouldn't have called her that.

She looks startled, but perhaps the surroundings have jarred her memory, because she simply replies, "That's kind of you, Rob."

"Seen enough?" Diane asks her, gesturing at our former home with one hand and turning the key in the ignition with the other.

"No!" Mom declares. "I want to walk to the house!"

The wind rustles the leaves of a maple at the yard's end, twisting their pale backsides upwards and giving them the aspect of panicked faces.

"We don't have time for that!" Diane says. "It's going to pour—maybe even hail—any minute! If you want to make it to Fort Hill, we need to leave this instant!"

Mom shakes her head. "I want to see the house up close!" she insists, her multi-colored scarf billowing like an animate spectrum. "It's where your dad and I began our family!"

"OK!" Diane relents angrily. "It'll take a few minutes to close the cartop anyway. Ian can help me with that while Rob takes you up to the house! But you'd better be fast about it!"

"Aye-aye, ma capitaine!" Mom replies with a shaky salute, which Diane ignores.

The wind rising, I help Mom out of the car and onto her walker and we make our way to the side porch—me, gripping the walker with one hand and her with the other, while she clings to me.

Once on the porch—which is smaller than I recall—Mom takes hold of her walker and we slowly head to the windows to look inside. The living room, once decorated with white wicker, pastel rugs, and floral watercolors, is now filled with teak, glass, and brushed-steel furniture more suited to an urban condo than to a seaside cottage. She sighs.

"What are you thinking?" I ask, hoping that whatever it is, I can respond in a way that will make her feel better.

"I'm just remembering when we lived here, when you and Diane were little," she replies. "We had such lovely mornings on the beach. But in the afternoons, I'd have to run around like a madwoman to get the cooking and cleaning done before your dad came home for supper." She sighs anew. "Your father was devoted but he could be a terror if he wanted."

As she gazes into the room, the wind-blown clouds briefly part and her pensive expression is reflected in the window glass.

"You two had some great times in this house, though, didn't you?" I ask, as Ian, finished helping Diane close the Caddy's roof, joins us.

Mom's expression lightens. "Yes," she

acknowledges, turning from the window. "We had lots of friends in the neighborhood—people from the university. You could rely on them for anything," she says with a smile. "Plus, they threw great parties!" Her smile vanishing, she concludes, "They're all gone now."

"They moved away?" Ian inquires.

"They passed away," she corrects him.

"All of them?"

Mom nods. "These days, Ian, I know many more dead than living. Everything changes," she says, contemplating her knotted, wrinkled hands, once as smooth as fine China.

I think but don't say, "Except the dead."

As the clouds re-close and the sky again darkens, Diane waves at us from the Caddy. "You'd better hurry back before it rains cats and dogs!"

"Êtes-vous prête à partir?" I ask Mom. "Because we really should be going."

"Oui," she replies. "There's nothing left to see here."

We go down the porch stairs, Ian descending in front of Mom and clutching her walker, and me behind, holding her shoulders. As we cross the rain-spotted drive, blasts of wind from the bay and marsh cut through it, causing my scarf and Ian's to flutter and Mom's to blow off entirely.

"Mon écharpe!" she cries as her multicolored

scarf shoots skyward then catches and hangs amid the maple's branches like a swathe of shimmering bunting or striated ribbon candy.

"Guess I was wrong about not seeing a rainbow today," Diane quips, while Ian and I help Mom into the car.

"Please get it for me, Rob!" Mom implores.

"There's no time!" Diane says, "It's going to rain to beat the band any second!"

"But I might catch cold!" Mom protests, as Ian and I hurry into the back seat.

"Here!" Diane replies, plucking a purple scarf decorated with an image of Caesar's Palace from the fabric piled at Mom's feet. "Put this on! It'll protect you from the drafts."

Mom regards the scarf disdainfully. "This awful thing! It'll make me look trashy!"

On the radio, the standards station is playing an Ella Fitzgerald version of "The Lady is a Tramp." Between bursts of static that break through her silken voice like a tear rends satin, Ella sings about wanting to wander free with the wind tousling her hair rather than be out on the town, gambling with the beau monde and slumming bedecked in jewels and furs.

"See?" Diane asks. "A true lady doesn't have to worry about what she looks like or what people might think—and you're the real article if ever there was one."

Mom shakes her head. "Wearing this is out of

the question!" she protests, letting the purple scarf fall back onto the floor.

"No problem," Diane replies, unfazed, as she opens the glovebox and more scarves tumble out. "Pick a scarf, any scarf!" she exhorts. "We've got a million of 'em!" Then, picking up a length of gold and magenta silk signed Ferragamo, she wraps it around Mom's neck.

On the radio, between spurts of dissonance, Ella intones a line about California being gloomy and East Coast beaches sublime.

"Speaking of which," Diane says, as the wind grows stronger, thrashing the maple and releasing Mom's scarf, "we'd better get out of here while we can!"

"Diane's right! If we don't leave right now, we won't be seeing any kind of beach—sublime or otherwise!" I tell Mom, as I watch her scarf now afloat above the yard, expand and contract like a Bird of Paradise moving its wings in flight.

Mom, following her scarf's disappearance over the marsh, nods her assent.

As Diane backs the car out onto the street, the radio crackles loudly one last time and the standards station gives way to uninterrupted noise.

"What happened?!" Ian asks.

"Probably a lightning strike on the station's transmitter," I answer.

"Just as well—I, wasn't looking forward to

hearing 'Stormy Weather,' " Diane wisecracks.

Ian and I laugh. Mom doesn't.

The closer we get to Fort Hill, the dimmer the light and the denser the clouds. Looking out, I see abandoned yellow and white parasols on the beach, some closed tight as hibiscus at night and others open and vibrating as if about to alight. When we start up the hill, a lightning bolt fragments the dark sky like an earthquake fissuring the frescoes of a Renaissance rotunda or fracturing a skyscraper's facade before knocking the building asunder. While the rain descends in heavy sheets, hitting the car as hard as sleet, I think of its impact on the sandy beach, the circular or contorted shapes it will leave in its wake, as transient as the traces of pebbles swept away by the waves' long reach or the lifelike shades of the departed that nightly disturb Mom's sleep.

A wind blast causes the Caddy to shudder then shake.

"We'd better start back!" Diane exclaims. "This isn't safe, and we can't see the ocean—or much of anything else!" As she turns the Caddy around, however, water streams in through the seams of its canvas roof and shoots out of the defroster and air-conditioning vents. Mom shrieks. The lights and engine go dead and, as Diane tries to control the now lifeless power brakes and steering, we silently slide down the incline toward a bend at the road's bottom, beyond which lies only rough, open water.

Mom begins to weep. I reach over the front seat and place my hands on her shoulders. "Ça va bien aller! It'll be all right—you'll see," I say, as reassuringly as I can manage.

"Rob's right—it'll be OK!" Diane echoes.

Then, as abruptly as it began, the rain stops. Bearing down on the Caddy's brakes and gripping its steering wheel as tightly as a boat pilot tends a ship's tiller, Diane guides the car onto the berm and halts it by a boulder without its suffering a scrape or scratch.

Ian is shaken. "Wow! How'd you manage that?" he asks.

Looking none too steady herself, Diane laughs. "I learned to helm barges as a midshipman at Maine Maritime."

"When was that?!"

"Before I worked in retail."

"Really!?" Ian asks.

"Yeah," she continues, pokerfaced. "The same year your father left the Air Force Academy to go to business school. His MBA wasn't help much today, though—proving that it's better to have good sea legs than your head in the clouds!"

"Are you putting me on about Maine Maritime and the Air Force Academy?!" Ian asks.

"Of course!" Diane replies. "We're just lucky the steering and brakes held without power!"

"But not without a lot of work from you," I remark.

"That's why I go the gym!" she smirks.

"Still think you'll get your asking price for this tub?" I ask, using my scarf to wipe the water off Mom's shoulders.

"If I sell it on a sunny day," Diane answers smiling.

"Sell what?" Mom asks as I pass the scarf over her wet hair.

"Your 'high-fashion' accessories," Diane gibes, waving toward the glovebox. "The Costume Institute at the Metropolitan Museum of Art has sent us a letter of interest."

"It has?!" Mom asks.

"I think not," I say. "But I'll tell you what we should be interested in," I go on, pointing to the vanishing clouds. "That it's getting sunny."

Mom looks out the window. Despite the tears on her face, she smiles. "It is, isn't it?"

In the bay's far reaches, breakers and rain from the receding storm mark the horizon—grayish-white sprays as expertly wrought as brushstrokes in a Winslow Homer seascape—while overhead a nascent rainbow appears in the sky's restored dome of porcelain-like azure.

I get out of the car to take a picture. Behind me, Mom lowers her window. "It's not my time to cross the river," she says as iridescent bands of color appear above us.

"Of course not!"

"Or go over the rainbow either," she continues, "but someday, 'that's where I'll be.' "

"Someday, that's where we'll all be," I remind her.

She peers at me as if I am far off instead of a few feet away. "If we're lucky."

"Which we are," I reply, walking back to her.

Smiling, she extends her right hand toward mine—gracefully echoing the bend of the varicolored translucent arc on high, the earlier spread of lightning bolts in the sky, the concave reach of old to young across the coved ceiling of the Sistine Chapel's venerable, endlessly vibrant heavens.

CHAPTER 45

Star Light, Star Bright

Long Take

As the cabin lights dim and the flight attendants ask everyone to stow their electronic devices before landing, I look out the window at Boston's pier-studded waterfront and the curving coastline of the bays and islands beyond. Relegated to a hold pattern by the control tower at Logan, the plane flies over towns and neighborhoods where I once lived—sandy Swampscott, cramped Charlestown, and the elegant Back Bay.

My seatmate, a long-haired young woman wearing a number of scarves and necklaces, looks over my shoulder. "It's something, isn't it? All those places and people crowded into such a small place."

"Where're you from?" I ask, turning.

"Chicago. It's more spread out."

"I'm from Cleveland. It's the same."

Perhaps put off by my comparison of Cleveland to Chicago, she smiles wanly.

"I'm surprised you're on this flight," I say. "I thought it was delayed by weather at O'Hare."

She nods. "It was. Lots of passengers bailed but

I hung on until take off. I had to—I'm attending a high-school friend's wedding at Harvard."

"Impressive," I remark.

"Not really. My friend's an Illinois State alum—but the groom just graduated from Harvard Law," she goes on. "Where're you headed?"

"To Maine to see Mom."

"That's nice."

"I hope it'll be. She's in her nineties and starting to fail," I explain, surprising myself with my candor.

"I'm sorry."

"Thanks," I reply. "She's had dementia for a while but now it's getting worse."

"That's awful!" the young woman responds. "My grandmother had dementia! It's tough!"

"It is," I agree, as the plane descends. "But a lot of things are, and we still have to deal with them."

"True," she replies, adjusting her Hermès, Louis Vuitton, and other, less easily identified scarves, a few of which have become entangled with her comparably expensive looking jewelry.

"Enjoy the wedding," I say to end the conversation.

"I hope your mother's OK," she responds.

"Thanks."

I look out the window as we approach the airport and fly over the North End and East Boston and, while the plane touches down, I silently recite the Catholic "Act of Contrition," which I always do during takeoffs or landings in case the untoward happens.

Once we've landed and disembarked, I wait on the jetway as the gate-checked luggage is brought up from the hold, eyeing each piece to see whether or not it's mine. When my bag appears, a young man with earbuds and a hipster haircut moves to take it but I block his reach. "That's my bag," I say.

"Can't hear you," he says, removing his earbuds.

"This is mine," I explain.

"You sure?" he asks irritably.

I show him the address tag.

"Uh, sorry," he grumbles with a frown.

I take hold of my bag. "No problem," I say, "happens to the best of us," suppressing the urge to add, "and even to those who aren't."

On the terminal's ground-transport level, waiting for the bus to the rental-car lot, I check my cellphone and find a text from Diane, who asked me to come and visit her and Mom this weekend—my third visit in as many months. Aware of my flight's delay, she wants to know when I'll arrive in Maine.

Hard to say, I reply. It's Columbus Day weekend—half of Boston will be driving north to see the foliage.

I forgot about that, she texts back.

How's Mom today? I ask.

The same.

What do you mean?

Not good, she answers, which is what I was afraid she'd meant.

I'll be there soon, I text. In the meantime, good luck.

You, too, she responds. Especially getting out of the city.

I pocket my phone and watch as MBTA buses marked Mass Pike, Water Shuttle, or Silver Line—none of which stop at the rental-car lots—pass by in near mind-boggling number. When at length the right bus arrives, it's predictably overcrowded. Still, I manage to board by wedging myself and my luggage into a door well. On the step above me, a tall, middle-aged blonde remarks, "Tight squeeze today," her Texas drawl unmistakable.

"Par for the course," I respond.

"I don't know how people live here," she says.

"It takes determination," I reply. Then, the bus driver turns a corner sharply and, thrown akilter, I fall toward her. She grabs me by the shoulders and manages to keep me from falling onto her and both of us from to the floor together. "And good balance—which I don't have today! Sorry!" I say, embarrassed.

"No problem, honey," she responds with a big

smile. "Where I'm from, we're used to bucking broncos."

Not sure whether she's referring to me or the bus, I blush and when the driver turns into my rental car lot and opens the doors, I gratefully start to make my exit. However, as I step out, the weight of my bag and the distance from the door well to the pavement make me lose my balance, and I start falling. Again, the blonde grabs and steadies me. Once sure-footed on the ground, my bag beside me, I tell her, "Thanks very much," and add, "Have a good day!" trying to seem nonplussed.

"You, too—and keep on bucking, bronco!" she responds with a laugh while the bus doors close and I blush anew. Still laughing, she waves as the bus takes off.

Since the express pick-up service is inexplicably closed, I enter the rental office, which is thronged with irate customers, most of them upset because their delayed flights and late arrivals have caused their car reservations to be canceled. So, I'm pleased when I get to the counter and learn that my reservation remains valid—that is until the agent, a pony-tailed young man, tells me the cost will be higher than quoted.

"Why?" I ask.

"Holiday surcharge," he replies, eyes focused on his computer screen. "Demand's high so the system's added an 'availability premium.'"

The woman in line behind me overhears. "Will I be charged that, too?"

Still looking at his computer, he answers, "Most likely."

"Your website doesn't mention premiums," she retorts.

"It's in the 'Terms and Conditions,'" he states without emotion.

"In other words, buried! That's not fair!" she protests.

Craning to look at her over my shoulder he tells her, "I don't make the rules, ma'am, I just follow them," and then slides the rental contract toward me. "Sign in the highlighted spaces, sir," he orders.

I comply and push the contract back to him. "Your car's in section A2, first door on the left," he says, pointing to an exit.

"What kind is it?" I ask, annoyed he hasn't already told me.

"Up to you. Just take any car with a green sticker—they're all in the same rate class," he says, dismissing me with a flip of his ponytail. As I walk away, he motions to the woman behind me to approach the counter. "About the surcharge . . ." I hear her begin. I don't look back.

Knowing the ride to Maine will likely take longer than normal, I step into the restroom before going to the lot to choose a car. Inside by the lavatories, a gray-haired, pot-bellied employee is shouting into a walkie-talkie. "Didn't I tell you to get that van out of the departure area?!" he barks in a South Boston accent. "It's blocking the VIP exit!"

"The customer's loading it as fast as she can but she's got little kids with her," his subordinate explains. "Plus, she's never been here and needs directions."

"The old, 'I'm not from here' story!" the first guy bellows back. "Heard it before! Don't give a damn! Get that van out of there!" he yells into the phone. Leaving the restroom, I reflect on how little I miss living in Boston.

In the lot, I choose the first green-stickered car I come across, a subcompact parked next to an SUV that the woman who was behind me in line is loading with her luggage.

"Here so soon?" I ask. "Did you get the surcharge waived?"

"I decided to save myself some trouble and just pay it," she says sheepishly. "You can't fight city hall."

"You've got that right."

I put my bag into the subcompact's trunk and close it, whereupon the taillights, probably already cracked, shatter and fall to the pavement in glittering fragments. "So much for my getting on the road fast," I say to the woman. "I'll have to go inside and report this."

She looks at me like I'm crazy. "Why?! They'll

just try to charge you for the damage! Take another car and screw the bastards!"

I consider the unexpected "availability" surcharge, the bad-tempered crowd in the rental office, and the traffic I'll be facing. "I guess you're right," I say and walk over to another subcompact which is identical to the first one I'd selected.

As I'm putting my bag in it, the woman backs out her SUV and rolls down the driver's window. "Have a good trip!" she calls.

"You, too."

"Oh, I will!" she answers with a mischievous smile. "You've already made my day!"

Waving goodbye, I slip into my subcompact. After having ensured its tank is full, I start the engine, drive through the lot's check-out gate, exit Logan, and get onto Route 1A, where the stream of cars is heavy but moving, albeit slowly.

Inching through the near North Shore's dismal landscape of industrial barrens, strip malls, and crowded hillside neighborhoods spotted with patches of orange and yellow fall foliage, I turn on a talk radio station to figure out how much longer than the usual two hours it will take to get to Mom's. The live reports from the station's traffic helicopter aren't encouraging. Beside the typical assortment of offbeat Boston traffic incidents—an overturned ice cream truck on one highway and a pile of discarded office furniture in the high-speed lane of another—the traffic on I-95, the next leg of my drive to Maine, is backed up from New Hampshire's Hampton tolls to upcoming Revere, a distance of forty miles. I switch off the radio and as the traffic comes to a halt before a roundabout, text Diane and tell her as much.

See you at Thanksgiving, she texts back.

It won't take quite that long, I reply. However, since it's already well into the afternoon, I add, but I probably won't arrive until evening.

I'll leave dinner in the refrigerator and the key under the mat in case we go to bed before you get here, she responds. Don't forget to disarm the security system right after you come in.

What's the code again?

I give it to you every time you visit, she complains, oblivious or indifferent to the number of client codes and passwords I must keep track of in my consulting business.

Nonetheless, I insist.

OK, she relents and resends it.

Thanks, I respond, putting down the phone.

The traffic stirs, and I make my way through the roundabout without incident. However, as I exit, I hear a crash immediately behind me. Through the rearview mirror, I spot a jackknifed sedan and minivan and, beyond them, a line of motionless cars as far back as the eye can see. Snaking along Route 1A toward the I-95 on-ramp, I count myself lucky even to be moving.

Because the interstate has six northbound lanes, the traffic, though congested, is no longer crawling. Still, it takes me an hour to reach the New Hampshire border, where a steady stream of cars coming out of central Massachusetts via I-495 causes another slowdown several miles before the Hampton tolls. At an overpass draped with banners welcoming fall visitors exhorting them to "Buy Local," the traffic comes to a standstill and stays that way. Ahead, in an adjacent lane, some college boys light a hibachi in the back of their pickup truck and begin barbecuing. I take a picture of the clogged roadway, hanging banners, and impromptu cookout, and post it to Facebook with the caption, "Autumn in New England—the Inside Story." It instantly garners a series of "LOLs," "likes," and "thumbs downs"—the latter mostly from my local connections.

When the cars ahead begin to creep forward again, I put down my phone, step on the gas, and resume the plod toward the Hampton tollgates. By the time I reach them, twilight has fallen, most cars' headlights are on, and the college kids in the pickup have extinguished their hibachi. Past the tollbooths, the traffic is only marginally faster and, as dusk descends in earnest and the landscape fades to black, I switch on the radio hoping for a traffic update. Instead, however, I find myself listening to a program on the challenges of caring for parents with dementia. "Dad won't focus on anything for more than a minute," laments a female caller. "And sometimes he's so confused he can't tell the difference between what he's imagining and what's really happening," she continues—which, I think to myself, is perhaps true of a lot of us. I turn off the radio.

Given Diane's description of Mom's accelerated decline, I wonder what awaits me. I hope my visit will help Mom but also doubt it. Crossing the Piscataqua River bridge into Maine, I catch glimpses of Portsmouth's lights, the dimly glimmering river, and the dark ocean further on. At the turnpike entrance, bright illumination from the high-mast streetlamps reveals that southern New England's yellow- and orange-leafed sycamores and birches have mostly been replaced by the north's green firs and red maples.

Turning the radio back on, I discover that the dementia discussion has given way to a review of hospice-care options. I switch the radio off again and focus on my surroundings. Passing Ogunquit and Kennebunkport, I recall my parents' favorite seafood restaurants in each and going by Biddeford, the seaside cottage where we once lived at Hills Beach. I reflect on how in the many years that have since passed, Mom has been an unshakeable source of support for Diane, me, and the rest of the family and know that after her demise, I'll miss her more than I'll ever be able to articulate or perhaps even bear.

When I pull into the driveway of Mom's house in Saco, all is dark except for the landscape lighting, which lends the trees and shrubbery on the yard's edge a shadowy, ethereal quality. Since it's almost ten, I assume Mom and Diane have long ago gone to bed.

I park the car in front of the barn and walk to the back door, my wheeled bag in tow. Taking the key from under the mat, I enter the house and deactivate the security system with the code Diane texted—Mom's and my father's birthdays, plus Dad's date of death.

In the kitchen, where the under-cabinet halogens cast the room in the same eerie glow as the exterior lights lent the landscaping, I notice a wheelchair by Mom's spot at the table—which saddens me since, until now, she's only used wheelchairs for outings. Not hungry, I forego the dinner Diane's left in the refrigerator and make my way to the family room, where I briefly consider turning on the television but instead walk over to the wall of family photos. Studying the black-and-white images of previous generations—my deceased great-grandparents, grandparents, aunts, and uncles—I wonder if Mom's photo will soon join them. Disheartened,

I carefully head upstairs to my room, making sure my suitcase doesn't bump against the banister and wake Diane and Mom.

In the second-floor hall, the sound of Mom's breathing as I pass her room assures me she's still living—just as, however far I've traveled or wherever I've resided, the thought of her presence in the world has always been comforting.

I enter my old room, whose mix of Colonial-style furniture, seascapes, and model sloops and schooners is little changed since I left for college. Unpacking my bag, I put my clothes in the closet and notebook computer on the desk. Afterward, I undress, pull back my old bed's nautically themed coverlet, and, lying down, again speculate as to what tomorrow might bring until I fall asleep.

Waking up in mid-morning to the sound of voices, I put on my robe and walk down the hall to Mom's bedroom. Diane is sitting at the foot of Mom's four poster, while Mom, supine amid the pillows and blankets, looks around the room in wonder as if it were new and unfamiliar—something which according to Diane she now often does, regardless of her surroundings.

Mom looks up as I enter. "What are you doing here, Rob?!" she cries, which catches me off guard, since recently she's been mistaking me for her late, elder brother Lucien.

"I missed you," I reply, unable to think of a better answer.

"You came all the way here from Cleveland just because of that?" she responds, surprised.

"It was worth the effort," I reply—which, as I speak, I realize is true.

She smiles. "You're sweet."

"When he wants to be," Diane says. "Are you ready to get up?" she asks Mom.

"No," Mom answers. "You two lie down here and talk with me. You don't have anything else to do, do you?" she asks playfully.

Since this is the time of day when Diane normally does housework, she frowns. Then, though, she says, "Sure, Mom," and lies next to her. Mom's smile broadens, and she beckons to me to lie next to her also.

"It's kind of tight for three people," I say, discomfited at the thought of sharing a bed with Mom and sister. "I think I'll just sit here," I go on, pointing to the slipper chair at her bedside.

"Comme tu préfère," she replies, acquiescing. "How was your flight?" she asks, as I seat myself.

"Fine, though getting out of Logan was a hassle."

"Logan?" Mom asks.

"The airport in Boston," Diane clarifies for me.

"The drive up here wasn't so great either," I add. "It was the usual holiday freak show, all the way from Revere to Portsmouth."

"It's a holiday?" Mom asks.

"Monday is Columbus Day," Diane explains. "Lots of people are coming up here to see the leaves turn."

"Your dad and I were married on Columbus Day," Mom says.

"Thea and I were married on Columbus Day," I correct her. "You and Dad were married on Memorial Day."

Mom's smile is replaced by a pained expression, presumably incited by her error. "Don't feel bad," I say, regretting that I pointed it out. "We all forget things."

"It isn't that," she responds unhappily. "I had a bad night."

"Couldn't you sleep?" Diane asks.

Mom doesn't reply.

"Did you have a headache? Cramps? An upset stomach?" Diane perseveres, ticking off potential causes in order of severity.

"No."

"Then what's bothering you?" she asks, knowing Mom's dementia makes any sort of response possible.

Mom doesn't answer, but instead declares, "You won't have to take care of me much longer," her eyes watering.

"What are you talking about?" Diane demands.

"I saw your father last night," Mom confesses. "I was lying here, thinking of all the people I've lost—my parents, brothers, and friends—when he showed up and said, 'Don't worry, Yvette—it's almost time.'"

"Time for what?" Diane asks—in my opinion, pressing her luck.

"For me to pack my bags and join him!"

Making light of this, Diane responds, "Come on, Mom, everyone knows you can't do that."

"Do what?"

"Take luggage to Heaven," she answers, straight-faced.

"Why not?"

"For one, Heaven doesn't have porters," I say, following my sister's lead.

Mom furrows her brow, unimpressed.

"Why are you so upset," I ask, taking another tack. "It was just a dream."

"Dreams predict the future," Mom replies and starts to cry.

"Most of my dreams are just about things that worry me or that I'm afraid of," I respond.

"Mine too," she admits.

This gives Diane an opening. "What're you afraid of? I'm always here to make sure nothing bad happens."

Mom looks down. "I'm afraid I'll be leaving you soon."

I'm afraid of that, too, I think.

To distract her, I walk to the window and pull open the chintz draperies. Across the way, the gilded domes of the Greek Orthodox church shine softly in the morning light, and the trees in the surrounding woods offer a palette of deep crimson, ochre, and russet foliage. "How lovely!" I remark.

"What's lovely?" Mom asks, since she's still lying down and her view is confined to the four poster's floral canopy.

"The woods are beautiful today!" I explain.

"How are they more beautiful today than any other day?"

"It's fall, Mom," Diane reminds her. "The leaves are changing."

"Fall," Mom repeats and then says, "I'm falling."

Diane and I frown. "Don't be silly," I say. "How can you be falling when you're lying flat on your back?"

"I've been falling for a long time," Mom replies soberly. "And nothing can stop me."

"What foolishness," Diane says, attempting to dismiss the topic.

Mom doesn't answer. Instead, she asks, "You know how we say 'to fall' in French?"

"Tomber," I reply.

"Like tombeau, the word, for tomb," she responds. "Every day I take one step closer to falling into mine."

Diane and I are momentarily speechless. "Aren't you exaggerating?" I ask.

Mom gives me a disinterested look. "I'm only

telling the truth. Soon, I'll be lowered into my grave and that will be the end of me—sayōnara, baby!"

"Since when do you speak Japanese?" I ask. "Did you hear that in a movie?"

"You told us a neighbor of yours said it at her mother-in-law's funeral," Diane reminds me.

"Really? I hope I moved afterwards."

Diane smirks at my remark. Turning to Mom, she says, "If you're going to talk this kind of nonsense, maybe you should go back to sleep for a while."

"But I'm only a little tired."

"A little is enough. Besides, that's not the point—the housekeeping staff has a lot to do this morning."

"We have staff?" Mom asks innocently.

"You're looking at it," Diane says, pointing to herself and to me. "And we need to get to work," she continues, standing up and closing the drapes. "So, stay in bed, and we'll come for you once we've finished making the Eggs Benedict."

"But I hate eggs," Mom responds.

"That's OK," Diane says, as she and I walk out of the room, "because we're actually having English muffins and orange juice." We hear Mom sigh while the door closes behind us.

In the kitchen, I take the English muffins out of the cupboard to put them into the toaster, only to find it's missing. "Don't tell me you've started selling the appliances?" I ask Diane facetiously, recalling how on my last visit I discovered she'd sold the family crystal and was planning on disposing of my father's old Cadillac to cover expenses.

"It broke, and I don't eat toast, so I won't replace it until I know how much longer Mom can stay here. Use the toaster oven instead."

"What do you mean by 'how much longer Mom can stay here?' Last month, you told me you'd never put her in a nursing home."

"That was then, and this is now," Diane replies flatly. "Like I said on the phone, she's gone downhill fast," Diane continues. "She barely eats, it's hard for me to get her in and out of bed, and she's started to use her wheelchair most of the time. Worst of all, some days she forgets who she is and doesn't recognize me either."

"She just recognized me," I say.

"That was a surprise, all right," Diane responds. "She's been confusing you with Lucien ever since I mentioned you were coming, and then when you show up, she recognizes you! Go figure!"

"Have you started making arrangements with a nursing home?" I ask apprehensively.

"No," Diane replies. "I had a public-health nurse assess Mom, and she approved her for home hospice, which means that Medicare will pay for a hospital bed and some help for me, among other things."

"That's good about the help but I don't think Mom will appreciate losing her four poster," I remark.

"She won't lose it. The hospital bed's going into the library," Diane replies, "which is one of the reasons I asked you to visit this weekend—to help me move the furniture out of the library before the bed's delivered tomorrow."

"Will Mom be OK with spending the night on the ground floor?" I ask. "It's always made her nervous."

"Which is why she'll be sleeping in the library. Between the casement shutters and damask drapes and valances, it's almost impossible to see inside that room, let alone from the outside in."

The toaster-oven timer rings, and I take out the English muffins, which look nearly the same as when I put them inside it.

"Are you sure this thing is working?" I ask Diane.

"Yeah—it's set on low because Mom could choke if the muffins are too crunchy."

"Oh," I say, placing two cups of coffee on the table while Diane fetches plates and flatware.

"This is striking," I remark of the sleek cutlery she's placed before me. "I didn't know we had such nice stainless."

"We didn't," she replies. "I sold the family sterling a few weeks back and replaced it with this stuff. It was on sale at Macy's."

"You sold the sterling! That set was over a hundred years old!"

"And in excellent condition," she says with an air of satisfaction. "I'm not going to miss all the polishing I had to do to keep it that way—plus, like I told you, we need the money." She holds up a bright, unblemished stainless-steel knife. "You just stick one of these in the dishwasher and, an hour later—presto, it's sparkling! And it costs a fraction of what the sterling brought at auction."

"I'm surprised you haven't sold my sloops and schooners," I remark acerbically.

"Your what?"

"The model ships in my room," I explain.

"You never know," Diane teases. "Life's full of surprises."

"Like selling the family silver?"

"I've told you what it costs to run this house," she says defensively. "I'm cutting back wherever I can. I've even cancelled the subscriptions to Mom's magazines—except for the French ones," she continues, putting an issue of *Paris Match* at Mom's place for her to browse through during lunch. "Things will get better soon, though."

"How's that?"

"The man from the bank agreed to my asking price for Dad's old Caddy—and he's got a client who wants to buy the field!"

"Last month, you said you were going to mortgage the field, not sell it."

"I know," she responds, "but the buyer's the developer who's building the subdivision up the road. He'll pay top dollar."

"And put up a bunch of McMansions," I counter.

"Most likely."

"I thought Mom said she didn't want any houses being built nearby."

"Honestly, Rob, at this point," Diane responds, "she probably won't even notice."

"That's another surprise," I say. "How could she get this bad so fast?"

Diane sighs. "Vascular dementia's like that. People 'plateau' then 'step down' to the next stage like they're dropping off a cliff."

And into the abyss, I think to myself.

"According to her doctor, she's in dementia's seventh stage, so she could live a lot longer or not," Diane continues. "That's why we need to be ready for anything—both at the moment and in the future."

"What do you mean?"

"Besides raising money, we have to rearrange a lot of the furniture to make the house more wheelchair friendly," she explains. "Can you lend a hand with that?"

"Sure thing."

Diane hesitates. "Could you also help me begin to clear out the barn? If we start now, we won't have as much to do after Mom passes."

Once again, I'm surprised. "You don't plan on living here afterwards?" I ask.

She shakes her head. "Too many memories."

"Where will you go?"

"I've already found a place," Diane answers. "When I was at the bakery buying maple-cream donuts for Mom the other day, Maeve Healy mentioned that her Dad's gone into assisted living, so she'll be selling his beach house. I told her I'm interested."

"Won't that be expensive?"

"It won't be cheap," Diane replies. "But Maeve said the property needs a lot of work, so she's going to let it go below market. Also, my guy at the bank offered me a low-rate mortgage."

My first objection shot down, I lob another. "Isn't it too soon? You and Mom might be here a while yet."

"Even if we're lucky and Mom lives a lot longer, the day's coming when I won't be able to keep up with her needs and she'll have to go into a facility," Diane replies.

"So, until then, you'll make mortgage payments on the beach house while it sits empty?" I remark, in a last attempt to discourage her.

Diane shakes her head. "I can rent it out. Lots of people want to live by the ocean, even in winter. And, if I fix up the place, it can bring in as much as five thousand dollars a week during summer."

Dismayed with how she's made the once-distant future alarmingly immediate, I nonetheless say only, "Sounds like a plan."

"Maybe, but not one I'm looking forward to executing," she reproaches me.

"I realize that—it's just a lot for me to process all at once," I admit, sensing a headache rising.

"That's another reason I asked you to visit again so soon," she answers. "To get you to really start thinking about everything."

"I'll try to reschedule my return flight so I can stay and help with clearing stuff out," I tell her—the only response I can muster.

"Thanks," Diane replies.

"Don't mention it." To avoid further discussion, I walk to the window and look out at the lawn, which, overgrown and blanketed with leaves of assorted colors, reminds me of a Jackson Pollock canvas. Its unkempt state surprises me, since Diane has always insisted on the grounds being immaculate. "What's up with the mess?" I ask.

"You mean the leaves and tall grass?"

I nod. "Did you let the mower guy go to cut expenses?" I guess. "No pun intended."

"Emmett?" she responds, shaking her head. "He should be here today—he's been upstate campaigning."

"Still running for governor?"

"Yeah—and still crazy as ever," she answers.

"So, despite Mom's advice, you've ruled him

out as a potential beau?" I tease, returning to the table and taking a sip of my coffee.

"What do I need a boyfriend for?"

"That cottage on the beach could get lonely."

"Things around here might not change all that much anytime soon," she responds.

"I hope you're right," I say, as my headache grows stronger. "But like you said, we've got to be prepared for anything."

"That's life," Diane replies.

Unable to dispute this, I look at my watch. "It's almost noon," I remark. "Will Mom be getting up soon?"

"Hard to say," Diane answers. "Sometimes, if she goes back to sleep in the morning, she stays in bed through lunch. That might be what'll happen today. It'd surprise me, though, because she's been excited about your—or, at least, Lucien's—visit."

I shrug. "She's probably just tired. Speaking of which, I'm still worn out from yesterday's trip. Do you mind if I take a little nap?"

"No problem. We can clear out the library when you get up."

"Thanks," I tell her and hope my expression doesn't betray I'd forgotten about that.

Passing through the living room on my way upstairs, I think it looks somehow different and then notice that one of the sofas and a few of the chairs and tables have already been pushed against the walls to accommodate Mom's wheelchair. Back in my room, I take some aspirin and lie down in the hope that sleep will cause my headache to retreat. Watching the sheers at the window rise and fall in the breeze like sea spray on the nearby bay, I wonder what it will be like when I don't have this house and Mom to return to. I don't know if I'll lose them tomorrow, months, or years from now—but lose them, I will, that much is certain. I close my eyes and, trying to push all this from my mind, eventually drift off.

Asleep, I experience a string of swift, plotless dreams, most of them simply images of former colleagues, friends, and neighbors—some close, others not, most alive, a few long dead. Suddenly, however, I find myself within a longer dream, strolling along the shore at Hills Beach. In the distance, a silver-haired woman, whom I take at first for Antoinette Robertson, is walking with a white Samoyed, seagulls scattering before them. As the woman approaches, I see that she's a somewhat younger version of Mom.

"Mom!" I call.

She responds with an enigmatic smile.

"What are you doing here?" I ask, as she draws nearer.

"J'ai n'aucune idée," she answers.

"No idea?!" I repeat.

She nods. "Les rêves sont comme ça—comme la vie et la mort aussi."

"Quoi?" I ask, shocked.

"Dreams are that way," she reiterates in English, "like life and death."

A gull passes overhead, distracting me, and when I turn my attention back to Mom, she's gone. Peering in the direction from which she came, I think I see the Samoyed romping at the water's edge but then realize it's only foam from the breaking waves. As I scan the empty beach, I'm overcome by grief.

I wake up in a cold sweat to a roaring, surf-like sound outside the window, so I walk over to investigate. Below, Emmett's landscape crew is clearing the flowerbeds and cutting the grass with leaf blowers and standup lawn mowers. Watching countless leaves fly skyward in defiance of gravity while multiple mowers crisscross the lawn's farthest reaches, avoiding trees and garden statuary, I wonder what all this is costing and start to share Diane's concern about expenses.

I glance at my watch and, seeing that it's late afternoon, hurry out of the room to help Diane clear the library. On the stairs, though, I encounter her carrying sheets and towels and see that the foyer below is already crowded with the library's furnishing. "I'm sorry—I overslept!" I exclaim. "Did you move all of that yourself?"

"No," she answers. "Emmett's crew did it for me."

Surveying the items in the foyer—a desk, a

reading table, and a small, rotating bookcase filled with volumes of a disused encyclopedia—I note the absence of the library's biggest pieces, two wing chairs and a matching sofa, and ask Diane about them.

"They're on Emmett's truck. He needs stuff for his campaign office, so he gave me five hundred bucks for the set."

"Just five hundred!?" I ask.

"At first he wanted to pay only three hundred—two hundred for the couch and fifty for each of the chairs, but I held out for a nice, round number," she responds, passing me.

"Five hundred dollars is dirt cheap for a set upholstered in Moroccan leather!" I object.

"Get with the program, Rob!" she retorts, walking to the linen cabinet. "Those things are so old-fashioned and heavy, we're lucky we didn't have to pay him to cart them away for us!"

I grimace.

"Just be grateful we didn't have to do it," she continues as she opens the cabinet. "If we had, we'd probably have wound up in traction."

Since this seems like a real possibility, I drop the subject. "Can I help?" I ask, as she places the sheets and towels inside the cabinet.

"Not with this," she answers, "but could you go downstairs and stay with Mom until I'm finished? She fell asleep at the table after lunch, and if she wakes up alone, she might be frightened."

I do as asked, however, on entering the kitchen I find that Mom isn't asleep but awake and petting the tiny plush dog Carrie gave her before moving to Boston. "Don't worry, Alfie," she advises the stuffed toy as she bends forward and rubs its neck. "I have to go on a trip soon but Diane will take care of you," she continues, her voice breaking.

"Hi, Mom," I say.

She looks startled. "Rob! I forgot you were here!"

"Can I get you anything?" I ask.

"No," she replies, turning her attention back to Alfie.

"How about him?"

Mom shakes her head. "He doesn't eat much."

"He doesn't look like he would," I joke.

"What?" she asks.

I repeat myself and explain, "He's so small."

Mom smiles. "Sorry that I didn't hear you at first. The surf is loud today," she remarks. "Could you shut the window so it's quieter in here?"

"That's not the sound of the ocean, Mom," I reply, closing the window. "It's Emmett's crew."

"Who?"

"Emmett, the landscaper," I explain. "When I woke up from my nap, I thought I heard waves, too," I continue, "probably because I dreamt about the beach."

"I know you did," Mom responds, which takes me aback.

"How?"

"I'm not sure," she replies, looking at the magazine Diane left for her. Then, she repeats her words from the dream, "Les rêves sont comme ça—comme la vie et la mort aussi."

Astounded, I walk over and find she's just reading a headline from the magazine. I wonder if I noticed this header earlier and that's how it ended up in my dream.

Diane enters the kitchen. "What're you guys talking about?"

"Life and death," Mom answers.

"Serious stuff," Diane remarks, glancing at me sternly.

"It's a headline," I explain and point to the magazine.

"Oh," Diane replies, mollified. "It figures. That's one of the few magazines I haven't cancelled."

"You cancelled some of my magazines?!" Mom exclaims.

"Not exactly—I let their subscriptions expire," Diane clarifies.

For whatever reason, this placates Mom. "Oh, that's different."

"And speaking of something different," Diane deftly segues, "how about a maple-cream donut for dessert?"

Mom shakes her head. "I don't think so."

"You know you love them," Diane coaxes.

Mom says nothing.

"Come on—I'll have one with you," I encourage her.

"All right." Mom relents. "But only if we split it."

"It's a deal." I cut a donut into quarters with one of the new stainless-steel knives—which, much as I hate to admit it, cut far more cleanly than the sterling. I take a bite and, watching me, Mom does likewise, though without evident enthusiasm.

"Delicious," I say, despite my dislike of sweets.

"Maybe to me but not to you," Mom responds. "As I recall, you don't much care for sweet things."

"I care for you," I reply.

Mom smiles.

"And I think it's important that you eat this," I persist.

She hesitates but gives in and takes another bite, inadvertently smearing maple cream over her lips, nose, and cheeks.

"Let me help," I offer and wipe the mess off her face, as she must have done for me in my early childhood.

"Eating these is harder than it used to be," Mom says.

"A lot of things are," Diane says, walking to the window and reopening it.

"It's so quiet now," Mom says between smaller and neater bites of her donut. "Is it low tide already?"

"Yes, actually," Diane answers. "Why?"

"Mom thought she heard the ocean earlier," I explain. "But it was Emmett's lawn equipment."

"Is Emmett the young man who's interested in you?" Mom asks Diane.

"He's not young," Diane replies flatly. "And if he's interested in me, the feeling's not mutual," she continues, removing Mom's empty plate. "Isn't it about time we visited the bathroom?" she asks her, again changing the topic—this time, less deftly.

"I'm not sure."

"Well, I am," Diane tells her. "It's been over two hours since you last went, and we don't want an accident."

"What kind of accident?" Mom asks.

"Any kind," Diane answers, wheeling her off to the bathroom.

While they're gone, I take out my phone and research next week's flights from Boston to Cleveland. Most are fully booked and those that aren't are inconveniently scheduled, so I begin investigating flights for the week after.

When Diane and Mom return to the kitchen, Diane asks her, "What would you like to do now? Have some tea in here or go into the family room to watch television?"

"I'd like to go to bed," Mom answers.

Diane frowns. "Already? It's only six o'clock, and we haven't even had supper."

"I'm tired," Mom protests.

"Even if you are," Diane replies, "you're not going to bed now just so you can wake up at midnight like you did last week. I've got enough to do around here as it is without watching 'Hallmark Hall of Fame' movies until dawn with you."

"I love those movies," Mom objects. "They always have happy endings."

"That's because their plots are all pretty much the same," Diane complains. "A recently divorced, middle-aged man meets his newly widowed high-school crush or vice versa, his Great Dane likes her poodle, the man and woman go hiking, skiing, and kayaking until, finally, they end up in each other's arms on the pristine shore of a mountain lake, watching a sunset so bright it almost blots out the closing credits."

"Maybe that's because the cast and crew want to remain anonymous," I joke, afraid Diane's candid assessment might have upset Mom.

Mom, though, seems unbothered. "Then, can we watch the news instead?" she asks my sister.

"OK," Diane acquiesces. "But only if it doesn't look like it'll upset you." She pushes Mom's wheelchair into the family room and positions it by the sofa, while I go and turn on the television. Sirens scream from the set as, onscreen, police-car and ambulance strobes streak beside an overturned tractor trailer.

Mom gasps, and Diane glares at me. I switch the channel, causing the sirens and flashing lights to give way to a multicolored roulette wheel and an audience yelling, "*Wheel of Fortune!*"

"Will this do?" I ask Diane.

"It should."

"What if the phrases the contestants have to figure out are disturbing?"

"Even if they are," she replies, "half the time Mom and I don't understand them. Isn't that right?" she asks Mom.

Staring at the screen, Mom nods.

"I usually don't either," I admit. "Maybe you've got to be attuned to popular culture."

"Or been dumbed down by it," Diane rejoins.

On the television, the show's host, a guy in his early seventies with a car salesman's chatty demeanor, asks the contestants about themselves, explains the rules, and then turns the proceedings over to his assistant, a model-pretty blonde of indeterminate age and endless, though mostly mute, affability.

"How long has this show been on the air?" I ask Diane.

"Almost as long as you and I've been alive," she answers, which isn't entirely accurate but close enough to give one pause. Watching the host call out clues and his assistant manipulate a board full of letters in response to the contestants' answers, it seems to me that, however many years the two have been at this, neither has much changed. I reflect that the rest of us should only be so lucky.

The phrase, "X XXXXX star" appears in subtitles, and the contestants—a young yet balding accountant, a perky blonde teacher of about thirty, and a long-haired, heavily made-up cosmetician in her forties—contemplate potential answers to the accompaniment of supposedly suspenseful background music.

" 'Dying!' 'A dying star!' " Diane exclaims.

"Gloria Swanson?" Mom guesses.

Diane harrumphs. "I'm saying that 'dying' is the missing word, Mom, not trying to guess who's dying!" she replies. "Besides, Gloria Swanson's been dead for almost forty years now."

Oblivious to Diane's explanation, Mom hazards, "Elizabeth Taylor?"

"Also dead," I say, humoring her.

"Sophia Loren?"

"Alive and healthy," I answer.

"Enough with 'The Parade of Stars!' " Diane exhorts us. "We're not supposed to guess what the phrase is about! We're supposed to find the word that completes it!"

Onscreen, the cosmetician yells, "Dwarf!" and

jumps up and down, her hair flying wildly about her. " 'A dwarf star!' "

For an instant, I wonder what this means but then recall it's a star that's collapsed and, consequently, is on the verge of falling into darkness.

While the host confirms the answer and the contestants move onto guessing another phrase, Mom, looking mystified, asks me to repeat the winning term.

"A dwarf star," I say.

"You mean like a munchkin from *The Wizard of Oz*?" she asks.

"Drop the movie stuff, OK, Mom?!" Diane snaps. "We're talking about the stars you see in the sky at night!"

"Stars are so beautiful and bright," Mom remarks dreamily, "like guardian angels guiding us through life." More somberly, she adds, "or souls alight in the afterlife."

Neither Diane nor I comment and, after a moment, Mom asks, "Is it clear out tonight?"

"Why do you want to know?" Diane replies.

"I'm hoping the weather's OK so Lucien doesn't have trouble getting here," she replies, suddenly pragmatic.

"He's already here," Diane says and points at me, presuming Mom has again confused me for him.

"Sometimes I worry about you, Diane," Mom

responds. "This is Rob—your older brother! Lucien's *my* older brother!"

Diane's brow furrows. "What's so great about Lucien coming, anyway?" she asks Mom. "Dad visited you last night, and that didn't make you very happy!"

Mom looks confused. "How could Henri have visited me? He passed away years ago! Lucien's still among the living," she asserts, though he died before my father.

Diane stares. "Dad came to you in a dream last night! Don't you remember?!"

"How do you know what I dreamt about?!"

Diane rolls her eyes. "Because you woke up at 2 A.M. and told us."

"What're you talking about, Diane?!" Mom responds. "First you tell me I slept until noon today, and now you're saying I woke up in the middle of the night!"

Because Mom's right, Diane doesn't attempt to deny this, and Mom gives her an exasperated look.

On the TV, the gameboard displays with the half-complete phrase, "Chain of XXXXX" and, as another irritating musical interlude begins, the cosmetician attempts to come up with the missing word. After a few seconds, she presses the buzzer and cries, "Chain of Fools!" and again starts jumping around crazily, her long tresses following likewise.

Diane smirks. "Easy guess—I mean, seeing that she's a link in the chain." As the host informs the cosmetician she's in the lead, she shrieks, and Diane amends her statement. "Or maybe the 'missing link.'"

"Diane!" Mom admonishes. "Being of unsound mind is hard enough without getting mocked for it!"

Diane and I are silent.

Suddenly plaintive, Mom asks, "Where's Alfie?"

"He's in the kitchen," I say and go get him. Returning, I put him in her lap. "You must've been afraid all by yourself," Mom says to the stuffed animal. "But don't worry—now that you're in here with us, nothing bad can happen to you."

On the TV screen, the phrase "XXX me XX the XXXX" appears, and the show's theme music resumes in annoying earnest. Since the cosmetician fails to take a guess, the bald accountant hits his buzzer. "Fly me to the moon," he says, calmly providing the correct answer.

"You won't fly off to the moon will you, Alfie?" Mom asks the plush dog. "We'll never leave each other alone," she declares, rubbing its stomach. Then, her eyes welling with tears, she continues, "Even if I have to leave here sometime soon, my spirit will always be with you."

Diane and I exchange glances, and she switches off the television. "The only place you're going now is to bed," she tells Mom. "You're way overtired."

"Am I?" she asks me.

"Could be," I say. "You kind of look like I used to after a long business trip to Europe or Asia."

"You went to Europe and Asia?" she asks, as if this is the first she's heard of it, though I've often shown her photos.

I nod. "Remember all my shots of Tokyo, Shanghai, and Paris?"

"You looked awful in those pictures," she declares, her about-face more startling than her candor. "So maybe I am tired enough to go to bed."

"Good thinking," Diane says, reaching to take Alfie away from her.

"I want to bring him up to bed with me," Mom protests, holding onto the toy tightly.

Diane shakes her head no. "Remember what happened the last time you kept Alfie with you overnight?"

Mom looks uncertain.

"He got lost in the sheets and almost ended up in the laundry. You don't want that to happen again, do you?"

"No," Mom answers but maintains her grip on the stuffed animal. "Will you look after Alfie until Diane gets back?" she asks me.

"Sure, Mom."

She hands me the toy dog. "Bonne soirée, Alfie," she says as Diane turns her wheelchair around, and they head to the foyer.

"Bonne soirée, madame," I answer for Alfie, adopting the high-pitched voice I imagine a small dog might have were it capable of speech.

Mom laughs, and Diane helps her out of the wheelchair and onto the chairlift. Pushing a button, Diane says, "Ups-a-daisy," and they ascend, Mom on the chairlift and Diane on foot behind it.

I walk into the kitchen and put Alfie on the table where Mom will expect to find him in the morning. Tired, I break my promise to her and go upstairs to change for the evening. After retrieving and putting on a pair of pajamas from my suitcase, I open the door to my old bedroom closet and look at everything I'll have to sort through when the house is vacated following Mom's passing—the outmoded yet carefully hung jackets and sweaters, the 1970s college textbooks lining the overhead shelf, the LPs of the same era stacked on the floor by the empty shoe rack. Since none serve a purpose other than in memory, I ask myself if I should simply dispose of everything before I return to Cleveland. But considering Mom's likely reaction if she found out, I think better of it.

Too restless to sleep, I don my bathrobe and return to the family room, where I turn on the television and scan the channels. Brassy women hawking mediocre jewelry, unqualified rehabbers disfiguring vintage properties, and well-practiced politicians blithely side-stepping reporters' questions pass by as rapidly as you'd wish they would if you ever had the misfortune to meet them. I settle on a channel displaying tropical fish in an aquarium, their streamlined forms and bright colors strangely soothing. As the fish swim from one end of their insular environment to the other, I rummage through the magazine rack's French-language publications and old issues of *National Geographic* for something worth reading.

Diane enters the room. "Can't sleep?"

I nod. "Probably napped too long this afternoon."

"Mind if I change the channel?" she asks, watching the fish pursue their limited travels.

I want to reply, "be my guest." However, as I'm in fact her guest, I say, "No problem—though good luck finding anything you'd want to watch."

"I think I'll manage to find something," she responds and clicks to coverage of the World Series, which I'd forgotten is ongoing. She turns the sound down. "Are you beginning to get an idea of what it's like around here these days?" she asks me. "I mean, between Dad's 'visit,' the confusion around *Wheel of Fortune*, and Alfie being treated like he's alive and breathing?"

I say nothing.

"And don't forget Mom's physical impairments," she presses. "Do you understand now why the land has to be sold and maybe, eventually, the house? Cash is king, and we desperately need a coronation."

"I get it," I admit. "But it's still hard to accept."

"It's tough, I know. You've got to, though."

On TV, the winning team's batter hits the ball into right field and begins to run the bases. He makes first, second, and third, then races home. The crowd rises, roaring.

"Too bad we aren't likely to have as good an ending," I remark.

Diane frowns. "It'll be as good as we make it."

"You're right," I concede. "I guess we just have to adjust our expectations to the circumstances."

"More or less—with *more* applying to the circumstances and *less* to the expectations," Diane advises.

Onscreen, a new batter repeats the previous one's performance, and the crowd's mood progresses from jubilation to near hysteria. Since I don't follow baseball, I ask, "Which team's favored?"

"The one that's trailing," Diane answers.

"How's that possible?"

"Their star pitcher is on disciplinary leave and their next-best one is out with an injury, so all they've got left are second-stringers," she explains. "Plus, the winning team has some new guys from the junior leagues who've turned out to be a lot better than anyone expected."

"I see," I say.

"Really? What do you see?" she asks, seizing yet another opportunity to drive her point home.

"That anything can happen."

"Exactly. And, like the winning team, we need to be ready!"

The ballgame is interrupted first by beer commercials and next by ads for local restaurants and car dealerships. "I think I'll go upstairs and try to get some sleep," I say.

"Pleasant dreams," Diane responds, without looking away from the television.

In my room, I open the window to catch the evening breeze, then turn off the lights. I lie down and reflect on everything that's happened in this house in the sixty years since my parents had it built—the holiday dinners, the summer brunches, my many leave takings and returns, first in adolescence and now approaching retirement. But mostly I think of all the wise advice Mom dispensed to the family over the years, whereas these days she can't even feed herself or tell a stuffed animal from a living one. Her illness—even though, like most illnesses, obviously unfair—is both undeniable and implacable. I listen to the rustle of the wind blowing through the autumn leaves and the tall, late-season field grass, a soft swishing sound like a wave at low tide as it gently ripples up onto the beach. After some time, I fall asleep.

Later, awoken by what I at first take for seabird cries but then realize is Mom sobbing, I throw on my robe and hurry down the hall to her room. There, I find Diane on the bed, holding Mom. "What's wrong?" I ask.

"She had a nightmare," Diane replies as she runs a hand through Mom's disheveled hair.

"It wasn't a dream!" Mom declares. "Your Uncle Lucien visited me like I said he would!"

Diane continues to smooth Mom's hair. "I don't see how he could've. I didn't let him in," she tells her.

"Rob might have," Mom replies.

I shake my head. "I've been sleeping."

"How he got in isn't important!" Mom continues, wild-eyed. "All that matters is that he was here!"

"Where exactly was he?" Diane asks, trying to re-ground Mom in fact.

Mom points to the ceiling above the Chippendale highboy. "There!"

"Was he sitting on it or floating above it?"

"Don't be ridiculous!" Mom scoffs. "How could a man Lucien's age sit on a chest of drawers that tall?"

"Here's a better question," Diane responds. "How could he float above it?"

Through her tears, Mom scowls. "I just said he was near it! Plus, where he was isn't the point! It's what he told me!"

"Which was?" Diane asks, taking Mom's hands in hers.

"That it's time for me to join everyone—him, my parents, your father!" Mom starts crying. "They're all waiting for me—but I don't want to go yet!"

"And you don't have to," Diane says, giving her a hug. "You can stay right here with me and Rob."

"And Alfie?" Mom asks anxiously.

"And Alfie," Diane reassures her.

Rummaging through the bed covers and not finding him, Mom panics. "Where's Alfie?!"

"Don't worry," I say. "I know where he is."

"Will you get him?"

"Sure thing."

"Please hurry," she entreats me.

Rushing to the first floor, I trip on the stairs but fortunately grab the railing before falling. Once I've got Alfie, I go back upstairs more slowly, as I doubt Diane could deal with an additional invalid. Approaching Mom's room, I hear music that I recall from my childhood, and entering find Mom sitting up in bed with Diane holding an iPad before her.

I place Alfie on the bedcovers beside Mom, who staring at the iPad screen, doesn't notice. "What's she watching?" I ask Diane.

"A *Captain Kangaroo* 'Storytime' clip on

YouTube," she tells me. "It's about an old circus dog who feels useless and runs away. But he's found by his trainer, who tells him how much he's missed him and brings him home. I show it to her when she's upset, and it calms her down."

Mom smiles as water-color renderings of a Dalmatian, a circus arena, and a mustachioed ringmaster cross the iPad's screen. "Feel better now?" Diane asks her when the video clip has ended.

Mom nods and pets Alfie. "I like that story," she says softly.

"What do you like about it?" I ask.

She ponders my question. "That the dog was lost and then found," she replies. Petting Alfie, she adds, "After all, home is where the heart is."

"Isn't it also where you make it?" I ask, as I think of the nursing home that might be in her future.

"I guess," Mom says, her eyes still on Alfie.

"Home is wherever you're surrounded by those who want the best for you," Diane comments. "Exactly where that is probably doesn't matter."

Mom doesn't appear to find this consoling, as she begins to weep again.

"But this is the only place I want to be!" she wails. "I'm not ready to join your father and Lucien! I might be a dwarf star but I don't want to disappear yet!"

"You'll never disappear, Mom," I say, sitting down on the bed.

"Rob's right," Diane agrees. "Wherever you are, you'll always be with us and we'll always be with you." She hugs Mom again.

"That's because you should never let go of what's most important," I say, taking Mom's hand in mine.

"You're right," she replies tearfully. "Because if you do, you're lost forever."

As her sobbing subsides, I let go of her hand and walk across the room to look out the window. Amid bare-branched treetops, the golden domes of the Greek Orthodox church gleam softly in the moonlight, while the sky above is starkly clear, a smooth black sheet seared with shimmering pinpoints of light.

"What are you looking at?" Diane asks.

"Just the stars," I say. "Some are so bright they look like they'll shine forever while others are so dim they seem about to disappear from sight."

Diane leaves Mom's beside and, joining me, gazes skyward. Sensing my mood and the thoughts it reflects, she says, "Don't worry. The majority will make it through tonight—and likely lots of other nights."

We turn away from the window and, since Mom has shut her eyes and gone back to sleep, head out of the room. In the doorway, we turn and take a last look to make sure she's all right. Then, stepping into the corridor, we switch off the lights.

Author's Last Words

My mother—the inspiration for this book's principal character, Yvette Allaire—passed away in late April 2021 at the age of nearly ninety-two. By then, she'd been ill for many years, her disabilities growing inexorably worse, so her death was neither sudden nor unexpected.

Nevertheless, perhaps because I lived so far from her and didn't see her daily, my mother's passing took a while to become real for me. I wrote her obituary and eulogy, delivered the latter, and watched as her coffin was lowered into a Maine cemetery plot on a cold spring afternoon. Yet, somehow, for a long time, I thought of her as still being present, as if she remained just a call or flight away. It took several months and visits with my sister in my mother's old house for me to confront the unforgiving truth that my mother was physically absent from the world and that, moving forward, her kindness, wit, and wisdom would be available to me only in memory and in those moments when I ask myself what she might have done in a situation and, as often as not, try to follow suit.

I think many of us go through life longing for the unattainable and that sometimes—if we were fortunate enough to have had devoted, caring parents—the object of our longing includes the unconditional love of our childhoods, the safety of the vanished venues and departed people who made up our first homes. This book has attempted to depict how my mother, whose gentle spirit survived even the ravages of a debilitating illness, was among the dearest and most influential of those people for me. Her eulogy, delivered on May 3, 2021, follows:

> My mother, Rita Gertrude Hebért Gilbert, was baptized and married here, in St. Joseph's Church, and will now be buried from it, as were her parents and most of her immediate and extended family. This church meant a great deal to my mother—as, indeed, did her religion. Every day, she said morning and evening prayers drawn from a variety of well-worn English and French missals, some of which had been in her possession long before she brought me or my six siblings into the world.
> When I was still a toddler, and the family was living in a cottage near here at Hills Beach, she would often read to me from religious storybooks and relate basic religious concepts. I remember one afternoon when, sitting by the water, I asked her how old God was and where he lived. She replied that he'd always been

and would always be and that he lived nowhere and everywhere. I must have looked confused because she picked up a beach ball, ran a hand over its surface, and explained, 'You see, just like this ball, God has no beginning and no end.' I stared at her and the ball and then replied that thinking about this made my head hurt, to which she responded, 'That's OK—it makes mine hurt, too.'

But I don't want to give the impression that my mother was preoccupied with religion. She wasn't. Much of the time, my mother, like most people, was busy just trying to keep her head above water, which—when you have a demanding husband, seven less-than well-behaved children, multiple pets, and a number of elderly family members in need of attention—was a pretty tall order. Some nights, after a particularly hectic day, she was so tired she'd fall asleep standing up, and some mornings, with two kids in as many bathtubs as she tried to prepare breakfast, she'd already be so harried that it was hard for her to keep track of who had to bring what to school or had to be chauffeured where afterward. Occasionally, this multi-tasking resulted in memorable mishaps like kitchen fires that led to visits from firemen or overflowing sinks that caused waterfalls to cascade down staircases and small lakes to form on hardwood and flagstone floors. But, somehow, she managed to take this in stride and to keep all our heads literally above water.

The demands of domestic life notwithstanding, my mother enjoyed being a housewife. In the 1950s, while employed in the office of a local manufacturer where she met our father Maurice, she was sometimes stressed by work or worried that she might fall victim to a layoff. In fact, one of the ways Dad persuaded her to accept his proposal was by telling her, 'You know, Rita, if you marry me, you'll never be out of work again.' Later, she came to feel that this was among the most honest things he'd ever told her.

Despite her domestic workload, my mother never regretted leaving her job to raise a family, which was the focus and joy of her life. She loved every one of her children, grandchildren, and great-grandchildren deeply and equally, and readily welcomed their spouses, significant others, and friends into the family. Wherever any of us lived, however far we traveled, we were in her thoughts and in her heart, which was large enough to accommodate all.

If there's anything that my mother believed in as much as she believed in God, it was in people and the need to treat everyone, whether she knew them personally or not, with the dignity that God had granted them. I seldom heard her speak critically of anyone, even public figures, and if she did, she immediately regretted and retracted her remarks. In my mother's view, there were no bad people, only bad actions, and it was not her place nor anyone else's to pass judgement on another. That would have been unkind and, my mother was unfailingly kind. This, she believed, was everyone's duty. Because for my mother, life and religion were first and foremost about fairness, kindness, and charity—about not thinking yourself better than someone else or placing your needs above those of others, but rather about regarding everyone with the respect and empathy that is owed all God's creatures.

So, I'll close by saying that, as my mother believed, all life begins with God, and, as is undeniable, most life begins with mothers. Now, our mother is leaving us to be with God, whose values she embraced and lived daily. But she will always be with us, a ceaseless presence in our thoughts and hearts, just as we were in hers.

Acknowledgments

Many thanks to my publisher Samantha Kolber, my editor Gary Miller, and my early readers Dr. Kenneth D'Amato, Philip Byrnes, Mary Gilbert, Dr. Nathaniel-Jordain Gilbert, Dr. Richard Litwin, Richard Oullette, and Arun Ranchod, without whose assistance and encouragement this book would not have been possible.

About the Author

Born into a New England family of Québécois descent, Ronald-Stéphane Gilbert is a retired global communications professional, who, after a career involving much travel, now lives in the Great Lakes region with his wife Leah, his son Nathaniel, and their aged rescue Pekingese, Reggie. *Conversations with My Mother* was inspired by his mother's gentle yet persistent descent into dementia and Alzheimer's, and by his family's attempts to care for her while cherishing what remained of her vanishing personality. He is a participant in the Cleveland Clinic's landmark Brain and Mind studies and a member of various dementia and Alzheimer's organizations.

Center Point Large Print
600 Brooks Road / PO Box 1
Thorndike, ME 04986-0001 USA

(207) 568-3717

US & Canada:
1 800 929-9108
www.centerpointlargeprint.com